YOURS
FOR
THE
TAKING

YOURS
FOR
THE
TAKING

a novel

GABRIELLE KORN

ST. MARTIN'S PRESS
NEW YORK

First published in the United States by St. Martin's Press, an imprint of St. Martin's Publishing Group

YOURS FOR THE TAKING. Copyright © 2023 by Gabrielle Korn. All rights reserved. Printed in the United States of America. For information, address St. Martin's Publishing Group, 120 Broadway, New York, NY 10271.

www.stmartins.com

Designed by Devan Norman

Library of Congress Cataloging-in-Publication Data

Names: Korn, Gabrielle, 1989– author.
Title: Yours for the taking : a novel / Gabrielle Korn.
Description: First edition. | New York : St. Martin's Press, 2023.
Identifiers: LCCN 2023023652 | ISBN 9781250283368
    (hardcover) | ISBN 9781250283375 (ebook)
Subjects: LCGFT: Lesbian fiction. | Social problem fiction. |
    Novels.
Classification: LCC PS3611.O74313 Y68 2023 | DDC 813/.6—
    dc23/eng/20230524
LC record available at https://lccn.loc.gov/2023023652

Our books may be purchased in bulk for promotional, educational, or business use. Please contact your local bookseller or the Macmillan Corporate and Premium Sales Department at 1-800-221-7945, extension 5442, or by email at MacmillanSpecialMarkets@macmillan.com.

First Edition: 2023

10 9 8 7 6 5 4 3 2 1

For my family

Have you ever committed any indecent acts with women?

Yes, many. I am guilty of allowing suicidal women to die before my eyes or in my ears or under my hands because I thought I could do nothing, I am guilty of leaving a prostitute who held a knife to my friend's throat because we would not sleep with her, we thought she was old and fat and ugly; I am guilty of not loving her who needed me; I regret all the women I have not slept with or comforted, who pulled themselves away from me for lack of something I had not the courage to fight for, for us, our life, our planet, our city, our meat and potatoes, our love. These are indecent acts, lacking courage, lacking a certain fire behind the eyes, which is the symbol, the raised fist, the sharing of resources, the resistance that tells death he will starve for lack of the fat of us, our extra. Yes I have committed acts of indecency with women and most of them were acts of omission. I regret them bitterly.

—"A Woman Is Talking to Death"
by Judy Grahn, 1974

The unfortunate truth is that climate change is coming for us faster than equal rights are. The data proves it: if we stay on our current course, women will not become truly equal to men before the world is made uninhabitable. What is urgently needed now, if we have any hope of changing our fate, is an immediate, complete restructuring of how gender dynamics play out in our culture. And rather than continuing to focus on *empowerment* for women, it is imperative that what is considered and worked toward, instead, is *power*—in its simplest, purest form. Did I lose you when I said that? I implore my female readers to stop for a moment and think about why you've been told to feel that *power* is such a dirty word. After all, an unequal distribution of power is what got us into this mess in the first place. If we're going to make it out alive, women must stop hesitating, and start claiming.

—*Yours for the Taking!: Reclaiming Female Power in a Changing World*
by Jacqueline Millender, 2045

YOURS
FOR
THE
TAKING

THE INSIDE PROJECT STARTED WITH THE BEST INTENTIONS.

At least, that is what I choose to believe, even knowing what I know now, even knowing that the very idea of Inside was based on the notion that some people are worth saving and some are not. Perhaps what went wrong Inside was a natural extension of that inherently broken belief system, making the destruction and chaos inevitable. Perhaps Inside's flaws were a natural consequence of trying something new, and we all became stronger because of what went wrong and what we learned from it. Perhaps it's much more complicated than that, and impossible to look at from a binary perspective, in black-and-white terms, or even good versus evil.

We can't understand what went wrong without first understanding why Inside was developed in the first place. It was a last resort: the planet was quickly becoming uninhabitable.

In New York, decades of unending natural disasters had pummeled what used to be Long Island, Queens, and most of Brooklyn into nonexistence so that the east side of Manhattan looked out directly onto the Atlantic Ocean. There were endless floods and tsunamis. Hurricane winds had knocked out the windows of nearly every skyscraper. Then there was, of course, the heat. Every day, it was only getting hotter.

It wasn't just the coastal regions of America that had been transformed by the weather, it was everywhere. Many people had moved toward the middle of the country, until the worsening storm situation made that unlivable, too ("Tornado Alley," it used to be called, until the alley became more of a highway, and then more of a parking lot, where tornadoes were so frequent that people stopped rebuilding their homes and moved away). Others had started going up north to Canada, where it was warm and sunny all year round, like Los Angeles had been in my childhood, back when you could still go there, before the fires burned it all down.

It also wasn't just America; in many countries around the world, tropical storms and hurricanes had become a constant. Elsewhere, droughts lasted for months at a time. Icebergs melted, causing historic tsunamis. The air quality suffered; people rarely ventured outside. Viral disease was ravaging vulnerable populations, taking lives faster than hospitals could admit patients.

Not everyone was suffering, though. The wealthy grew wealthier as they profited off fear, monetizing false promises of safety with manipulative marketing: *You, too, can survive if you just buy one more thing.* Violence increased as desperation grew.

Worldwide, an estimated 700 million people were displaced by weather-related disasters. They had nowhere to go.

The one thing that hadn't gotten worse was global conflict—there was too much for governments to worry about domestically for them to engage in international warfare. A United World Government was established as a response to the climate emergency; their initial goal was to slow down the climate's ongoing deadly transformation, but once it was determined to be too late for that, they shifted focus to how humanity could survive it. They promised a solution for everyone.

Maybe we should have known that was impossible. Maybe we just wanted to believe that we could all be saved. Whatever the case, we bought into their story. I did, anyway.

So it went: a team of scientists came up with the idea of highly fortified, city-size structures that could, quite literally, weather the impending storms, and the global project known as Inside was initiated.

Ground was broken in Singapore, Nairobi, Auckland, Moscow, São Paulo, and New York City. To create an Inside, the cities were sealed up: Sidewalks were encased in round tubes of weatherproof glass, becoming tunnels, and then more glass tunnels were built above them, looping between buildings like the legs of a jellyfish. The buildings were reinforced, and almost every open space was filled with more housing until the city, or at least the part that was becoming Inside, looked like one giant mass of metal and glass.

In Manhattan, the subway system was converted into a mazelike storage facility, and the vast majority of what once had been entrances to the stations were sealed up to prevent future flooding. Central Park had long since lost most of its centuries-old trees in one mega-storm or another and was now filled with cube-like Inside housing developments, each apartment optimized down to the square inch. The highest levels had skylights, but beyond that, views of the outside were rare. The tallest buildings were connected by passageways, woven tightly, and beyond were added layers of protective metal and reinforced glass, sealing the whole thing up, so that unfiltered air and heat couldn't penetrate the structure. Most windows simply looked into other windows.

In order for Inside to be completely self-sufficient for an undisclosed period of time, the entire West Wall, facing the now moat-like Hudson River—and beyond that, the rest of what was left of America—was made up of an enormous, sloping garden, with tiered layers of horizontal land dedicated to the crop that would most benefit from the angle of sun that filtered through the thick glass. Because the gardens stretched across the entire west side, Inside simply looked, if approached from the mainland, like a big green hill: a large, lumpy triangle. It was an inelegant solution to the problem of protecting the future of humanity, but it was a solution, nonetheless—albeit an expensive one.

Even though Inside was a government-initiated project, each location was largely funded by private investors, like the elusive multibillionaire/women's rights activist Jacqueline Millender of JM Inc., who invested heavily in the New York City project before joining other wealthy luminaries in space, on the cruise ship–like stations that orbited the earth while the planet's remaining inhabitants hurtled toward an uncertain future. Each shuttle was connected to a different Inside to obtain resources, like food, creating an extraterrestrial umbilical cord between Earth and its now-distant children.

Up until this point, there were a few things Jacqueline Millender was known for, aside from the simple fact of her enormous wealth, much of which was inherited. Her grandfather, James Millender, had been the original JM Inc., and the initials were passed down in her family, first to her father, Joseph, and then to her. But unlike her predecessors, who grew their empires largely in the oil business, Jacqueline had a gift for innovation, and made a lot of money very quickly after she came up with the idea for Refillables, an automatic home refueling system designed to minimize plastic waste and increase convenience.

But the project Jacqueline was most proud of was her book. *Yours for the Taking!: Reclaiming Female Power in a Changing World* was written by a team of well-paid professional ghostwriters, but it was based on her ideas. It was an international bestseller, translated into too many languages to count. It spurred a luxury product line, an award-winning podcast, and worldwide members-only, women-only coworking spaces called Yours! And ultimately, profits from the Yours! brand were what allowed her to fund Inside.

Jacqueline told me she thought of New York's Inside as a love letter, and also an apology, to the planet. She was happy to be able to leave such a concrete legacy. On the days that she could make out the East Coast of North America from the smudged circular window in her new quarters, she said she liked to imagine she could see "her" Inside. Sometimes I saw her pressing her hand to the glass, as though greeting it. When I first saw her doing that, I was moved by the gesture, thinking I was seeing a flare of emotion in Jacqueline's otherwise steely facade. Now, I'm not so sure.

Out of the millions of applications sent in by people desperate to escape a roiling world, the press announced that three million people would be approved to move into Jacqueline's Inside. It took five years for the applications to be processed. The people who had been accepted were alerted simultaneously, their phones lighting up with a jarring buzz. From afar, it sounded like the cicadas that now descended every summer, their once seventeen-year life cycle having shortened rapidly, the nightly dissonant symphony becoming increasingly frantic. I was not one of the lucky ones who had been accepted, but I had won another kind of lottery: Jacqueline had offered me a place alongside her on the space shuttle.

At that time, we thought there were only two truly safe places to be: Inside or in space. There were no protections anymore for people who were neither wealthy enough for space nor lucky enough for Inside, and the government had washed their hands of the matter. Communication between the people who lived Inside or in space and those who lived in the wilderness all but ceased. At first, those people had been monitored by the United World Government, in case they decided to rise up against the injustice of their fates. But the government didn't have much to worry about from the shutouts. After the initial riots had been quelled, nothing else followed—at least not from the people outside.

As it turned out, the cracks that started to form in the fortresses known as Insides were not external, they were foundational—but it would take years for anyone to realize they had been there from the beginning.

PART ONE

PRONE TO ROOT ROT

2050–2055

1

A GROUP OF TIRED, RUMPLED YOUNG PEOPLE SPILLED OUT of the lab's double doors and onto the glittering, gum-encrusted sidewalk. They rubbed their eyes in the hazy afternoon light, which was thickly speckled with floating white bits of who-knows-what, and though the city smelled of dirt and rot, the light was aesthetically pleasing, like a photo filter that turns everything grainy and sepia toned, like a memory. It was Friday, and the students hummed with unforetold promises of the weekend ahead. Among them was Ava, the teacher's assistant for the plant biology class the kids had just fled. Students clustered into small packs around her, talking loudly about their evening plans. She wasn't much older than most of them.

When Ava rounded the corner, breaking off from the group of students, she reached into her nose and pulled out the gold, horseshoe-shaped septum piercing that had been hiding upside-down in her nostrils since the morning. Her long, curly brown hair was parted down the middle, which she always felt made her look more approachable during the workday. She briefly stopped walking to adjust her part to the side, revealing an undercut shaved around her left ear. She took her glasses off and stashed them in her backpack, blinking as her eyes adjusted. Her students didn't need to know that this was what she normally looked like when she wasn't working. It was easier if they read her as a bookish academic.

Her stuffed backpack was pulling her shoulders down. It was hot out; well, it was always hot now in Manhattan, but it was an extra-oppressive kind of heat that afternoon, and Ava felt like she was moving in slow motion. Sirens wailed in the distance.

The lanyard with her employee ID was still around her neck, and the plastic was sticking to her skin. Her hair was electrified by the humidity, frizzing around her head in gravity-defying ways. She felt a pimple brewing painfully on her cheek, trapped by the grease on her face. Her armpit sweat was getting the best of her deodorant. There was nothing pleasant about being in Manhattan. She couldn't wait to get home to Orchid.

She'd have to rush to get to the station before the next aerial tramway departed. Always creaking and moaning its way across the water, it was the only good way to get back and forth from her home in what was once Brooklyn (residents now called it Brook, an abbreviated name that suited the newly tiny, crescent moon–shaped land) to Manhattan; there were no bridges left, and the subways no longer functioned. There was a ferry, but the water was so choppy it made Ava sick, a feeling that always reminded her of being a kid trapped in endless silent car rides with her parents, nauseous and alone.

She made it into the Brook-bound tram just as the doors closed behind her. Packed in with dozens of other nine-to-fivers, Ava finally breathed a sigh of relief. She'd soon make it home, to the air-conditioning, to the sweet little living room she shared with the woman she loved.

She took out her phone. Its background was a selfie of her and Orchid; Ava's whole face was buried into Orchid's neck while Orchid squinted in the sun, looking just past the camera's lens with the kind of half smile that Ava adored. As Ava settled into her seat on the tram she examined this photo, even though she'd seen it a million times. She could have spent the rest of her life looking at it.

They'd met by chance. Now, though, as Ava considered the millions of decisions that had led to the exact place and time when her life intersected with Orchid's, it felt more like an inevitability than an accident.

Ava had been walking down the street between classes. She was lost in thought, much as she was now. But in that moment, her daydreaming was interrupted when a voice out of nowhere said, "Oh shit, watch out," and then a warm hand grabbed her by the arm and pulled her sharply to the left just as a drone carrying a box labeled REFILLABLES zoomed by.

"Oh my god," Ava had exclaimed. The hand was still locked onto her arm, and as Ava caught her breath she took in the tall, broad-shouldered woman it belonged to. She was white and appeared to be around Ava's age. Her short, reddish-brown hair shimmered with sweat. A smattering of freckles danced between pitted acne scars on her cheeks, which gave her a roughness that negated what would have otherwise been a disarming prettiness. She was wearing a toolbelt slung low on her hips and an orange reflective vest. An active construction site churned and beeped behind them.

"Those things are such a fucking hazard," the woman had said, shaking her head. She dropped Ava's arm, though where she'd grabbed still felt tingly and hot. "You okay?"

"I'm fine," Ava said. And then, she added, "You saved me." As if on cue, the woman turned pink, holding Ava's eye contact for a beat longer than necessary, telling Ava everything she needed to know about what was going to happen next.

Despite herself, Ava had laughed. The stranger grinned. "I'm Orchid," she said, and extended her hand. She didn't ask Ava's name; she knew Ava would tell her.

They shook hands, a warm squeeze. Ava had giggled more. She couldn't help it. Meeting like this, being so clearly on the same page about what *this* was; being so attracted to someone that it rendered her uncharacteristically bold; having that attraction clearly be so mutual, and so random. If Ava had used the bathroom after class (and she almost did), they would not have met at all.

"Like the flower?" Ava said, immediately regretting it. It was probably what everybody asked her.

Ava had never seen an orchid in real life before; the wild ones had been wiped out by a virus. She knew that they had been known for their beauty and that the most beautiful among them were also the rarest. Some people still kept them as houseplants, but they were delicate and finicky, prone to root rot.

"Something like that," Orchid replied, and then gestured to the nearby science building. "Did you learn about dead plants there?"

Ava nodded.

"Cool," Orchid said.

Ava laughed. "Is it?"

"I think so," Orchid said.

There was a pause. Ava, anxious to keep the conversation going, said, "So, are you building something?"

Orchid nodded toward the construction site. "We're putting the campus on stilts because of all the flooding. Apparently this whole avenue is going to be a canal soon. I'm just an assistant carpenter, but, you know."

Ava did not know, yet she had nodded again. She'd never done much work with her hands. But she wanted badly to understand the person standing in front of her. She felt impatient about it, like the parts of her life that happened before meeting Orchid had all been a waste of time. She handed Orchid her phone. "Give me your number." Orchid did as she was told.

Remembering this moment on the tram, Ava smiled to herself. Now, five years later, Ava was, for perhaps the first time in her whole life, something adjacent to happy; adjacent because it was that very happiness that worried her, as she obsessively followed the news of the climate crisis and wondered, often, if the world was truly ending, and what that would mean for their future together. Their love gave her something to fear losing. She couldn't remember feeling this worried before she had someone.

This was something they had in common: they were both alone. They'd discovered it on their first date, while they'd sat together at a beachside bar at the southern edge of Brook, the waves crashing urgently into the seawall.

"Where's your family?" Ava had asked, between sips of beer.

"My mom left when I was a kid, and then it was just me and my dad," Orchid said. "He had a heart attack a few years ago. It's been just me ever since."

"My parents died in the hurricane last year," Ava said. Orchid placed her hand over Ava's and gave it a squeeze as a mutual understanding settled over them.

The light pollution was less intense over Brook, and a few stars glinted above them. "I love being able to see the planets," Ava said, pointing to Saturn's soft glow. "It's so comforting to know there are some things humans can't destroy." Orchid squinted up, following her gaze.

Orchid paid the bill and led Ava by the hand to her apartment. She unlocked the door with a retinal scan and said, "My roommates are out." Before Ava could even look around, they were kissing. Orchid's mouth tasted like ash and salt, and her arms felt solid and warm.

She guided Ava to her bedroom, and then she pushed Ava playfully onto her unmade bed.

On her back, Ava held Orchid with all of her limbs, her arms and legs squeezing as tightly as they could, and she imagined that if she could just touch enough of Orchid's skin with a maximum amount of her own, they might fuse. It was just a matter of surface area.

There was a layer of dimpled flesh across the backs of Orchid's thighs, and Ava dug her fingers into it. This feeling, she remembered with the utmost clarity; how it turned her on more, knowing that Orchid had cellulite and pimples and a stomach. She was real. She smelled like sweat and sawdust and when Ava bit her lip too hard, she winced.

Ava tried, a few times, half-heartedly, to get on top, but Orchid wouldn't let her. "You don't actually want me to get off you, right?" Orchid said, and Ava acquiesced.

Her first orgasm at Orchid's hand felt like jumping off a cliff. Her second one felt like her body had turned inside out.

When Ava was so raw and reeling that she couldn't stand to be touched anymore, she reached for Orchid, but Orchid moved her hand away, pressing herself into Ava's thigh instead.

"I want you like this," Orchid said.

They were still awake and kissing when Orchid's alarm went off for work.

Ava spent the day sleeping in Orchid's bed, her long curly hair spilling all over Orchid's pillows. She was still there when Orchid returned that night. She had wanted to be there every night when Orchid came home.

And from that moment on, she was. She'd be there tonight. She'd looked forward to it all day.

The windows of the tramcar were cracked open, but the sliver of fishy wind that came through did nothing for the heat. Sweat trickled down her back as she glanced through the news, which—as always—was bad. She hardly absorbed any of the information. Headlines blurred into one another. The tram swayed in the wind.

She was wearing a pink dress made from recycled bottles. The dress was so short she could feel the sticky plastic of the seat touching her thighs. Holding her phone in her right hand, she used her left hand to tug at its hem, trying to get the material to lie flat between her skin and the seat. It was no use; the fabric had no give. She longed for the days of cotton or even polyester. The technology that aimed to fix fashion's waste problem hadn't factored in physical comfort. The man sitting next to her made a performative coughing sound and she realized she'd been bumping him with her elbow.

"Excuse me," she said, but he didn't make eye contact.

As she scrolled idly, her phone screen turned red and began buzzing. All around her, phone after phone lit up the color of blood, the simultaneous vibration echoing through the tramcar. She jumped, her heart pounding loudly in her ears.

> Congratulations. Your application for
> Inside has been approved.
>
> Please await further instructions.

She pressed her phone to her chest, smiling up at the ceiling of the tram. Next to her, the man began to sob. She straightened, trying to conceal her excitement from his devastation. Besides, she was excited, but she wasn't feeling relieved. She hadn't heard from Orchid yet.

With shaking hands, she texted: I got in!!!!

She watched Orchid start and stop typing several times.

At last: I didn't.

They'd first heard about Inside one evening a few years ago. Ava was lying on the couch with her legs in Orchid's lap, when suddenly everything changed.

They got the alert at the same time; a push notification that overrode whatever else they were looking at, expanding and flashing urgently.

> Announcing: The Inside Project.
> Please swipe for more information.

"The fuck?" Orchid said.

"No idea," Ava said, sitting up. They both swiped on the message.

Their phones were immediately flooded with words about the need for this new level of protection, and about what might happen to those who weren't accepted.

A summer hailstorm raged outside; every now and then the wind hurled pieces of garbage against the window, making Ava jumpy and on edge as she read about this strange new initiative.

"We should apply," Ava said.

Orchid shrugged. "I guess it can't hurt."

The enrollment office for Inside was at City Hall. They'd waited in line for two days, nestling together in Orchid's tattered sleeping bag on the sidewalk and eating protein bars for meals. The weather held up, somehow, though they'd packed raincoats and, at Ava's insistence, hard hats, in case it hailed more. They took turns using the grimy public bathroom in the park, while the other held their spot in line.

Once they got through the door, it was as though they'd hit fast-forward, a flurry of signatures and stamps before they were rushed off to the Inside techs, who took their blood and gave them passwords to the Inside mobile app, unlocking the hundreds of pages of forms to be completed at home. The whole application process would take months thanks to the thorough psychological evaluations needed. Nobody knew when acceptances—or rejections—to Inside would be announced. Probably not for years.

But Ava wasn't even thinking about that as she giddily clutched Orchid's hand, sweaty with anticipation and with a new prickling sensation in her stomach that felt weirdly romantic, or maybe just like hope.

She had reason to feel optimistic about their chances because they already had a connection to the project—Orchid was one of the thousands of people helping to construct Manhattan's Inside. She was hired through the union, and then was quickly promoted on the site from an assistant to a foreman. ("Forewoman," Ava liked to correct, while Orchid rolled her eyes.)

Orchid came home from work full of stories for Ava about the looping tunnels and endless, windowless rooms that made her feel dizzy, leaving her constantly nauseous as she fortified the glass against the gale-force winds.

"I'm actually not sure if this whole thing is a good idea," she told Ava one night, eating piece after piece of pizza. And then, grinning with her mouth full, she added: "But I guess there's a reason it's not up to me."

Ava shrugged, not wanting to be confrontational, but the truth was that she thought Inside was a *great* idea. When she wasn't guiding small groups of students through other peoples' curriculums, Ava began to spend her free time obsessing over Inside, and about their chances of being accepted. She'd streamed the mayor breaking ground on her phone, and then had watched in person as the walls went up, squeezing to the front of the crowd on her lunch break.

Inside felt like their best bet for survival. They would both get in, she decided. They had to.

Though, sometimes, if she was being honest with herself, Ava felt a small, creeping doubt. Inside's screening process seemed to be looking for certain markers of intelligence, and while Orchid was street-smart, she wasn't educated. Ava worried it would hurt her chances.

She shook these thoughts off whenever they came. There was only one option, and that was being accepted together.

But now, with Inside's final decisions about her and Orchid's future still warm in her hand, Ava exhaled, the last bit of hope leaving her lungs. They had decided long ago that they would only go if they could do it together. There had been no promise that unmarried, childless couples wouldn't be separated. They were evaluated as individuals. But it still came as a shock. To not be able to move Inside meant . . . Well, who knew what it meant? That was the scary part. There would come a day when Brook would no longer be livable. Everything they knew was about to become something else entirely.

Besides, they were in love, and that was the most important thing. Ava knew they'd figure it out. They always did.

Ava shivered. She wasn't sure she felt relief or terror. Perhaps both. At least they finally knew.

She got home to an empty apartment. As she paced around the living room, she texted Orchid a few times, but didn't hear back, which was odd. When Orchid finally appeared in the doorway Ava jumped into her arms and they held each other tightly.

"Where were you?" Ava whispered into her neck, inhaling the smell of sawdust.

"I'm sorry," Orchid said. "I got stuck at work."

They sat down next to each other on their small sofa, their phones perched between them. The walls of their living room were covered in art and odd objects they'd found and mounted quaintly, a loving hodgepodge of pressed flowers that Ava had found, and unusually shaped screws that had no obvious partners from Orchid. Their apartment was small, but it was theirs, and it was Ava's favorite place to be.

"Why do you think they picked you?"

Ava didn't answer. She was picturing the endless forms and tests, how carefully she'd written her answers. She'd had a feeling she would be chosen but hadn't paid much attention to it; it felt naive, like how a child might think she's special. But still, she was not surprised that she was accepted.

Ava's phone buzzed again. This time, the screen was pink.

Congratulations, from Inside.

Over the next month, we will be welcoming you and your new community in staggered groups.

At your designated time, please bring only yourself (no belongings of any kind) and report to the main entrance at 34th Street.

At check-in, please be advised:

For sanitation purposes, all hair will be shaved by our medical team.

You will be given a full panel of vaccines.

We will be drawing blood upon entry, and
on the first of every month therein, to keep
track of your well-being.

Upon entrance, you will be assigned a new
address.

Once you enter Inside, you may not leave,
for your own safety.

Double-tap to accept the terms of your
residence.

Thank you, and welcome to your new,
safer future.

"It doesn't matter," Ava said. "I'm not going."

Orchid looked at the ceiling, picking a hangnail on her thumb. The silence in the room seemed to swell, and then Orchid said, "Ava."

The urgency in Orchid's voice made Ava flinch. "What?"

An infinitely long moment passed before Orchid met Ava's eyes. When she finally spoke, she sounded serious, stern. "I love you more than anything, but I think you need to do it."

"What are you talking about?" Ava stood up, wiping her palms on her jeans. They'd gotten so sweaty.

Orchid reached out and grabbed Ava's wrist. Talking louder now, sounding more panicked, she said, "It's the only way to make sure you survive."

Ava pulled away from her. "We've been talking about this for, like, ever," she said, her voice rising in frustration. "You can't change the plan at the last second."

"I can't bear the thought of you not going because of me," Orchid said, in a voice so small that Ava almost didn't hear her.

"And what are you going to do?" Ava demanded. "Bike to Canada, and then live in the woods forever?"

"Yeah, I am," Orchid said, brightening and sitting up straighter, as though the idea had only just occurred to her when Ava said it. "That's exactly what I'm going to do."

"You're going to die."

"I think I'm going to die either way."

"Orchid," she said, in that way she knew made Orchid bristle. "What is going on right now? I'm not going without you." And then it occurred to Ava that although Orchid was saying one thing, what she meant was something else entirely. "Is there something you'd like to tell me?" Ava asked.

"Please don't make this harder than it has to be."

Ava felt all the blood rush out of her face. "What?" she said, and then said it again. "*What?*"

"I—I'm sorry," Orchid stammered. "I'm sorry. I'm so, so sorry."

Ava started to cry. "You want me to go in there alone?"

"I want you to survive."

Ava said, "If you wanted to leave me, you could have just said so."

"That's not what I meant," Orchid said, but Ava had stopped listening. She was sobbing uncontrollably now, still standing, her arms wrapped tight around her own torso as though her organs were about to fall out. She felt certain they might.

"Is there someone else?" she asked.

"No," Orchid said, offended. "Of course not."

Shakily, Ava walked out of the living room and into their bedroom, flopping facedown on the bed. Orchid called her name a few times, but Ava didn't answer. She didn't know what else to say.

After a few minutes, she heard Orchid rummaging around in the coat closet. Then came the sound of the front door opening and clicking shut. And then—quiet. Orchid was gone.

2

IT WAS ALMOST MIDNIGHT, AND FOR A FEW MOMENTS, THE only sound in the kitchen was the ticking of an old wall clock. The ongoing scream of sirens in the distance didn't even count as noise anymore.

At a small, round table, directly across from her daughter, Shelby's mother sat stricken. She let out a long exhale and asked: "What do you think *that woman* can teach you that the university can't?"

"*Mom*. I'm not dropping out of school forever. It's an internship—an opportunity."

"But it's instead of class this semester, right?" Shelby nodded. "How can you throw away that scholarship you worked so hard for?"

"I'm not throwing it away! I don't understand what your issue is."

"Shelby, honey," her mom said. "I think you know exactly what the issue is."

Shelby did know. Jacqueline Millender was basically the embodiment of capitalist achievement, endless ambition, and a winner-takes-all, binary view of the world—everything her parents stood against. But revealing that she understood their argument would mean giving in, and she wasn't willing to do that. Her dad sat next to her mom in silence, as usual.

It was stuffy in the kitchen; the permanent smell of fried garlic and onions hung in the air. Shelby pushed her thick brown bangs off her forehead. She wished they had air-conditioning. *No one should be this uncomfortable inside*, she thought.

She rubbed her eyes, smearing her black eyeliner onto her fingers. It was supposed to be waterproof, though no amount of chemistry could create makeup to withstand the heat in the kitchen, or outside, for that matter.

Shelby lined her eyelids with smudgy black kohl every day. It was her signature. She liked the look of smoldering eyes peeking out from behind her overgrown bangs. As a tall white girl from the Midwest, it was hard to feel enigmatic; she did what she could to create an air of mystery.

Under the kitchen's cheap fluorescent lights, Shelby's parents looked much older than they were. She felt a pang of guilt, thinking of all they had sacrificed for her. But she also felt relief; now, she'd be able to pay her own way, maybe get an apartment with air-conditioning, and even a dishwasher.

First, though, Shelby needed to have this talk with her parents, and let them know that she had managed to land an interview for the highly coveted internship at JM Inc. Why couldn't they see that this would be good for her? That she was essentially securing her future?

"No one needs to be a billionaire," her dad said, finally speaking up. "She's a wealth-hoarder."

"Yeah, but," Shelby pleaded, "JM Inc. does so much charity work! I could help with that. They have all of these amazing initiatives that support young women. I could have a real impact."

"Lots of people do charity work."

"Okay, but she invented Refillables! That's a once-in-a-century innovation."

"Civilian space travel is a once-in-a-century innovation," Shelby's mom said. "Refillables are a convenience."

"You *guys*."

Shelby knew her mother had a point, though she was not about to admit it. Refillables was a smart-home refueling system. If you ran out of, say, toothpaste, you simply put the empty tube into a special chamber that was installed in an exterior-facing wall. One press of a button, and your toothpaste would be automatically refilled within a few hours by one of the countless drones that swirled overhead. The chambers, of course, could only be purchased from JM Inc. Refillables could have potentially helped alleviate some damage to the environment, had anyone thought of it a few decades before; the idea of a new plastic container for every time you ran out of something was now so outlandish, it was politically incorrect to suggest. But it had hit the market just half a century too late. The landfill situation was already out of control.

Shelby heard small footsteps running down the hallway. Soon her little sister, Camilla, appeared in the kitchen doorway, rubbing her eyes.

"Honey, what are you doing up?" their mom said.

"I had the dream again," Camilla said, and then climbed into Shelby's lap. Shelby wrapped her arms around her.

Camilla started to cry. "The climate refugees." She sniffled. "I dreamed they came to our apartment and slept in the living room and you told them to go and they wouldn't. They just stayed here."

"Never gonna happen, kiddo," their dad said.

"But aren't you guys scared?" Camilla said, while Shelby stroked her sister's silky seven-year-old hair. "The kids at school say the world is *ending.*"

"Every generation thinks the world is ending," their mom said, trying to be reassuring, but her voice gave her sadness away. "We did, and look. We're all still here."

"You should believe our parental units," Shelby said, tickling Camilla to distract her. "If the resident Zoomers aren't worried, we shouldn't be, either."

Their parents laughed.

"You know we hate being called that. It's ageism," their mom said.

"Zooooomers!" Camilla giggled.

Hearing Camilla's voice, Pesto jumped up on the table, stretching his tiny body, purring and reaching out a paw toward Camilla, who held her hand out and stroked his back while he slinked by.

"I really wish you wouldn't encourage him to walk where we eat," their dad said, but he reached out a hand to pet the kitten, too.

Camilla rested her head on Shelby's shoulder, and Shelby felt her sister relax. She rubbed slow circles on Camilla's back. Shelby was thirteen years older than Camilla, and she felt more like a mom than a big sister.

"You know," their dad said, "I have an old social justice friend whose kid got an internship with the NYPD. I think I know how he feels."

Shelby rolled her eyes as dramatically as she could. "God, Dad!" she said. "At least Jacqueline is a feminist."

Shelby's mom shook her head. "Jacqueline Millender feminism is not actual feminism."

"No," Shelby said. "It's *better.* You should read her book."

"I don't need to read that book to know what's in it," her mom said. "I remember the era of the girlboss. I lived through it. I don't care to see the propaganda it has evolved into. Aren't kids interested in socialism anymore? What happened to intersectionality? We used to want to *eat* the rich. And you want to, what, be just like her?"

"You don't understand," Shelby said. "She's not a *girlboss*. She's literally a woman who is a leader. There's a difference."

"You're right, I don't understand," her mom said. "You've worked so hard in school. Please don't lose sight of your own dreams."

"This *is* my dream."

"No. It's Jacqueline Millender's dream. You'd just be helping her with it. I can't believe someone as smart as you could be fooled by all this."

"Fooled by it?" Shelby cried, laughing a little bit at how dramatic her mother sounded. "I'm inspired by it. I thought you wanted me to have strong female role models."

"I don't think you should get involved with all the gender unrest, anyway," her dad chimed in again. "It seems dangerous. Those men's rights organizations are out for blood."

"But that's why I want to get involved. Don't you see? It's important to be on the right side of this."

"I'm not sure there is a right side, honey," her mom said. "Both are arguing against equality."

"Maybe there's something to that," Shelby said. "It's not like men have made the world *better*."

"How can you say things like that in front of your father?"

"I'm sorry, Dad," she said, but he wouldn't meet her eyes. "I didn't mean *you*."

The conversation ended there. Shelby carried Camilla back to her bed, tucked her in, and made sure to leave the door open a crack for Pesto, who loved to sleep with Camilla.

Shelby's own room was just as it had been in high school. Although she was almost through with college, Shelby still lived at home. Cramped as it was, the family apartment had seemed like her only choice, financially—until now, with the potential for a job at JM Inc. on the horizon. As desperate as she was to make it on her own, Shelby was grateful for her parents, who had supported her in much more profound ways than just money and shelter. At nine years old, just a little older than Camilla was now, Shelby had told her parents that she no longer wanted to be called the name they had given her at birth, and she requested Shelby instead. It had been her grandmother's name. She also told them that she wanted them to use female pronouns.

When Shelby clarified what her gender was, though, they still lived in the Midwest, in a region where the worsening tornado situation meant that resources were limited. The government's focus was on community storm shelters, and while the hospitals were massive and multiple, they were mostly set up to treat urgent injuries. There were no clinics within driving distance that were equipped to get Shelby the right kind of care.

And so, the family moved to New York City, where there were still doctors who focused on things other than emergency injuries, and they started over. Once settled into city life, they saved and borrowed and fundraised until they had enough money to get her blockers and, later, hormone replacement therapy.

Her transness was never an issue in her family. Their first real disagreements started when Shelby wasn't interested in the activism that her parents participated in; when she instead spent her time shopping and collecting print magazines from decades past, when her idols became women who ran their own companies. For Shelby's radical, lower-middle-class family, this was an affront to everything they had worked for. But Shelby had different goals than her parents had for themselves—she wanted to prioritize her own needs and ambitions and see what could come of them.

Shelby was a business major, a choice that was usually met with a simple question: "But why?" The economy had been in freefall for most of her life. But Shelby was interested in the larger picture: in the way that corporate CEOs seemed to have more power than politicians. She thought it was a shame that more of them weren't women. She had a vision of herself at the head of a massive table in a boardroom high up in the sky, everyone gathered around her, listening to her every word as she voiced her plans for making a better world.

Her search for women who felt similarly led her to Jacqueline Millender, who quickly became her hero. Shelby found her work to be an inspiring challenge. The concept of women rethinking power spoke to her; she didn't want to have to dance around the issue of her own abilities anymore, as she so often had to do in class, surrounded by sensitive boys who couldn't handle a woman being smarter and more capable than they were.

A few nights after the late-night conversation with her parents about the internship, as Shelby stood in front of the mirror practicing her most professional "Nice to meet you," there came a knock on her door.

"Come in," Shelby said.

Her mom pushed the door open and handed Shelby a navy-blue skirt suit. "I thought you might want to wear this," she said.

"Is this a peace offering?" Shelby said, taking the suit. The silk felt cool and soft in her hands. All of Shelby's clothes were very hip—one of her talents was finding discounted vintage items that still looked relevant—but nothing she owned was necessarily professional. She needed the suit as much as she needed her mother's support.

"I just want what's best for you," her mom said, her eyes turning glossy. "If you think that means working for that woman, I won't get in the way."

She turned around while Shelby tried the outfit on. "What do you think?" Shelby asked.

"I would hire you in an instant," her mom replied, and pulled her in for a tight hug.

The next morning, Shelby arrived at the JM Inc. headquarters at exactly 8:45 a.m., fifteen minutes before her interview. She knew to expect some security, but by the time her bag had been searched, her whole person scanned, and both her IDs verified, it was a quarter past nine. She was flustered and anxious when she finally stepped into the elevator.

The doors dinged open into a light, airy lobby, where a receptionist was already waiting for her. "Shelby Silver?" Shelby nodded. The woman said, "You can wait in the conference room."

"I'm so sorry I'm late," she said, breathless, but the receptionist only nodded.

"There's water if you want it," she said, gesturing to a gold bar cart, and then left Shelby alone in the air-conditioned silence.

Shelby drummed her fingers on the table. She crossed and uncrossed her legs. She took her résumé out of its folder and placed it on the table. She smoothed its edges. She scanned it for typos. Finally, running out of things to fidget with, she checked her phone. It was almost 10:00.

At last, the door opened, and a woman who was definitely not Jacqueline Millender breezed in.

In the end, Shelby had five interviews with different JM Inc. employees before she got an email asking her to come in and meet with Jacqueline herself. She wore the blue suit each time.

By now, she was prepared. She knew to arrive an hour early. But after the security check, instead of being escorted to the conference room again, she was directed to a different set of elevators.

"These will take you directly to Ms. Millender," the security guard said, and then winked. "Good luck."

Shelby's knees felt weak as the elevator dinged and then flew upward. She closed her eyes and tried to steady her breathing. *You can do this*, she told herself, and then repeated the thought each time the elevator passed another floor. By the time the doors opened, she felt certain she could.

The room she found herself in was surely too big to be Jacqueline's *office*. With soaring ceilings and dark hardwood floors, amber-tinted lights, and a warm, floral scent in the air, it felt more like the lobby of a luxury hotel (at least, how Shelby imagined one might look). But there in the corner was an oak desk, and on the other side of the room were two pink sofas that faced each other. Sitting in one of them was a slight figure in a black dress.

"Shelby!" Jacqueline called brightly across the expanse.

"Hello," Shelby said, and walked as confidently as she could to where Jacqueline was perched.

Jacqueline grinned, a genuine, warm smile, and Shelby felt herself begin to relax. "Please sit," Jacqueline said, gesturing to the other pink sofa. "Everyone here loves you. I imagine I will, too." She sounded sincere. Shelby had imagined Jacqueline to be a lot of things, but *nice* wasn't necessarily one of them. It was a delightful surprise.

In her press photos, which Shelby had practically memorized, Jacqueline

Millender appeared tall, ageless, and impeccably dressed in cream-hued layers of cashmere, with a simple string of pearls, or sometimes diamonds. Her head was often tilted just slightly to the left, revealing a strong, square jaw and smooth neck. Her body, or at least what could be seen of it beneath her couture, was lithe; the kind of muscles you get from twice-daily sessions with a personal trainer. Her shiny white hair was razor-cut into a bob, angled sharply beneath her chin. Her lipstick was always matte red.

As Shelby drew nearer, it became clear that Jacqueline was probably just over five feet tall. The skin around her neck had a bit of a sag to it, and her eye sockets were slightly hollow. She was in aggressively good shape, that much was accurate, but it wasn't really doing her any favors; she was all jagged edges.

But her presence was larger than life. Shelby felt so starstruck that, later, she couldn't even really remember the rest of their conversation at all, up until the moment that Jacqueline revealed the true purpose of their meeting: "I know we spoke about an internship, but I'm wondering if you'll consider coming on as my full-time assistant."

Shelby did not tell her parents when she dropped out of school to work for Jacqueline full-time. She knew they would never understand. Instead, she simply told them that she'd saved enough to move out and found a studio apartment near the office where she could go to work without their judgmental eyes following her everywhere.

Her apartment was small and cramped, just like her family home—but it was all hers. She was on her way to . . . something. She wasn't sure what this job would lead to, but at least it was leading her forward. At night she fell asleep beneath a water stain on the ceiling that seemed to bloom wider whenever she looked at it. It didn't matter. Her life already felt bigger.

One morning in the office, Jacqueline brought Shelby over to a table that was overflowing with packages.

"This is the free table," she said. "These brands are all begging me to endorse them on social media. As if I'd advertise them for free!" She laughed, and Shelby laughed, too. "Not that they could afford my rate," she said.

"That reminds me," Jacqueline said, not laughing anymore. "Do you want to start running my accounts for me? I trust you to write in my voice. Don't give too much away; I must maintain some sort of mystery. I know it's important for my brand, I'm just tired of doing it myself."

"I'd be thrilled to," Shelby said, and she was.

"Great," Jacqueline said, and then gestured at the pile of goods on the table. "Let me know if there is anything I'd like in there. But otherwise it's yours."

It seemed strange to Shelby that companies were being so wasteful and excessive with their gifting. But there was a lot of denial here, in these monied spaces. It was almost contagious. If she tried hard enough, she could pretend like she thought everything was going to be fine, too.

The free table, Shelby quickly learned, was replenished almost every day when the mail came. Shelby accumulated designer robes, comically large candles, high heels she'd never wear, perfume that made her cough. Sometimes Shelby sold the things she found and used the money to buy food; she loved splurging on the oversized green grapes that were only sold at the high-end grocery store, because she could eat a bunch slowly over the course of an hour and not feel full. Mostly, though, she saved the nicer stuff from the free table for her mom and Camilla, and when she saw her family for dinner every few weeks, she made a point to always slip something into her mom's purse.

JM Inc. was in the midst of a hiring boom. The Yours! franchise was so successful that they needed to bring on more people to staff the coworking space. Jacqueline asked Shelby to screen the applications, and then, to Shelby's surprise, Jacqueline spent her days observing the interviews from behind a two-way mirror. She was present for conversations with even the most junior hires.

Shelby realized that Jacqueline must have been secretly observing all of *her* interviews, too. Shelby wondered what Jacqueline had seen, and what she had thought of the nervous girl in the navy-blue suit alone in the conference room—what it was about her that Jacqueline felt was worthy of bringing into her very carefully curated inner circle.

Shelby came with Jacqueline for some of these observational sessions, and after she'd seen so many that the candidates started to become hard to keep track of, Shelby noticed something unsettling: Jacqueline was staffing the Yours! spaces with almost exclusively women of color. Meanwhile, the higher-ups of the company were mostly white.

One day, she tried to ask Jacqueline about it directly. "None of the people you've chosen for the more menial jobs are white."

"Why wouldn't we be hiring with an eye for diversity?" Jacqueline replied.

"That's not what I meant," Shelby said. "It just seems like . . ."

Jacqueline cut her off. "It's important that we give opportunities to all women," she said, ending the conversation, and clearly not understanding Shelby's point. Shelby was too nervous to bring it up again.

Up until this moment, Shelby had regarded Jacqueline's work with a kind of wide-eyed wonder. Suddenly, though, Jacqueline was starting to seem more human than Shelby had anticipated; flawed, even. Shelby had wanted to take Jacqueline's mission statement at face value, wanted to believe that when Jacqueline said "all women," she meant it. But how could she, given what Shelby herself had witnessed?

It made her anxious about what Jacqueline's true politics around trans women were, too. Was it possible Jacqueline's persona was all just lip service?

But in practice, Jacqueline was keeping Shelby too busy to really give her time to analyze the situation. And if Shelby focused only on the kind, almost maternal way Jacqueline treated her, it was easy to forget the rest.

A few days later Jacqueline called Shelby into her office. "Shelby, what do you think about joining me in my home?"

"What for?"

"I get more work done there," Jacqueline said. "And I'd like to have you around during the day. You soothe me."

Shelby flushed with pride. "I'd love to," she said. "I'd be honored to."

The first day Shelby worked out of Jacqueline's penthouse, she couldn't stop staring at the view of the city below. Once she was able to tear herself away, she found herself enchanted with the endless walls of books, the dramatic, classical sculptures of naked women displayed around the apartment, and then, the ultimate surprise, the spa-like bathroom with a heated floor.

From the living room, Jacqueline called out, "Shelby, can you come sign books for me?"

Shelby spent the rest of the day forging Jacqueline's signature. While she worked, she kept an eye on Jacqueline's email, taking a break every few minutes to schedule meetings and make sure her calendar was organized.

Jacqueline watched her from the other side of the room, sipping a martini.

"Come to an event with me tonight," Jacqueline said.

"Really?"

"It's just a boring cocktail party. You'll be the youngest person. But I think it would be a good learning experience for you. Lots of feminists there. You should be meeting people."

"I don't have anything to wear," Shelby said. She had on a simple, loose-fitting linen dress.

"You look very cool today," Jacqueline said. "You should wear what you have on."

"Where's the party?"

"I put all the details in a draft in my inbox," Jacqueline said.

Shelby pulled up Jacqueline's draft folder and found thousands of saved files filled with Jacqueline's nearly incoherent note-taking; lists and out-of-context paragraphs and links.

"This isn't a good system for keeping track of information," Shelby said, alarmed but laughing; it was endearing that someone so rich and powerful was so disorganized and so bad at technology.

"Why do you think I hired you?" Jacqueline said. "Anyway, it's easy for me, and I've been doing it like that for years. Can't stop now. I'm too old to make major changes to my habits. At least I always know where my draft folder *is*."

They took a black car to the party downtown, and Jacqueline's body-guard loomed over them while they pushed through the men's rights protesters outside. To Shelby, the protesters were frightening; their rage felt childlike, unpredictable. As though they were mad about things they couldn't fully understand, having this public tantrum as their only means of self-expression.

"They always do this," Jacqueline shouted to Shelby over the noise of the crowd. "Every event we plan."

Inside the gilded walls of the cocktail party, older women in pantsuits peered curiously at Shelby, who orbited nervously around Jacqueline.

"Okay, that's enough," Jacqueline said, finally, her tone more abrasive than it had been all day. "Stop hovering. Go talk to someone. Find me when you want to leave." And then Shelby was alone.

She took a glass of champagne from a tray. She nibbled a small fried appetizer that was handed to her. She listened to the women around her complain loudly about the men outside. She felt deeply out of place.

It was possible, she thought, that Jacqueline had brought her here to make a point to these women; to prove how progressive she was. She didn't want to think such a negative thought about her boss, but it was hard to ignore the possibility that her identity was being used to further Jacqueline's brand—something that was always top of mind for Jacqueline.

She took her phone out and texted her mom. What are you doing?

Her mom wrote back, I was just thinking about you.

Jacqueline materialized in front of Shelby before she could respond to her mom. "I see you haven't met anyone," Jacqueline said. "Come." She dragged her by the arm over to a corner where Jacqueline's ghostwriters were standing around a cocktail table.

"I love what you're wearing," one woman said to her. "Where can I find a dress like that?"

"I got it at a thrift store," Shelby said, and the small group laughed as though she was joking. Shelby blushed. The truth was there was nothing special about her dress. It was simple and boring. But she'd noticed that cis women loved to compliment her clothing. It was an interesting way to bond. Superficial, but also somewhat telling; as though they felt the need to show her that they approved of her femininity. Jacqueline also did it.

"We were just discussing feminism's fifth wave," a woman with a bright orange bob and a fleck of lipstick on her front tooth said to Shelby. She appeared to be in her sixties. "Are you familiar?"

"Very," said Shelby.

"And what do you think of it?"

"I think there's a lot of damage we have to undo because of it," Shelby replied.

Jacqueline smiled as if to say, *See? I told you she gets it.*

Orange Bob nodded. "The word *feminism* has been stolen by the very people it was invented to challenge. It's become meaningless."

"Well, I don't think it's exactly *meaningless*," Shelby said.

"I'm aligned," Jacqueline chimed in. "The problem isn't feminism, it's that the fifth wavers said it was feminism's job to fix the global crisis of masculinity. Apparently, men falling behind was our fault."

"But the fifth wavers didn't fix it," Orange Bob said. "They just rolled back progress."

"Yes. And that's why the old issues returned," Jacqueline said. "Sexual harassment, assault, pay gaps. Domestic violence incidents. All our reproductive rights, gone." She was ticking the issues off on her fingers, and flashes of her glossy red-pink nail polish caught the light. "Women haven't been this disadvantaged in a hundred years."

Shelby was already familiar with the ins and outs of the sociopolitical circumstances that had led to the gender unrest, but she knew these elder-millennial women liked feeling as though they were teaching her things, so she listened and nodded and asked questions when it was clear they wanted her to.

"It's the climate crisis," Orange Bob was saying.

"How so?" Shelby asked, on cue.

"It distracted everyone. No one wanted to hear from the feminists while the coasts were flooding. Our rights were low on the hierarchy of needs."

"The same thing has happened for queer people," Shelby said.

Orange Bob gave her an approving nod. "I know. I'm queer, too," she said. "Though you probably think I'm just some boring old cis white lady."

Shelby laughed. That was exactly what she was thinking, though being called out for it made her change her mind.

Shelby began to regularly attend events with Jacqueline, and she figured that Jacqueline liked having her there as much as Shelby liked going. For all of Jacqueline's talk of women's independence, she seemed to do better when she had a person whose only job was to support her.

Jacqueline looked, by all accounts of those closest to her, *"Amazing!"* But Shelby had learned that the only person whose opinion she cared about was her dermatologist.

She hovered in the doorway and watched the doctor peer into her boss's face.

"We should really do something about those under-eye circles," he said. He was in her living room—he only did house calls.

"Get rid of them," Jacqueline said.

Shelby had observed Jacqueline paying out of pocket for cosmetic procedures many times by now. But regardless of how much she spent fixing one area, as soon as it healed, another alleged issue would pop up. If it wasn't her jaw, it was her mouth, and so on and so forth until there was nothing on her face that hadn't been altered in some way. Shelby couldn't tell the difference, but she'd never say so. It made her feel self-conscious about her own face. Could Jacqueline see imperfections there, too, or did she only care about her own invisible flaws?

The dermatologist injected Jacqueline with a needle that, to Shelby, appeared to be nearly the length of her forearm. Jacqueline didn't flinch, though Shelby did, just watching. "Is that all you got?" Jacqueline said.

He laid a frozen eye mask over her face. "Don't move for an hour," he said, and saw himself out.

When the door closed, Jacqueline said, "Shelby, can you turn on something for me to listen to while I lie here like a corpse?"

"Of course," Shelby said. "What mood are we going for?"

"Business," Jacqueline said. "I need some inspiration."

Shelby pulled her phone out and began scrolling through podcasts.

"You know," Jacqueline said, "the most important lesson my grandfather taught me was to not think about our corporation in terms of the present. We must think about the future."

"That makes sense," Shelby said.

"Soon, we'll need something new. Something for the more dangerous decades ahead."

"Do you have any ideas?"

"I have nothing but ideas."

Shelby turned on an audio recording of two CEOs discussing the relevance of capitalism in a post–climate change world, and Jacqueline settled into her velvet chaise lounge.

When the timer dinged, Jacqueline removed her eye mask and touched her hand to her face.

"Shelby, can you bring me the hand mirror?"

Shelby handed Jacqueline a gold-framed mirror, and Jacqueline brought it close to her face as she examined the doctor's work.

"Do you see a difference?" she asked.

Shelby bent down to study Jacqueline's under-eye bags. "I thought you looked beautiful beforehand," she said. "But this looks great, too."

"You can leave early," Jacqueline said. "I have the world's most boring meeting tonight. You know the one."

Shelby did know it. She'd told the government officials no at least a dozen times before Jacqueline told her to just schedule it.

"Actually," Shelby said, "do you mind if I hang around? I'm curious about what they want."

"Sure." Jacqueline shrugged.

A few hours later, Jacqueline sat across from a row of drably dressed men on the plush rose-hued couches in her office. A chandelier twinkled above them in the golden-hour light that trickled through the row of floor-to-ceiling windows. Shelby sat on a chair in the corner, poised to take notes.

She could tell that Jacqueline was impatient. She'd had no interest in the research these men were working on. But Shelby *was* interested. It was unlike any meeting she'd ever scheduled.

"I must begin by telling you that I worship your work," the man on the left said.

"That seems clear," Jacqueline said, and Shelby recognized the forced smile. Jacqueline tapped the pointy tip of her shoe on the marble coffee table between them. "What can I do for you?"

The man who spoke first continued. "We want to talk to you today about the climate emergency. But, first, I do want to mention, I think it's absurd that you don't get more credit for the way you've solved this country's recycling overflow issue."

"On that, we definitely agree."

"We'd like to discuss the Inside Project with you," the man on the other side of the couch said. He had awful sideburns, Shelby noticed.

"You need money," she said, and they all looked equally startled. Jacqueline laughed. "What, you think anyone makes a meeting with me without asking for money?"

Shelby smirked to herself.

They looked at each other nervously. "All the Insides are seeking private investors," the first man said.

"How much control would I have?"

He looked confused. "You want to be involved?"

"I only give my money to projects I can have control over," she said. "Make me the director, and you can have all the money you want."

Shelby tilted her head to the side. The director? Of Inside? Perhaps this meant she and her family had a chance of getting accepted. They'd applied like everyone else, but her connection to Jacqueline meant she was no longer just anyone. Jacqueline liked her; surely she'd help her out with something so monumental.

"We were prepared to offer you something else," he said. "If you invest in us, I will secure a spot for you and your team on the US space shuttle. The other Insides have done similar things for their own investors."

"I'd like both of those things," Jacqueline said.

Shelby's head was spinning. Jacqueline? Fleeing to space? She'd stopped taking notes and was staring, mouth half-open, at the confident, calm way Jacqueline was dominating the meeting. As though she'd planned for it.

Before Shelby knew it, Jacqueline put her glasses on the tip of her nose and scribbled out a check for a number that most people wouldn't even recognize as anything other than a fantasy.

"Take all my money!" Jacqueline said, laughing. *They have no idea what they are getting themselves into,* Shelby thought. To be fair, she wasn't sure what they were getting into, either; it was clear to her that Jacqueline had an ulterior motive, though what it could be, she had no idea.

The man said, not laughing, "We'd love to."

Jacqueline started to pass him the check, but then pulled back. "So you'll agree to my terms, then," she said. It wasn't a question.

"Of course," he said. "We'd be honored to have you join our leadership."

Jacqueline handed him the check and took her glasses off. She winked at Shelby, and said, "We live so many lives, don't we?" Above them, the crystal chandelier bounced rainbows onto the wall.

3

ALONE IN HER KITCHEN, OLYMPIA MADE A CUP OF TEA USING the fancy, organic Darjeeling her brother had sent her for her last birthday. He'd bought it on his last tour through India. She never forgave him for joining the military, but even she had to admit that the gifts from far-flung destinations were nice. She always saved them for special occasions.

And that night, Olympia was indeed celebrating. On the table lay several different job offers, glossy folders thick with information about health insurance and bonuses and PTO. It was only the fall semester of her final year of medical school, but already, opportunities were pouring in.

Thanks to the recognition her research was finally getting, Olympia was feeling better about herself than she ever had. It was showing up physically: her posture had improved, her skin had cleared, her cuticles were healed after a lifetime of picking at them.

Though Olympia had always been on the masculine side of androgynous, she often felt that the parameters of gender—even, or maybe especially, gender as expressed by other queer people—never really fit her. They were always trying to label her. Other Black women called her a stemme, though she didn't feel a personal connection to the words femme or stud, while white women called her an LHB, for long-haired butch, as though the length of her box braids was a sufficient qualifier to indicate something about who she was as a person. The way she defied category used to make her feel out of place, but these days, she was coming into herself, finally realizing that the things that made her different also made her appealing to certain people.

She could tell by the way women were looking at her. Shy smiles as she passed. Not that she ever had a girlfriend. She was too busy. No one could have accomplished what she had if they were also dating, she thought.

Eyeing the offers splayed out on the table, she raised her chipped mug to cheers the empty air in front of her, and then, feeling a little foolish at this display, took a sip. This was what she'd been preparing for all her life.

In many ways, she couldn't quite believe that someday, medical school would be over. For nearly a decade her life had been lab work and exams and doctors to be shadowed, a total blur of organs and blood and medicine. All of this came easily to Olympia. She felt she was born to be a doctor, and the flood of offers proved it.

On her table, next to the paperwork, lay a book. The cover read *Yours for the Taking!: Reclaiming Female Power in a Changing World*, by Jacqueline Millender, with a gaudy INTERNATIONAL BESTSELLER sticker slapped across the top. It wasn't the kind of thing Olympia was usually drawn to, so pink and fierce and popular. The book was a gift from one of her prospective employers—a perk of one of the jobs was a free membership to Yours!, owned and operated by the author of this book. Olympia had no intentions of ever going to the all-female coworking space, though. It wasn't her thing.

But that night alone in her modest apartment, she had nothing better to do, so she brought the book with her to her favorite armchair. She removed the glossy outer jacket and began reading.

"If we stay on our current course," the introduction to *Yours* warned, "women will not become truly equal to men before the world is made uninhabitable."

Five hours later, she was still reading. Her feet had fallen asleep, curled under her legs.

Though she imagined she wasn't part of the target demographic—she doubted Jacqueline Millender had pictured someone like Olympia when she addressed *women* in her writing—she found herself nodding along, relating deeply. Olympia's academic career was marked by achievement but missing the fanfare and splashy accolades that the men in her class had acquired. These men were her peers, but while they were graduating into jobs as CEOs or global leaders, she would be proud to simply get a mention in the alumni newsletters.

And, anyway, there was a newfound concern with how damaging certain waves of feminism had been to men. As far as Olympia could tell, it had become almost politically incorrect to point out sexism as it happened, because god forbid you make a man feel as though he wasn't important. There was so much tiptoeing that had to be done that it was hard to communicate directly at all. Even when, in a clinic, Olympia's much older boss had followed her into the bathroom, pushing his hands up her shirt while she begged him to leave her alone and instead he told her to stop making so much noise—she kept it a secret. She knew what the response would have been. She'd seen it happen to her coworkers: Their own motivations for telling on their abusers were always questioned. She'd be accused of wanting to take his job, of playing the victim when really she was the one taking advantage of an older man. He was the kind of white man who liked to talk about how all the good jobs were being taken by marginalized people, people like Olympia, and were she to try to get justice, she already knew exactly how it would be spun. It wasn't worth it, and so she never told anybody, at all. Her success had been too hard-won; there were too many obstacles she'd faced to throw her reputation away.

At every turn, there had been people who didn't think she had what it took to be successful. But she did. She knew she did. She had to assume that therefore it was her queerness, her masculinity, or her Blackness—or, as was generally her experience, the combination of the three—that caused people to treat her as though she wasn't good enough. Everything she had, she'd worked two, three times harder for than her straight white colleagues.

It was a lesson her parents had taught her: she'd have to be better than every white person in the room to get ahead.

Olympia had been very badly wanted by her parents. Six years—that's how long they'd tried to get pregnant before adopting her. Olympia didn't know much about her biological parents other than they'd likely been climate migrants passing through Texas and had left her in a basket with a note at the fire department. She'd been only a few weeks old, so she had no memory of it other than the stories she was told. The handwritten letter read simply, *"We can't give her what she needs. Please find someone who can."* Olympia's new parents had told her those words meant that she'd been loved, and because these adoptive parents also loved her, so purely and so unconditionally, she believed that story to be true.

Instead of feeling that she had been abandoned, she felt she'd been found.

Her new parents taught Olympia how to advocate for herself, how to succeed in a world that often felt rigged against her—just as they had. Despite the decades in between her adulthood and theirs, it seemed to Olympia that the racism they faced operated in very much the same way. It was perhaps expressed more subtly in Olympia's lifetime, but that didn't make it any less potent.

Her parents had less advice for her when it came to navigating the world as a queer person, and this at times made those two identities feel separate to her, even though in her experiences outside of her family, they were completely intertwined.

Progress for queer people in general had stagnated over the course of her life. It was as though the general population was only capable of focusing on one major issue at a time, and the climate crisis took center stage. Rights were being stripped away and it hardly made the news.

She slept in her armchair that night, the book in her lap, and when she awoke the next morning, she beelined straight to her computer and pulled up the Yours! homepage. She decided she couldn't wait for a complimentary membership and signed herself up, sweating with excitement.

Later that week she carved out time to visit the space, agonizing over what to wear. Finally, she landed on a modest outfit: black slacks, a white silk button-down, sensible leather loafers. The slacks were designed to be loose, but they were a little too loose-fitting on her; she'd always been thin. She grabbed a belt to secure them in place, the top of the pants becoming like a paper bag crinkled around her frame. She pulled her hair into a ponytail at the base of her neck.

Yours! was located in Lower Manhattan, where nearby, a university was being put on stilts. The entrance was hard to find, a nondescript metal door on the side of an enormous brick building. She took an old utility elevator up to the tenth floor, and when she emerged she found herself bathed in sunlight, with windows all around, and well-dressed women everywhere she looked. Women who were chatting, working, laughing to each other, touching up their makeup in the vanities that lined one of the walls. It was beautifully decorated, the air nearly vibrating with feminine energy. The art on the walls was vaguely vaginal.

The group of people before her were not as diverse as Olympia would have liked, which didn't come as too much of a surprise: straight white women like Millender always neglected to factor in anything other than their own identity. But as she stood in the entryway, she found she was not discouraged but rather motivated by what she saw. She could help bring in other women of color. She could think of a dozen off the top of her head to recommend. Olympia always liked to believe that everything had a purpose that was larger than her. Helping improve the diversity of Yours! could be the purpose of her joining.

She also felt inspired. There was something about this place that made her feel hopeful for the future. When she got home, she curled up in her armchair with her laptop, Jacqueline Millender's book tucked next to her, and an essay flew out of her fingertips and onto the screen about the mental health bene-fits of community during this uncertain time. She'd always liked writing, but academically speaking, it had taken a back seat to her other ambitions. She couldn't even remember the last time she'd written an essay. Certainly, she'd never written one for fun. But that's exactly what this was: she felt a joyous sort of energy rushing through her as she laid out her argument, developed it, backed it up with facts.

Her roommate popped her head out of her bedroom. "I can hear you typing from all the way in here," she said.

"Sorry!" Olympia called, and tried to type more quietly, but it was hard. She was fueled by something larger than herself.

When she was done, she submitted the essay to a feminist newsletter she subscribed to. It became the first of many that Olympia would pen, and soon she'd made a name for herself as the medical school student with strong opinions. She often stayed up all night in order to finish her coursework and meet her writing deadlines. That was fine; she thrived on the anxiety. She always had.

In the spring, Olympia wrote an essay she was particularly proud of.

It was published on a popular feminist website and was about how the hardest part of learning to be a doctor, for her, wasn't the science—it was the implications of the science. Or, rather, the implications of the *lack* of science—there were certain things that no one had answers for. She argued that climate change was causing a health crisis: viral pandemics, a rise in asthma, mysterious new autoimmune diseases—the changing planet made everything worse. But more than that, she wrote, all these issues showed up first in women of color. If wealthy white men had suffered equally, in the beginning, they would have prioritized climate change relief programs back when it could still have made a difference. And maybe there would be a solution by now. Not just for the diseases, but for climate change itself.

She sent the link to a few friends. The response was positive; she'd struck a nerve.

The next day, Olympia received an email so surprising, she wondered if she was dreaming.

I'd like to take you to dinner, it read. I feel that we have much in common. It was signed, Yours in solidarity, Jacqueline Millender.

Was it really Jacqueline Millender? Olympia conducted several searches to try to verify the email address, but of course Jacqueline's personal contact info was not listed anywhere. The brevity of the note made Olympia think it was legitimate; only someone with nothing to prove would say so little.

But if it really was Jacqueline, what did she want from her? Olympia read it over and over again until the words blurred together. The tone was impossible to glean. Was it friendly, or an accusation of sorts?

She showed the invitation to her roommate, who said, "I feel like this could go either way."

Olympia agreed to the meeting, and spent the rest of the night lying awake, staring at the ceiling. What in the world was Jacqueline Millender after?

They met at a candlelit, secluded restaurant at the top of Manhattan, where people spoke in elegant murmurs and even the quiet clinking of the silverware against the plates sounded luxurious. Olympia arrived early but even still Jacqueline was there before her. There was already a bottle of wine on the table.

"Ms. Millender," Olympia said as she slid into the leather chair.

"Please, call me Jacqueline," came the reply. And then, she got right to it: "I am very interested in your work. Particularly the way you synthesize ideas, drawing connections that your older peers are too afraid to make in public." Jacqueline took a sip of a full-bodied red wine. Olympia gulped some water, and then shivered. Nice places were always so cold.

When Jacqueline mentioned Olympia's work, Olympia knew she wasn't talking about her achievements as a med student. Yesterday's essay, which as of this morning was going viral, made reference to Jacqueline's writings.

The waiter appeared, refilling Jacqueline's wineglass. Jacqueline waited for him to leave before she began speaking again. "I'm wondering what you think about our future," she said.

"When you say *our*, who do you mean?" Olympia asked.

Jacqueline chuckled. "Great question. I can already tell we will get along."

The waiter returned with a basket of small warm rolls. "Can I get you anything to start?" he said.

"Whatever the chef thinks," Jacqueline said. "Just nothing with butter." She waved him away.

"I meant women," she said to Olympia, when the waiter was out of ear-shot. "What do you think the future holds for women?"

"At this point? Nothing good," Olympia said. She and Jacqueline held eye contact for a moment longer than was comfortable, and Olympia looked away first. This was a very strange meeting, indeed.

Jacqueline finished her glass of wine and began pouring another. "As I assume you know," she said, "I've invested in North America's Inside, and as such am the acting director. We are only in the very beginning phases of research. But the main issue I've been stumped about is how to restart civilization so that it won't simply repeat itself, dooming humanity to play out the same old story."

"Ah," Olympia said. She had been wondering about that very problem.

Jacqueline continued, "Most models for Inside that the government has explored are recreations of the world as it already exists. They've been trying to figure out how to keep the current balance of power, of gender, of class, without disruption. As though some idea of normalcy is the best way to keep people happy."

"Normal only sounds good if you benefit from it," Olympia said.

"Correct," Jacqueline said. "So what would you say to a proposal for a completely new societal structure?"

"I'd say I am still listening."

"Good." Jacqueline lowered her voice. Olympia had to lean all the way forward to hear her. "And what would you say if that structure didn't include any men?"

Olympia paused, unsure if she had heard correctly. "I would have a lot of questions," she said.

"I promise to answer all of your questions to the best of my ability," Jacqueline said. "But first, I'll need you to sign an NDA, and then I'd love for you to come visit the lab in person. I have a feeling you'll be as moved as I am by the work the team is doing."

The waiter returned with two steaming bowls, but Olympia found she couldn't eat. There was a sinking feeling in her stomach that was part curiosity and part dread. She *needed* to know more; and also, she was aware on some level that the more she knew, the more wrapped up she'd become in whatever this was. Still, she couldn't help herself. The questions left her mouth before she could hold them in.

"But how will society continue on? Assuming you mean cis men, this is a plan that will only last as long as the generation is alive, right?" she said.

Jacqueline took a bite, chewing slowly. She seemed to be considering how much to reveal. "Man is not a natural species," she said. "He is a historical idea."

"Simone de Beauvoir." Olympia nodded. "Though I believe she was paraphrasing someone else."

Jacqueline dismissed this. "Don't let your imagination hold you back from what is possible in this life."

"All-female societies don't work," Olympia said. "For a number of reasons."

"Maybe." Jacqueline nodded. "Or maybe the idea has just never been properly funded."

The essay was going more viral than Olympia's writing usually did. Over the next few days, people she hadn't talked to in a long time reached out to say how proud they were. There was some backlash, of course; she'd expected dissent. It was a controversial stance to take. She'd known that going in. But it wasn't exactly a *new* take; she'd just been adding her voice to the chorus, from her specific perspective. So she wasn't worried. The argument was a well-worn path.

Then one morning she awoke to an anonymous text message: This is bullshit. Don't you think we have bigger things to worry about? Like the end of the fucking world. It was early and she was still struggling through her first cup of coffee. She flipped her phone over and didn't look at it again until sunlight filled her room.

But by that point, it was too late. She had thousands of texts and missed calls. Her phone battery was almost completely drained. With a growing sense of dread, she opened her laptop and did a search for her own name. All of the results that popped up were from a men's rights organization. She held her breath while she clicked on the first hit. They had linked to her article. And published her phone number alongside it.

If they had her phone number, she wondered, what else did they have? Was she in physical danger? Her heart was pounding. She didn't know what the protocol was in a situation like this. She didn't know who to alert, who to go to for help. The authorities would obviously not care. She was terrified, but more than that, she felt completely alone.

Olympia also didn't understand why *her*, why *this essay*. What about the countless other women who had said the same thing elsewhere? Why not any of her other essays?

Still, none of this would have really been that big of a deal to her—
Olympia knew women were harassed online all the time—except that she
hadn't yet chosen from one of the many job offers that had come the semester before. Now, if someone searched for her name online, the first few
pages of results would be from men's rights forums, talking about what an
alleged fraud she was.

She was right to worry. One by one, over the next week, every clinic
she'd been talking to about a residency retracted their interest. They didn't
have to explain why. She knew they didn't want to bring controversy into
their already underfunded walls. The curse of being a woman with an opinion in public. It was devastating.

"These fucking men," Olympia cried to her mom on the phone. The calls
and texts from the men's rights groups hadn't stopped. "They've ruined my
career."

"No, they haven't," her mom said. "You will get through this. You always do."

"Mom," she said, "it's out of my control. Everything is."

She hung up, not feeling any better. If anything, she felt worse. No one
seemed to understand the gravity of her situation.

A few days later, Olympia skipped her graduation ceremony.

She didn't plan on missing it. Even though her family, who lived in Texas,
wasn't able to come, she had ordered her cap and gown and made plans with
some friends to celebrate at a bar afterward. But that morning, she found
she couldn't overcome the feeling of disillusionment. What was there to celebrate? She'd be graduating into an industry where there didn't seem to be
a place for her.

She shoved the cap and gown into the garbage and went for a run along
the river. She turned her music all the way up and tried to soothe herself by
concentrating on her feet hitting the pavement in time to the beat.

But even that wasn't satisfying. The heat made it impossible to move as
quickly as she wanted to, and eventually she had to slow to a walk, drenched
in sweat and feeling light-headed. The air quality had gotten so much worse
recently. She'd read somewhere that an hour spent outside was like smoking
multiple packs of cigarettes.

As she slowly made her way back to her apartment, she passed the library, a grand building where she'd spent countless hours. *So much squandered potential*, she thought.

She took off her tank top and tied it around her waist. Her skin underneath her spandex bra was starting to itch from the heat. She stopped on the corner to catch her breath, stretching her calves against a lamppost, and a man running by whistled.

"Fuck off," she shouted, but he was already out of earshot.

When she got home, she opened her laptop, and read everything she could find about the global project known as Inside.

ASIDE FROM THE PHYSICAL ASPECT OF AGING, JACQUELINE didn't mind being older; the wisdom that came with it made her feel calm and in control.

Her marriage, for example, taught her how resilient she was. She'd been in her late twenties. She'd had a very large wedding on the glass-covered roof of a hotel owned by one of her relatives. She wore a vibrant magenta pantsuit. Her hair was in the platinum-bobbed style that she'd later have to commission a wig to be designed after, once she'd bleached it so severely that it all fell out. Nearly extinct blooms were flown in from all over the world. Pedestrians could smell the party from a block away. Intensely floral, decadent, romantic.

In the immediate years that followed, they were happy, or so she thought, taking trips to far-flung islands, before those islands disappeared into the ocean. There were parties and business dinners and long, languid days stretched out on velvet furniture doing absolutely nothing at all, watching the sunlight cast dramatic shadows on the city below.

It was around this time that she had the idea for Refillables, and their wealth skyrocketed. They spent nearly a decade like that, and then Jacqueline got sick.

She'd never really believed that people like her could get the same diseases that regular folks got. But she lived in what was commonly referred to as the "cancer belt," an area that stretched along the East Coast of the United States that had disproportionate rates of breast cancer—thanks, probably, to the toxic waste in the water. Not that Jacqueline drank the tap water. But she did shower in it.

Jacqueline's husband was supposed to meet her at her first doctor's appointment, but he didn't show up. And despite how many times she told him she wanted him there, he didn't come to any appointments that followed. In fact, after that, he was around less and less, with excuses about business trips and friends in crisis. Jacqueline was stunned to find herself alone, battling her own body.

It was a battle she won. Many surgeries and chemo treatments later, she was completely cancer-free. And then she was husband-free, too. She kicked him out. He went without much of a fight.

But then, with forty fast approaching, she realized nothing in her life felt right. She'd always assumed that by this point she'd have a family. She'd always wanted children, but she'd never done anything to make sure her life was going in that direction, not really. She realized that it wasn't enough to assume the things you wanted would happen; you had to make them happen. The things that she wanted were hers for the taking, or not taking, but either way, action and choice were imperative. Passivity would never yield the intended results.

Which was, coincidentally, the same line of thinking that led to the birth of something else: her book.

Yours for the Taking!: Reclaiming Female Power in a Changing World was sometimes criticized for being overly corporate and light on nuance, but she didn't read the criticisms. She didn't really engage with the dialogue surrounding her work at all. She believed in it, and as her own book prescribed, as a woman, believing in yourself sometimes had to be enough.

Jacqueline became a leading voice in the latest wave of feminist thought, a cohort of women who wanted to reclaim the movement, focusing on the concept of *power* for their gender, rather than *empowerment*. Feminists before them—the fifth wave—had been too soft, too willing to let *anyone* benefit from women's success.

Jacqueline and her peers avoided labeling their thinking "the sixth wave," though, because they wanted to transcend the idea of waves of feminism entirely; this would be the final wave, eclipsing everything that had come before it.

"More like a feminist tsunami," Jacqueline once said to me, with her legs stretched out over her desk as she admired her red-soled high heels and then picked at the spot where a cosmetic injection had shriveled a juicy varicose vein on her right thigh.

"Women need to remember how powerful they are, plain and simple," she said.

Jacqueline, for one, never forgot.

PART TWO

CALL IT WHATEVER YOU'D LIKE

2051–2055

4

INSIDE'S WORKING LAB WAS IN A HUGE, SPRAWLING WARE-
house near the piers in Midtown. Olympia was finding it hard to breathe
as she approached it. The combination of excitement and terror was intoxicating.

The night before, Jacqueline's assistant had emailed Olympia an NDA. It
was pretty straightforward, if lengthy, and after reading it a few times while
she paced around her apartment, she decided to just sign the damn thing. It
didn't mean she had to commit to Jacqueline; it just meant she had to keep
quiet about whatever it was Jacqueline was planning. She could do that.

When she arrived, a security guard appeared and whisked Olympia
through the doors and into a lab where Jacqueline was standing over a young
woman typing furiously into a computer.

It took the two of them a few moments to realize Olympia was there. But
when Jacqueline saw her, her face lit up.

"You came," she said.

"Of course I did," Olympia replied. She couldn't imagine anyone ever
saying no to the heiress of JM Inc.

"I understand you've recently been doxed," Jacqueline said, with an expression on her face that somewhat resembled a smile.

"I was wondering if you knew about that," Olympia said.

"It was hard to miss. But I do think it means you might need me as much
as I believe I need you."

"I do seem to need a job," Olympia said, trying to keep her tone light, not
wanting to allow Jacqueline to see the desperation that had begun to brew.

"This is not a job in a traditional sense. It's more of a mission."

"Say more," Olympia said.

Jacqueline walked slightly in front of Olympia while she gave her a tour of the facility, and Olympia kept catching whiffs of her hair, which smelled like baby powder and, oddly, glue.

The desks and lab stations were all occupied by young women. Most of them seemed too busy to even look up while the duo passed. The energy in the air felt electric. Olympia thought of the way Jacqueline had said it was a mission, not a job. That seemed to be true for the people under her, as far as Olympia could tell.

"Who are they?" Olympia said, gesturing to the women sitting at their desks.

"My team," Jacqueline said. "I've hand-selected every single one of them, the same way I found you."

That seemed believable enough. Olympia couldn't imagine Jacqueline outsourcing such important decisions as who to keep in her inner circle.

"They all have impressive qualifications," Jacqueline continued. "You'll see when you get to know them."

"Did you take each of them out to dinner, too?"

Jacqueline smirked. "Many of them, yes. But not everyone has needed that much convincing."

They reached an area with some couches and sat down.

"Olympia," Jacqueline began, "you must understand that I have the opportunity to do something very important here."

"Being an Inside director is a huge undertaking," she replied. "And a huge responsibility. It was generous of you to invest."

"Certainly." Jacqueline grinned. Her teeth were so white, they were nearly translucent. "But I've been thinking about it as more of an opportunity. You see, each Inside is its own little world. It's up to me to set the rules for that world. And why would I follow the rules that currently exist, when those rules are what got us here?"

"I see your point," Olympia said. "So, tell me how you envision it working."

Jacqueline crossed and then uncrossed her legs. Her cropped black slacks revealed a hint of pale ankle. "Don't worry about the *how* in this moment," she said. "Let me tell you the goal. If we can reimagine society as being woman-originated—not just matriarchal, but truly have women as the foundation—their children of all genders would be born into a world free of patriarchy. Free of oppression. Are you following?"

"Uh." Olympia hesitated. "Sure. I'm following."

Jacqueline continued, "And those children will give birth to a subsequent generation that is then that much further removed from the oppressive circumstances of their grandmothers. And so on and so forth. Each generation born from the original group of women will get closer and closer to being totally free of the things that hold us back today."

"Just to clarify," Olympia said, "do you mean that you won't accept men into Inside?"

Jacqueline beamed. "Precisely."

"I have to be honest," Olympia said. "That all rests on an outdated understanding of sex and gender, no?"

"Don't think of it like that," Jacqueline said. "We're just omitting *men*. That means we're including everyone else. It's only binary if you think that the only two genders are *cis man* and *cis woman*. Obviously there are other kinds of people."

"And those people will be accepted?" Olympia asked.

"Yes," Jacqueline said. "Everyone but men."

"I guess I'm confused because you keep saying *women*," Olympia said.

"What would you like me to say?"

"How about *people*?" Olympia said, and Jacqueline laughed, though it hadn't been a joke. "What about trans men?"

"Well, that's a good question," Jacqueline said, though by the tense way she said the words, Olympia wasn't sure she actually thought it was a *good* question. "What do you think?"

"Um." Olympia hesitated. "Trans men are men. I guess *you* have to decide whether you're saying the problem of men comes from masculinity, or the gender someone is assigned at birth, or testosterone, or chromosomes, or something else. That will get very complicated very quickly. I, for example, could be described as masculine. And women naturally produce testosterone. We know that chromosomes don't dictate gender. If you think about it long enough, you can't really create parameters around gender at all."

"I'm not here to define what makes a man or a woman," Jacqueline said. "That's on the individual to decide. But I do think if one connects to and identifies with the *concept* of being a man—in the context of our current world—that's what the problem is. For what have men proven that they are, in this day and age, except for sources of destruction and pain?" Her voice took on a new tone, as though this was a speech she'd practiced. Olympia guessed every new recruit had heard a similar monologue.

Jacqueline continued, "What have men done except systematically dismantle our rights so they can abuse us, impregnate us, outearn us, and ruin the planet—all with no repercussions? And yes, of course I know *not all men*. But enough of them. Enough to prove the point. And I'm not saying no to men forever. It's the context for men that we need to change."

"Fair enough," Olympia replied. "But statistically, cisgender men are the ones responsible for the issues you listed out. And specifically conservative white ones."

"So then you think we *should* include trans men?" Jacqueline's mouth twisted into an unreadable little smirk.

For a moment, Olympia put her face in her hands. They were talking in circles, and she wasn't sure if it was by design.

She lifted her head. "It doesn't make sense to group people into *cis men* versus everyone else. There's something very retro about that kind of thinking. It kind of reminds me of how feminists used to spell *woman* with an x to include nonbinary people instead of, like, acknowledging trans identities as separate and real."

Jacqueline laughed. "I always thought *womxn* was annoying, but could never put my finger on why," she said.

Olympia nodded. "If we're to separate out *man* as a category of gender, it has to be everyone who identifies as a man, no matter how they arrived at that identity."

"I completely agree," Jacqueline said, as though she'd been waiting for

Olympia to reach this conclusion. "Admission will be based on identity, *not* any sort of biological sex testing."

Olympia was quiet for a few moments. She studied the room around her. She listened to the hum of conversation overflowing from the labs. Something was still not sitting right.

"And what about their cultures, their ethnicities?" Olympia asked. "Are the people you accept just supposed to abandon their upbringings and become some homogeneous race?"

Jacqueline's hands were folded in her lap, but Olympia noticed they were shaking. The woman's voice, though, gave no hint at anxiety. She said, "What if I could create a world that is post-race? We can do a race-blind application process."

"That's not a thing," Olympia said quickly. Maybe working with Jacqueline wasn't a good idea after all. She didn't seem to get it. *It* being, well, everything.

"Is it not? This is how we structured the Yours! admissions process."

"Right, and the Yours! spaces are not exactly beacons of diversity," Olympia said, choosing her words carefully. "I couldn't help but notice how overwhelmingly white it is in there."

"It's hardly my fault if Yours! attracted a specific type of woman."

"I disagree," Olympia said, thinking to herself: *Fuck it.* "You created a barrier to entry with that membership price, and the qualifications to join. You could have sponsored people. Brought them in. Given them the experiences and contacts they'd need to have careers that would allow them to afford that world."

Jacqueline's face was impossible to read, and for a moment they just sat there, the weight of Olympia's criticism hanging above them.

At last, Jacqueline's shoulders softened. "Fine," she said. "I see your point. What do you suggest?"

"Equal representation of every race and ethnicity present in North America," she said firmly. "If we're reinventing the world, let's reinvent it. True equality. And none of this post-race stuff. That's bullshit, I'm sorry. Who they are and where they come from is important. It'll impact how they see themselves and each other."

Jacqueline's eyes sparkled. "I love it. And I especially love that you feel comfortable challenging my ideas. Not everyone would have the courage."

Olympia gave a curt nod. She wouldn't be distracted by flattery. "And are you concerned at all that the people you'll choose for this won't want to participate?"

"I'm so glad you asked," Jacqueline said. "The psychological portion of the application allows us to screen out people who wouldn't thrive in these circumstances."

"Interesting," Olympia said. She wasn't convinced.

"We're being incredibly selective," Jacqueline said.

"Surely it will be hard to find the right candidates," Olympia replied. "First of all, you'd need people who aren't predisposed to bias, so that they see each other as equals when they walk through the door. But it seems to me that almost everyone feels some sort of bias about something, whether or not they're aware of it."

"That's true," Jacqueline admitted. "We're not accepting very many people."

"What do you mean?" Olympia said.

"Fifty thousand," Jacqueline said. "Max."

Olympia had to stop herself from exclaiming. "But we've all been told three million."

"Everyone has been told a lot of things," Jacqueline acknowledged with a shrug. She stood up and walked to the other side of the room. When she returned, she had a glass of red wine in hand. It wasn't even 3:00 p.m., but Olympia didn't say anything.

"What else are you screening for?" Olympia asked, instead.

"It's a very sophisticated algorithm," Jacqueline said. "It would take a long time for me to explain. But basically, we're looking for people who are best equipped for communal living. They need to have the right level of intelligence, specific politics, values. Feminism. It's a specific profile."

"And how do you imagine reproduction working?" She'd been holding in this question for the whole tour.

Jacqueline returned the question with a question. "How much do you know about the plan for Inside's biological screening process?"

"Enough," Olympia said. "I read the news."

"So you know that people who are able will be required to give a sperm sample as part of their application."

"Sure. Everyone knows that."

"We'll simply save the samples in order to provide the residents with the option of intrauterine insemination."

"Saving, or stealing?" Olympia said.

"Call it whatever you'd like," Jacqueline said.

"How are you going to get away with it?" Olympia said.

"We're going to lie," Jacqueline said. "Mostly by omission."

Olympia accepted that answer. She'd been expecting it. There was no other way to do what they were doing.

"But, my dear," Jacqueline said, "whether or not we get away with it is beside the point. We'll definitely get away with it. You're asking the wrong question. The real question that you should be asking is, *What if it doesn't work to allow men to be born Inside at all?*"

Olympia stifled a laugh. "Excuse me?"

"I'm serious," Jacqueline said, and from her stern tone it was clear that she was. "The experiment we're doing here is the addition of boys in the first generation. We'll have to see how it goes; if the maternal influence is strong enough to remove the echoes of patriarchy. I sincerely hope that it is. But if that doesn't work, we can simply pivot from IUI to in vitro fertilization, which will allow us to be more intentional about the eggs that get fertilized. In case it turns out we function better without men altogether."

"Wait," Olympia said. "Isn't that the opposite of the plan you just laid out? If you only allowed *female* zygotes to be created, you still wouldn't be eliminating all men, based on everything we just talked about. And you'd be preventing the existence of transgender women."

"Well," Jacqueline said, "I know it's extreme. That's why I'm hoping we don't have to get to that point."

Olympia was stunned into silence. Jacqueline's understanding of gender sounded archaic. Olympia wondered, too, what Jacqueline really thought about the nuances of gender beyond biological sex; would she seek to lift up *all* women assigned female at birth, or just the ones that fit Jacqueline's idea of what a woman should be? But the truth was that up until the moment Jacqueline disclosed this experiment of hers, Olympia had been pretty much on board. She made a mental note to bring it up later. It was too big to let it slide, but it also seemed very far-fetched. They wouldn't need to resort to such extreme measures, not if everything went according to the plan that had been laid out. She'd challenge Jacqueline on it if it came up again.

Much like the feeling she'd had standing in the doorway of Yours! for the first time, Olympia thought to herself that she could fix this. She could be involved while making the changes she wanted to. She could prevent Jacqueline from creating a world that was only for people assigned female at birth. She and Jacqueline didn't have to agree on everything. Plus, it seemed as though Jacqueline listened to her, at least a little bit.

"I guess I just have one last question," she said. "Why do you want *me*?"

"To be our medical director, of course," Jacqueline said.

This took Olympia by surprise. "Director? Don't you want someone with . . . experience?"

"No," Jacqueline said, so forcefully that Olympia jumped. "What good is experience? I don't want someone who has grown bitter from a lifetime of glass ceilings. I want someone who is talented but not jaded by the state of the world. Someone fresh, with all the knowledge and none of the baggage. I want *you*."

Olympia remembered the cold shock of finding that her personal information had been shared online, the horror and fear she had felt the past few weeks all because some men felt threatened by her opinion. The devastation that all of her hard work—a lifetime of effort—had been destroyed so quickly, as though it was nothing. She remembered the man in the clinic with his hands up her shirt, knowing there'd be no repercussions for him. She would never trust men again. She never should have in the first place.

But should they be excluded from this last chance at survival? She didn't feel that was up to her to decide. And there were holes in Jacqueline's thinking; that was clear. But there would be time to address those things. She could make these changes from the inside—no, from Inside.

For the first time since she arrived, Olympia didn't have to force a smile.

"So, are you in, or what?"

"I'm in," she said.

The plan was confidential. Under Jacqueline's guidance, Olympia would prepare a version of Inside to appease the UWG. It would be almost laughably easy to fool the men who sat at the top of the Inside Project. They were so desperate for help that they'd believe anything Jacqueline and Olympia told them. As for the people she was working with? They turned out to be women she trusted; women who believed in the work. They would all play crucial roles in bringing the dream to life.

Even though Olympia's job was, technically, to run the medical program, she found that Jacqueline began to treat her as more of an equal. They made plans together. Olympia was allowed to delegate to people outside of her own department.

Power flowed from Jacqueline to Olympia. It filled her up. It made her forget.

Olympia sank into the soft rose sofa in Jacqueline's office, where the two women now spent most weeknights drinking white wine and discussing the future. Well—Jacqueline drank. Olympia never did.

"Olympia, I've been meaning to ask you. How do you identify?" Jacqueline asked, swirling her wine around her glass.

"How do I what?"

"*Identify.* How you describe yourself. I want to know how I can describe you to other people."

It was an odd question, but Olympia decided to humor her. "I identify as a Black woman," she said.

"But," Jacqueline said, fishing, "is that all?"

"I'm also a lesbian, if that's what you mean."

"So you'd actually say *lesbian*? You wouldn't say, for example, queer? Please be patient with me, I'm just trying to get the words right."

"Sure, sometimes. But I've always liked the specificity that the word *lesbian* provides," Olympia replied.

Jacqueline clapped her hands together. "Wonderful," she said. "I had hoped as much. I've always admired lesbians. All the strength of our gender, without any influence from men. I'm a bit jealous, if I'm being honest."

Olympia laughed. "That's certainly one way to put it," she said. She wasn't sure if she should be offended or flattered.

"I suppose we should get back to work, then," Jacqueline said, abruptly switching her tone. "I'd like a lot of the structural things to come from you. You're the expert when it comes to keeping people healthy. I promise not to interfere with that. In exchange, I've decided there are two things I need," Jacqueline said.

Olympia raised her eyebrows. It didn't seem likely that Jacqueline would be able to resist telling her how to run the medical center, regardless of her expertise. After all, Jacqueline was the director of everything Inside; Olympia was her employee. If Jacqueline noticed her skepticism, she didn't address it, and instead continued talking. "First, I'd like to help imagine this women-only Inside; it needs to have my stamp on it if it's to be built with my money."

"Great," Olympia said. She'd gotten used to the way Jaqueline used the word *women* in place of something more accurate. "What do you imagine?"

Jacqueline smiled as though she'd been waiting to be asked that question all her life. "I see a color palette of clean white, soft baby pink, gentle mauve, and beige," she began. Olympia could barely conceal her eye roll. For all Jacqueline's ideas about gender, her vision of what women preferred tended to land squarely in the realm of the traditionally feminine.

There was no time to dwell on this observation, though, because Jacqueline was still rambling on. "I want the women to be clothed comfortably and fed according to a strict diet—no fried food. They'll need adequate vitamin D since they'll be lacking direct sunlight. We must build state-of-the-art workout facilities and libraries and art studios. There should be a signature fragrance. Something floral and earthy."

Olympia was taking vigorous notes on her tablet, though she quickly realized that Jacqueline's stamp was largely superficial and wouldn't require much work at all. "That all sounds very reasonable," she said.

"The second thing I'm imagining is a little less conventional," Jacqueline said. She paused for a long time, staring at an invisible spot on the wall. Olympia's heart rate quickened.

"I would like one of the women chosen to live Inside to carry my child," she said. "My eggs are already frozen."

"Oh!" Olympia exclaimed, relieved it wasn't a bigger ask.

"It would be a my-bun, someone-else's-oven sort of thing," Jacqueline said. "I want my baby to have the opportunity to live in our feminist utopia."

Olympia nodded. "We can find a surrogate."

"Yes. Good."

"And what do you think we should tell the child about you?" Olympia asked. "Do you want an open adoption sort of situation?"

Jacqueline tilted her head to the side. "No," she said. "I imagine that would be very sad and confusing. I don't want to make the child's life harder."

Olympia made a note on her tablet, though there was no chance she'd forget this request.

"Imagine," Jacqueline gushed, growing emotional, "a little girl who has my genes, but grows up without the obstacles I've faced. Who knows what she could accomplish?"

Olympia looked around the room at the hardwood floor, enormous windows, fur throws, and priceless art. She thought about questioning what, exactly, Jacqueline thought the obstacles she'd faced were; she wondered if Jacqueline cared that this child would grow up being lied to about who their mother really was. But then she thought better of it. Best to be on Jacqueline's side as much as possible, not challenge her on the things with low stakes.

As long as she made sure Jacqueline's child was cared for by adoptive parents, this could work out. She could find people Inside who wanted the baby. If the baby could have parents half as devoted as hers had been, it would be one lucky kid, indeed.

In fact, Olympia's parents loved her so much that, recently, they'd expressed relief when she told them she had a way to go Inside, though she'd lied to them about almost every piece of the circumstance. She told them about the job running the medical center, but not about Jacqueline, and certainly not about what they were turning Inside into. They just wanted her to be safe.

Her parents had decided to stick it out in Texas. It was their home, even though the lakes of her childhood had long since dried up, revealing reddish-brown basins that looked like the surface of Mars, and even though some winters it remained hot as summer and other winters the freeze came so quick and sharp the pipes froze and broke. They were just too old to try to relocate, and where would they even go? Her brother was going to live on the military base at the border of the US and Canada, where the space shuttle would leave from. Out of all of them, she knew she had the best chance for survival. *But*, she thought, looking around Jacqueline's office with a sinking feeling in her stomach, *at what cost?*

"And," Jacqueline said, resuming her serious tone and snapping Olympia out of her thought spiral, "in case this wasn't clear, I'd like to have a female child, so that we can use her as a point of comparison."

"What now?"

"To prove my theory," she said. "I'm willing to have my daughter be the basis by which the progress of every child is measured."

"You mean to decide whether or not you want to allow babies with Y chromosomes to be born."

"Exactly. And maybe there's a chance my hypothesis is wrong. Maybe it'll work just fine to have only one generation raised without the influence of men, and we'll never have to talk about this again. But we need to test it, don't we? And since it was my idea, I'm fine to use my own offspring to prove it. My guess is that she, and the other girls, will prove superior."

There were so many flaws in this line of thinking—not just the politics of it, but also the fact that it just wasn't how experiments worked. But Olympia sighed, already sensing that logic wouldn't help her argument. "You're not going to let me talk you out of this," she said.

"No." Jacqueline smiled. "Plus, it's just a test. It's just observation and data."

Olympia looked at the ceiling, thinking. Surely there was no harm in allowing Jacqueline to run her wacky little "experiment." There was no way her theory would be proven right, because it wasn't based on anything other than Jacqueline's own bias, and because her methodology was broken.

"And anyway, if anything goes wrong," Jacqueline continued, "I can always swoop down from space and retrieve the child."

"What do you think could go wrong?"

"Oh, honey," Jacqueline said. "Things can always go wrong."

Olympia groaned. "You're making me so nervous."

"You know, I've always wanted to try to play god," Jacqueline said.

Olympia finally let her guard down and laughed. "Not god," she said. "Goddess."

A few times, Jacqueline visited the labs in person, wanting to see the progress they were making with her own eyes. On these visits, Olympia rolled out a proverbial red carpet, and Jacqueline was treated to spreads of cookies, fruit, and cheese—none of which she touched—as well as presentations customized just for her, given by the young women who were hard at work making the dream a reality.

Jacqueline brought Shelby with her but left her in the reception area; what they were working on was confidential, even from Jacqueline's most trusted assistant. Olympia took Jacqueline's word on this, even though she liked Shelby; the young woman was very sweet and paid attention to Jacqueline in a devoted, tender way that struck Olympia as how a daughter might care for her aging mother.

It required some extra work to keep Shelby in the dark about the real purpose of Inside, but Jacqueline was convinced that it was for the best, and Olympia had no choice but to agree. Perhaps it was true that Shelby, for all her sweetness, had a sense of right and wrong that was not as flexible as Jacqueline's was; maybe she lacked what Jacqueline called "the moral creativity" to understand the work.

"You should stop having her check your email for you," Olympia advised Jacqueline. Security needed to be a priority if they were to get away with this.

The Inside developed by Olympia and her team was, in a lot of ways, like a supersized version of the Yours! spaces, albeit with a much more involved application process, no membership fee, and, of course, it being permanent. They implemented many of the tools that Jacqueline had developed for Yours! to decide who would be chosen for Inside; emotional intelligence was valued as highly as IQ, and strength of character was measured through a series of tests, to be taken over a period of time.

Olympia knew Jacqueline thought little of the women who would not be chosen for Inside. They were simply not up to par, and it was not her problem. In time, Olympia came to feel that it wasn't her problem, either.

5

THOUGH AVA HAD BARELY SLEPT SINCE ORCHID LEFT, SHE
also found she couldn't get out of bed.

She knew the sun must be rising by now, but when she opened her curtains to look out the window, the sky was so smoggy it was impossible to tell.

She tried to check her phone, but the battery had been drained by nonstop news alerts. She plugged it in and scanned the headlines. The announcement of who would be accepted Inside had triggered wide-scale rioting. Around the world, the cities that housed Insides were consumed by fighting and destruction.

In New York, cars were set on fire, stores ransacked, and homes abandoned by terrified families and turned into meeting places for the military police, who appeared in Lower Manhattan in enormous clusters, delivered from the sky and clad in black and yellow like a swarm of murder hornets. Crowds of people were tear-gassed, shot with rubber bullets, corralled, and arrested by the hundreds. Tanks showed up on Fifth Avenue, mowing down anyone in their path. The sky turned orange with fire and then black with smoke until it became the dense gray Ava now saw out her window.

Those last few days before she moved Inside, she'd been hiding in her apartment, terrified of the hordes of enraged people who would not be joining her. They had nothing left to lose, so they were destroying everything. She understood their anger. If circumstances had been different, she might have protested alongside them. Now, she couldn't help but know she was different from the people in the streets, the people who weren't selected for survival.

✣　✣　✣

Ava had grown up on the highest hill in a neighborhood so idyllic that it was, in fact, famous—or, rather, infamous. Inside its gates, old Victorian-style mansions sprawled proudly with wind chimes on their porches and stained glass decorating the oversized front doors. There, protected by their wealth, people could pretend that, even in the face of climate change, life would go on just as it always had, that the deteriorating earth and the crumbling economy were simply more storms to be weathered.

Ava hadn't known what it was to worry about money, or a lack of it. The only thing she'd lacked, really, was love. Her parents had worked long hours during the week; on weekends they holed up in their separate studies, ignoring each other and her. Ava was largely left to her own devices and had been for as long as she could remember.

By the time she'd seen the blurry video clips of the hurricane ripping through the town where she grew up, causing house after house to crumble right off their foundations, she couldn't even remember the last time she'd spoken to her parents. She tried to reach them but got no answer. She called again and again, long past the moment she knew they would never pick up.

There were no lingering signs of her parents, no indication that they might be watching her from beyond. She'd always imagined that having a dead loved one might feel like hearing a voice in the next room, a room you can't get into. But it wasn't like that. There were no muffled voices. There was nothing at all.

Her despair felt shapeless. She didn't know where to put it; she wasn't sure of its borders.

Ava had no idea what love was supposed to look like, only what it wasn't. But she knew enough to know that love was what she wanted in her life, and she'd vowed to never treat anyone the way her parents had treated her. She would never reject anyone who needed her.

Ava, it's true, had felt Orchid start to slip away long before she actually left, but she'd ignored her intuition because she didn't understand what could possibly be wrong. Instead of confronting the problem, Ava did what she always did: She held on tightly. She showed her love effusively. She left very little breathing room for Orchid. No one had ever told her that this was a problem. Instead they just left. Or died. Which was also a kind of leaving.

* * *

The morning of her Inside check-in, when it was finally time to go, Ava took one final look around her apartment. She'd cleaned it, because it had felt important at the time. Now, though, she didn't know why she'd wasted so many of her last remaining hours in the outside world dusting and sorting. She touched her clothing to say goodbye to it, rubbing her favorite shirts between her fingers. She couldn't bring herself to look through her photos or the book of notes from Orchid she'd saved. She was still wearing the silver bracelet Orchid had gotten her several years ago, which she never took off. She didn't remove it now; not because it was a gift from Orchid, she told herself, but simply because it felt like part of her arm. She'd deal with it later.

When she left, she didn't bother closing the door behind her. There was no point. Besides, she thought, maybe someone who needed a home would find it. She left some canned food out on the counter just in case, along with a note: *Please take whatever you'd like.*

Ava took the sky tram to Manhattan. The uprising had been quelled, and the city was quiet. There weren't any other people on the automated three-level cable car, and she chose a seat on the roof deck, in the corner. As the tram creakily made its way across the East River below, she watched piles of garbage thrash in the waves. The smell was almost unbearable out on the deck: dead fish mixed with sewage and salt. Hard to believe this had ever been a beautiful sight to behold. Hard to believe there'd ever been any beauty in New York at all. But she wanted to feel the wind in her face one last time, even if the air was sour.

She realized she was still wearing her septum ring, and with only a moment's hesitation she pulled it out of the small hole between her nostrils and tossed it into the river. It didn't make a splash. She wondered who she would be without all these little markers to define her.

The tram arrived at the edge of Chinatown, and she refilled her water bottle at a public filtered-water repository to prepare for the walk up to 34th Street, the entrance to Inside, where Penn Station used to be. She pulled her medical mask up from her neck, bending it in place around her nose. She wore athletic shorts and a tank top and was already sweating. Her hair was in a tight ponytail, but small pieces of it were sticking to her neck, and she felt itchy all over.

The city was too quiet; evidence of the rioting was everywhere. Broken glass littered the street, burned-out cars still smelled of melting rubber and plastic.

Graffiti was scrawled across boarded-up windows: *LET US IN*.

A defaced wall read: *INSIDE LIES*.

It took her an hour to walk uptown. She could have taken the electric bus, which ran on cables with or without people, but she wanted to savor her last moments outside; wanted to remember how the sun felt on her skin. Her arms began to burn, and her forehead ached from squinting. She walked by a few people who didn't look up to say hi. Even through her mask, the smell of the city was sticking to the insides of her nostrils so that every breath felt toxic.

Perhaps, she thought, *this really is for the best.*

As she walked up to the looming structure, she saw security guards in riot gear standing behind a table where a row of Inside employees were checking people in on large electronic tablets. It was a surprisingly calm scene, the backdrop of destruction holding only the ghosts of protest. A line of people had started to form; some looked nervous, but everyone looked excited. They were saved, after all. Chosen, somehow. And yet, no one spoke to each other. Her phone was warm in her pocket, and she touched it absent-mindedly, even though she knew no one was trying to reach her. She wasn't sure why she'd even brought it.

Finally, it was her turn. The woman at the table, wearing pink scrubs and a matching pink face mask, barely looked up. "Name?" She took Ava's fingerprint on a screen to verify her identity and then, before she knew it, Ava was greeted by a security guard who gently took her by the elbow and guided her around the table and through a door just to the side of the massive gate. The door blended into the wall so well she hadn't even noticed it was there. With a click, it slid open.

Ava stepped inside, and felt her old life—her parents, Orchid, her job; all that heartbreak and uncertainty and loneliness—shedding like an old skin. She knew, with the utmost clarity, that this moment marked the clear divide between a before and an after, though what the after would look like was still a question mark. The door closed behind her. She didn't even hear it shut.

6

IT WAS TIME TO SAY GOODBYE, BUT SHELBY COULDN'T GET
the words out.

Their applications to Inside had been declined. Instead of offering to
help her family, Jacqueline had asked Shelby to join her on the space shuttle.

Now, Shelby sat across from her parents at the kitchen table, the whole
family in almost the same arrangement they'd been in when Shelby first told
them about the internship for Jacqueline so many years ago. But nothing
else about this moment was the same. Camilla was almost a teenager. She
didn't want to sit in Shelby's lap. And Shelby was leaving.

Shelby was devastated, but she was also angry. Her resentment flowed
in all directions: toward Jacqueline, for asking her to leave her family, and
toward her family, for not being able to guarantee her safety should she stay
with them. (The impact of the sadness would hit later, tidal waves that left
her unmoored.)

She knew her family needed her, and that she was breaking their hearts
by leaving them. But she also knew that they did truly want what was best
for her, which meant leaving the planet with Jacqueline. On the space shuttle, she'd have access to food, water, shelter, estrogen. None of that was
guaranteed to her outside, not anymore.

Most of Manhattan had been turned into Inside, and the rest of it was
rapidly sinking into the ocean. Soon, her family would have to flee New York
City. They'd been lucky that their apartment wasn't in the area zoned for
Inside, but unlucky because that meant that soon the ocean would overtake
the land it sat on. They still hadn't figured out where they would go, or how.
They would become climate refugees, the shapes of their lives dictated by

the unpredictable weather. If Shelby didn't have to live like that, why would she?

In the end, like most people pulled into Jacqueline's orbit, Shelby was left with the feeling that it wasn't really a choice at all.

"I know you are doing what is best for you, but I still want you to come with us," her father said.

"I'm sorry."

Her mom's head had been lowered, but at last she raised it and looked into Shelby's face. "I just want you to live," she said. "Promise me you'll be safe."

"I promise."

Shelby had a present to give to Camilla. It was a tiny harness and a leash.

"For Pesto," she said. "I know he'll want to go with you."

"Pesto wants you to come, too," Camilla said.

Shelby had a present for her parents, too, one that she'd been saving up for. It was an off-grid, analog communication device that used solar energy, created a couple of decades before, once it became clear that most power grids weren't going to be reliable indefinitely. She'd bought a leather case for it and slid it across the table to her dad. "So you can reach me," she said. "If you need anything."

When Shelby hugged them all goodbye, she couldn't let herself think that it was actually the last time she'd see them. *This is just temporary*, she thought, while her mom buried her face in Shelby's neck. *I'll see you again someday.* Camilla wrapped her arms around Shelby's torso. *You'll call.* Her dad's cheek left a puddle of tears on her forehead.

"I'm so proud of you," her mom said.

7

WHEN AVA FOUND HERSELF IN A WHITE, STERILE WAITING room with pale-pink seats, the first thing she noticed was the smell. The air was so clean it nearly stung her throat, but it carried with it a scent of something deeply floral and dewy, like roses in the morning, like a memory from her childhood—or was it a dream?—in which she was playing outside, dirty with earth and kid sweat, her mom glancing out the kitchen window. It smelled like that brief moment of eye contact, a small reassuring smile. Like she was safe and loved, like her bare feet were sinking into damp grass. This memory, Ava knew, was more of a wish—a revision of history. But then that was also the effect that the smell had on her; it made her imagine something positive out of thin air.

Inside was alarmingly quiet—so quiet that her ears felt nearly muffled. She turned around to look at the door that had let her in, but it was no longer visible. She felt as though she'd been hermetically sealed in a frosty pink jar of potpourri.

At the front of the room a woman sat at a desk. She handed Ava a ticket, and then told her to sit down. The soothing scent in the air became too sweet, almost nauseating. Flowers from a lab. The sum-total smell of a wall of cheap perfume at the mall.

Ava took a seat in the sterile waiting room, which felt like a very chic DMV, if such a thing was possible. Her heart was beating so loudly she thought it was going to jump out of her throat, and her armpits felt damp and cold. She knew that everyone needed to be processed before entering, but she didn't expect being processed to feel so impersonal. She was just a body who would be taking up space.

Ava did some quick math in her head to distract herself. She knew from the news that three million people had been accepted to each Inside location around the world. If that many people were to be processed in one month, that was about a hundred thousand people a day, and a little over four thousand per hour. No wonder they had it scheduled to the minute. But there must have been only about a dozen people in the waiting room with her. She tried to picture four thousand people moving through every hour. She couldn't fathom it. Perhaps, she thought, there were other waiting rooms somewhere else.

A voice called out, "Thirty-two?" It was Ava's number. A woman around the same age as her, maybe a little bit older, appeared at a door to the side of the front desk. Clothed in those same pink scrubs, she had a shaved head, and she wore no makeup. *The aesthetic of Inside,* Ava thought.

The woman smiled and motioned for Ava to come with her. With legs like spaghetti, Ava made her way over, and they went down a very long, narrow hallway. Their footsteps were silent on the thick, oatmeal-colored carpet. They walked past dozens of closed doors before opening one, walking into what appeared to be a doctor's office. Ava perched nervously on the exam table and the woman grabbed a stool.

"I'm Dr. Quin, but you can call me Olympia," the woman said. "I'm going to be your doctor here."

"Nice to meet you," Ava said, in an accidental whisper. The sound of her own voice made her realize how terrified she was.

"So, as you know," Olympia said, "I'm going to give you several vaccines. Then we'll take some blood and get you shaved."

Ava nodded and put her arm out. She saw Olympia notice her bracelet.

"I'll need to take that," the doctor said.

"Oh," Ava said, while Olympia unfastened the tiny silver clasp and pulled it from her wrist.

"Sorry," Olympia said. "I know it's hard to part with these things."

"It's for the best," Ava said. "In a lot of ways."

With the bracelet gone, Olympia began the vaccinations, jabbing needles into her arm. It hurt, but Ava found that she liked the pain. It was a welcome distraction.

A hot tear slid out of one closed eye and landed with a silent splash onto the doctor's hand.

"I'm sorry," Ava whispered.

"Don't be," Olympia said. "I get it." Ava still felt afraid, even though she sensed the doctor was trying to extend kindness. The whole process took under five minutes, leaving her entire left arm sore and throbbing. Then Olympia told her to undress. While Ava self-consciously removed her pants and T-shirt, Olympia took out an electric buzzer and a linen garbage bag.

"Do you really have to shave my head?" Ava asked, touching her ponytail.

"What, are you scared it won't look cute?" came the reply, in a tone that sounded like teasing.

Ava looked at her feet, embarrassed. She knew it didn't matter how she looked anymore. The only thing that mattered was surviving.

"Don't worry," Olympia said. "Forget about the hair industrial complex. When everyone is bald, the beautiful people will still be beautiful."

At this, Ava laughed. "You sound like a liberal arts student," she said.

Olympia said, "Just a concerned citizen." She was laughing a little bit, too.

"Was your head shaved before you came here?" Ava asked.

"Me?" Olympia said. "Oh, no."

"That's funny," Ava said. "It suits you so well, I just assumed you were always a short-haired person."

Olympia smiled. "Thanks," she said. "It'll suit you, too."

Ava blushed. There was a sort of soft-butch elegance to the doctor. Ava had been too nervous to realize it until this moment, but now it was all she could focus on.

Olympia took out a pair of scissors and, with one dull-sounding snip, cut off Ava's ponytail at the base. Then she shaved Ava's head, and then her legs, and then everything else.

"You can grow it all back," Olympia said. "It's really just for sanitation purposes. We don't want anything toxic from outside hitching a ride on you."

As the doctor worked, she explained to Ava that she'd be her assigned health tech, for the rest of her life. Both their lives, Ava thought. Olympia took Ava's phone and placed it into a drawer, atop a pile of other phones.

"You won't be needing it," she promised, and handed Ava a folded set of pale-mauve linen pants with a matching tunic, and white canvas tennis shoes without laces. The clothes were soft and comfortable. The pants had an elastic waistband. It was like wearing pajamas.

"Here," Olympia said, handing her a digital tablet.

It was a familiar model. Ava immediately noticed the small lens of a camera next to the blinking light that told her the tablet was on. "Am I to take pictures?"

Olympia laughed. "Quite the opposite. You'll soon find that there's no real need to take pictures here. Your worth is no longer dependent on what a camera can capture."

"Well, that's very cryptic," Ava said.

"The tablets will help everyone navigate Inside. And we disabled the camera function anyway," Olympia said. "It's just there because these are recycled. We didn't want to make new ones. That would kind of destroy the goal of being eco-conscious."

Ava nodded, accepting this as the truth. A different Inside employee appeared to lead Ava to her new home, and Olympia left before Ava had a chance to thank her or say goodbye.

The route to her housing was filled with so many twists and turns that it was hard to tell exactly where it was in relation to anything else. To get there from the doctor's office, they walked silently through multiple glass-encased sidewalks, up several flights of stairs, down a tunnel that connected two buildings, through another glass sidewalk, and then up a final flight of stairs. By the time they arrived at the right door, Ava was sweating and out of breath.

"Surely there's an easier way to get up here," she said. "Like, for people with mobility issues? An elevator maybe?"

"You don't have mobility issues," the employee replied.

"Well, not for me, but . . ." Ava trailed off.

"I'll leave you to it," the employee said, and then Ava was alone.

The studio apartment, which unlocked with her fingerprint, had a full-size bed and a nightstand. There was a window that looked into the hallway, with a flimsy white curtain drawn over it. The walls were white and bare, and with a pang of sorrow, she pictured her cluttered, colorful living room. Ava wondered if Orchid had laid this plaster herself, if her hands—those big, strong hands that used to make Ava feel light-headed—had touched anything in this room. If Orchid had been here, she never would be again.

On the bed was a package containing her regulation items: a travel cup, a single set of dishes, a menstrual cup, a toothbrush with organic, plant-based toothpaste, an unscented brown bar of soap, an extra set of clothing, and a tote bag in which she could carry the dishes to and from the dining halls. Ava placed the items on the floor and got into the bed. She was surprised at how comfortable it was. She quickly fell into a deep, dreamless sleep, and when she opened her eyes, she had no idea how much time had passed.

She reached for the tablet on the floor and turned it on. It was the next morning, nearly twenty hours since she'd checked in. How had she slept so hard and for so long? The screen flashed pink, with white cursive: *Welcome*. A map appeared, showing Ava as a small pink dot. She found the nearest place to eat, which was illustrated with a fork icon. She dragged herself out of the apartment and down the flights of stairs, watching her dot move on the map. The technology was so seamless and intuitive she hardly thought about using it.

For three weeks, Ava didn't speak to anyone, and barely even looked around her. She felt as though her blood had been sucked out. While the administrators of Inside welcomed the other residents in staggered groups, Ava kept her head down. There would be an orientation once everyone was in, and until then, the tablets had maps that would show them the places they could explore. Ava, though, did nothing but eat in one of the massive dining halls—vaguely spiced vegetable-based meals that came out of a fancy vending machine—and then return to her apartment to sleep. Time felt like putty, malleable; days blended into nights blended into days. She had never felt so sad.

Ava noticed that sometimes in her room the smell in the air was stronger, and on those days she felt more like sleeping, lulled into a sort of blissful dream state that she didn't have the energy to fight. Other people around her seemed to be similarly affected. No one tried to talk to her. They floated around, disconnected and aloof.

Finally, orientation day came, and Ava received a message instructing her to report to the main meeting hall, in the space that used to be called Madison Square Garden. It took her an hour to navigate the tunnels and stairways to get there, until at last she found herself in a sea of bald heads, quietly walking down a wide tunnel to enter the venue. The inexplicable brain fog that had plagued her all month was lifting. She took her seat and, for the first time in weeks, really looked at her surroundings. MSG had been remodeled in the clean white-and-pink aesthetic of the other Inside resource rooms; all the flashing lights and advertisements were gone, replaced with the gentle, warm glow of energy-efficient, solar-powered bulbs. The arena's walls had been extended upward; it looked like there were maybe double as many seats as the last time she was there, for a pop concert. As she looked around, she noticed that not every seat was occupied. But everyone was bald, wearing the same loose linen clothing.

As she continued to study the people around her, something began to feel very, very off. The first thing she noticed was that everyone appeared to be in their early or mid-twenties. The amount of smooth, early-adulthood skin was nothing short of alarming. Where were the old people? The children? It was like a graduate seminar.

There were countless races and ethnicities present, but that was where the differences seemed to end, as the second thing she realized—and this was harder to deduce thanks to the shaved heads and the androgynous clothing—was that there were seemingly no men.

How many people could the space hold? Ava wondered, scanning the rows and sections. Whatever the number, it was far less than the three million residents Inside had promoted, and as far as she knew, there was only one orientation.

She bumped elbows with the person sitting next to her.

"Sorry," she said, not looking to see who she'd hit.

"That's okay. Weird in here, right? I'm Ira, by the way. They/them."

Ava turned toward Ira, despite herself. They had a full figure and kind brown eyes. "Hi," Ava said, trying not to blush.

The huge screen above the stage flickered on, and a face appeared. The crowd hushed. The face cleared her throat, and then began to speak. She had preternaturally smooth, pale skin, cheekbones that defied the laws of gravity, and bright red lipstick. The edges of her white bob looked like they'd be sharp to the touch.

Jacqueline Millender needed no introduction.

"Hello, and welcome to the future," she said.

She was smiling into the tense quiet, her gleaming white teeth taking up the screen. "For the last five years I have been in charge of the most important, most top-secret project in all of human history. You have known it as the Inside Project. For our sister organizations on the other continents, that's exactly what it is. But along the way, we became something different."

Jacqueline Millender was a politically connected, mysterious billionaire-slash–women's rights activist, who was always in the headlines but rarely in photos. Ava shivered as she wondered what her agenda was.

"You represent the fifty thousand people who are most qualified to be here. You are the smartest, most evolved, most emotionally intelligent people we reviewed. You are also the ones who are most likely to agree with what our mission here is. As you may have guessed, it's slightly different from the original mission of the Inside Project."

She gave a little snort, clearly pleased with herself.

She continued, "While we, of course, are interested in the long-term survival of the human race, our research revealed that a radically different approach would be the most effective. You see, when studying the reasons why the earth is in its current state of disrepair, all of our work pointed to one answer. We approached this from all angles: scientific, anthropological, sociological, mathematical. And in every study, our results were conclusive: the problem, again and again, has been men." She paused dramatically, as though she'd rehearsed this part a thousand times.

Next to Ava, Ira whispered, "Oh, fuck." Ava couldn't tell if Ira sounded thrilled or terrified. To be fair, she couldn't tell which she was, either.

"It was men that took us to wars that never ended. Men who invented the technology that polluted the planet. Men who put themselves in charge and then created systems to remain in charge. Men who ignored the damage they were doing to the planet and continued to do it until it was too late. Acts of violence are almost always committed by men. Many of you, in fact, have survived abuse at the hands of men. You've been harassed, overpowered, raped, abandoned, controlled, manipulated—by men." Jacqueline let her words hang in the air.

Ava tilted her head to the side. Harassed, definitely. Abandoned, sure. The validation felt like electricity in her blood. She looked sideways at Ira, who had begun nodding vigorously.

With a sharp inhale, Jacqueline went on. "You know on some level that the only way forward is to radically reimagine the entire world. Your testing indicated that. And we know you aren't leaving men you care for behind. You're estranged from your fathers and your brothers. You don't have a lot of male friends, because why would you? Most of you are unmarried. Some of you are divorced. Some of you are trans. Some of you are nonbinary. Many of you are lesbians. Many of you are not. Many of you are not . . . yet," she said, and laughed at her own joke. Someone in the audience cheered, and it echoed into the otherwise-silent arena. "Perhaps you've left behind a little nephew you love, or a friend's son. But babies are hardly the problem. The problem is what they'll grow into. And we've got a plan to address that."

Here we go, Ava thought, bracing herself for whatever this speech was building toward.

"Our plan, simply, is this. We have collected and saved sperm samples from every man who applied to Inside. We've studied them, sorted them, and created a system in which only the best male DNA will be kept; the men who have psychological profiles closer to women, whose intelligence hit a certain marker. If you are able to, and you so choose—and trust me, that this is your choice—you will have the opportunity to be inseminated with the sperm that best complements your own profile, and you will help give birth to a new kind of person. One raised free of the influence of men from the outside world. And we believe that in this new environment, with a new societal structure in place, we can eliminate patriarchy—and its reverberations—in a single generation."

There was some scattered applause. Ava held perfectly still, save for her lower left eyelid, which was twitching rapidly.

"Let's talk more about how our new society will work, shall we? First, we will operate on a barter system; there is no money here. Second, we will prioritize nurturing and caretaking. Teachers, cleaners, chefs, and, of course, mothers will be rewarded the greatest for their labors. After this meeting you will be allowed to apply for a job, and you will shortly be notified of your assignment. All food and access to facilities is free as long as you work. Again, mothering is considered a job like any other, and those who choose to have children will not be required to complete other work until their children turn twenty-two. When you retire, you will also be fully taken care of."

More applause. Some people wept with what appeared to be joy. Others were all-out sobbing. Ava began to dig at a loose cuticle on the side of her thumb.

Jacqueline said, "You may have noticed that there are significantly fewer of you than you expected. That is because we intend to rapidly grow a new civilization to fill these walls. Our hope is that by the time our grandchildren are born, our matriarchal culture will have fostered the kind of creativity we need to come up with a new way to continue living on our planet, in safety and in peace."

Jacqueline Millender gave a little head nod that served as a bow. On the huge, high-definition screen, tears were visible.

Ava closed her eyes. She'd never felt any great tenderness toward men. They *were* a problem, a systemic, insidious problem; that much the Inside scientists had gotten right. But now here Ava was, veritably trapped inside by a powerful woman who believed that leaving *all* of the men out in the world to die would solve the problem. And maybe it would. There was a certain grim logic to it. But it also felt like a wildly superficial approach—and it ignored the specifically elite aspect of Inside, which didn't save *everyone* who wasn't a man, just the "best" of them.

She tried to picture a generation of children raised with no adult men around. What would they be able to accomplish? Learn? Love?

What would they fear, without men?

But even though she felt the string of logic begin to pull her toward a conclusion, all she could think of was Orchid. Men had objectified Ava, at times even demonized her, but it was a woman who had basically ruined her life.

And now that woman was trapped outside with all of the men who weren't allowed in. Men—and everyone else—who would not be too pleased when they realized what had happened.

Not that any of that mattered now, Ava reminded herself, as she looked at the sea of faces around her. Orchid wasn't chosen, and she was.

Her anger wasn't serving her, she admitted to herself. It was time to move forward, in a new world created just for people like her. She belonged here, and Orchid didn't. Perhaps going Inside alone was the choice she was destined to make after all.

From: Dr. Olympia Quin
To: team@Inside.com
Subject: Congratulations
March 1, 2055

Hello, all,

First, I want to congratulate you on a successful first month Inside. As always, I am impressed and inspired by your dedication and brilliance.

I imagine there will be an elevated amount of anxiety post-orientation, though not much and definitely not from everyone. Please flag in the system who among them seems to be struggling to integrate and adjust to the new information.

Additionally, as you get to know the residents, please be sure to maintain your professional boundaries.

If you feel you lack a sense of community, remember that you always have one another, and me. And ultimately, you have the work—it anchors all of us.

Any questions, please let me know. I'll see you in person at the end of the week for orientation.

Warmly,
Olympia

From: Jacqueline Millender
To: Dr. Olympia Quin
CC: team@Inside.com
Subject: Re: Congratulations
March 1, 2055

Hi, ladies, just chiming in to say how PROUD I AM of ALL OF YOU. What an INCREDIBLE achievement . . .

Also—now that we've closed the doors, it's important that you all keep an eye on the medicinal levels in the resident rooms. It's a fine balance. We want them calm, not complacent. You should feel free to customize the levels as per the individual, as you see fit. I trust you to use your best judgment here. Ask Olympia if you need help.

As always . . . I'm cheering you on from way up here. xx JM

PART THREE

PARTY FACE

2055–2056

8

WHEN THE SPACE SHUTTLE CONTAINING NORTH AMERICA'S
wealthiest people left Earth, it went straight into its preestablished flight
path hundreds of miles into space, where it would stay orbiting the planet indefinitely; turbulent blue and green below them, thick blackness dotted with
glowing orbs around them. Safely above the dying earth. Removed, waiting.

There was less for Shelby to actually do than she'd anticipated. A few
weeks in, her work had slowed to an unbearable lull. She didn't know what
she'd been expecting, but she certainly had not pictured boredom. She'd
certainly never been bored working for Jacqueline before. She never had the
space—mental or physical.

But here, Jacqueline was surprisingly self-sufficient, taking calls from
Olympia in private, and her calendar wasn't so complicated that she needed
a ton of help anymore. For the first time in years, Shelby all of a sudden had
hours to herself.

"No one prepares you for how dull it is to just survive," she said in passing
to an assistant of another billionaire.

He laughed, almost sadly, and she realized he was kind of attractive.
Maybe not the kind of attractive that would have caught her attention in a
previous life, but now, with a limited pool of people to choose from, there
was an understated charm to him that sent a tingle down the backs of her
legs. Later that night she found herself wandering over to his room. He welcomed her in as though he had been waiting for her, and after a few hours of
talking and laughing they made their way to his bed, where she found him
to be sweet and tender, which wasn't exactly what she was looking for, but

it was nice, nonetheless. And it was doubly nice to know how easy it was to have sex with someone, if she wanted to.

Over the next several months she engaged in various affairs with other support staff members on the ship, simply to try to entertain herself. She found that sex was a great way to pass the time, at least at first. But she felt nothing emotional for any of the people whose bodies she touched and who touched hers back.

That was the effect being in orbit had on her; she felt disconnected, reckless. Her actions had no consequences. No one kept track of her. There was nothing to be working toward. What would she do if she were to actually fall for someone? Have a space wedding? The thought made her laugh. She was bored by getting-to-know-you conversations; she couldn't bring herself to care about the details of the people with whom she was now stuck.

She talked to her family often through the off-grid she'd given them. But the calls were staticky because the device seemed like it was from another century, and awkward because she never had any real updates for them. Everything was always the same for her. And they seemed hesitant to tell her what life was really like back on Earth. She could tell they were holding back, but she felt too guilty to press it. She wasn't sure if she could stand to hear about their hardships.

She gained a bunch of weight, and then lost it, just to see if she could. But then she accidentally got too skinny and Jacqueline, always aware of women's body sizes, said to her in a yoga class, "Do I need to worry about you?" Shelby pretended to not know what she was talking about. She gained the weight back.

About six months into her new life in space, Shelby woke up to the feeling that someone was pricking her with a needle. She threw her blanket on the ground and found that her ankles were covered in red lumps, grouped in threes, itching as though she was on fire. She knew instantly what they were. She'd had them before. Most people who grew up in large apartment buildings had, too, at one point or another. With a sob, she stripped the sheets off her bed, and flipped the mattress over.

The underside of her mattress was dotted with bugs.

Shelby went straight to the ship's cleaning director, who put out a message to the entire population over the intercom: "Check your beds for signs of a bedbug infestation immediately."

Shelby was taken to the laundry room, where she stripped off her clothes and put them directly in the washing machine, wrapping a towel around herself to wait for it to get hot enough to kill the bugs and their eggs. She was so embarrassed.

It didn't take long for Jacqueline to discover that Shelby had been the first bedbug victim. A few nights later, she called Shelby into her office but refused to let her in more than a few steps past the door.

"How could you bring that filth here, after everything I've done for you?" Jacqueline bellowed.

Shelby stuttered. "I—I didn't do it on purpose."

"Don't get defensive," Jacqueline snapped. "It's not a good look on you."

Shelby lowered her head. She felt very exposed. Jacqueline had never spoken to her like this before.

Jacqueline continued, "And now look. You've probably spread it to the entire ship. I know what you've been doing at night, the way people come and go from your room. Did you ever think about them? About what they'd be carrying from your bed into theirs?"

Shelby ran out of her boss's room as quickly as she could, so that Jacqueline wouldn't see her crying.

It was not, in fact, Shelby's fault that the ship had bedbugs; the military base at the border of Canada where the ship had launched from had been infested for years, and the little bugs had jumped onto the legs of the people boarding the ship while they walked in a line through the loading area. But Shelby, in a group of wealthy people and their prodigious support teams, was an easy scapegoat. She was stunned to find herself ostracized.

It took several months to eradicate the problem fully, but even once the bedbugs were gone, she was subject to sidelong glances. Conversations halted while she walked by. She was still friendly with the other assistants, who were sympathetic to her plight, but that was as far as her socializing went. Jacqueline engaged with her only digitally, sending her emails of to-do lists. Shelby ached to go home.

But her home was gone. Her family was somewhere she'd never see.

Had her path been the wrong one? She felt abandoned by Jacqueline. Over time, that hurt turned to hatred of Jacqueline—and anger at herself. She'd barely known Jacqueline at all, but she'd given up everything to go with her.

She thought of her family. She missed them all the time.

And perhaps, she thought, staring out into the black void of space, her mother had been right. Perhaps Jacqueline's whole girlboss thing *was* insidious; a symptom of a greater darkness. She'd been so naive not to see it before.

As the months stretched out ahead of her, Shelby had an idea for a book. It was part memoir, part manifesto—and part tell-all—and she wanted to call it *From Yours! to Ours: Moving Away from Narcissism and Toward the Collective Good.* She knew, though, that if it was too obviously a rebuttal of Jacqueline's work, Jacqueline would end up taking credit for it. Still, the name made her smile. Most days it was satisfactory to just entertain herself.

9

AFTER ORIENTATION, AVA CURLED UP IN HER NEW BED WITH
only the glow from her tablet illuminating the small room. The words that
Jacqueline Millender had bellowed into the stadium still rang in her ears.

How had the Inside team pulled off such a scam? And was it true—were
men the problem? Would a generation born without their influence be better equipped to care for the planet? The morality felt murky at best. But Ava
was also so tired. There was nothing really to do but go along with it. For
now, at least.

Following the instructions that appeared on the screen, she applied to
work in the gardens, caring for the plants that the population would rely on
for food. It was the option that felt the most familiar.

Within seconds her tablet made a little pinging sound, and words appeared in a swooping pink font across her screen: Your job request has been
approved.

She was, she knew, something adjacent to qualified for the role. She'd
studied plants; she'd taught others about them. But she'd never really become a scientist in the way she had imagined. She had de-prioritized her
career as soon as Orchid showed up. Who knew what she would have become if she hadn't been rushing home every day after work, leaving early,
opting out of networking events in order to spend time with the girl who
would someday leave her?

She shook off the thought spiral, trying to refocus on the moment. She
could do this job. The only real challenge would be the physical labor. She
loved nature but had never worked to foster it. The natural world was likely
better studied by her than tended to by her.

Then again, this wasn't exactly the natural world. She reported for her new job in the morning.

There was a group of people gathered quietly at the entrance to the gardens when Ava got there, and a few of them smiled at her. An Inside employee appeared in front of them, and began calling out names, assigning people to different plots of land.

Ava heard her name called, along with a number that corresponded to a specific tier. She pushed her way through the group, entering the gardens. The air here was humid, pumped with vitamins to make the crops grow, and it made Ava's head swim. She followed the signs that took her to a cluster of plants growing low to the ground. A woman with a clipboard was walking up and down the tiers.

"Ava," the employee said, when she reached where Ava stood. "You're responsible for strawberries, garlic, spinach, and thyme."

"Really?" Ava said, startled by the breadth of the vegetation. "I haven't tasted strawberries since I was a kid."

The woman responded with a quick nod. "The seeds have been sown for you," she said. "You'll see some have sprouted. We've already calculated the light and accounted for it, but you'll have to track it. We'll check in again once it's ready to harvest."

"What do I do in the meantime?"

"Keep an eye on them," the woman said. "Water them. Trim them. Talk to them. You'll have plenty more to do once it's time to pick what you've grown."

The woman handed her gardening gloves and work boots, and then left. Ava could hear her giving similar instructions to the people on the tiers around her, where they were growing corn, quinoa, sweet potatoes, tomatoes, chili peppers; some tiers had fruit trees, already starting to flower. Some people were responsible for cotton, others for coffee beans. Each tier had its own little custom ecosystem.

She spent most of that first day crouched down on the ground, tenderly caring for her vegetable plot. She couldn't wait to watch the sweet little green leaves grow strong. As she patted the warm dirt around her plants, she was forced out of her own head. It was almost soothing. By the time night fell she was so tired that she went to sleep right away.

She woke up in the morning and did it all over again. And again and again. Time was passing so strangely. When tiny, pale-green strawberry buds appeared, it felt like a personal victory. It was nice to focus on something other than her broken heart. Sometimes she even forgot all about it.

There were areas of Inside that she passed on her way to work that were made to look like the outside, with VR projections showing fields of tall green grass and clear skies. Sometimes in the morning, in the glass-tubed walkways, bird sounds would play through invisible speakers. Ava found it annoying to the point of insult, and while the others would gather in the spaces where screens showed images of sandy beaches and fluffy clouds, she stuck to her routine. She went to work, came home, and went to work again.

But after a few weeks of the same routine, the loneliness set in, a bitter aftertaste she couldn't brush away. Her hair started to grow back in, unruly and thick, like the top of a stalk of broccoli. Others had chosen to keep their heads shaven, but Ava missed her hair. She missed the concept of vanity in general; she missed worrying about her appearance as though it was consequential. Here, they were allegedly liberated from their physicality—their worth wasn't determined by the shape of their bodies or the luster of their manes. It was great in theory, but in practice, it was incredibly boring. Even in theory, actually, it felt like a straight woman's fantasy of what it would be like to live without men. If anything, with no men around, Ava spent *more* time contemplating her physicality—as well as a considerable amount of time every day wondering if the others were having sex with one another.

She wondered about those others a lot, what they thought of this place, what they did after she went to bed. She knew friendships—and probably other relationships—were forming without her, and she felt left out. It made her want to withdraw further within herself. But instead, out of sheer desperation, she started to say hello to her coworkers on the tiers of land above and below her. They were friendly enough back, if a little surprised; she'd been quiet for so long.

She tried to think of questions to ask them in passing. "How's your avocado tree doing?" or "Do you like your new apartment?" She had the distinct feeling that they were always laughing at her, but she asked these rehearsed questions anyway. "What are you growing over there?" and "Have you found

the library yet?" The others tolerated these attempts at conversation, and
Ava assumed that on some level they all felt a degree of awkwardness.

Eventually she got up the nerve to join her coworkers during lunch. She
spotted Ira sitting with five other people around a small picnic table, eating
piles of root vegetables and quinoa. When she approached, they immediately made room for her, seemingly unfazed by her sudden presence.

As Ava settled into a seat next to Ira, one person said, "Well, I'm thinking
of doing it."

"Really? Me, too. It seems like a pretty good deal: you get a bigger, better
room, and better food, too," said another woman, as she pushed her uneaten
vegetables from one side of her plate to the other.

"Do what?" Ava asked.

"Have children," replied the woman who had been talking when Ava first
sat down. "Pregnant people can spend their days doing whatever they want."

"Doesn't seem worth it to me," someone else chimed in; some of the
others nodded. "I'd rather enjoy my own life while I still can."

"I wonder if anyone has done it yet," Ava said.

"We're all too young to have kids," insisted Ira. "Let me have my
twenties."

"What do you need your twenties for?" the first woman responded.
"We'll be Inside forever. Might as well get those perks."

"What about the girls who can't have kids?" someone across the table
asked. "Like, I'm trans. Unless Inside has invented a way for me to get pregnant, it seems like my rights here aren't the same as yours."

There was a heavy silence. Finally Ira said, "Yeah. You're right. That's
fucked."

Everyone nodded. Ava didn't know what to say. The benefits for pregnancy suddenly seemed like a cruelty.

The woman across the table sighed. "I guess we'll just have to wait and
see." And then, as though she didn't want sympathy, she changed the subject. "Think there's anything fun to do around here?"

Ira's leg was touching Ava's under the table, and every time their eyes
met hers, Ava's heart rate quickened.

The lunch hour ended, and everyone at the table got up to return to their tiers. As Ava turned to leave, Ira touched her elbow. "It's nice to see you again," they said.

"Yeah, you, too," Ava said, though it was an understatement. It was more than nice to see Ira.

Every day at lunch for the next week she and Ira sat next to each other, and Ava found herself flirting, at first nervously and then unabashedly. Ava was always disappointed when the lunch hour ended and they went back to their separate levels.

But one day as they parted, Ira said, "You should come to C later."

"What's that?"

"I'll tell you, but you can't tell anyone else."

"I swear," Ava said.

They took a step closer to Ava, speaking so quietly that Ava had to lean toward them. "So, no one knows who started it, but it's kind of like an underground bar."

"But there's no rule against something like that, right? We're allowed to drink and gather wherever we want."

"Sure, but this is a place we can go without *them* watching." Ira gestured to the Inside employees who were having lunch in a separate area. "And there's none of that VR bullshit. We don't have to pretend we're outside."

"Why do you call it C?"

"It's shorthand. We used to call it Sea Bar, because of the view, but we realized if we just called it the letter C, no one would know what we were talking about. Like, if I said to someone, *Are you going to C?* and you overheard, you might think I said, *Are you going to see?*" Ira pointed at their eyes to indicate the difference.

"Sneaky," Ava said. "I like it."

Ava was so excited that she could barely eat dinner that night. She paced around her room, waiting for the evening bell signifying the end of the day, and then came a quiet knock at her door; Ira and their friends from work, scooping her up on their way down.

Ava thought to herself that with their matching mauve tunics, they looked like members of a cult.

One by one, they quietly made their way down the tubed sidewalks to the ground level, through a hard-to-find doorway in a brick wall, down several flights of stairs, and into a windowless room. There, they found the latch on the floor that lifted up a door, and when it opened, the windowless room filled with the sounds of punk rock and laughter, the smell of smoke and sweat. They ushered Ava down the ladder first. She found herself in a room that had one enormous window that looked directly into the dark, murky waters of the Atlantic Ocean.

Ava didn't realize how starved she was for the real sea. The tranquil turquoise water that Inside re-created digitally in rooms meant to simulate the beach held none of the power, none of the soul of the ocean. On Brook, she'd been able to see and smell it from her apartment. She even missed her seasick tram rides back and forth, from home to work and back home again, suspended across the churning waves. Now, finally, it was inches away, and glorious.

And then someone was pouring wine into her mug, and she was drinking it, and drinking more of it, until her head was spinning and there were warm hands resting on her hips, and she was so happy to have physical contact that she thought she might burst into tears. Instead, she started laughing, head thrown back, arms wide toward the thick gray-green water. *I could be happy here*, she thought. *I don't need more than this.*

The space's walls were painted black, no doubt with materials lifted from the public art studio. A bar cart that looked like it had been stolen from the kitchen was in the corner. Pillows lined the floor, and people filled their regulation mugs with wine from jugs on the cart and then sat on the floor together, laying their heads in each other's laps, watching the occasional misshapen fish bump into the window while garbage floated by, cans and bottles and sewage. The space was lit with candles.

Ava lay down on the ground and watched the room spin around her. Someone handed her a joint. "Is this actually weed?" she said.

"One of the gardeners grows it in the West Wall," the person who handed it to her said. "But it's a secret that she's been harvesting it for us."

Ava was starting to realize that there were many secrets among the people who lived Inside, all kept from those who worked there. Despite the barter system and the pink pillows and the well-rounded meals, all designed for everyone's comfort, a very specific "us versus them" dynamic had begun to unfold. She wondered if she should worry about it.

But before she could give her worry another thought, Ira materialized in front of her and took her hand.

"Come," they said.

Ira led Ava back to their own apartment, where they kissed her in a room with blank walls. As they lay down on the bed together, Ava marveled at how unfamiliar Ira's body was. She'd gotten so used to Orchid's specific angles and bones. It felt good to lie on someone new. Ira was soft and warm. Ava wanted to nestle all the way into them.

Ira said, "I want your mouth."

Ava froze.

"Oh god," Ira groaned. "You're not straight, are you?"

Ava laughed, nervously. "Definitely not. It's just honestly been a while since I've gone down on anyone."

"What? Why?"

"I was with the same girl for years," Ava said, unsure how much to disclose. "She was . . . kind of too much of a top? If that makes sense. She never wanted me to do anything for her."

"I hate that shit," Ira said. "It's, like, what's the point of being queer?"

"Amen."

"Don't worry," Ira said. "It's like riding a bike."

To Ava's relief, it was exactly like that—only, of course, wetter. Ira tasted like the ocean.

"Well?" Ira said, as Ava climbed back up the bed.

Ava wiped her mouth with her fingers. "I honestly can't think of a better place for my face," she said.

"I think that's the sweetest thing anyone has ever said to me," Ira said, laughing.

Hours later, when they'd exhausted themselves in the bed made of light-pink linen, Ira gestured that Ava should lay her head on their shoulder, and Ava tucked right in, feeling relaxed and safe in the ample arms of this relative stranger. Almost as soon as her cheek pressed into their skin, she fell asleep, and awoke to the sounds of the morning bell, telling her it was time to do it all over again.

"Maybe we'll meet up later," Ira said.

But while they did see each other at work and then again at C that night, Ava was relieved that Ira seemed to silently agree it was best if they didn't go home together again. Not because they didn't enjoy each other—Ava was certain they had—but because the untapped potential that everyone else offered was too great.

So it went for week after week: Ava went to work each day, and then to C each night, drinking the sticky red wine until her stomach hurt, dancing with her face toward the depths of the trash-filled ocean, and then lying on the ground, listening to the voices around her as they laughed and bickered. Sometimes she went home by herself, but more often than not she went home trailing behind some beautiful short-haired stranger, someone whose name she rarely remembered.

There had only been one person before Orchid, a girl in college who was so similar to Ava that sex was sweet and easy, intuitive and tender. Sex with Orchid had been the opposite; rough, carnal, surprising.

Now, Inside, she found herself sleeping with all kinds of people. There were women who were more feminine than her; masculine women who reminded her so much of Orchid she had to keep her eyes open to remind herself that Orchid was gone; trans women who showed her ways to make love that were new yet achingly familiar. She had a lot to learn about how to make love to bodies that were different than hers, but she had a lot to learn about bodies that were similar to hers, too. She felt the need to prove herself worthy to everyone she slept with; to prove that she could provide them with pleasure, that she wanted to, that it turned her on. She'd spent so many years with Orchid moving her hand away, receiving but never being trusted to give. And she had so much to give. She wanted to give to all the people Inside.

And then one night it all ended. Ava arrived at C's door to find a small crowd gathered around the entry. The sound from below was louder than usual, the smell of bodies and smoke thicker.

"It's full," Ira said to Ava, their voice full of surprise. "Everyone found out about it, and now we can't fit."

"Fuck," Ava said. "That really sucks."

More people arrived behind them, and their voices became louder as the group grew.

"We have to keep it down," Ira hissed at the rapidly expanding crowd.

Unsure what to do, they dispersed, retreating to their separate quarters. Ava went to sleep—alone and disappointed.

The next morning, an Inside employee asked Ava to retrieve a tool from an office that was on the top level. Ava took her time running the errand; it was nice to get a break from the monotony of gardening. After she found the pruning shears, as she made her way back through the hallway on the highest floor, she passed a door that was slightly ajar. She hesitated briefly, looking around, and then pushed it open. Light immediately flooded out of the room and spilled into the hall—real light, from the sun, not some high-definition re-creation.

Ava entered the room and found herself standing beneath three square skylights. She hadn't seen the sky in so long that the blue made her ache, and her eyes filled with tears. She lifted her face toward it.

She stood there in silence for a few minutes, awestruck. Her shadow played across the room's wide, empty walls, the afternoon light casting a golden glow. She tore herself away from the skylights and ran back to the gardens, and within a few hours everyone who worked in the gardens knew about the room in the sky.

Memories of the overflowing Sea Bar were quickly forgotten. They planned to meet at the room that Ava had found that night, though they agreed to be very careful about who else they told. Warm hands squeezed Ava's arm in passing throughout the day, and her cheekbones hurt from grinning. She'd never felt so appreciated, so seen.

Over the next few weeks, they realized that the room with the skylights was a much more exciting place to drink and dance anyway. They could sometimes see the moon, bathing in its white gleam, and often there were stars visible, though through Inside's thick glass they looked like bright white smudges. Mostly it was stormy, but that was okay, too. They could hear the rain. And they could see the dawn approaching, as the sky turned from inky blue to shades of smoky orange and pink, the air pollution lending itself to a sight that was beautiful and strange, almost alien.

Could we really be happy here? Ava wondered to herself, night after night, as she drank and danced, and during the day, as she touched the tender leaves of her plants and laughed with her friends on break. It became her refrain.

Once, she even accidentally said it out loud to her friends on their way up to the skylight room: "Do you think we could be happy here?"

"Are we not already?" Ira teased, but not unkindly.

10

OLYMPIA'S NEW APARTMENT INSIDE WAS MORE LUXURIOUS than anything she could have imagined. But, then, all of the top-level employees were given prestige accommodations. That was part of the deal. Still, she hadn't expected something so large, designed so thoughtfully. She felt a little embarrassed by the opulence. She had certainly not become a doctor to live like a queen. But she didn't complain about it, either. It was comforting to be so well taken care of, and so appreciated.

All of the people from their original team worked within Inside itself. Olympia was friendly with some of them, but she wasn't *close* with any of her colleagues. They all had too much work to do to form those kinds of bonds. Working Inside was a 24/7 job, but Olympia didn't mind; she believed in what they were doing completely, and that was motivation enough. They were saving the world by reimagining it.

Every morning on her video call with Jacqueline, Olympia shared her findings from what felt like the most progressive lab experiment of all time. She was thrilled with how well the residents were doing; they were already healthier and happier in the highly controlled environment.

The calls always ended with Jacqueline assigning Olympia some task. Often it was simple enough, like testing someone's blood levels to see if the medicinal air was being administered appropriately. The drugs were customized per person and pumped through the air vents in the residents' rooms so that the administrators wouldn't risk inhaling it.

Other times, Jacqueline's requests seemed to have nothing to do with Olympia's scope of work, like making sure that certain residents interacted with each other, or helping the other administrators manipulate the residents into thinking there were spaces where they could go at night to party together, unobserved; and when those spaces became too crowded to observe clearly, Jacqueline requested padlocks on the doors, and it was up to Olympia to figure out how to guide the residents to new spaces without them realizing there was any sort of intervention happening. And even though Olympia felt she was beginning to be a bit stretched thin, she always said yes. Until the day she didn't.

"I would really appreciate you hearing me," Olympia said to Jacqueline's face on the screen, as firmly as she could. "This is the first time I've ever said no to you."

Olympia was appalled at what she was being asked to do, but she knew by now that showing her hand wouldn't help her in a conflict with Jacqueline. It was taking everything she had to remain calm.

It was early in the morning, before Olympia's Inside patients would start to arrive, and she was still working her way through her first cup of coffee. Jacqueline's signal from space was spotty, and her face looked pixelated. Still, her expression was clear: she was extremely displeased.

"This is so much bigger than you, Olympia," Jacqueline said, not even attempting to hide the condescension in her voice.

"You brought me here to do a job," Olympia said, trying to channel reason. "I can't be the medical director if I am also a mother. It's simply too much work, and one or the other would get neglected, and both things are too important to not have my full attention."

"*I* would be her mother," Jacqueline said, sounding wounded.

"You'd only be her mother biologically," said Olympia. "Someone Inside does need to raise her." There was no way in hell Olympia was giving up her job to birth and then take care of a baby that wasn't even technically hers.

"I imagined this was a sure thing," Jacqueline said, as if Olympia weren't even there, which was more telling than she knew: it meant that Jacqueline probably didn't actually care that she was there. If Jacqueline could have impregnated her without her consent and without any consequences, she likely would have. This white woman really thought she was entitled to Olympia's body.

This conversation should not be coming as this much of a surprise, she told herself, thinking about the very real, racist roots of Jacqueline's work; those super-white Yours! spaces haunted her. But, still. She'd thought on some level that Jacqueline had evolved, and that she herself had helped her get there. It seemed now that she'd been mistaken. Jacqueline was exactly the person Olympia had originally judged her to be.

"I thought you'd be flattered by the opportunity," Jacqueline said.

"What?" Olympia exclaimed. She was so angry that she thought she might cry. Instead, she started to yell. "This is outlandishly offensive," she snapped. "You can't use my body like that. Do you have any respect for me at all?"

The connection glitched and Jacqueline's face momentarily flickered. "Sorry, I didn't hear you," Jacqueline said, though Olympia doubted that was true. "Say that again? This time, with perhaps a little less combativeness?"

"Look," Olympia said, with a heavy sigh. Jacqueline was giving her a chance to redo what had just come out of her mouth, and she knew she needed to take her up on it, even while she felt her whole body recoil. Even the word *combativeness* was so loaded. "We just picked the fifty thousand most capable people in North America to live here," Olympia said. "Surely one of them fits the profile you're looking for."

"I really can't stand the thought of one of the residents thinking they are her actual mother," Jacqueline replied.

"There's a new community of women forming who are talking about raising children collaboratively," Olympia said, sitting up straighter as she spoke, because she knew that this idea would work. "We can have them look after her."

"That sounds awfully experimental," Jacqueline said.

"This whole thing is an experiment," Olympia said. "We can simply implant your embryo in someone who is already planning on getting pregnant. She doesn't even have to know about it. What difference does it make?"

Jacqueline was silent. Olympia continued, "And then the child will be raised by the group. I really do think this is for the best."

Jacqueline didn't look happy. Olympia took a sip of coffee while she waited for the response.

Finally, Jacqueline nodded. "Maybe," she said.

At least I won't have to carry it, Olympia thought.

"But what if it doesn't work?" Jacqueline said, the panic in her voice escalating all over again. "What if it turns out children need one mother, not twenty?"

"If that happens, we will find someone who has a similar psychological profile to you and have her raise the child instead. We can even have that person be the one to carry her," Olympia offered. "So that there's already a built-in bond as a fail-safe."

"I have to say, I hate this plan," said Jacqueline.

"Everything is going to be okay," Olympia said, though she wondered whether or not that was true.

"Maybe this is for the best." Jacqueline sighed. "Maybe you don't have the maternal touch."

"Maybe you're right," Olympia replied. "Maybe your definition of maternal doesn't fit me. You probably want the child to be carried by someone more like you, at any rate."

"You owe me one," Jacqueline said, as her way of signing off.

Olympia sat, stunned, her mug of coffee growing cold in her hand. Before this moment, she'd thought Jacqueline respected her; she'd felt, in many ways, like she was the exception to the rule of Jacqueline's pathological superiority. She'd known from her flippant asides in prior conversations that she didn't regard all the residents of Inside, or even all the executive staff, very highly, but she hadn't felt like that disdain encompassed her, too. She always thought they were peers. She was shocked at her own willful ignorance.

11

AFTER A FEW WEEKS OF DRINKING RED WINE EVERY NIGHT, a butterfly-shaped rash appeared in the middle of Ava's face, bumpy red wings across each cheek.

It only took one friend saying, "Hey, Party Face" for the name to stick.

She drank as much as she wanted and slept very little. Every day her body felt more bloated and tired. Her monthly bloodwork regularly showed that she was dehydrated, and she was told to drink more water, which sometimes she did and sometimes she didn't. It didn't seem to matter; her days all took the same form regardless of how she treated her body, and so she did whatever she wanted with it.

But during the day, the physical labor of her job sometimes made her want to throw up, especially if she stood up too quickly after tending to a crop. And then one day she got so dizzy, she slipped.

She'd only gotten about three hours of sleep the night before and was out of it, not paying attention, and when she stood up the ground felt like it was moving beneath her. She lost her footing, careening forward, with nothing to steady herself upon. *Shit*, she thought, as the ground rushed up toward her face. She thought it probably looked like an intentional pratfall from afar and was still thinking about the absurdity of it all when she somersaulted over the edge of her tiered garden and dropped a full four feet into the next one. She landed on her knee, and then rolled over onto her back, looking up at the thick sloping glass.

Ava was helped to her feet by her coworkers and then gingerly rushed to the doctor's office, where the woman who had shaved Ava's head on her check-in day was waiting.

"Been spending a little too much time under the skylights, huh?" Olympia said, while she examined Ava's knee, and then her abdomen.

"How did you know about that?" Ava said.

Olympia just frowned and said nothing else. She turned her back to Ava and took her gloves off, washing her hands vigorously.

Ava was silent. *Of course they knew.* Did they have cameras? Spies? Probably both. But why?

Olympia took her glasses off and pulled up a chair to Ava's bed. She sat with her legs open, her elbows resting on her knees. "So, Ava. I can't let you work like this."

"Obviously," Ava said, trying to be cute, but the doctor didn't laugh.

"You might remember that one of the few rules of this place is that in order to eat and use the facilities, you have to work in some capacity."

"But, I can't."

"Well," Olympia said, "there is a different job you could do."

"Why can't I just go back to the gardens when my knee heals? I like it there. I'm good at it."

"Because there might be a better option," Olympia replied.

"Okay," Ava said, trying to be a good sport. "Maybe I could be a researcher, or something more academic."

"That's not what I had in mind," Olympia said. "Besides, once you've been assigned a job we can't really put you in a completely different field. It wouldn't be fair to the others. But you *could* choose to be a mother."

"What? No," Ava said. "No. That's insane." She covered her face with her hands. She wasn't ready for this. She felt as though she couldn't breathe.

"Listen," Olympia said. "I know it's a big decision. Believe me, I know. It's a terrifying prospect if . . . if this isn't something you've considered before." She paused, as if wanting to say more, but stopped herself. She looked conflicted; her face held sorrow, as though she didn't want to be making this suggestion at all. "I'm sorry," she said, and it was clear that she meant it. "But this is the safest place in the world to have a baby right now. You'll have everything you need." She resumed her professional tone. "All the support and resources you could ever want for them and for yourself. You can move to the pregnancy wing immediately."

"Where is that? What is it?"

"It's a part of Inside reserved for people who are doing the most important job—making a new human. You'll love it. It's really wonderful in there. You'll be fully taken care of in every way. Plenty of people are there at this very moment."

Ava's mind raced. She didn't want to be a lab rat. *Am I already a lab rat?* she thought. At least for now she was a lab rat in her private, pink-lit room, where she could nestle into her clean linens and eat the freshest fruits and vegetables she'd ever tasted. This new proposal wasn't like that: it was darker, clinical, the scariest kind of science. She wondered where the pregnant people were being kept, how many of them had actively sought out this option, and how many were presented with it as being their only option. It wasn't really an option for her, she knew that. If she couldn't work, she wouldn't be contributing to the little society that she'd grown to love. And then what would happen to her? She'd be denied Inside's benefits. She'd be lost.

But . . . a baby? She hadn't even daydreamed about having a baby Inside. It would change everything. She thought about raising a child without a partner. Ava felt a pang of sadness so sharp that she made a small noise and brought her hands back to her face.

And then Ava thought about how maybe she didn't need a partner— especially one who might break a promise to her and set off on a bike to Canada of all places, or who, at the very least, would just disappoint her. As a mother, Ava would have someone who would love and need her back, who she could protect, and who would never run away—who couldn't. She had never pictured herself having babies. But maybe she hadn't ever pictured it because if she let herself, the want would become too overwhelming.

No, she corrected herself. *That can't be right.* Her thoughts were taking on a life of their own.

Olympia was watching her, with her head tilted to the side, expression unreadable.

After a long silence, Ava said, "When would you want to do it?"

"We can start right now, if you'd like."

"No," Ava said, aghast. "Let me try to go back to work first."

Olympia agreed, but her lowered eyebrows revealed her trepidation. A health tech helped Ava back to her apartment, where she found herself unable to rest, though she lay in bed for hours, her knee wrapped in bandages and throbbing with pain.

In the morning, swollen and sad, Ava limped to the gardens. Ira greeted her with alarm.

"What are you doing back so soon?" Ira said, rushing to her side and putting an arm around her waist. They guided Ava over to the picnic table.

"My options weren't amazing," Ava said, and then she told them what Olympia had offered.

"I don't understand," Ira said.

"Me, either," Ava said, relieved to have someone on her side.

But then they continued: "Why wouldn't you just have a kid?"

"Because I don't want to," Ava said.

"I honestly don't get it," Ira said. "It seems like it would just be easier to do whatever they tell you to and reap the benefits."

"You don't get why I don't want to sacrifice my body?" Ava couldn't believe Ira's callousness. "I kind of thought you and I were on the same page about this."

Ira rolled their eyes. "I just think it's not worth putting up a fight, that's all."

"They really got to you, huh?" Ava said. "I feel like we're being brainwashed."

Ira looked dumbstruck. "I'd never let myself be brainwashed," they insisted.

"You would probably feel differently if it were happening to you," Ava said, looking at Ira as though she was seeing them for the first time. She had truly thought they had a connection. But now she knew that Ira didn't care about her at all. Not even as a friend.

"Untrue," Ira said. "I just think you're not really thinking about the privilege you have right now. Most people would never get the chance to have a baby and be fully taken care of. Not even everyone *here* has that privilege."

Ava was speechless.

Ira continued, "Well, I guess maybe that's not what it was like for *you* out there. Maybe things were still good for white women."

Ava turned bright red but tried to sit in the discomfort of what she was being called out for. "Whatever white privilege I had outside, in here it seems like we're all about to be fucked equally."

Ira laughed. "Maybe so," they said. "Though it does seem like having a child would only benefit you."

Ava got up and went to her own garden. She was furious. Whether or not she had a baby should not dictate her worth. But after a few moments of trying to do her work, it became clear to Ava that she was indeed useless, at least in this state. She couldn't even crouch down to tend to her plants. She held back tears of frustration. It seemed the decision was making itself.

Ava made her way back to her apartment early, before the workday was up, and got back into bed. She knew that her entire life was about to change, but it was hard to imagine it changing any more than it already had. What would it mean to be a mother? What would it mean to be a mother *here*? She didn't know what she could teach a child about being alive. There was still so much she had yet to figure out for herself.

But Ava knew she didn't really have a choice. She'd agreed to the laws and systems of this world, one of which was that she would work in exchange for . . . well, everything, and motherhood was a job here. Perhaps it was only a matter of time before this became her only option. Perhaps none of them had a choice about it. Maybe it was best to just surrender to the fact that now there were forces larger than her steering the course of her life. She had a part to play like everyone else. Her part was just not what she'd expected. But she could adjust. She *would* adjust. There were so many more pros than cons. Inside had given her everything she'd ever wanted. She could overlook the parts that didn't feel exactly right. She skipped dinner and fell asleep on top of the covers.

When she heard the sounds of her neighbors waking up and leaving for breakfast, she hoisted herself out of bed and slowly limped her way back toward the medical center. Olympia met her in the waiting room as though she'd been expecting her, and guided her to an operating table.

Ava lay back, and a series of new doctors entered. An IV was attached to her arm.

Everything will be different now, she thought, fighting back tears. But that was a pointless line of thinking. Everything was already different.

12

THE PREGNANCY WING WAS MORE LIKE A LUXURY SPA, though Olympia didn't have anyone to say that to. She was committed to maintaining professional boundaries with her coworkers, which meant no complaining; no poking fun at the sometimes-ridiculous details of the world Jacqueline had created. It was a lonely way to be.

Each morning before her shift in the medical center started, she walked through the special, luminous mauve hall, making small talk with the pregnant people and using her presence to wordlessly remind the administrators that, though this wasn't her exact department, she was watching. This tactic was Jacqueline's idea: "It's always important that workers feel there's an authority figure nearby," she'd said to Olympia, and while Olympia thought Jacqueline's adherence to capitalist values was a bit stale, in this case she agreed. Keeping the pregnant people safe and happy was the most important thing they were doing here, which meant making sure the administrators did their jobs well. The future relied on it.

And after Ava was inseminated, Olympia herself took her patient by the hand and brought her to the room she'd live in for the better part of a year. The large bed was lined with pillows of different shapes and sizes to keep her comfortable as her body changed. A personal fridge was stocked with Popsicles—a common request—though there was also a chef on call to make whatever Ava might crave. But Ava was having no reaction to the amenities before her. Instead, she sat on the bed and stared at the wall.

Olympia sat next to Ava and took both of her hands in her own. "Ava, please look at me."

Ava slowly redirected her hollow gaze to meet Olympia's. She looked pale.

"It's going to be okay," she said.

"Is it?" Ava's voice was barely a whisper.

Olympia squeezed her hands. She was overwhelmed with compassion for the beautiful young woman beside her, though it was the beautiful part she was trying hard to ignore.

"I know this isn't what you had planned. But I will take care of you. We all will. And you'll see. Having a baby will bring more love into your life. I promise."

Ava flinched, breaking eye contact. "Okay," she said, but it sounded like defeat, not like an actual agreement.

"Do you want me to leave you for a bit?" Olympia asked, and Ava nodded. Olympia wiped the sweat from her hands onto her scrubs as she stood up, taking one last look at Ava frozen on the bed, before she left, closing the door quietly.

Within a few days, they would know for certain whether or not Ava was pregnant, both with her own child and Jacqueline's. Though there wasn't much doubt in Olympia's mind. Their success rate had been nearly one hundred percent so far—with the exception of a few patients who turned out to have surprising, unforeseen fertility issues—and she didn't see why this should be any different.

Olympia had provided Jacqueline with several options for a surrogate, and once Jacqueline had read Ava's profile, the decision was made. Jacqueline had insisted Ava was perfect. Olympia had immediately regretted including Ava in the list—there was something so vulnerable about her—but Jacqueline had made up her mind, and Olympia was trying to choose her battles more wisely.

As she walked out of Ava's room, she took a peek into the bathhouse. A humid waft of rose hip oil and eucalyptus filled her nose. A small cluster of people were gathered in the tepid saltwater pool; next to it, prenatal massage beds lined the wall. *Ava will be fine*, she told herself. *This is the best thing for her. She might even enjoy her stay.*

But no matter how hard she tried to tell herself that what she was doing was right, she couldn't overcome the sense of dread and guilt welling up inside her. For if this was the best thing, surely she'd be doing it herself, instead of allowing her patient to not only sign up for a child she didn't want, but unwittingly carry Jacqueline's baby as well.

The irony of all this weighed heavily on her. There was a history here that was going unacknowledged; a history of forced birth, which had uniquely impacted Black women, especially after abortion became illegal in America. And here she was, helping repeat, or at least continue, that pattern. At least that was one way of looking at it. The other way was that she had to choose between herself or someone else, and she'd chosen herself and her freedom over that of a white woman. In a way, that was changing the narrative. In another way, it wasn't changing anything at all.

A few weeks in, and Ava—who was successfully pregnant with two—was as depressed as ever.

The patient wouldn't participate in group activities. She wouldn't take advantage of the classes or the library or even the spa treatments. It was beyond alarming. She was hardly eating.

Olympia could not put her on mood stabilizers because of the pregnancy, so she tried to urge her to talk to the therapist, but Ava refused.

"There's no point," Ava said, in a monotone voice. "This is happening no matter how I feel about it."

Olympia found she could not argue with Ava, and instead tried to give her all the options, and to just be consistent and kind. She also decided not to tell Jacqueline what was happening. It wouldn't be worth the fight.

Instead she made sure to visit Ava every day, to touch her arm gently, to ask her questions even though the answers were always the same. She brought her books she thought might help, though they went untouched. It seemed Ava was more content staring at the wall. The others attended classes and practiced their care skills on dolls, but Ava stayed in her room.

When Ava's pregnancy became visible, Olympia noticed that she kept her hands on her belly at all times. As though she was keeping them safe, maybe, or trying to hold them in.

"Don't make me push it out," Ava said one morning while Olympia was checking her vital signs. "I know you guys are really into natural births, but I don't think I can handle it. Can't you just cut it out of me?"

"We can schedule a C-section," Olympia said, choosing to ignore the way Ava only referred to her baby as *it*. She had already planned on a C-section for Ava, but it was good that the patient came to this herself. It would be easier to hide Jacqueline's baby this way.

"And I don't want to be awake for it, either," Ava continued.

Olympia took the stethoscope buds out of her ears and grimaced. Her empathy for Ava was making her sick to her stomach. "I'm sorry you're still feeling so badly about this."

"Thanks," Ava said, in a way that felt more like a bite than like gratitude.

Other people from Ava's cohort in the gardens began to move to the pregnancy wing, but Olympia knew better than to mention it to Ava, who clearly had no interest in finding community at the moment. A resident named Ira, whom Olympia knew Ava had had an early-days tryst with, moved in just down the hall, and Olympia felt a surprising surge of jealousy when she thought about the chance they might reunite. But they didn't. Ava just stayed in her room.

The irony of obsessing over Ava wasn't lost on Olympia. After pushing Jacqueline so hard to make sure that Inside represented as many people as possible, and equally at that, Olympia found herself most concerned with someone who had occupied one of the more powerful positions in the outside world; a feminine cisgender white woman. She'd come from money, too. At least she was gay, Olympia thought, while also knowing Ava's identity should be irrelevant to the care she received. But, still. Surely there were other people who needed this kind of attention. Instead, all her thoughts flowed toward Ava.

Not that she cared any less about her other patients. But it was different with this one. Ava was like a wounded bird, and Olympia always had a weakness for those who needed help. It was why she was a doctor. And that's what she was, she reminded herself regularly: Ava's doctor. Nothing more.

That wasn't what it felt like, though. It was starting to feel like she was much more than that. Olympia needed Ava to be okay in a way that transcended the boundaries of a doctor-patient relationship. But there was no future for these feelings; no place to direct the growing warmth she felt at the mere mention of Ava's name. She tried her best to leave the feelings where they were. She was only mildly successful.

✦   ✦   ✦

One night, Olympia awoke to the emergency alarm on her tablet. She flew out of bed. Something had happened to Ava.

She ran to the pregnancy wing, her breath coming in gasps, heart pounding so hard it hurt. She found Ava sitting up in bed, blood between her legs.

"I think it's dying," Ava said, her eyes wide and wild.

Other health techs appeared in the doorway with a wheelchair and they pushed her down the hall to the exam room, where Olympia quickly determined via ultrasound that the babies were perfectly okay.

She felt herself exhale for the first time since the alarm sounded. Ava looked pale as a ghost.

"Everything is fine," Olympia said, and gestured for the nurses to leave. "Some bleeding can happen at this stage. I promise you the baby is okay. This is normal."

To her surprise, Ava began to cry.

"Oh," Olympia said, grabbing a tissue and pushing it into Ava's clenched hand. "It's okay. Really. I know it's scary."

"Is it my fault?"

"Why in the world would you think that?"

"I don't know. Maybe I'm not healthy? Was I drinking too much before?"

Olympia smiled. "I'm going to tell you a secret," she said, and leaned in closer to Ava's ear. "It's not really wine."

Ava abruptly stopped crying and started laughing, an unhinged, shaky giggle. "What is it?"

"Grape juice and water."

"Why did it make my face look like I had a wine rash?"

"Could be anything," Olympia said. "Lack of sleep. Stress. You might even be allergic to something you were growing. An allergy to strawberries is known to cause a face rash."

"This fucking place," Ava said.

"I know," Olympia said, wanting to apologize to Ava for all that had happened, but refraining. "I know." And then, despite herself, she added, "Please don't repeat that."

✧   ✧   ✧

Ava did start eating more, eventually. The cravings were too great. She requested the usual odd combinations of flavors that the other pregnant people wanted: pickles, raw onions, kumquat jelly out of the jar with a spoon. She gained weight, which Olympia measured with a sigh of relief. She took her prenatal vitamins. Her hair began to grow quickly, filling in around her face with shining, bouncy brown tendrils. The paleness in her face was replaced by a healthy glow. Only her frown remained.

Ava never asked to see her ultrasounds. She didn't inquire about the sex of her baby. Olympia had worried it would be hard to conceal the fact of twins from her, but Ava showed so little curiosity that it wasn't a problem. Even when she was clearly growing so much larger than everyone else, she didn't seem to notice. She hardly saw anyone else, anyway.

One day during her visit, when Ava was nearing the end of her term, Olympia said, "Do you want to talk about what is happening inside your body these days?"

Instead of answering the question, Ava began to weep. A gush of compassion rose in Olympia's throat. She had to stop herself from pulling Ava into a hug.

"I hate this," Ava said, between sobs. "I hate what you've done to me."

"I know," Olympia said.

Ava wiped her snot on the back of her hand. "I mean, I know it's not *your* specific fault. I get that *you* care about me. It's this place. It's just really fucked up, you know? Everyone pretends that we're in heaven here, that it's so great without men, blah blah blah. But is it? Do we really have more control of our bodies in Jacqueline Millender's little world?"

Olympia bit her lip. Ava was right, but to agree would be to call everything into question.

Instead, she said, "Ava, do you feel ready to start talking about how to care for the baby once they're born? It will be hard but manageable. There are things you should know about what your child will want from you. I'd be happy to walk you through it. The other pregnant people have been taking classes, but I'm sure you and I could get through the material quickly."

But before Olympia could say anything else, Ava let out a groan. "Ow," she said, doubling over. "Fuck."

13

IT WAS TIME. AVA TRIED TO COUNT HER BREATHING TO CALM her nerves as the birth team surrounded her bed. Another contraction gripped her, and she cried out. She was grateful that she wouldn't have to push, and even more grateful that they'd be putting her under for the procedure, which was now an emergency C-section rather than the planned one she'd been counting on. A nice break from her own thoughts.

Before she could think any more about it, she was told to inhale, and then to count to ten, and when she got to four it was like a lever was pulling her eyelids down, and she couldn't fight it. She didn't want to, anyway. She welcomed the abyss.

But as quickly as her eyes closed, she felt them open. And now she was sitting up, shirtless.

In her left arm lay a naked, screaming baby girl.

In her right arm, a feeling of warmth and lightness, and also a strange sort of yearning, as though something, or someone, had very recently been there, tucked into the crook of her elbow, and then taken away.

PART FOUR

YOU'VE ONLY JUST ARRIVED

2056–2078

14

NOT LONG AFTER INSIDE CLOSED ITS DOORS, THE NEW world was moving along at a dizzying, dazzling, better-than-expected pace. It exceeded all of Jacqueline's expectations.

Jacqueline watched the surveillance footage, enraptured, while she sipped her wine in her ergonomic desk chair. She listened to the sounds of the space shuttle staff clamoring down the hallway and shivered in her ice-cold, air-conditioned room. But her mind was always far from her body. She felt her whole soul was Inside.

The tubes, tunnels, glass-encased sidewalks, and endless stairways were filled with toddlers, clothed in identical cream-colored linen onesies. Their laughter, screams, babbles, and cries bounced off the walls. Their sticky fingers left small handprints. The administrators of Inside beamed down at them. Jacqueline grinned at her screen.

She was even relieved that, in the end, the embryo made from her egg was implanted into a woman who would never know that she carried an additional baby to term. It was for the best. The fact that Olympia had said no meant she truly was not the right one for the job.

Jacqueline's baby's first memories would be of groups of other children, of singing, of being passed around and held and loved. There were many babies who were raised like that. She belonged to everyone. And also, to no one. She was a daughter of Inside.

There were boys born Inside, too. Boys, girls, and nonbinary children would be raised alongside one another by the strong, smart people who had been chosen to shepherd a new generation.

For now, though, it was just babies. And soon it would be kids. Jacqueline imagined the kids racing each other from the top of Inside to the bottom while their mothers and other caretakers yelled after them to be careful. They would be told scary stories about the before times, when men had power and women did not. They would fear nothing because there was nothing to fear, long for nothing because everything they'd need was available to them, their universe guaranteed never to change.

All this stood in stark contrast to what was happening in the other Inside locations, where—Jacqueline learned from the directors—gender roles had become more pronounced, and violence was endemic. The other directors believed strongly that traditional social hegemony was the best way forward, and it was proving predictably catastrophic.

Jacqueline knew that one thing was certain: this world she'd created needed to be protected at all costs.

15

AVA DIDN'T KNOW WHAT HER DAUGHTER WANTED FROM her, except to consume her, and even that didn't seem like it would be enough.

She named her Brook, after the home she'd left behind. She'd hoped that, just like the island she used to call home, Brook the baby would bring her happiness. But she didn't. She only brought misery.

To say Ava had no idea what she was doing would have been an understatement. She had zero experience with babies—no little siblings, no younger cousins, no neighbors who needed watching. Her gestation period would have been a great opportunity to emotionally prepare for the task in front of her, or even to read some books about what babies needed. Instead she'd spent the whole time wallowing in sadness.

It felt like a nightmare she couldn't shake, like she was trying to scream but when she opened her mouth there was no sound. She had never even changed a diaper before.

"Please stop crying," she begged Brook, who squirmed and turned splotchy with rage in her arms. "Why do you hate me? What do you want?" But Brook, who was, after all, a baby, only answered in screams.

"I love you," Ava tried, but it was as though Brook could sense that she didn't mean it and screamed some more.

Everything was always covered in baby shit and spit-up and pee. And Ava couldn't even take a proper shower without the baby wailing so loudly that her neighbor would bang on the wall. She was being held hostage, and no one was going to pay her ransom.

"She's like this little vampire, draining me," she cried to Olympia during her weekly checkup. "I honestly think she wants to kill me. That's the only thing that would make her happy."

"Now that it's safe, I'd like to start you on some antidepressants," Olympia responded, and Ava accepted the little bottle of white pills without question.

After a couple of weeks, she found it helped, some, but mostly made it harder to cry. Her own body felt foreign to her. She tried several different medications; weeks of pills that made her throw up or caused her to be insatiably hungry all the time. The worst one made her brain feel as though it was being electrocuted in the night with little zaps that would wake her up.

Olympia took notes of Ava's symptoms with a small frown.

Then, two weeks into a combination of a few different pills, she woke up feeling calm. She walked over to the crib where Brook slept.

Her baby was so beautiful. She was so small, but she seemed so wise. Sensing Ava, Brook stretched and yawned awake. Brook gazed at Ava and she gazed back, and Ava felt that the two of them were floating in their own warm little bubble.

Her sadness was quite suddenly replaced with a love so intense, she wasn't sure if she could bear it. As quickly as the depression left, she forgot about it entirely.

She could not believe the miracle before her. How did she get so lucky? And how had she not seen it before? She strapped Brook to her chest and went on a long walk, smiling at the other mothers and explaining the sights. "That's where we'll eat when you're older," she said. "These are the walls that will protect you." She had the urge to sing to her, and so she did, humming the melody of a song that felt like it was from another life.

That night, instead of putting Brook in her crib, she moved her mattress onto the floor and pulled Brook into bed with her. They started sleeping together every night like that on the floor, and Ava didn't even mind that Brook woke her up every hour: she loved opening her eyes to Brook's sweet face. She wanted to do it for the rest of her life.

At her next doctor's appointment, she said, "I think the drugs are finally working."

Olympia smiled. "I noticed," she said.

Months steeped in joy started to fly by.

Brook was getting chunkier. Ava's arms were getting stronger each time she lifted her into the air. Brook was growing smarter, too, more aware of her surroundings. Ava loved nothing more than to watch Brook observe the world, taking it all in, organizing the new information in her mind.

When she was seven months old, one morning while Ava lay on the floor reading to her, Brook stood up.

"Oh my gosh." Ava clapped. "Look at you." She wished there was someone else there to witness it. Brook immediately fell back down on her butt, but she was grinning and giggling. A few days later, she took her first step into Ava's arms.

Two months later, Brook stared excitedly into Ava's face and said, "Mama."

Ava vowed to never let her daughter feel as alone and uncared for as she once had.

In the afternoons, Ava joined the other parents. Together, they sat on the floor and sang songs while the children climbed all over them. Sometimes they took the babies to the space where the VR mimicked a park, and they picnicked in the fake grass.

"This is the best," Ava said to a mother sitting next to her, and the woman agreed.

"Heaven," she said.

The only person Ava knew in the group of parents was Ira. Ava was not in the least bit surprised the first time she saw her former lover among them, a baby in their lap. They greeted each other in a way that felt friendly enough, and sometimes they'd even sit by each other, letting their babies play, but Ava knew by now to keep a boundary. She didn't know when Ira might turn on her again.

There were plenty of people who did not have children. These people continued to do the manual labor required to keep Inside running.

Meanwhile, the mothers were treated to perks that the childless were not privy to—pristine open spaces in which to gather, custom-cooked food, ongoing spa treatments.

Ava sometimes saw the childless groups walking through the dining halls, snickering to each other as they passed. The difference between the two groups was palpable. Most of the time, they wouldn't meet her eyes.

But once, while they walked by, someone said, "Hey, Party Face," and they all laughed.

"Ignore them," Ira whispered to her. "They're just jealous."

Ava felt as though she was watching elevator doors close on an alternate universe of a life she could have lived, a life in which these people respected her and liked her and even wanted her.

But none of that mattered, because Ava finally had a real family.

Ava's original thoughts about having kids—that it was unethical to do so when the world was ending—had changed. She began to think about motherhood as the *only* ethical thing to do. She believed in Inside's mission, and she felt proud that she could support it. She even felt okay about her suspicions that they were being watched. It added a welcome layer of safety.

Time was moving too quickly. Before Ava knew it, Brook was no longer a baby; she was a child. Ava tried to savor the moments when Brook still crawled into her lap, wanting to be cuddled. She knew these years were precious and finite. At some point Brook wouldn't want to be in her lap at all.

Eventually, when Brook started school, Ava met her after class each day, and most of the time, her friend July would come, too.

Ava knew her daughter couldn't even remember a time when she didn't know July, who had been born into the well-loved pile of babies that was part of the collaborative model some gravitated toward but was mostly raised by Ava herself. As soon as July was old enough to say what she wanted, she made it clear where she belonged: with Ava and Brook. She spent less and less time with her own community and tacked herself on to Ava's family instead. Ava didn't mind. July being there just meant more love.

July sparkled with prettiness; she was tiny, with huge blue eyes and straight brown hair and, Ava thought, always looked like she'd just woken up from a very satisfying nap. There was something otherworldly about the girl. Brook, though, was definitely of this world; she took after Ava, with wild curls that couldn't be tamed and an adorable chubbiness to her face that Ava remembered from when she was that age. She'd hated it on herself, but looking at Brook's cheeks, she was glad her daughter had some extra padding. It would protect her.

Ava liked having the two girls so close to her. She loved being surrounded by their fluttering chatter and giggles. They anchored her; they gave her purpose.

"What did you learn about today?" she asked, as they walked toward the dining area.

"Seasons," July chirped.

"Oh!" Ava gushed. "Tell me more."

"The four seasons used to be more pronounced," Brook said. "The earth orbits the sun on an axis. It made some of the year very hot and some of the year very cold and some months were in-between."

"But not anymore," July said. "Now everything outside is hot and bad."

"Can you imagine it?" Ava said. "Can you try to picture what the changing seasons felt like?"

The girls were quiet. "It must have been nice," July said.

"It was. I don't know how to describe it," Ava said.

"*Try*," Brook said, sounding annoyed.

"Okay," Ava said. "The year starts with winter. Everything dies in the winter—well, the plants, at least. The animals go to sleep for a little bit. But then, in the spring, the birds would come back, and suddenly you could hear them singing in the morning again. The leaves on the trees would start off so tender and bright, and when summer came they'd turn dark green. It would get so hot out, your head would swim. Then in the autumn, the leaves would turn the color of fire and fall to the ground. When I was your age I loved crunching them under my feet."

The girls stared at her, blankly.

She continued, "We'd eat different foods in the different seasons. In the summer we'd have watermelon and barbecue. In the fall we'd have cinnamon and pumpkin. By the time I was your age, winter didn't feel much colder than fall but all the leaves would be gone. Everything would be sort of gray and cool for a few months until spring came. And then there'd be a lot of rain. I liked the spring rain when I was a kid. When I was a little older than you, though, the rainstorms turned into something much worse, and then . . ." She stopped herself.

The girls looked antsy and confused. Inside was always the same temperature. They'd never know what she was talking about. They'd never even know the feeling of the sun on their faces—a forbidden pleasure, in those last years, because the UV levels had gotten so high.

"We learned about the stars, too," Brook said, as they reached the dining center.

"Do you two want to eat, or what?" Ava asked, and the girls nodded.

"But the stars, Mom," Brook whined. "What were they like?"

"They were the best," Ava said, and they both stared at her, waiting for her to continue. "Okay. The universe goes on forever. We can only see a very small portion of the stars and the planets because most of them are so far away. A lot of the ones we can see are already dark, but it takes their light so long to travel that they still look bright from Earth. When you're outside at night, the sky is full of them. They're like little pinpricks of light. Sometimes they shoot across the sky. I know you've seen images of them in the virtual reality spaces, but they're so much more beautiful in person."

"I want to see them," Brook said.

"You can see them from some of the skylights," Ava said. "I'll take you when you're older. It's not the same, though, so don't get your hopes up. The glass is too thick to see them well."

"Did you know that things would be different in here?" July asked.

"What do you mean?"

"They told us that Inside was supposed to be different from the outside," July said. Her voice seemed quiet and small, though these questions were huge. "But that it was kind of like a surprise. That you didn't know."

"It was definitely a surprise." Ava nodded.

"A good surprise?"

"Yes and no," Ava said. "Let's go eat, okay? We can keep talking about this later."

"Would you have still come here if you knew?" July asked.

"Oh, sweetheart," Ava said. "I don't know. Yes. Probably."

July furrowed her brow but dropped it.

Nothing Ava ever told them was enough. Ava had never seen kids who were so excited about learning—she wished she'd known them when she herself was that kind of kid, several lifetimes ago.

The girls were encouraged to write poetry, to read novels, to paint, to sing, and to dance. They studied a carefully curated version of history that made sure to highlight the stories of women and marginalized people. They learned about the earth and what men had done to it. They learned about consent and pleasure, about their bodies, without shame. They practiced hard skills that would prepare them for life after school; cooking, farming, sewing, cleaning. They were learning how to inherit the world, or at least what was Inside.

It was the opposite of what Ava had been taught, which was to be fearful of her future. She grew up familiar with death and destruction. Hopelessness defined the world Ava grew up in.

When Ava's daughter thought of her childhood, she would remember soft gold light and softer pink linen; an abundance of friendly-faced people with laughter that bounced through the halls. Brook had never been anywhere that didn't smell of synthetic gardenia; to her, that was just what air smelled like. Ava barely noticed it herself these days, except when it would inexplicably intensify, making her mouth taste swampy and her head grow cloudy, the sharp edges of her thoughts smoothing out.

The days went by slowly—an endless whir of getting the girls up and taking them to classes and meals and snacks and group activities and getting them ready for bed and then doing it all over again—but the years went by quickly. Life became a dreamy blur.

They were both hers, she felt strongly. No one corrected her when she started referring to July publicly as her daughter.

For a time, Brook and July appeared to be all noses and legs, like sweet little horses, and Ava sometimes imagined that they were in fact a family of horses, frolicking together in a beautiful meadow. That's how it felt to raise children: mammalian, primal. She was the mother horse and they were her colts.

But eventually July and Brook stopped looking like baby horses, as the rest of their faces and bodies caught up to them, and they transformed into fresh-faced, independently minded people. It was shocking to Ava that her children weren't simply extensions of her but their own whole selves, with internal landscapes that she couldn't just plug into and understand. They would soon have secrets of their own. They maybe already did.

She missed the littler versions of her girls, even as she loved the young women they were becoming. And she missed how she felt when she took care of them; she missed the purpose it gave her, the way she felt anchored by their need for her. Soon they wouldn't need her at all. But she still needed them. No one had prepared Ava for how heartbreaking raising children was, even while it was rewarding, even though they loved her back. Their love for her would just never be the same as what she felt toward them, by design. Of all her unrequited loves, this one stung the most.

But the exquisite, rewarding pain of motherhood rendered all previous heartbreak dull and unimportant. Every now and then, if Ava thought of Orchid, it was only because she knew Orchid's hands had built the walls that were keeping her and her family safe, and she felt a passing sort of gratitude. She sometimes wondered if Orchid had made it to Canada. Despite how things had ended, she hoped she had. She hoped she was all right.

When Brook was eight, Ava noticed something odd: her daughter had a series of rituals that she did before leaving and entering rooms.

For example, before going into the bathroom, Brook would stand in the doorway and press her palms into the frame, whispering something to herself. When she left, she closed the door behind her, and tapped its knob exactly three times.

At night, when she went to bed, Ava could hear her counting out loud.

Once she asked her about it: "Baby, what are you doing?" And Brook was so embarrassed that she locked herself in the closet. Ava never heard her counting out loud again, but sometimes she'd see Brook's lips moving. *One, two, three.* Brook also started failing classes in school, which was surprising, since she was so smart. It seemed to Ava that she'd simply stopped trying.

As Ava observed Brook mouthing numbers over her breakfast, she felt a flash of anger; a feeling she hadn't felt since that awful year she'd first gotten to this place. For a brief moment, everything came rushing back—the way she'd been forced to have a child, how terrible and lonely it was. Her rage had melted away so quickly as soon as she'd fallen in love with motherhood. But was it possible her original feelings had been appropriate? Was Inside failing her daughter, as she had once believed it was failing her?

Instead of bringing the behavior up with Brook again, Ava asked Olympia at her next doctor's appointment.

"That is alarming," Olympia said. She and Ava sat across from each other in Olympia's office, where it was quiet and they could be alone.

"What do I do?" Ava was at a loss.

"I'm not a psychologist," Olympia said. "But I have some thoughts. I'm not sure if they'd be helpful to you."

"Please, tell me," Ava said. She valued Olympia's opinion more than anyone's in the world.

"I don't know if it's good for the children that they're being raised with no risk."

Ava flinched. "I thought that was the whole point of living here."

"Sure," Olympia said. "But if they never have to figure out how to protect themselves, they'll never learn that they *can*, and then how are they to form a strong sense of self? I imagine that it must be very anxiety-inducing to never be challenged. It's . . . it's the opposite of what we wanted for them, but in hindsight the outcome feels very obvious."

"Are there other children with similar issues?"

"Yes," Olympia said. "But I can't tell you more than that, for their privacy."

"Of course. But what am I supposed to do in the meantime?"

Olympia looked directly into Ava's eyes, and Ava felt her stomach do a surprising twist. Olympia was so intensely attractive. Even more so over time.

"You're supposed to just love her," Olympia said, holding eye contact. If she noticed Ava turning red, she gave no indication. "Even—no, especially—when she's doing things you don't understand. Be there when she says she needs you, but also when she says she doesn't. I'm not sure what else you can do. Keep her alive."

Ava nodded. "Thank you," she said, but the last part of what Olympia said haunted her for a long time after: *Keep her alive.* As if anything bad could happen here.

In school, the kids were separated by learning styles, but luckily, the two girls were kept together. Ava hoped they'd be able to stay together in all things, forever. She had always imagined that having a sister would be like having a built-in soulmate, and watching Brook and July, she was sure that was true. Most days, she even forgot they weren't really sisters.

But although they were placed in a group together, they were different. When it came to their studies, Brook continued to struggle, and July emerged on top.

The intense competition could have seemed a little out of place in their equality-focused world, but Ava had read Jacqueline Millender's book, and she knew that this was part of their director's philosophy; women were encouraged to be as powerful as possible.

Not that they were measured in the usual metrics. If she was being honest, Ava didn't fully follow how the kids were being ranked, but it was clear that July would have shone regardless of the methodology. And she was so exceedingly likeable. Ava knew it probably made Brook a little bit jealous, but Brook also was not immune to July's charms. Like everyone, she just wanted to be around her.

One night when Ava sat down with Brook and July at dinner, she caught them in the middle of an intense conversation. "I think you even scored higher than *him*," Brook was saying to July.

To Ava's surprise, July looked flushed. "We'll find out soon," she said.

"Scored higher than who?" Ava said, cutting up her steamed broccoli.

Brook rolled her eyes and groaned. "Mom, don't listen," she said.

"What else am I supposed to do?"

"We were talking about Ellery," July said, always more generous with Ava than Brook was.

"Ira's kid?" she asked. "Why?"

"He's the top of one of the other groups," Brook said. "He and July are tied."

"I'm sure you'll beat him," Ava said, but by the embarrassed look on July's face she had a feeling it was more complicated than that.

But she didn't try to press it. She didn't need to know more about Ira's child. The only kids she cared about were her own.

16

SHELBY'S EYES WERE STILL CLOSED WHEN HER ALARM WENT off, an awful, jarring buzz. Like every morning, there would be no sunlight to signal the start of the day, just this noise, then the endless black of space out her window, then a list of tasks from the boss. She reached an arm out toward the other side of the bed. It was empty, but still warm.

She groaned as she sat up, wrapping her blanket around her shoulders and shivering as her bare feet touched the cold metal of the space shuttle floor. She pressed the button on the wall that would fill a mug with coffee and opened her laptop. She saw her reflection in its black screen; hair greasy and matted, leftover eyeliner from last night haunting her eyelids.

"Well, you're a small mess this morning, Shelby," she said to her reflection, which quickly vanished, replaced by the home screen.

The outline she'd been making for her work-in-progress book showed up first. She'd been researching Jacqueline's early life and starting to put the pieces together of how the roots of JM Inc. had led to what Jacqueline built. She couldn't help but feel like she was missing something major, though she always considered herself to be an expert on the details of Jacqueline's existence.

Her clothes were still in a tangled pile on the floor, where someone had pulled them off of her before they collapsed into bed together. She flushed and smiled at the memory of their hands on her body. Last night's lover must have slipped out while she slept. It was for the best.

An email from Jacqueline appeared with an annoying pinging sound. It contained no greeting and no thank-you, just a bulleted list of things she needed "immediately." Though urgency for Jacqueline on the space shuttle was relative; there were no true emergencies for Shelby to attend to. Jacqueline's dry cleaning; a dentist appointment; more pictures posted online. Shelby pulled up Jacqueline's social media page and uploaded a photo she'd taken of the stars through the window of the dining hall, which felt like a pointless thing to do since the only people who still used social media were the ones on the space shuttles, but she didn't care about doing a great job, just getting the job done. Marveling at the abyss, she captioned it. That sounded like Jacqueline, or at least like an approximation of the Jacqueline that Shelby had created online.

Shelby knew that the things Jacqueline asked her to do were things her boss could do for herself, probably in the time it took to email Shelby about them. But that wasn't the point. The point was that Jacqueline liked to delegate, and that's what Shelby was there for. It was a fair price to pay for survival, she thought.

She closed the computer and headed into the shower, where she lathered her hair and did her best to scrub off the last of her eye makeup.

She was sitting on her bed in a towel when the off-grid began to beep, and she ran over to it, thrilled to hear from her family. They hadn't spoken for a few weeks, which was her own fault; sometimes she just felt like she had nothing to say to them.

"Hi!" She almost screamed it. "I miss you guys so much! Tell me everything." Her hair was dripping down her shoulders.

There was a pause, and some static. The sound of a throat clearing. "Hello?" Shelby said. "Can you hear me?"

"Hi, Shelby," Camilla said, but her voice sounded very small and very tired.

Something was wrong. She could tell from Camilla's voice, even though it was a world away. She brought a hand to her mouth. "What happened?"

There was a crumpling sound that Shelby couldn't identify, and then she realized that Camilla was sobbing.

"Baby," Shelby said, starting to cry with anticipation of the news. "Tell me."

"Mom died," Camilla said, at last.

Shelby thought she might be having a heart attack; the pain was so quick and so severe. She clutched her chest. This was an impossible piece of information to understand.

"What happened?" she said, when she could speak again. "Where are you?"

"So. Mom has this second cousin in New Hampshire. Do you remember her?"

"Of course," Shelby said. "Harriet? Though I don't think she is an actual cousin. Grandma's friend, maybe?"

"Well, whoever she is, she said we could come stay with her," Camilla said, and then paused for a long time.

"Go on," Shelby begged. She was shaking.

"So we were driving there, with all our shit in the car, and then we ran out of gas," Camilla said, and it occurred to Shelby that Camilla's voice sounded exactly how it used to sound when she was describing a nightmare: bewildered. "There was none left anywhere. We had to pull the car off to the side of the highway and just walk. We left all our stuff. There were tons of people walking. And then, I don't know. One day Mom woke up and was sick, and just kept getting sicker. We think she might have eaten something bad or caught a virus from one of the other migrants. They say there might be another pandemic soon, something about viruses being released from the ice melting. I don't know. Anyway, it started as, like, digestive stuff? But then she had a fever and then she was coughing so much. She was too tired to walk anymore, so we camped in the trees for a few days. Her face felt so hot. She was delirious."

"Why didn't you call me sooner?"

"Because I didn't think she would actually die!" Camilla shouted. "And besides, what the fuck could you have done anyway?"

"I could have said goodbye," Shelby said. The tears were coming faster than she could wipe them and the room around her turned blurry. She would have given anything, everything, to see her mom one last time, to smell her hair and hug her soft middle. She'd never felt so far away.

"Well, I didn't get to say goodbye, either," Camilla said. "We woke up this morning and she was just gone."

"Oh my god," Shelby said. "I'm so sorry. And Dad?"

"Too heartbroken to talk to you," Camilla said, and then her voice softened. "I'm sorry, Shells. I'm not trying to be an asshole. This is just all too much, and I wish you were here. I can't believe you left us. But I'm so glad you're safe up there. It's such a disaster here."

"I wish I was there, too," Shelby said, and she meant it with every cell in her body. Camilla would have to care for their aging father on her own. It didn't seem fair.

Her computer made a dinging sound, signaling another email from Jacqueline, but Shelby did not move toward it. Her knuckles were turning white from how hard she gripped the device connecting her to her sister.

"I heard that," Camilla said. "You can go if you need to."

"What about you? What are you going to do now?"

"Bury her," Camilla said. "And then we have to keep moving. It's so fucking hot out and it's only getting worse. We're going to try to get to Mom's cousin's house anyway. Hopefully she'll still want us."

"I'm sure she will."

"That is," Camilla continued, "if we can even make it there on foot. It's not like Dad and I have literally any wilderness skills."

"Mom was the one who knew all that shit," Shelby said, flooded with memories of camping as a kid, watching her mom string food from a tree so the bears couldn't get it.

"And she up and died on us."

"I'm so sorry, Camilla. I'm so sorry I'm not there."

"You did what you thought was best for you," Camilla said, sounding too wise for her age. "I can't fault you for that. We're all just trying to survive."

"I think I chose wrong," Shelby said.

"You only think that because I'm telling you that Mom died."

Shelby was still weeping, but at this she laughed. "Maybe, you little jerk."

"Go answer your email from Jacqueline," Camilla said, the pinging in the background only getting louder. "I'll call you next time we stop somewhere."

"Tell Dad I love him."

"He knows," Camilla said.

17

WHEN BROOK WAS TWELVE, SHE WOKE AVA UP IN THE MID-
dle of the night. "Mom," she said, "I'm bleeding."

"Oh!" Ava cried, sitting up and reaching for the light switch. "That's so wonderful."

"It hurts," Brook said.

"I know, baby," Ava said. "But now you can enjoy all the perks at the Blood Moon celebration tonight."

Ava heard a stirring from July's nest on the floor. "What's happening?" she asked.

"I got my period," Brook said, and Ava thought she detected some smugness in her voice. The girls had become so competitive recently.

"Oh," July said.

"You'll get yours soon, too," Ava said. "Don't worry."

"I'm not worried," July said, but the small shake in her voice gave her away.

That morning, when Ava went to the bathroom, all the toilet paper was gone. "Brook," she called. "Did you use all the TP?"

Brook poked her head in the doorway, her face dark with shame. "I'm sorry," she said. "I just felt so dirty."

"Your period isn't dirty," Ava said. "It's natural."

"No," Brook said. "It's disgusting and I hate it."

"Maybe you'll feel differently tonight," Ava said, hopefully. Brook said nothing and slunk back to her bed.

Most of the people Inside who could menstruate got their periods when the moon was fullest. Celebrating together was one of Ava's favorite traditions. That evening, Ava helped Brook braid her hair into a crown, while July watched from her bed, sullen and quiet.

Ava had been taking July and Brook to the Blood Moon celebrations since they were babies, holding them both at once for as long as she could until they became too big, and then as the months and years passed, she'd crouch down, the three of them holding hands in a circle. Each month she noticed that she had to crouch down a little less, until they were as tall as she, and then they didn't want to spend the evening with her at all. But they at least would still arrive with her.

When they reached the festivities, the air immediately filled with the sounds of laughter and intense conversation.

Brook said, "Mom, can we go do our own thing?"

Ava tried not to show how hurt her feelings were. "But it's your first time having your period at the Blood Moon. Don't you want to hang out with me for just a little?"

Brook squirmed. "Do I have to?"

"Fine," Ava gave in. "Go." Brook vanished into the crowd.

"How about you?" she said to July, but July was not paying attention. Ava followed July's gaze toward Ellery, who had recently become so beautiful even Ava took note of his huge sad eyes, his angular bone structure. Ava started to say something to July about it, but before she could, July was already wandering off, too, following Brook.

Ava sighed. There was a buffet set up, and she made her way over to it. It was the usual Blood Moon food: dark leafy greens with beans and ginger turmeric stew. She piled some of it onto a plate, but then noticed another buffet station with dandelion tea and ceramic plates of chocolate chip cookies. She abandoned her greens and went for dessert instead.

Ava knew that the Blood Moon rituals weren't for everybody, and she felt regret that there was no single holiday they celebrated that all of them could enjoy. People who didn't menstruate still participated in the celebrations, but Ava knew it meant something different for them. She hadn't thought that those people might feel ostracized here until she had become a mother and realized that Inside was absolutely designed to cater to those who could give birth. For a world that claimed to not be based on hierarchies, there seemed to be a very clear social structure, indeed.

She ate her plate of dessert, and then joined hands with her friends in a large circle. Her worries were soothed by the rhythmic sounds of someone beating a drum. She threw her head back as they danced and danced. She was happy her daughters would have this ritual to anchor them, as it had done for her. She loved them so much.

18

THE OTHER INSIDES WERE BEGINNING TO POSE A PROBLEM
for Jacqueline, ideologically, as she sat in her luxury quarters in the space
shuttle while it orbited the dying planet.

She patched into her video call with Olympia. She'd just finished her
weekly meeting with the other Inside teams.

"You should hear the way the other directors talk," she said, shaking her
head. "I feel very sorry for the women in the other Insides. It all sounds very
chaotic."

"I'm sure," Olympia said.

"But you know," Jacqueline continued, "they really aren't our concern."

"I suppose not," Olympia said.

Jacqueline went on. "My question is this: What is the point of this project
in which I've invested heavily if, when future generations return to the outside, there are millions of people who *haven't* had the same kind of cultural
reboot we've manufactured?"

"It's a good question," Olympia said.

"I have a feeling I know exactly how the people of our Inside will be treated
by the others. It's not hard to predict: their descendants might very well become even more marginalized than our generation was," Jacqueline said, more
to herself than to her colleague on the screen. It was a horrifying hypothetical.

Jacqueline's quarters on the space shuttle were decorated precisely as she
had requested. There was a shag rug, oversized pink couches that were
nailed to the floor to avoid moving in turbulence, a bed dressed in down pillows and white fur. She had a computer filled with every book ever written,
and sophisticated communication devices with which to reach Earth.

Her little window looked out into the abyss, the most beautiful sight she'd ever seen: endless stars, the unknown, the unknowable. It was humbling—a new feeling for Jacqueline.

"I worry for July, too," she said. "She's so precious."

Olympia nodded.

The name reminded Jacqueline of waking up to thunder and hot rain, of petal-soft slip dresses and frizzy ponytails. Not that July would ever know what the month she was named after was once like.

"I'm not even slightly surprised that she's been gravitating toward the woman who carried her to term," Jacqueline continued. "There seems to be some spiritual force larger than the rules of Inside pulling them together."

"Do I detect some jealousy?"

"Never," Jacqueline lied. "I'm relieved. I'd like her to have a more structured family life. You know how I feel about those experimental communities. But don't get me wrong," she continued. "I still believe in what we are doing, obviously. I've used my own DNA to lead these people into the future, after all. Someday I imagine July will take over for me as director, and she'll be fabulous."

As far as Jacqueline could tell, July was perfect. The girl was only a child, but still. *A mother knows these things*, she thought. July was the ideal specimen to use as they tracked the progress of everyone else; the gold standard to which every other child could be compared.

"July is hitting all of her developmental milestones early," Olympia said, which Jacqueline already knew, but it was nice to hear again. "She's quite bright, and very well-liked by her peers. And she's as healthy as she could possibly be."

Jacqueline grinned. "I knew it."

"But," Olympia said, and Jacqueline immediately sensed that something was off.

"What?"

"July is doing better than anyone else, I'll give you that. But the other children . . . It's not *just* that July is doing better than them. It's that many of them are actually doing quite poorly. There's no real biological reason that July should actually be superior."

"Isn't there?" Jacqueline smirked. "She is my daughter, after all."

Olympia didn't take the bait. Instead she said, "My best guess is that July is only doing better than the others because she's getting so much more attention from us. You know I adore her. But it's possible a lot of her success is due to the fact that we're investing the most resources in her and giving her the least amount of room to fail. It's hard to compare her progress when she's being treated so differently. It's impossible for the team to invest this kind of time and energy into her and make sure everyone else is keeping up. Everyone is bending over backward for her—her teachers, her caretakers. They're all acting like she's an extension of you. It's not fair, and it certainly won't allow us to accurately read how this system is working."

"Tell me more about the other children," Jacqueline said, begrudgingly.

"They seem more anxious than they should be. Many of them are displaying early signs of OCD and other anxiety disorders. They're having panic attacks."

"What in the world is there for them to feel anxious about?" Jacqueline said, aghast, but it was a rhetorical question; she didn't want to know the answer. Instead she said, "That's the most ridiculous thing I've ever heard. Can't you just increase their dosages?"

"I think we need to be more conservative with our use of that," Olympia said. "If we turn it up too much, they'll just be zombies."

"Then I'm really not sure what you want me to say. Please don't come to me with problems unless you also have solutions to suggest."

"But, Jacqueline," Olympia said, "your theory was that July *and the other girls* would be doing better here. The girls and the nonbinary children are flailing just as the boys are."

"Well then, fix it," Jacqueline said.

"I'm worried the damage is already done. These are very formative years."

Jacqueline didn't know what else to say, so she ended the call.

She sat at her desk for a while, pondering the years to come. She wasn't worried about the children. Children had always been prone to anxiety. They'd get over it. This information didn't change what Jacqueline felt: Inside's future would be brilliant.

Yet it was a future that still felt like it was in danger, especially considering the fact that their society would not be the only one left. She could not control what happened within the other Inside projects—her sphere of influence was limited to the location she'd invested in. And she especially couldn't help what would happen hundreds of years in the future, when everyone returned outside.

The lack of control terrified her.

What if the people from the other Insides tried to harm July? She was no stranger to destructive envy. She'd found herself a target of it, again and again. Throughout her career, and even her whole life, men and women had attempted to take her down because of jealousy, pure and simple.

She'd need a way to protect what she'd built, especially if she could turn it into an all-female world, as she'd originally envisioned. But maybe the move wasn't to wait to be attacked. Maybe eventually she'd need to go on the offensive. Maybe there shouldn't be any other Insides allowed on Earth, at all.

Jacqueline didn't realize that she had cocked her head to the side to consider this idea until her neck began to throb. She'd need to see the massage therapist soon.

Jacqueline thought about Shelby. Her assistant had been at her side for so many other messes to be cleaned up. How was she doing? She thought about sending her a message. But she didn't. She had other things to do.

19

ONE NIGHT, WHEN THE GIRLS WERE FIFTEEN, BROOK ASKED,
"Mom, have you ever been in love?"

Ava was sitting on her bed reading a book, while Brook and July lay on the floor doing their homework.

"Yeah," she said. "A long time ago." The girls immediately sat up.

"Who was it?" Brook asked.

"She was just some woman," Ava said, not wanting to go into detail. Her life with Orchid was a million light-years away.

"What happened to her?" Brook asked.

"She didn't get accepted to Inside," Ava said. "So we split up."

"That sucks," July said.

Ava laughed. "It really did suck," she said.

"Do you miss her?" Brook said.

"I miss some things," Ava said. "But she wasn't who I thought she was."

"Who was she?" Brook asked.

"She was someone who was in a lot of pain, I think. Actually, we both were. My parents had died only a year before we met. I think I underestimated how much I was still grieving when we met. I just wanted someone to be my family."

"Do you love anyone now?" Brook asked.

"Just you two," Ava said, while the girls rolled their eyes and groaned.

When Brook and July turned twenty-two, they received little pings on their tablets to tell them their new housing placements. Ava couldn't believe they were going. They'd only just arrived.

But Brook, at least, wasn't going far. Her new apartment was in the same area of what used to be Central Park, a few floors away. Still, Ava felt that she might as well be moving to the other side of the world. She didn't know how she'd fall asleep without the sound of the girls' tiny snores.

She didn't know where July was placed. Brook had come to gather her things alone.

"Mom, stop staring," Brook whined, as she stripped her bed and packed her tote bags.

"No," Ava said, and Brook, despite herself, laughed.

"I'll still see you all the time," Brook said. "We can still have dinner together."

"You better still have dinner with me!" Ava said.

Brook made a groaning noise. "I obviously will. You can calm down."

Ava was glad that Brook was being mean to her. It would make it easier to say goodbye. She wondered how solitude would feel now. So much had changed. Within her, and around her.

She hugged Brook tightly, and then pushed her gently toward the door. "Leave before I change my mind," she said, and then she was all alone again.

The night after the next Blood Moon celebration, Ava awoke in her empty apartment with cramps, a hot doughnut of pain wrapped around her lower half. She limped her way down to the medical center, where she knew there must be something Advil-adjacent. The tea and the chocolate were nice, but those perks never really helped her symptoms. She'd kill for a glass of real wine. It had never again had the placebo effect on her once she learned what the dark red substance really was.

As she walked through the tubed sidewalks, she could hear some celebrations still going on, laughter and shouting in the distance.

Olympia was the only one working. She took one look at Ava and seemed to know exactly what was wrong. "Menstrual cramps?" she asked, and Ava nodded.

Olympia guided Ava gently by the elbow to an exam room in the back, and then she took out a balm-tipped stick and began rubbing it in gentle circles over Ava's abdomen. It felt cool and warm and tingly all at the same time, and to Ava's embarrassment, she accidentally let out a small moan. Olympia gave her a little squeeze and continued working.

The CBD worked quickly on her cramps, and she soon felt sleepy and coddled. She watched Olympia's slender, strong fingers as they massaged her, and felt heat rise to her face.

Ava asked, "How come I never see you at the Blood Moon events?"

"We like to maintain our boundaries," Olympia said, though Ava thought she detected loneliness or even regret in her voice. She imagined it must be hard to be an employee of Inside, and she pictured Olympia, alone and hardworking, while the residents that she looked after coupled off and started families.

"You know," Olympia was saying, interrupting Ava's thoughts, "at one point we thought that we could get rid of PMS."

"Why didn't you?" Ava said.

"We couldn't figure it out," Olympia said. "But wouldn't that have been great?"

"Very," Ava said, and the conversation ended, because Ava was so overwhelmed with a feeling of tenderness that she didn't know quite what to say.

Olympia wrapped up the treatment and brushed her off when Ava started to thank her. "Go rest," she said, and turned rather abruptly around to her desk. The invisible wall between them rematerialized, but Ava knew with certainty that she had, for a moment, seen through the professional barriers Olympia kept in place. Even if it was just a glimpse.

Ava went back to her apartment in a trance. She climbed into bed and touched herself while she thought about Olympia's hands on her, coming so quickly that she immediately fell into a deep, dreamless sleep.

The girls moving out meant it was time to go back to work.

Ava applied to work in the school as a science teacher. When she was denied, she was dismayed, and dreaded what assignment she'd be given instead.

So when the familiar pink cursive looped across her tablet's screen, Ava steeled herself, only to find herself taken aback by the words it revealed: On behalf of Inside, you've been offered the position of: Manager, Gardens.

She hadn't even considered something like that would be possible for her—management was strictly for the original employees, not the residents. But then her tablet pinged again: You have been matched with this role because of your ongoing leadership and scientific knowledge.

Ava realized that within the context of her new life, she maybe had blossomed into someone other people looked up to. She felt a renewed sense of purpose.

Because, even though she knew the plan was to live out the rest of her days Inside—not just the plan, but the whole point of it, really—she had never stopped feeling as though Inside was transitory, like she was there until she was able to return to the *real* world. She supposed that was the effect the endless waiting had; waiting for the outside world to get worse, for their culture to turn into something new and better, for the next generations to rise up. Now, though, her perception had adjusted, and the waiting felt normal. It was her new baseline.

There was a bittersweetness to going back to work—it meant being a mother was no longer her full-time job. But she was thrilled to have gotten such an elevated work assignment. And the people who worked in the gardens accepted her back into the fold without any awkwardness. Once she was back working among them, the differences between them melted away. They acted as though their years of silence had simply never happened.

It hurt Ava's feelings to not acknowledge how they'd dropped her, and sometimes she thought about challenging them on it, but then she grew nervous, not trusting that their bond was strong enough to survive confrontation. So, she just accepted them, and they accepted her, and she continued on with a feeling that at any point they might drop her again. That, she thought, was better than being alone.

Some of them, though, reported to her now at work, and she felt that they respected her, at least in a professional capacity. Some of them had also had kids and, like her, had recently returned to work, but many remained childless and had continued to work the gardens since the beginning. Inside had fulfilled its promise that people with children or people in nurturing roles would be rewarded, and so some of them enjoyed larger apartments and more access to the food that was harder to grow, but from Ava's vantage point those things didn't seem to make that big of a difference.

Most of her new job made sense to her, but some of it was still confusing. One day she was asked to bring a very large quantity of produce into a room on Inside's lowest level, on the outer edge, where an old subway tunnel used to be.

The room had two doors; one that she used to enter, and another one that led somewhere else, though it had a cautionary sign on it: DO NOT OPEN. ALARM WILL SOUND. She was instructed to sort the produce on a table and then leave it. She was asked to repeat the process again the next week. When she went back to the room that she had so recently filled, it was empty. She repeated this process every week—bringing fruits and vegetables and grains to the room in the subway tunnel.

She assumed that they were testing the food, or maybe a different department was drying and canning it for the future. She still didn't ask questions. She didn't try to open the other door.

The rest of her job was largely administrative; each tier of farmland had its own team, and that team captain updated her daily about the crops. She logged their information and tracked it, occasionally looking for disturbances, though there weren't ever any. The system was flawless. She was impressed with it, and it made her feel more at home—the more she learned about the way the food system worked Inside, the calmer she felt, trusting that this was truly the safest place on Earth. Not that she hadn't felt that before, but there was something to be said for being in a leadership position. The power it came with was like a salve for her busy mind.

PART FIVE

THE THINGS
YOU DIDN'T SAY

2070–2077

20

THE HEAT ALONE MADE IT HARD TO BREATHE IN MOST PARTS
of the world. But up north, where Orchid settled, it was still pleasant—
beautiful, even. Warm but not too warm, as though it was perpetually about
to be summer. The air was holding its breath, the sunlight danced on the
edge of what was comfortable. No one knew how long that pleasantness
would last, and Orchid tried not to take it for granted.

Orchid had thought that living in the wilderness would be dangerous.
She was part of that doomed fourth category, the unprotected humans who
weren't chosen for Inside, nor rich enough for space, nor devoted enough for
the military. The UWG had washed its hands of them. But what she found
instead was that there was peace. United by the need to survive, the last
remaining people found that they weren't one another's enemies anymore.

Orchid had stopped counting time, but she knew middle age was upon
her. Her short hair had grown long, and she wore it in a thick braid down
her back. Her body hair was long and sumptuous: arm hair, leg hair, a patch
of little black hairs under her chin. Her hands were calloused and spotted
from the sun. Her clothes had become threadbare, thin and loose, perfect
for the warm afternoons and the physical labor. Her legs were scarred from
bug bites.

There were other small communities of people living off the land, and
sometimes they'd send someone over to trade for materials. Orchid liked
meeting these new people and hearing their stories. It gave her a sense of
time passing, of her world continuing to expand even while she stayed put.

There was companionship, too, and intimacy, though it was fleeting.
There were many nights when she'd meet someone's eyes across the fire

where they all gathered for dinner, and later would find that person in her doorway, and they'd drink each other in, their bodies moving hungrily and quietly under the stars. But those women would inevitably end up choosing other partners, pairing off and never appearing in Orchid's little house again.

She was sick of being used. She longed for something stable, for a body she could get to know over time, not just a few frenzied hours.

She often thought about Ava in the moments after someone had just left her bed. She wondered if Ava had actually gone Inside or if she, too, was somewhere out in the wilderness. There was no way of knowing what had happened after Orchid left.

The day Orchid met Ava, she floated home as if in a dream. She put her phone on the kitchen counter while she heated lab-grown hot dogs in the toaster oven for dinner, but she didn't take her eyes off the screen, in case Ava texted. Her housemates were making noise in the other room, and their laughter was rising and falling through the thin walls. She felt wide open to whatever would happen next.

As always, the adrenaline rush of new attraction was intoxicating. Better than any drug. She was addicted; she loved meeting new people and dating them right up until the moment those urgent feelings sizzled out. She'd never stayed beyond that point. She figured this was just what dating was. After all, she'd watched her dad do the same. Her mom had left when Orchid was seven, joining some sort of climate change denial cult and driving out of her life in a huge, dilapidated bus. Her mom's face in the window looking wild and free was the last memory Orchid had of her before she vanished forever.

After that, her dad had bounced from person to person, always introducing Orchid as though the new woman was a big deal, until Orchid finally understood that it didn't matter *who* her dad was seeing, just that there was a warm body holding her mother's place.

Orchid and Ava fell quickly into a relationship. Ava was hot and interesting. And also such a nerd, which was new and different. Orchid had never met anyone as smart as Ava.

In the beginning, even the sound of Ava's voice turned Orchid on. The familiar clunkiness of a New York accent frosted with the pretentious lilt of academia. Logically speaking, someone like Ava should not have been interested in Orchid; this, Orchid knew with certainty. Ava was way out of her league. So Orchid did everything she could to distract Ava from realizing it. She fucked Ava for as long as Ava wanted her to, whenever Ava wanted. Sometimes her shoulders would cramp or her jaw would lock, and she welcomed those aches with pride. She was earning the right to keep Ava around.

Orchid loved looking at Ava. It didn't matter what Ava was doing—lying quietly with her virtual reality headset on, catching up on work, sleeping, leaning over to pet a dog in the park—Orchid followed her every movement.

One Sunday, at the beach, she found she couldn't take her eyes off Ava's skin, which was rapidly tanning and sparkled with sweat and flecks of sand. They were lying side-by-side on a tattered old quilt, the competing sounds of other people's music and the crashing of the waves in their ears, an electronic joint passed lazily between them. Ava's one-piece swimsuit was a muted yellow, the color of mustard, and the shiny jacket of the textbook she was reading was a brighter, more lemony yellow. The sun was beating down on them so bright and hot that Ava, bathed in the glow of her yellow things, appeared luminous; heavenly, or maybe radioactive. She caught Orchid staring.

"What?" Ava said, but she was grinning, and before Orchid could think about what she was doing, the words escaped from her lips: "I love you." She immediately put her hand over her mouth as though she could put the sentence—and the implied commitment—back in. But there was no turning back.

Ava tossed her book to the side and pounced on her, pinning her into the hot sand, knocking Orchid's aviator sunglasses off, and they kissed, laughing into each other's mouths. "I love you, too," Ava said, when she could catch her breath.

When they moved in together, Orchid took it upon herself to assemble their new furniture. This was the one thing she knew she could do better than Ava, and she wouldn't let Ava help. She knew Ava was watching her as she hammered the bed frame together and hung their shelves. She felt proud, then. *See?* she told herself. *You know how to do things. You're not totally useless.*

Orchid's admiration for Ava made her want to be a better person, or at least closer to Ava's idea of a better person. So, she started reading books on the way to work instead of staring at her phone; she folded her clothes and put them away after she washed them. She got as close as she'd gotten in years to quitting cigarettes. It was hard, though, so she began keeping mouthwash in her locker at work to conceal her smoke breaks. She didn't want Ava to see her weaknesses.

She saved money for months until she could finally afford to buy Ava a real present, the kind she figured a girl like Ava would expect: a dainty silver bracelet. Instead of wrapping it she clasped it around Ava's wrist one morning while they lay in bed together. Ava never took it off.

When the Inside Project ramped up, Orchid started working longer hours, taking on extra shifts to make more cash and prove her worth. There was certainly enough work to do. She was helping drill Inside's roof in place, and the task seemed endless.

The material that covered the top of Inside was a hard, impenetrable metal, dotted with solar panels and the occasional skylight at the top of a building. While she worked, she noted how odd it was that the skylights could only be opened from the outside, but she wasn't there to ask questions, and nobody was volunteering any explanations about who—or what—would ever need to open the skylights from the outside, thousands of feet up into the air.

Orchid was focused on other things as she worked on the roof, things that made her sad. Like the fact that, once Inside, residents would barely be able to see the sky. No clouds. No sunsets. No stars for Ava to gaze up at, if they were to get in.

And the sadness that came in that moment of understanding stuck to her, coating her brain. The hopelessness was inescapable. They were all fucked, regardless of who went Inside and who didn't. There was no longer anything to look forward to.

If she was accepted, if she wasn't accepted—the outcome would be the same.

In the weeks that followed, Orchid found that the strangest part about living through the beginning of the end of the world was she began to fantasize about it finally just happening already. She couldn't tell if helping to build something that was supposed to protect some people from the worst of the oncoming apocalypse made her feel better or worse. She didn't know if it mattered.

Hypothetical global chaos had more appeal than the slow-burn anxiety of going through the motions of normalcy when you knew, in no uncertain terms, that the world was actually going to shit. Her existence had begun to feel devoid of substance. She wasn't sure how she'd arrived at this moment in time with her life laid out as it was. She had the feeling everything had sort of just fallen into place around her, and she didn't know how she was supposed to care about any of it.

Even the option that was supposed to give her hope—Inside—filled her with dread. Orchid preferred to have some semblance of control over her life, and she knew that Inside, with its impenetrable walls and government-designed structure, would only take control away. She didn't think she'd be able to endure it.

"I have a bad feeling about Inside," Orchid said to Ava one night over dinner. She didn't really have the words to fully communicate her dread.

"I don't know," Ava had replied. "I like that Jacqueline Millender is working on it."

Orchid nearly choked, spitting out bits of food as she said, "That woman? Isn't she, like, the definition of white feminism? Like, *the future is female* bullshit?"

"That's cute," Ava said. "I don't think people have said that for, like, thirty years."

Orchid felt her muscles tense, as they always did when Ava condescended to her, but she laughed it off. "I feel like I should be offended that you think it's cute when I know things. You're lucky I like you."

"I'm sorry." Ava sighed. "But now that you bring it up, maybe those millennial feminists had a point. I mean, what is the future, if not female?"

"Fucked," Orchid said. "The future is fucked."

She didn't bring it up again, and instead retreated further into herself.

In one dream she kept having, she tried to drive a car from the back seat. In others, she had to land an airplane on a highway, or tried to breathe underwater. She always woke up right before she died, the post-nightmare panic quickly replaced with disappointment. She was safe in her old bed, like she always was.

"What is it?" Ava would murmur next to her, sensing Orchid awake and tense, throwing an arm around her, a tether.

"Nothing." Orchid tried to keep the annoyance out of her voice, but she didn't know how successful she was.

Perhaps because they couldn't have a real conversation about what Orchid was going through, Ava instead started doing things for Orchid, things that were supposed to be nice. She no longer let Orchid pick up the tab at dinner. She started buying Orchid little presents on her way home from work—a new T-shirt, socks, expensive-smelling face lotion, augmented-reality glasses. Without asking, she switched all the utility bills over to her account.

This triggered an anger in Orchid that she didn't know she had. She wondered if Ava looked down on her. She assumed that she did.

Once, after Ava offered to let Orchid use her credit card, Orchid said meekly, "I wanted to be the one to take care of you."

"Why?" Ava said, laughing. "Because your hair is shorter?"

If Ava didn't already get it, Orchid didn't think she could explain it to her, so she didn't try. The more Ava gave her, the more Orchid felt her sense of self evaporating.

Eventually, when they'd have sex, Orchid stopped letting Ava touch her. She couldn't stand to give away any more control. And after some time, she started leaving her sports bra on, too. There was no need to feel more naked than she already did.

But she never tried to describe the way she felt wrung out with fear and powerlessness. It was unspeakable.

She used to think that at least if a catastrophe finally happened, she could stop pretending that things like work and money and clothing *mattered*. She already knew they didn't. But catastrophes had happened, and still life continued. Orchid just didn't know if *she* could continue. Not like this, anyway.

Everything suddenly felt like too much work—including her job. It wasn't that she didn't love her line of work—she did. In a city that ran largely on robotics, she liked how physical her job was. There were so few things left for people to actually do, versus just pushing some buttons. She looked forward to the conclusive satisfaction of starting a project and finishing it; of using her hands and her body to make something, touching the materials, feeling the sun on her face. She even loved the soreness in her muscles. But the thought of getting up at 6:00 a.m. every weekday for the rest of her life to drag her tired body onto a construction site filled her with existential dread. Is that really all that life held for her?

"Maybe you should go back to school," Ava said, the few times Orchid complained about work. A laughable, offensive comment.

Orchid had dropped out of high school when her dad died. There would be no going back for her. School, at any rate, had largely lost its meaning, not just for her but for most people. *All that matters*, Orchid thought, *is learning how to deal with whatever comes next, and there aren't any books for that.*

But as things continued on as ever before, Orchid realized that the world wouldn't ever *end*, insofar as nothing really ever ends, it just changes. And since people were adapting to all the changes, no matter how catastrophic, Orchid knew that she couldn't wait anymore for a disaster to come and shake up her life. She'd have to do it herself.

And then, the night they sat on the couch together reading Ava's acceptance notification from Inside, the opportunity presented itself. She knew what she needed to do, but the thought of hurting Ava was just about the worst thing she could imagine.

Actually, it wasn't: the worst thing she could imagine was having to live with the guilt of Ava turning down a safe haven in order to spend her life with Orchid, when Orchid wasn't even sure that a life with Ava was what she wanted. She had never been able to fully conceive of a future with Ava, even while going through the motions of planning one. In fact, she hadn't been able to imagine a future for anything at all.

She'd tried to arrange her thoughts and feelings into words that could be uttered into an explanation, but she opened her mouth and all that came out was, "I'm so sorry."

What she meant to say was this: *I think we would be better off apart, and it's something I've been feeling for a long time, and I didn't have the courage to tell you sooner.* Instead, what she kept saying, again and again, was that she was so sorry. She felt like her brain had broken. It had been a relief that Ava had stormed out of the room, ending the conversation, allowing her to avoid the obligation to try to express herself more fully.

As Orchid fled the apartment, she'd managed to grab her go-bag and some supplies. She carried her bike on the tram and then pedaled north through Manhattan, and eventually she got on the highway that was the last remaining way to get to Upstate New York, and after that, Canada, where the weather was supposed to be safer. Along the way, she joined other people heading that way on bicycles. Eventually her group grew to a dozen and then more. The highway was full of abandoned cars; people who had driven for as long as they could until they ran out of gas. They zigzagged between the empty cars, sometimes stopping to raid open trunks for food and supplies.

Sometimes Orchid saw people walking on the road's shoulder, their faces bleak and full of desperation. Mostly, though, there was just emptiness; long stretches of highway where their group comprised the only living things in sight. Their one constant companion was the smell: burnt rubber and garbage. Orchid kept a faded black bandana over her nose and mouth.

And as they rode through abandoned towns and miles of makeshift tents where people with sad eyes and crusty skin peered at them suspiciously, she thought—as she so often did—about dying. She wondered if anyone would miss her.

One night when they were making camp at a rest stop, a grizzled man appeared out of the darkness. He approached Orchid and tried to thrust a fuzzy yellow bundle into her arms. She jumped backward out of his grasp and realized with horror that the bundle was a baby wrapped up in a blanket.

"Jesus," she exclaimed.

"You have to take her," the man said, his voice heavy with desperation, his eyes feral and glinting in the light from the campfire. "I'll never make it north on foot. The storms are getting so bad. You have a bike. You can carry her there."

Orchid put her hands up, shaking her head as she continued to back away. "Sir, I can't hold your kid and ride my bicycle at the same time," she said. "Do you have, like, a carrier or something she can go in?"

He shook his head. "Please," he said, trying again to shove the baby into her arms.

The others saw what was happening and began to walk over, standing behind Orchid like security guards. The man looked stricken and small. His baby began to wail.

"I'm so sorry," Orchid said, his grief making her soften. "I would if I could."

"Fuck you," he spat. "You fucking worthless dyke." He wandered back toward the freeway, the baby's cries fading into the wind.

Other startling encounters happened along the freeway; they grew to be so many that they began to lose their impact. One morning Orchid heard screams from the sky and looked up to find more birds than she had ever seen in her life hurtling north in huge, endless groups. The sky was so dotted with swooping black shapes that it looked alien, like an invasion. It took more than ten minutes for the birds to pass, and when they were gone their cries were replaced with a deafening silence. Orchid heard no more chirping again along the freeway, not even when the sun was coming up.

The weather made the journey take longer than it should have. Torrential downpours that turned to hail came without warning and they'd have to disperse, jumping into empty cars for shelter. Sometimes the heat was so intense it felt as though they were biking through hot soup and so they'd wait under trees for the sun to set, making up the miles in the night.

When she reached Toronto, it was nothing like Orchid had pictured. She had imagined the Canadian city from her childhood: pristine, bustling. Safe. Instead, it was more like what New York City had become. Hollowed out. Rotting. Full of people who looked terrified, and hungry. As her group slowly wandered the garbage-covered streets, it became clear that they couldn't stay there. There were too many tall buildings swaying dangerously in the gale-force winds.

They continued heading north, way north, into the woods. They biked for days, desperate to get the dying city out of their minds. The air was thick with smog and smelled of sewage. Abandoned campsites lined the road. Groups of migrants walked along the median slowly, weighed down by their belongings, and Orchid sometimes tried to make eye contact with them, to communicate some sort of shared hardship, but they rarely met her gaze.

As the city faded from view, the woods became denser, more alive. After a few days the air felt cleaner, and soon they even began to notice wildlife darting by. At last, they could hear birds again.

And now, so many years after she'd left Ava, too many years to count anymore—Orchid was alone, and the world was ending, or changing, and there was nothing to do but try to survive.

Wasn't this what she had wanted? Wasn't this the apocalyptic scenario she'd daydreamed about on the way to work so long ago? Shouldn't she feel as though she'd accomplished something by dreaming it into existence? The feeling of waiting for something awful to happen had turned out to be the common denominator, a base-level dread that didn't go away even though she had changed every single detail of her life. The worst had yet to happen, and they were just preparing for it. She might be preparing for it forever. She would likely die not seeing the end of the world. She knew other people might think that was a good thing. But Orchid found it extremely anticli-mactic. She wished she had a crystal ball. The curiosity and the uncertainty were the hardest parts.

So when it came time to visit a neighboring community, Orchid gener-ally nominated herself, searching the faces as they emerged from their own homes for a spark of familiarity. Sometimes she thought she saw Ava in a face that was turned away from her; other times the back of a strange woman's head would be tilted at an angle that was so like Ava, Orchid had to stop herself from calling out.

Once Orchid was able to admit to herself that she had indeed made a mistake, the feeling never left, like a side cramp from running without breathing deeply enough, sharp and painful and inescapable. There was nothing to do but feel it.

It seemed to her that her life had been more shaped by the things she hadn't said to Ava than the things she had. Perhaps if she had been able to tell Ava how she was feeling when she was feeling it, Ava could have changed the behaviors that were pushing Orchid away. But by not saying anything at all, Orchid hadn't even given her a chance to try.

And what was more—when she broke up with Ava, it had never occurred to Orchid that no one would ever love her again, but here she was. She had squandered her last chance of romantic stability. There was no one after Ava, not really, and probably never would be. She'd die alone. She supposed she had incidentally arranged it that way. Her newfound self-awareness made everything feel worse. What was the point of self-actualization if you had no one to share that self with?

21

ORCHID HAD DEVELOPED A REPUTATION IN HER ENCAMP-
ment as being the one who knew how to build things so they would last.
People came from all around to seek out her help; money didn't mean much
anymore, so Orchid bartered for her skills, and had managed to accumulate
a treasure trove of items; some useful—a pair of scissors—and some that
she simply accepted because it seemed like the polite thing to do, which was
how she acquired sunglasses that didn't fit her face and books she wouldn't
read. It was more about the symbolism of bartering than the benefits of it;
teaching people cost her nothing.

One day, an old man and a young woman came through looking for Orchid. They didn't have anything to trade with. Instead they offered her the
use of an off-grid in a faded brown leather case.

"You can use it to call whoever you'd like," the man said. "I'm sorry I
don't have anything to actually give you."

"Does it still work?" Orchid said, taking it into her hands.

"It does; it's solar-powered," he said. "But the reception isn't great. It's
about as clear as one of those old walkie-talkies."

This made Orchid laugh. She said, "Who do you think I'm trying to
talk to?"

The man who was offering it to her looked embarrassed. He said, "I'm
sorry. I know it's not much. But it can connect to just about any location,
even space, and I thought maybe that would be useful to you."

Orchid heard a small meow, and she looked down to see a very old cat
rubbing itself on the woman's legs. The cat was on a leash.

Orchid laughed with surprise. "Well *that* is something I've never seen before."

The young woman looked embarrassed. "We needed a way to take Pesto with us," she said. "He would have run away otherwise."

"Pesto is a good name for a cat," Orchid said. She felt bad for them. It seemed like they were willing to offer her something meaningful, when it would be no cost to her to teach them how to build a house. But she sensed that this man was proud. And she liked them; she didn't want them to feel embarrassed for having nothing useful to trade with.

"I have no reason to call someone—in space or on Earth," she said. "But thank you for offering to let me use it. Maybe we can work something else out. Maybe the two of you could stay awhile and help out around here. There is plenty to do."

The man and his daughter immediately relaxed. "It's a deal," he said. She handed the device back to him.

She spent the next several days teaching them everything they needed to know about building a shelter. And then, so that they could feel as though they were giving her something in return, she assigned them menial tasks, like holding her tools while she patched up someone's roof or accompanying her on trips to the landfill site to gather new materials.

But after they had more than settled their debt, instead of moving on, they stayed. They built two small houses the way Orchid had taught them to, not far from Orchid's, and Orchid got used to seeing them every day.

The man was not unlike how Orchid's own father had been—though her dad had had a layer of gruffness concealing the sensitivity and pride that this man wore on his sleeve.

The woman, whose name was Camilla, was easy to be around; she didn't seem to want anything from Orchid other than her company.

"You must have been so young when everything fell apart," Orchid said one morning while they gathered wood in the forest. Camilla was still so young, but Orchid didn't say that. She didn't want to embarrass her.

"I was twelve or thirteen," Camilla said. "We lived in Manhattan. Every-thing was so different. I don't think we had any idea how close we were to the end. I remember going shopping, going to the movies. Things that seem ridiculous now." They paused so that Camilla could adjust Pesto's harness. "I can't believe Pesto has lived through all of it. He's the oldest cat on Earth."

"So, you dropped out of school?" Orchid teased, as if formal education had any meaning anymore. "Well, don't worry. I did, too." She began gathering dry branches into a pile. A bird nearby began chirping, and as she dug around for loose branches, a small chipmunk darted across her path. Orchid smiled. It was so peaceful here.

"Did you have a family?" Camilla asked her.

"It was just me and my dad," Orchid said. "Like you guys." She threw a log into their pile and wiped the sweat from her brow as she realized her faux pas. "Unless . . ."

"I had a mom and a sister," Camilla said.

"I'm sorry," Orchid said. "I'm an idiot."

"It's okay," Camilla said. "My sister is still alive, somewhere, but I'll never see her again. We talk sometimes, but I feel like you're more of a sister to me now than she is."

"You're gonna make me cry," Orchid said, and they both laughed, though she wasn't joking.

Years went by like this. In time, Orchid couldn't remember what it was like to not have them there.

Her friendship with Camilla was a welcome surprise in what was otherwise a very dark period of Orchid's life. Recently, she'd found herself wondering if she was going insane. Her evidence came in the form of a nonstop feeling of absolute dread over the fact that soon they would all be dead and the earth would simply be just another uninhabited rock hurtling through space; space that was infinite, space that didn't care.

She often thought of Ava's obsession with the stars. Maybe this kind of existential longing had haunted Ava, too, and Orchid had been too self-absorbed to see it. They probably had so much more in common than Orchid ever thought. She knew in her heart that Ava wouldn't have judged her for the anxiety she felt about the solar systems above them. Ava would have been able to tell her facts that might have calmed her down. But Ava was long gone, and it was all her fault.

Sometimes Orchid even indulged in letting herself wonder about extra-terrestrial life, though the sheer horror of that particular unknown was like a dark black pool and she felt herself teetering dangerously on the edge of it. So she tried not to wonder, except when she was feeling reckless, when she didn't care if reality became far away, as far away as the other planets, where maybe there was life or maybe there was just more nothing.

One morning, Camilla confronted her.

They were walking through the woods when Camilla stopped and said, "Orchid, we need to have a conversation."

The light, filtered through the leaves, was casting shadows across the younger woman's face, giving her a kind of whimsical glow even as Camilla was looking at her with such concern.

"This isn't easy to say," she said.

"Just say it."

"You're one of the most important people in the world to me, and I'm really, really worried about you."

"About me?" Orchid was taken aback. "Why?"

"Orchid, I'm sorry, but . . ." She trailed off. "You seem lost."

Orchid hadn't thought that anyone had noticed how she was struggling. She didn't know what to say, so she looked at her feet.

"Do you want to talk about it?" Camilla said.

Orchid sat down. Camilla sat down, too, facing her, and waited.

"My mom went crazy when I was little," Orchid said, when she found the words. "I think that might be happening to me, too."

"What kind of crazy?"

"I'm not sure. The kind of crazy that makes you name your kid Orchid."

"I'm serious," Camilla said.

Orchid could feel that secret dark part of her sealing back up, protecting itself, and she willed it to remain open. "We didn't really talk about it. She thought climate change was a conspiracy. She started talking to people who weren't there. I was really young, but I remember some things so clearly. She stopped bathing. The smell of her—that's what I always think of. And then she left us. Found her people, I guess."

"I'm so sorry," Camilla said.

"And recently, I can't stop thinking about, like, insane shit. I feel haunted."

"What kind of insane shit are you thinking about?" Camilla asked.

"Like . . ." Orchid paused, and then started to laugh. "Aliens."

Camilla wasn't laughing with her, and Orchid quickly adjusted her tone. "I know how it sounds. I just can't stop thinking about how much we don't know, and how small we are, and I think it's driving me insane."

Camilla nodded and picked at some grass. She waited for Orchid to continue.

"Did you ever fly on an airplane?" Orchid asked.

"Once," Camilla said.

"Do you remember what landing felt like? Like, the first couple of seconds when the wheels hit the ground, you can feel the brakes trying to battle with the speed, and there are a few moments when you're not sure if the plane can stop? Like maybe it's going to veer off the runway and crash into something at full speed? That's how I feel all the time. Like I've just landed and I'm not sure if my brakes can hold me back."

"I think you should move in with me," Camilla said.

"You want to be my bunkmate? After I told you I'm losing my mind?"

"I want to keep an eye on you. So, yeah. What do you think?"

"It can't hurt to try," Orchid said, and for the first time in a long time, the weird, rambling voice inside her head was quiet.

"You know," Camilla was saying, "I get your whole thing." She had finished helping put Orchid's belongings away and sat down on her bed.

"What's my whole thing?"

"You act all calm and cool, but you've got a storm brewing in there. It shows if anyone so much as scratches the surface."

"Jesus," Orchid said. "Who asked you?"

Camilla gave her a withering look. There had never been a more accurate read of Orchid, and she wasn't sure what to do with it. So she let it hang in the air, and as she adjusted her bed so that it fit neatly in the corner, she thought about how Ava would have loved to hear Camilla analyze her inner life.

IT HAD BEEN MANY YEARS SINCE I'D BEEN ABLE TO MAKE out the nighttime glow of cities on Earth from my window on the space shuttle. Everything was dark, as though the earth was reclaiming what had been taken.

On the ground, though, on the nights when the moon was full, the dead city around Inside was illuminated. There was no more electricity in Manhattan, nor were there many people—the buildings and streets had emptied out within a few years after Inside closed its doors. The moon's white light reflected off the metal surfaces of Inside, and if it wasn't storming and the sky was clear, the city almost looked just like it used to, minus, of course, the crowds.

Occasionally, though, some people would pass through New York on their way north, setting up camp for a few days in abandoned buildings in Lower Manhattan, south of Inside. Other times, people came to the city specifically to see Inside, for it was a new wonder of the dying world.

Oftentimes, people came to break in—or try to, anyway. The full moon was a perfect time to make an attempt; Inside, illuminated gloriously and viciously in the dark, demanded attention.

There were rumors about what went on within this Inside location, though they were impossible to confirm. Even on the space shuttle, everyone knew of at least one well-educated, upper-middle-class young woman who was accepted. Had they accepted any other type of person? It was mostly conjecture, and then myth, but still—on the ground, the stories drew people toward it, curious to confirm the scandal they'd heard about in whispers.

Men in particular tried to scale the building from all sides. Using rock-climbing gear, they crept like spiders up the east side, the side that had solar panels, but what they did not anticipate was that Inside had a very effective security system designed to deter people who tried to break in, and once they reached a certain height off the ground, they'd find themselves suddenly flung into the air, as though Inside was a person who was swatting them like a fly. Most of them fell to their death or were otherwise so hurt by the fall that they died of the injuries, their bodies left to rot. Other people tried to climb the smooth glass side where the farms were, on the west side, but they found that it was not possible to grip the glass, and they'd slide right off, never getting higher than ten or twelve feet.

Over the years, as thousands of displaced climate refugees passed through the city, people eventually learned that there was no use trying to break into Inside, and while they accepted it, it didn't deter the migrants from defacing it as they traveled by. As a result, as time went by, the entire exterior perimeter of Inside became covered with graffiti; names and poems and swears.

The most common recurring phrase, besides the simple *FUCK INSIDE* and the lewder *INSIDE YOUR ASSHOLE,* was *INSIDE LIES.*

It wasn't just graffiti, though. Rocks were thrown at its shiny gray base, gum was stuck to it, and occasionally dead animals were nailed to it, which in the heat would quickly decay, becoming skeletons. The defacement went as high as people could reach and wrapped around the structure almost entirely. The water level rose, so that Inside could not be approached on foot, and then people would come in boats up the Hudson River, leaning out as far as they could in order to leave a mark on this structure that represented the beginning of the end.

Aesthetically, it was an intense departure from the glorified, glittering achievement that had been unveiled so many years ago. Its creators would have been horrified to see what had become of its base.

And as the waves of climate refugees passed, seeing Inside's terrifying ugliness, many of them began to feel relieved that they hadn't been accepted after all, for they assumed that anything as hideous and threatening as that on the outside must be much worse on the inside.

PART SIX

SIX

WHAT IT MIGHT MEAN

2078

22

JULY AND BROOK SPRAWLED OUT ON THE FLOOR OF A PRI-
vate study pod under a blinding azure-blue sky, marred only by scattered
dark spots where the virtual reality panels glitched. The two women, who
at twenty-two were more like sisters than best friends, were going through
the motions of reading the book that marked their final college assignment.

Brook was on her back, legs stretched up against the curved wall; July
was next to her, flat on her stomach, face in her hands. They radiated youth;
their skin luminous from never seeing the sun. Their voices—even when
they were complaining or gossiping, as they often were—sounded sweet
and naive, never bitter, never burdened by the hardness of life. Their lives
weren't hard, had never been hard; they were promised safety and care, if
nothing else.

Peering at Jacqueline Millender's headshot on the book's jacket, July
said, "She's kind of scary looking."

"But in, like, a hot way?" Brook said.

"Ew." They both giggled.

July drew a curled mustache over the photo. Brook flipped over onto her
stomach and added a unibrow.

As they colored in Jacqueline's teeth, Brook said, "I think she looks much
better now."

They were lying so close to each other that Brook's long, dark brown hair
spilled onto July's shoulder, tickling her. "You really need to get that mane
under control," July said, brushing the curls off her.

"What am I supposed to do with it?"

"We could shave it."

"So that I can look like one of the old ladies?" Brook shook her head, laughing. "No way."

"I think it would look nice," July said. "Maybe we can just shave part of it."

Brook rolled her eyes so hard that her irises nearly disappeared into her skull. "You don't really think it would look nice. Leave me alone," she said, and pulled her hair into a ponytail. A few wild curls remained on Brook's neck, defying the hairband's will, but July decided not to point them out.

"Look," July said, nodding toward a small figure down the hall. "There goes Ellery."

Brook didn't look.

"I wonder where he's going," July said, ignoring Brook's melodramatic sigh. "He always looks so busy."

July had recently become hyperaware of her own body and the way people around her reacted to it. If she held her head at a certain angle or smiled just so, she could get whoever was staring at her to blush. It was an odd and unsettling power. She wasn't sure she liked being able to manipulate people so easily. It made her feel even more alone than she usually did.

Except, Ellery had no reaction to July. He was totally unmoved by her. Or at least, that's how it seemed. It was probably why she liked him so much, she knew. He was a challenge. One she was determined to win.

Ellery had been a pretty kid, and then a beautiful teenager, his body like a lean pile of sharp angles, and his face overtaken by huge, soft eyes. July—and others, she knew—couldn't resist his pull.

"Who cares?" Brook got up and closed the door to their pod, obscuring July's view.

July poked Brook in the ribs. "I care," she said. "Don't be jealous."

For as long as July could remember, she had been painfully aware of him. She didn't know him, not really, because she'd never had the guts to talk to him. They had been placed in different classes within the same year—though they were the same age, their dispositions and learning styles meant they were taught separately. But they'd each emerged at the top of their own section. The kids were discouraged from measuring and comparing one another, but everyone knew that Ellery was the smartest in his unit and July the smartest in hers. It would have been a rivalry, if that sort of thing had been tolerated;

instead, they were encouraged to express admiration and support. It made July's blood boil to have to praise him. Even now, when they were, allegedly, entering adulthood.

But then there was also the fact of his thick dark hair and smooth, olive skin, his low voice, and the way he sometimes grinned at her in passing as though he might be taunting her. Sometimes, though, July suspected it might be more innocent than that, like he was just trying to get her to smile back. She never did, though. She couldn't do it. She was too nervous.

Brook closed the book and tossed it to the side, startling July out of her daydream. "I can tell you're thinking about him," she said. And then, in a whine that July could tell was only half a joke, she added, "Pay attention to *me*."

"What do you have in mind?"

"Want to give each other tattoos?"

"What?" July exclaimed, laughing. "How? Why?"

Brook opened her tote bag and pulled out a small vial of black ink and a needle. "Before you freak out, I overheard some of the women talking about how to do this, and it seems really easy."

"Did you steal all this from the art room?" July asked.

"Borrowed," Brook said.

"Will it hurt?"

"Nah," Brook said.

July dug around in her bag and pulled out her water bottle. She poured some into her mouth, and then handed it to Brook. "Have some of this."

Brook took a sip, and grinned. The wine was warm and bitter.

July winked. "It's our last week of school, forever," she said. "I wanted us to celebrate."

"Speaking of which. Are you ready?" Brook said.

July nodded. She pointed to the squishy bit of flesh at the top of her hip. "Do it here, so no one will see."

"Good idea."

"What are you going to draw?"

"The moon," Brook said. "Will you do me after? So we can match." July nodded, and then held her breath as Brook began poking her with the needle.

"Ow," she said. "Fuck."

"Do you want me to stop?"

"No. Just hurry up."

Each prick of the needle felt alarmingly violent, and her hip grew white-hot with pain. She closed her eyes tightly and focused on the familiar smell of Brook's hair—soap and sweat.

"Are you done yet?"

"No, sorry. I just need to make it perfectly even." Making things *perfectly even* was a preoccupation of Brook's, and July knew it was pointless to try to argue with her about it.

"There," Brook said, after what felt like an eternity. "You can look now."

July examined the pristinely wrought crescent shape. Her skin was swollen and pink around it. "I love it," she declared. "Your turn."

As July began, she found it oddly satisfying to push the needle into Brook's skin; she was surprised by the quiet pop as the skin broke and the needle entered the pliable flesh below. "Are you sure this is okay?" she asked.

"It's too late to stop now," Brook said. "Can you make sure it's the same size and shape as the one I did?"

Little red beads of blood appeared where July poked the needle in, and she wiped them off with the corner of her tunic. Neither of them realized how quiet they were being, how caught up in the intensity of the moment, until their silence was punctured by the sounds of familiar laughter and shouts of their classmates coming from a few levels down. July could make out Ellery's distinct, booming laugh. "Do you wish we were with them?" Brook asked.

"Literally never," July said, a half-truth that was probably obvious to Brook.

"You could just, like, ask him to hang out with us."

"I truly could not. It's way too embarrassing to even think about."

"Fine." Brook shrugged. "He's probably studying anyway. He's such a nerd."

July raised an eyebrow. "You know, I bet if you ever actually studied, you wouldn't have been assigned a job in Refillables."

"Hey! It's not like you ever studied, either. How'd you get such a good work assignment?" July had been placed on the prestigious medical track, where she'd study under Olympia.

"We'll never know," July said. "Stop talking, you're making this harder."

Brook shifted, ignoring her. "I can't believe school is over. Do you remember when we liked going to class?"

"Barely."

"Same. But I feel like it was fun in the beginning."

"I remember we liked learning about the outside," July said. "I feel like it turned a corner when we also learned we could never leave here."

"Totally," Brook said. "It's like, who cares about something we'll never see?"

As July put the finishing touches on the crescent moon, their tablets dinged in unison.

"Oh!" Brook said. "Our new housing assignments. Finally!"

July dropped the bloody, inky needle on the ground and grabbed her tablet. She couldn't wait to find out where she was placed. Once they had their assignments, they'd have to move immediately, which was fine with July; she was dying to start this new chapter of her life.

July had grown up in a cavernous apartment with many babies and almost as many people looking after them. In the beginning, in her murkiest memories, she was raised by a group of women who were all her mothers, though she didn't call any of them "Mom." Her early childhood was mostly chaotic, sometimes ecstatic, other times stressful. But in the background of everything was the unsettling feeling that she was always being monitored.

As a child, whenever July had hurt herself playing, someone would swoop in and rescue her immediately, no matter how mild her injury. Administrators always made room for her to cut the lines for food and supplies, so she never had to wait for anything. When she was walking somewhere alone, it wasn't only that she felt like she was being trailed, but she'd also often catch sight of someone's pink tunic rounding a corner ahead of her, as though her path was staked out, as though she was surrounded at all times.

July never told anyone about this. She thought it might make her sound insane.

As she got older, she slept over at Brook's as often as she could, making a nest on the floor next to Brook's bed. Eventually Ava got July her own bed. She liked it better at their place, where it was usually quiet, though Ava was always around if they wanted something. July was used to having lots of adults around getting her whatever she needed, but it was nice to have just one person to ask for things. Ava treated July like she was one of her own.

But now, they were adults, or something approaching some approximation of adulthood, and they would all have their own apartments, which meant no more sleeping in the same room as Brook. July wasn't going to miss much about being young, but she was going to miss that.

"I actually have all my shit with me," July said, gesturing to her tote bag. "I can go right now."

"Okay. I'll find you after we move," Brook promised. "I'm just gonna go get the rest of my stuff first."

But July was not assigned to an apartment that Brook could have found.

July followed her tablet's instructions and headed first to a staircase she'd never encountered before. She went up one flight of stairs, and then another, and then another. She began to sweat. By the time she reached a large metal door with a keypad in the center of it, she felt like she'd climbed so high that the other side of the door might actually lead to the outside. Her tablet pinged again, instructing her to put in a nine-digit password. She had never seen a door with a password before; all the locked doors Inside used facial recognition technology. Then, as the door slowly swung open, she laughed, followed by an annoyed sigh: another set of stairs.

She was excited for her new place, wherever it was, but she also had a feeling she couldn't shake that she should have been able to choose it for herself. She thought about choices a lot, and how little they had here. Even though the choices made for her usually felt right.

When she reached the top, she found one more door, but it was already slightly ajar, as if welcoming her. She pushed it all the way open and stepped into the largest private space she'd ever seen. A huge bed sat directly underneath a row of square skylights, from which sunlight streamed through, dancing across the walls. And it was real sunlight, not computer-generated. She flung her tote bag of regulation items into a corner and laughed at how little her belongings were compared to the expanse of her new home. She stretched her arms out and spun around in the sparkling light, kicked off her shoes, and jumped on her bed. *This is all mine*, she thought.

She lay in the bed for a while before bouncing up to go to the bathroom. She had never had her own bathroom before. When she turned the lights on, the tiled floor grew warm beneath her feet. She washed her hands with the rose-scented soap and smiled at herself in the mirror over the sink, as if she were sharing a secret with herself, a secret about how lucky she was to have gone from never being alone in her life to having her own palatial space under the clouds.

By the time she was done drying her hands on the gossamer-soft towels, her smile had dimmed a bit. July was afraid to tell anyone about this. It wasn't just that she was embarrassed by her good fortune, although it was partly that, but mostly, she was worried about what it might mean for her future. And what it might indicate about her past. Maybe there *was* a reason July felt she was always watched, and given different, unspoken rules to live by. Maybe she wasn't so crazy after all. And maybe her new home meant she'd soon find out what the truth was.

When she met back up with Brook, who was excited to tell July everything about her new place, which was a one-bedroom with a window that looked into the hallway, July just shrugged and said, "It's fine" about her own. "Nothing special." She hated lying to Brook, but she didn't think she had a choice.

That night, July couldn't sleep. The wind was whipping against the skylights, sounding like it was alive. She tossed off her blankets and jumped up, running across her room to grab a chair to stack on top of her bed so she could get closer to the skylight and see what was up there.

July climbed up carefully, getting her face as close to the glass as possible. She could almost touch it with her fingertips. The moonlight caught the soft hairs on her arm and turned them silver.

As she stood there, arms outstretched and face craning upward, something took shape in the darkness above: a hand from the outside reached back toward her own. For a moment, July thought it was the reflection of her own arm. It mirrored hers perfectly.

But then it slammed down on the glass.

She screamed and fell off the chair, landing on the bed.

She looked up. The hand was gone. She thought she heard something—a body?—bouncing along the roof, but she couldn't be sure. She couldn't be sure of anything, not what she had heard and not even what she had seen.

She looked at the sky through the thick glass and began to feel very small and very alone. She flopped down on the bed and began to cry, a frustrated, angry sob. *Why am I even here?*

Then, everything faded into black.

When she woke up in the morning, she didn't remember having fallen asleep, but she did remember dreaming of a field of gardenias that she had sunken into, like a flowery ocean. She remembered feeling very afraid, but it seemed no more real to her than her dream, and as the day wore on she convinced herself she hadn't really been that upset at all.

She met Brook for lunch. "Come over tonight," July said, in between bites of salad. "I want to show you the space. It's so random that I even got it. I still can't believe it."

Hours later, Brook and July were already out of breath by the time they got to the password-protected door.

Brook said, "There's no way they gave you this place by accident."

When they got to July's actual apartment, Brook wasn't even talking anymore; her mouth was just hanging open in disbelief.

"Say something. Do you hate me?" July asked.

Brook had closed her mouth, at least, July noticed, but was still silent, just wandering around the apartment, running her fingers across the opulent furniture, her eyebrows raised in what July was pretty sure was suspicion, if not scorn. Then, Brook stopped moving. She turned to July and gave her a wicked grin, kicked off her shoes, and ran at full speed toward the bed, jumping up high at the last minute so she landed with a belly flop into the fluffy comforter and stack of pillows. Feathers floated around her.

She regained her ability to speak, and howled, "What the fuck, July?"

July felt defensive. "I don't know!" she said. "I didn't ask for it. I don't know what it means."

"Don't worry. *I* know what it means," Brook said, laughing. "It means even with my dumb job, we're still going to have a lot of fun together, because if this kind of apartment exists? Then so do all the other places we've heard about."

Brook had good reason to be excited, July knew. Top-floor apartments Inside had seemed almost mythical; it was hard to imagine that anyone actually got to live in them, let alone even visit them. But as Brook and July knew, many of the sky-high residences had been turned into private nightclubs, where Insiders danced and drank until the sun came up, where they got away with illicit things that the girls couldn't yet imagine.

July lay down on her back next to Brook on the bed and stared up at the deep skylights. "So, you think it's okay that I live here? You don't think it's, like, a conspiracy or something?"

Brook sat up, flung her leg over July, straddling her, and looked straight down into her friend's face with total seriousness. "Oh, I definitely think this is a conspiracy," she said, and then started laughing. "But I also think it is practically our job to enjoy it while we can."

July laughed, too, then got up, pushing Brook back into the pillows. "Okay, you jerk. Then, you know what we should do?"

"Uh-oh," Brook said. "What should we do?"

"We should try to find what else is up here." July tried to look serious but couldn't control her grin.

Brook rolled her eyes. "If we're going to get in, you need to know what you're talking about."

"Okay, but don't pretend that you know what you're talking about, either."

All they knew were the rumors they'd heard as kids about an original Sea Bar—or was it simply called C?—on the lowest level, and they'd thought it sounded cooler than anything they'd ever experienced. They'd missed its heyday, though, and felt a strange kind of nostalgia for a bygone era that they hadn't experienced. *If only we'd been in the first group of people*, July thought. That was when the fun had really happened.

"Let's go tonight," Brook said. "What are we waiting for?"

"Agreed." July grinned. "Let's go as soon as we can see the moon from this bed." She lay down next to her again and put her pinky over Brook's while they waited for the moon to rise.

It wasn't technically sneaking around—now that they were done with school and enjoying a few weeks of break before work began, they were largely left to their own devices. But they knew that the space they were trying to find was a secret, and they suspected that going there would be forbidden if the people who ran Inside found out. But that was part of the fun: the fact that it was a secret made it more exciting.

They did not, as it turned out, find anything that night. Or the nights that followed.

They spent the better part of a week lurking around Inside's top floors, pushing on doors. Soon, the excitement began to wear off. They were tired of staying up so late. Maybe, they thought, it really had all been a story. Or maybe Inside had found out about the secret partying and had ended it.

And, at any rate, they'd both have training for work soon. July knew that her nights of wandering around with Brook would soon be too much stress; they'd need to be wide awake, early, for their new roles. They decided to search for the bars in the sky up until their first day of work, and if that time went by and they didn't find anything, they'd give up.

If she was really being honest with herself, July didn't actually care about finding the rooms as much as she cared about not wasting what was left of her time with Brook. She knew that once she went to work in the medical center, she wouldn't see much of her friend anymore, and she felt a weird kind of pre-sadness, knowing the feeling was coming, trying to treasure every moment before it arrived.

She knew Brook felt the same, though they didn't really talk about it. They didn't need to. July could tell by the way that Brook was never more than an arm's length away that she was savoring their proximity, too. Every time their hands bumped each other's while they walked through the glass sidewalks, the feelings were confirmed. *You're going to miss me so much*, July thought.

July and Brook had spent nearly every day of their lives together. Working different jobs meant they'd no longer be a pair. July wasn't even sure if they'd ever spent that many hours—the length of the workday—apart.

But once she arrived to her post in the medical center, she forgot to be sad about missing Brook, because walking past her was Ellery. She nearly dropped her tablet. He didn't seem to notice.

"Good morning, Ellery," an administrator greeted him.

"Hi," he said. "I've been assigned here." The deep monotone of his voice made July shiver. She pretended to read the welcome message on her tablet.

"Come on in," the administrator said, unlocking a door that July hadn't realized was there. They disappeared inside a room. She got a glimpse of the back of his head, the black ringlets that hugged the nape of his neck.

This meant that there was just one wall and one door of separation between July's new desk and the department where Ellery was stationed, whatever it was. July thought to herself that maybe they would finally have a conversation.

It was hard to focus that first day, not just because of Ellery's distracting proximity, but because of the sheer volume of information being thrown at her. There was so much she was supposed to be learning, and she tried hard to listen to Olympia while she showed her various procedures and processes, but by the afternoon her eyes were starting to cross. It was too much to take in at once. She felt they'd overestimated her by giving her this job.

And then, suddenly, it was the end of the day, and Ellery was emerging from the room with the locked door. Their eyes met. Instead of looking away, he smiled and said, "See you tomorrow, July."

She was too blindsided to answer. All the blood in her body rushed to her cheeks. By the time she could open her mouth, he was out the door. But a "See you tomorrow" meant that he did, in fact, *see* her, and paid enough attention to know that he'd see her the next day, too.

She was tingly and pink as she floated down to the dining hall to meet Brook for dinner.

"What's wrong with you?" Brook said, eyeing her suspiciously.

July laughed. "You'll just yell at me."

"Do you deserve to be yelled at?"

"It's Ellery-related."

Brook groaned. "Tell me what he said."

"He said *See you tomorrow, July.*" She put her hands over her mouth to hide her grin.

"Oh my fucking god." Brook rolled her eyes and pushed July. *"That's your news? He said See you tomorrow?"*

"He said my name, too," she said, unwilling to allow Brook's jealousy to bring her mood down. "He's never said my name before."

"That can't be true." They picked up their trays and walked toward the vending machines. July's stomach was growling.

"Believe me," she said. "I remember everything he's ever said to me."

Brook filled her bowl with quinoa and beans. "Okay, actually, I believe that."

23

ELLERY SAT QUIETLY, ALONE IN A SMALL ROOM, FOLLOWING
instructions on his tablet. He read from a checklist, idly turning knobs
and pouring different amounts of a fragrant pink substance into the many
tubes that snaked around him. He could not have been more disinterested
in the task at hand but tried to maintain focus; he heard the voice of the
administrator in his head telling him this work was a science, not an art.
He needed to be exact in his measurements. Inside depended on it, or so
he was told.

The door to the room where he worked was always locked, and for the
time being, Ellery was the only resident who was allowed in. They didn't tell
him much about what exactly he was doing; better if he didn't know, they
said. It would make the work easier to not think about it. He was not important enough to be let in on the *why* of the work, just the execution of it.

But he knew more than they gave him credit for. One day he spilled a
couple drops of the pink substance onto his hand and, without thinking,
licked it clean. Within minutes, he felt a joyful rush, followed by a heavy sort
of calm, a feeling he not only recognized but strongly associated with the
floral smell that still lingered on his skin.

He figured they were having him funnel some sort of drug into the air
vents, and that it was being distributed to the residents' rooms in various
doses. The doses were determined by the instructions on his tablet, which
ran in a never-ending feed throughout the day.

He had no urge to tell anyone else, though. He knew it would be upset-
ting, and he was okay with shouldering the burden of this knowledge, at
least for now, until they hired someone else to work in the vent room with

him. But no one else had made the cut, so for the foreseeable future, he was alone, both in this room and with the truth.

He was also hungover. That was nothing new, at least not as of late. He had started stealing the small pink tinctures and taking them back to his room at night. Eventually he had discovered that if he mixed enough drops of the concentrated liquid into some water, he'd hallucinate. He gave some of it to his friends, without telling them where he got it. They didn't seem to care much anyway; they just wanted something to do. It was the most exciting development of their lives. They took to tripping almost nightly.

When the substance wore off, though, Ellery would feel the lowest of lows. He grew used to waking up devastated and exhausted, spending his days looking forward to the evening privacy that allowed him to return to the concoction that would not only lift his spirits but propel his consciousness into another universe.

He was in a particularly bad low this morning and was thankful that no one was around to see it. He rested his head against the wall, pressing the side of his face into the cool plaster and closing his eyes. He wanted quiet, but to his surprise, his ear was filled with muffled sounds from the adjoining room, which was in the medical center. Curious but mostly bored, he held his breath and pushed his ear harder into the wall. He could hear chairs squeaking on the floor and footsteps and voices greeting each other. After a few moments, the commotion quieted, and a single voice was audible, but obviously digital, as though it was coming through a computer speaker.

"Now that she's twenty-two, it's time to assess the totality of the data," the voice said. "If the subject's metrics are better, I think we know what to do next."

Ellery had no idea what this meant. He knew it probably had nothing to do with him. And why should it? It didn't matter. Nothing really mattered. Least of all him. Like everyone else he was simply a placeholder, a tally in a population count. And no one else seemed to grasp that—the meaninglessness of it all.

Ellery's depression had never been severe enough to keep the attention of the medical team. He did so well in school, and he was so well-liked. The doctors told him the malaise he reported was hormonal. He was too high functioning to be depressed, they told him. He suspected that they just didn't want to have to bother with him. He didn't blame them for this. He wouldn't want to have to bother with himself, either.

Later that night, alone in his apartment, Ellery flipped his tablet over. He hated its screen, which always told him what to do.

Then, without giving it much thought, he unscrewed a tincture and drank the mysterious pink concentrate straight up. He finished the whole thing in a few big gulps. He'd only ever had a few drops at a time. Within a few moments the floor began to tilt and the walls around him appeared to turn into vapor.

His skin felt numb. He pinched his arm, at first gently and then harder, harder, laughing with surprise at how little he felt. He raked a fingernail into his forearm. Still no feeling. It was like touching rubber.

There was a tingling sensation in his jaw as a wave of nausea hit him. He was throwing up on the floor before he even registered the vomit rising in his throat.

He wiped his mouth on his sleeve. He felt very dizzy and so, so tired. More tired than he'd ever felt in his life. The need to lie down was urgent. He could clean up the puke later.

In the moments before he lost consciousness, Ellery hallucinated his parent, Ira, standing before him, and he reached for them.

24

GETTING ASSIGNED A JOB IN REFILLABLES WAS BROOK'S
worst nightmare, but she wasn't about to admit it.

She knew it was her own fault, anyway. She'd stopped trying in school
years ago, once she realized that there was no point to working hard. Besides, Brook had other things to focus on; like counting the tiles on the floor
to make sure that the number was the same every day, or the number of
steps it took to get home. She kept track of her place in the world by mapping out the numbers of little repeating patterns around her.

Brook loved being twenty-two—she'd looked forward to it since she
was eleven. It was the most soothing number she could think of; those two
double curves so neatly in line with each other. She'd imagined that being
twenty-two would feel as comfortable as the number looked; so sensible and
predictable. You could divide it up so many ways. She wasn't as excited for
thirty-three, which, while more visually satisfying, had less routes to get to it.

Sometimes Brook was interrupted in her counting. To her teachers, it
looked like daydreaming. But then they'd move on and she'd resume. *Ten
plus ten is twenty, one plus one is two, two plus twenty is twenty-two. Two
times eleven is also twenty-two. Two plus two equals four; four times six is
twenty-four; minus two is twenty-two.* When left to her own devices, it was
nearly impossible for Brook to get through her homework. There were too
many patterns to sniff out.

She didn't really worry about slacking off so much. It's not like they were
ever punished for anything. She could pretty much do as she pleased, and at
the end of the day still be told how great she was. It all felt like an elaborate
joke. Only no one seemed to be laughing.

But now, she knew, there were consequences. She'd been evaluated based on her behavior. She had no one to blame but herself.

"How's work been?" Ava asked on one of the nights that she met Brook and July for dinner. The warm din of conversation hummed through the dining hall as the residents picked up their meals from the vending machines and brought them back to the tables. Brook felt relieved to still get to see her mom regularly, though she was embarrassed to admit it. Even though they'd moved out, she wasn't ready to be completely without her.

"It's fine, Mom," she said, mashing up a sweet potato with her fork so that it flattened into an even orange mush across her plate, touching both sides equally, smoothing out any anomalous chunks. "I don't really care." Brook felt both annoyed at the question, and glad that her mother noticed she was upset. She liked the attention, the concern. But that didn't mean she was willing to be truthful. She had too much pride to admit how disappointing it was.

The truth was that her job was anything but fine. It was terrible. All day, every day she had to push around a huge cart stocked with Refillables, sneaking into people's apartments and refilling their empties before they returned.

She'd heard from one of the other Refillable workers that, outside, homes had technology that had allowed them to refill automatically. Flying machines called drones delivered the supplies. What they did Inside was a cheap imitation of that sort of magic. It felt insulting to Brook that it had the same name. And stupid. There was no magic to the way Refillables worked Inside. It was just labor. Her labor.

"You can tell me if you're upset about it," Ava said.

"I'm not," Brook said. "It sucks, but it's fine."

Ava didn't look convinced. "Okay."

"And besides, I can always change jobs, right? I'm not doomed forever."

Ava's brows knitted together. "I am actually not sure," she said, and Brook's stomach dropped.

"Are you mad at me? Do you wish I was put in medical with July?"

"Of course not," Ava said. "I just want you to be happy."

"I'm happy," Brook insisted. "It's whatever."

Before her mom could say anything else, July piped up to ask if Ava had done something new with her hair, and Brook was flooded with gratitude that at least the topic had been dropped.

But, Brook conceded, July didn't fully understand, either. Everything always seemed to work out for her. Brook couldn't even be mad that July had been given such a good job assignment based on nothing. It felt almost inevitable. The only thing that annoyed Brook was that July refused not only to acknowledge that she was everyone's favorite but also to enjoy it. If Brook were that lucky, she knew, she'd make the most of it.

But July was Brook's favorite, too, and as Brook spun around to face her, she couldn't help but notice that the golden light from the solar bulbs was making July's hair appear to glow.

"What's new with you?" Brook said. And then she added, in a voice that held equal parts admiration and annoyance, "Why do you look so pretty right now?"

July blinked her heavy-lidded eyes and tilted her head to the side. "Which question do you want me to answer first?" she teased.

"You know which one, asshole." Brook laughed.

"I learned how to take blood today," July said.

"You weren't squeamish, were you?"

"Please!" July cried. "You're the one who couldn't hold still when . . ." Brook kicked her under the table. "Ow! Fuck."

Ava looked up from her pile of vegetables. "What are we talking about?"

"Nothing," Brook groaned.

After dinner, when they all parted ways, Brook went back to her apartment alone and got into bed. It was so strange living by herself. She wondered if she'd ever get used to it.

On the other side of her bedroom, Brook's secret collection was growing larger. When she lived with her mom, she'd had to hide it under her bed. But now, she could put the little things she stole from around Inside on display; other peoples' cups that they'd forgotten about, the errant baby shoe, small bars of soap and shriveled-up food. She arranged these objects by color and within color, by theme. Every now and then she searched for a missing piece to complete a section, and often wouldn't sleep until she found it. From the bed, she gazed at her collections with a satisfied smile. It was nice to control this one little corner of the world.

Brook pulled out her tablet and opened the map, zooming in and out of areas that she knew by heart. Once, when they were younger, she and a group of kids had taken turns blindfolding one another and walking from one end of Inside to the other. She'd been the only one who could do it. She'd memorized the steps, of course. She wondered if that was part of the reason she'd been put in Refillables. Her one skill—mastering layouts. She put her face into her pillow and groaned as loudly as she could. The future seemed to stretch out before her, endless and empty. As blank as the walls of her new room.

Brook yearned to understand how they'd all gotten here, and why this world was how it was. But in the place of a proper explanation, there were only more questions, and in the empty space where answers should have been, she wrote her own; found patterns where there weren't any; invented rituals as though she had some sort of power over what happened to her.

The rhythm of her own counting began to lull her to sleep. The tablet slipped out of her hands and landed with a dull thud on the floor as she nodded off.

Brook was on her morning rounds a few days later, pushing her huge cart of supplies around when she opened an apartment door to refill the toothpaste, and realized the resident was still home. A dark pile of short hair was visible from underneath a mountain of blankets.

Brook was only supposed to go into people's rooms when they were out; part of the gig of Refillables was maintaining some sort of mystery, as though the products simply refilled themselves.

"I'm so sorry for barging in," she said. "I can come back later." But the figure didn't move. It was odd that they were home at this time, when everyone else was at work.

"Hello? Are you okay?" Brook walked closer to the bed, the hairs on her arms standing straight up. She stepped on something that crunched beneath her foot, and she bent to pick it up. It was a shattered vial. She plucked a piece of glass from the bottom of her shoe.

It didn't feel right in this room. The air felt heavy and smelled so sour it made her eyes water. She held her breath as she reached the bed and yanked the blankets down.

It was Ellery. He still didn't move.

Then she noticed the vomit. Chunky brown puddles on the concrete floor, flat brown stains on the bed's pink linens. Everywhere her eyes landed. She put her hands on his shoulders and shook him, at first gently and then harder. "Wake up," she whispered. "Fuck, please wake up."

He was breathing, but barely.

Hands shaking, she hit the emergency call button on her tablet.

She forced herself to look at Ellery: His face was gray. His mouth hung open. She sank to her knees in front of him and watched his face for movement while she waited for help to come. The object of July's affection looked like nothing more than a fragile cluster of bones.

She glanced around for something to count, but her eyes kept filling with tears, and the fact that she couldn't see clearly enough to keep a proper tally of the objects around her made her heart start to pound.

Within a few minutes she heard footsteps and shouting, and then about a dozen people appeared, some she recognized, and some she didn't. Brook was pulled to her feet and passed between hands until she was out in the hallway, a warm arm around her shoulder guiding her away. She looked behind her one last time and saw a swarm of mauve linen tunics and shaved heads surround the boy in his bed, and then she couldn't see him anymore through the thick circle of administrators. She felt light-headed with shock.

Brook was taken down into the medical center, where Olympia was waiting.

"Are you okay?" Olympia asked, guiding Brook into the privacy of her office.

"I'm fine," she said. But the truth was she couldn't stop thinking about Ellery's pale face, his eyes closed, mouth open. His arm hanging off the bed, like he was reaching for something. "What was wrong with him?"

The doctor swallowed and paused for a long time. Brook shifted impatiently. "Food poisoning," she said.

Brook raised an eyebrow. It sounded like a lie. "What did he eat? Did anyone else get sick?" she challenged.

"I'm sorry," Olympia said. "This really isn't appropriate for you to hear about. You should take the rest of the day off."

"I won't argue with that," Brook said quickly, trying to get the older woman to crack a smile, but it didn't work. "Is July here? Maybe I could go talk to her."

"July has too much work to do," she replied. "Maybe you could go find your mom instead."

"I'm an adult now," Brook said. "I don't need to run to my mommy every time something bad happens."

But, as it turned out, that was exactly what she needed, and exactly what she did.

THE COMPUTERS INSIDE WERE LIMITED. EACH PERSON WAS given a tablet, and those often were in need of repairs. Children were given tablets when they were old enough to start playing with toys, so they were used to the touch screens and the maps, and the occasional announcements. But most of the technology was reserved for the administrators of Inside, to help keep things running smoothly.

The people who lived Inside did not know about the room filled with computer screens, where their behaviors were recorded and analyzed. They did not know that each tablet had a camera on it, always recording them. They did not know that there was an experiment unfolding in real time, that the value of their lives was measured by how well the experiment was going.

The residents did not know, also, that how often they broke their own tablets by accident meant that the surveillance—though thorough in design—was spotty in practice. The Inside team was having a much harder time keeping track of everyone than they'd anticipated.

Plus, the transfer of power was about to get complicated. The original team would soon need to pass along the torch to the next generation, and they were selecting young people from the first graduating class to mentor.

But some of those young people weren't able to stomach what they'd need to do in order to keep everything running smoothly. The boy, in particular, was not built for the work, though no one realized just how poorly equipped he was until the accident. Someone with a greater maturity level would not have been tempted in such a grave way. It derailed things considerably, but not entirely.

I didn't learn of his death until later, when everything began to unravel.

At this point, from my position on the space shuttle, I only had access to the most superficial information about Inside; most of my research was still focused on Jacqueline and her impact on the culture of a pre-Inside United States. I was deep into the archives uncovering information about how she'd pivoted the company away from the oil industry. But still, I should have seen it. Everything Jacqueline did on the outside had an echo Inside.

Much like how Jacqueline had taken the reins from her father, Inside's administrators knew that a generational shift of power would be the ultimate defining moment for Inside. If they did it successfully, it was likely that their new world could continue on exactly as planned.

If they couldn't—if for whatever reason the daughters of Inside didn't want to carry out the vision of its creators—well, there were other ways they could be controlled.

PART SEVEN

FALLING THROUGH THE CRACKS

2078

25

AVA WAS IN THE LIBRARY STUDYING NEW INFORMATION
about how best to cultivate root vegetables when she felt eyes upon her. She
looked up from her tablet. Before her stood Brook, pale and trembling.

Ava flew out of her chair, reaching for her daughter. "What happened?"

Brook began to sob, burying her head into Ava's shoulder.

"I was doing my rounds," she said, sniffling. "And I found him in his
room, and he wouldn't wake up."

"Who?"

"Ellery," Brook said, crying harder. "That guy that July is obsessed with."

"Okay," Ava said, holding her tightly, immediately thinking of Ira, and
how impossible it would be to recover from this loss. "Okay."

Ava took Brook back to her apartment, the apartment she'd raised the
girls in, and put her in her old bed.

"Was he dead?" Ava asked.

"I don't know. How would I even be able to tell?"

The question startled Ava. "You just know," she said. "They don't breathe.
They don't move. They feel cold."

Ava sat on the edge of the bed and stroked Brook's hair until she eventually fell asleep, an endearing puddle of drool forming on the pillow. For
all of Brook's resistance to being coddled, she seemed to need Ava so much.
It was almost as though Brook's bad attitude was a test; as though she was
saying, *Do you still love me if I treat you like this?* Brook was always looking
for the limits of Ava's love. But Ava's love had no limits. Brook must have
known that, on some level.

And then Ava sat there some more, staring at her daughter's face, which looked so much like her own. How had Inside allowed this to happen? Weren't they supposed to be safe and well-taken care of here? The thought of anything happening to Brook made Ava want to tie her daughter up and hold her hostage for the rest of her life, though this idea made her remember the time, so long ago, that Olympia had suggested Brook's anxiety was perhaps related to how little risk her life held. But that was beside the point in the moment, because nothing bad would happen to Brook and that was the end of that. Brook wouldn't die. Brook wouldn't ever be allowed to come close to dying.

She knew that Brook's life would be forever changed by what she'd seen in that boy's room. Her girls lived in a world that was centered around a brighter future. Hope, not despair, was their foundation. She was glad that they hadn't experienced what she had, that they didn't think about death as a monster that loomed behind every moment. But as such there were things about Ava that her children would never understand, and vice versa.

Ava couldn't empathize with this being Brook's only reference point for tragedy. Ava's traumas were so great, she still couldn't quite comprehend them herself.

26

"**I NEED YOU TO TELL ME WHAT HAPPENED TO HIM**," JULY said to Olympia, whose furrowed brow was the only indication that she was stressed out. The rest of her face was annoyingly neutral. It was a few days after Brook had found Ellery unconscious in his room, and the not-knowing was driving July insane. It was all she thought about.

Sitting across from July at her desk, Olympia sighed. "I do think you have a right to know," she said, "but it needs to stay between us."

July nodded, holding her breath.

"He died," she said. "I'm so sorry. We didn't get to him in time."

July brought her hands to her face, as though she could keep the sadness in. She got up and fled the room before Olympia could say anything else.

In the days that followed, July's grief traveled from her head to her heart before settling in her stomach, twisting her insides painfully. She found herself forgetting to eat. She tried drinking more water, and she tried going to bed earlier, but the gnawing feeling only worsened. Dark circles appeared under her eyes.

She didn't want to have to talk about it, so she lied, endlessly, like she always did. At noon, when her tablet pinged to say, How are you feeling right now? she always selected Good.

The only thing that mattered was that Ellery was dead. July would never figure out if her feelings had been jealousy or attraction or some intoxicating combination of both.

July didn't tell anyone about this storm of feelings happening in her brain and in her body, not just because she'd been sworn to secrecy, but because July never really liked to tell anyone anything real. It didn't make her feel better to share the secret parts of herself with other people. Nothing anyone ever said to her was smarter or more helpful than what she could say to herself. She learned how to mask her fury with quiet, realizing that people were eager to project whatever was most convenient in the moment on a placid-faced child. They didn't guess that inside, she was raging. Even Brook didn't really know her.

Long before Ellery died, July figured that she had a lot to be angry about, and she didn't understand why more people didn't seem to feel similarly. She knew the entire basis of their world was bullshit. For a culture that taught consent so intensely, it seemed ridiculous to July that the first generation hadn't even consented to being here, not under these terms. Because they had learned that you can't fully consent to something if you don't have a full picture of what you're saying yes to.

The more she learned about what the outside world had been like, the angrier she became. It would have been so easy for people to save the planet, to stop the wars, and to curb the influx of disease. Instead they had all been selfish and ignorant. They'd done nothing until it was too late. July and her peers had inherited the damage previous generations had done. And now as a result, the people who remained alive were stuck inside, where they would all die before seeing the earth heal itself. And no one was talking about how miserable that was.

27

"IT WAS HEARTBREAKING," OLYMPIA SAID. "HE WAS SO YOUNG."

Jacqueline adjusted the angle of her screen, tilting it so that it would show a more flattering view of her neck. Shelby had recently helped her tinker with the lighting around her computer so that the lines on her face seemed softer than they were. "It seems to me that he brought this on himself," she said.

The connection glitched, freezing on Olympia's face. She looked horrified, which seemed a little bit dramatic. Jacqueline refreshed the page. While she waited for the connection to come back, she glanced out her window. It was always nighttime in space. Someone should have warned her how sad that would feel. Worse than any seasonal depression. Olympia's face reappeared.

"Lost you for a moment," Jacqueline said. "Please continue."

"This is a disaster," Olympia said.

"It's bad," Jacqueline admitted. "But it's nothing we can't handle."

"Really? It already feels like we can't handle it."

"It was one person," Jacqueline said. "Surely it's not the end of the world."

"We should have caught it sooner. This was clearly not the first time he tried something like this. It makes me wonder what other self-destructive behavioral patterns we're missing. My team tells me he might have been giving the substance to his peers. We need to look into all of them."

"Maybe," Jacqueline said. Her staff should have known better, but Jacqueline had compassion for them. There were more important things for her employees to be thinking about.

Olympia said, "You know I've been concerned about Gen A overall. This is a worst-case scenario."

Jacqueline arched an eyebrow. Olympia had made this point several times over the past fifteen or so years. Now, though, with a death on the books, Olympia had evidence to support her claims, which meant Jacqueline needed to steel herself for an argument.

"Well, let's hear it. Tell me what you want to say." Jacqueline sat up straighter to brace herself for impact.

"In prioritizing July, we've let others fall through the cracks."

"I really resent the implications of that," Jacqueline said. "It's not July's fault that this boy decided to end his life."

"I'm not saying it's July's fault. I'm saying it's ours. The team has been caring for her at the expense of everyone else."

Jacqueline dismissed this quickly. "Anyway," she said, trying to deflect with a quick pivot, "you do bring up a good point about Gen A's lack of progress. We might disagree on the reason they are falling behind, but the fact is that they *are*. We always knew this could happen, that there was a chance July's progress versus everyone else's would prove that boys aren't necessary. At this point I think it's clear my vision would be better served by a permanently all-female population."

Olympia made a sound that was part cough, part gasp. "Excuse me?"

"Yes?"

"No," Olympia said. "We can't do that. It's not ethical. There's no way the residents would agree to this."

"Why do we have to tell them about it?"

"You don't want to give them a choice?"

"That's the beauty of the IVF technique, isn't it? We could simply fertilize only female zygotes and make it seem like, oh, I don't know, a fun coincidence that everyone has daughters. We have enough sperm samples saved for a million years. We would quickly evolve past the need for a male species."

Olympia shook her head. "First of all, that's not what *evolve* means. Second, not everyone will need us to help them get pregnant. What's your plan for people who want to do it the old-fashioned way? Plenty of Gen A is interested in heterosexuality. Even July seems to be mostly straight, as far as we can tell."

"Surely this is a question your medical team can answer," she said. "Can't you just, I don't know, go in and *alter* the organic pregnancies that don't align with the goal? Swap things out, so to speak."

"If you're saying what I think you're saying, I really, really don't think we should do that," Olympia replied. "It's wildly unethical on every level."

"It's extreme, yes, but we always agreed that if introducing men into the population didn't work, we'd take extreme measures."

"But that's the thing. We have no way of knowing whether or not it actually worked," Olympia said, her voice rising. "The test results have been sabotaged. There's no real control group. This is really starting to feel like a self-fulfilling prophecy. Who are we to say that the reasons July is doing better aren't due to the fact that this world is set up for people like her?"

"This is hard to hear, especially from you," Jacqueline said. "The time to voice these opinions was decades ago."

"Well, honestly, this is the first time it's come up in a real way," Olympia said. "I think I was hoping you had changed your mind about forcing an all-female future. Not just an all-female future—an all-*cis*-female one."

"I think you know me better than that," Jacqueline replied.

"Yes. I know you very well. Enough to know that you underestimate your own bias," Olympia said. "It's like you have this plan, and you only see the data in a way that supports what you want to do."

"Yikes. Are you serious?" Jacqueline said. "Did you really just say that to me?"

"I'm sorry," Olympia said, but it was clear she wasn't.

Jacqueline was losing her patience. "Are you making an argument for men's rights? That's a little bit shocking."

"Never!" Olympia said, firmly. "But you know that this is a regressive way to understand gender, right?" Jacqueline stiffened. "We need more diversity than people who are assigned female at birth. AMAB people belong here. We designed this whole system so that they *could* be born, and then raised under new circumstances, whether they are cis, or trans, or nonbinary, or otherwise have identities outside of the heteropatriarchy governing everywhere else on Earth. Trans women belong here. They're an important part of the community." She took a breath. "You would be eliminating *all of them*. And what about AFAB people who aren't women? Would they actually be welcome here? Would you also force them to give birth to girls? I never wanted to be part of something that was all cisgender women. It wouldn't work. It's not right. It's not the point of all this." She threw her hands up in the air. "And where would you draw the line around what a woman can and can't be? What about gender-nonconforming women—what about women like me?"

"Not to use an antiquated word here, but are you calling me a TERF?" Jacqueline could hardly believe what she was hearing. "I'm not *invalidating* trans identities."

"No," Olympia said, her voice somber and disappointed. "You're just saying they don't belong here. That's not any better."

Jacqueline was seething. "You know I support trans people. Shelby has been my assistant for decades now."

Olympia sighed. "Having one trans woman working for you does not negate what you're trying to do here. If anything, it proves my point. She's always been a token to you, hasn't she?"

Jacqueline was quiet. She didn't have a retort. The truth was, she hadn't really stopped to think this point through, and she hadn't realized it until this conversation. She'd need to recalibrate a bit, which was a very unfamiliar process.

Olympia said, "All I'm saying is we need to be thinking about everyone. And . . . specifically, people who aren't July."

"Have I not thought of them?" she cried, defensively.

"I'm not accusing you of anything," Olympia said, even though it was clear to Jacqueline that she was. "I just think maybe it's time to rethink a few things. I'd love to be able to have a real, honest discussion with you about these issues."

Jacqueline did some deep breathing to steady herself.

"And," Olympia said, with an air of finality, "it's my medical center. I decide what we do to people's bodies. And we're not doing this. This is the hill I'll die on."

"Okay," Jacqueline said, trying hard not to sound as defeated as she felt. Olympia made a good point; there was nothing Jacqueline could do, medically, without Olympia's buy-in. "I don't like it, but I hear you."

"You do?"

"Yes. You can stop yelling at me."

"I wasn't aware that I was yelling at you, but I'm sorry," Olympia said. "So what do we do now?"

"Here's what I'm thinking," Jacqueline said, pausing for a bit longer than necessary for dramatic effect. "We've had this experiment in the works since the 2050s. You can't expect me to throw it all away, to give up on my goals, simply because you say so. You have to give me something in return. If you don't want to move forward with this program as I imagined, surely I can at least continue my dream on a personal level."

"What does that mean?"

"It means I have plenty of my own frozen female zygotes, and we can find new surrogates."

"Jesus," Olympia exclaimed. "Will you ask their permission this time?"

"I don't see why," she replied. "The first mother we used never knew the difference. Don't you think it would just make things unnecessarily complicated?"

"No," Olympia said. "I don't think that at all." She was shaking her head vigorously. "You don't have an ongoing right to other people's bodies. It was bad enough we did it once."

"I don't know," Jacqueline said, feeling pleased for the first time since the conversation began. "I actually think it might be a good compromise."

"You'd barely be alive to see your children reach adulthood," Olympia tried.

"You don't know that." Jacqueline smiled. "I'm feeling rather eternal these days."

Olympia groaned. "That was not what I was trying to accomplish in this conversation."

"So it's decided," Jacqueline said. She was thrilled with this outcome.

"I suppose you'd be happy if we could go right to cloning all the original women," Olympia said. "Or, rather, if we just clone you. An Inside full of little Jacquelines. How does that sound?"

"I don't have time for sarcasm," Jacqueline said. "Let's start looking into new surrogates immediately. How many embryos should we begin with? Four or five, perhaps?" She grinned, enjoying watching Olympia squirm. "Twenty, maybe? Thirty?"

"I can't talk to you when you're like this," Olympia said. "I can't tell if you're serious or just trying to torture me. And we still have to talk about Ellery."

"I suppose we do," Jacqueline said, though the truth was she'd been hoping to get out of it.

Olympia said, "His death doesn't bode well for how we've been using drugs for resident control. I don't want anyone else to get hurt."

"Don't exaggerate," Jacqueline said. "It's harmless if used correctly. The mixture for the air is mostly rose water and chamomile."

"And Xanax!" Olympia said, laughing a little bit at the way Jacqueline was downplaying the situation, which struck Jacqueline as very rude. "And a little bit of MDMA. And sometimes psilocybin. You know this. It works on the gen pop because it's microdoses. Ellery died of an *over*dose. And we don't really know how much of it he gave away, or to whom. I'm concerned about the kids becoming little drug traffickers."

"Is there a reason the team isn't able to track this?" Jacqueline asked.

"My feeling is that the surveillance isn't as reliable as it was in the beginning. The original residents knew how to take care of a tablet. But now, the young people are constantly breaking them, or losing them, or flipping them upside-down just when we need to see what's going on. It gives us a very fractured picture of what they're up to."

"The residents just need more structure," Jacqueline declared with confidence, brushing Olympia off. "We can give that to them." Jacqueline heard the sound of the ship's support staff working nearby, clattering and shouting. It was irritating, but also somewhat inspirational. *If these morons can get it together,* she thought, *the residents of Inside can as well.*

"No one can know why," Jacqueline added. "If word were to get out, I don't know if the population would ever recover."

"I'm concerned about his parent, Ira," Olympia said.

"Let me handle that," Jacqueline said.

"Fine. And other than Ira, the only resident who knows is July," Olympia said. "I fully expect her to tell Brook any day now, and for Brook to tell her mother. But those three are a pretty closed loop. I believe they mostly just talk to each other."

"Good," Jacqueline said. "Let's make sure it stays that way."

"I know July didn't have a personal relationship with him, but she seems truly shaken by what I told her. I've watched her cry herself to sleep," Olympia said.

"I saw that, too," Jacqueline said. "I do think Brook is a comfort to her."

"No surprise there," Olympia said.

The girls, of course, had no idea they were being watched, just like they didn't know why their bond was so unbreakable. It was interesting to observe, which was easy since the girls didn't know why anyone would care what they were up to. Jacqueline was counting on it. And anyway, maybe with future daughters, instead of bonding with a peer, they could simply bond with *her*.

A few days later, after giving it some thought, Jacqueline called a team meeting with all the Inside administrators.

"We'll need to implement some structure," she said, trying to read the dozens of pixelated faces on her screen. Alas, it was impossible to interpret the mood from so far away. "There's been a tragedy, and I'd like to prevent it from happening again."

She saw Olympia's face in a tiny box on her screen. Jacqueline would never admit to Olympia directly that she had been right about a few things, and this was as close to an apology as she'd give her, as close to an admission that maybe some things could stand to change. And though Olympia had said it out of anger, and likely didn't mean it, she'd had a point: Inside would function better if it contained fifty thousand clones of Jacqueline. Not that Jacqueline would ever utter that thought to a soul. Even she knew how it sounded.

Instead, she tried her best to be reasonable. "Let's begin twice-weekly individual therapy, and group therapy for the ones who don't seem to be coping well." She tapped her fingers on her desk. "Does anyone else have any other ideas?"

Someone from the tablet team came off mute. "We can redesign the digital check-ins," she said. "We could track their feelings more thoroughly throughout the day. Change up the questions, make them more in-depth than the usual *How are you feeling right now?*"

"Good," Jacqueline said. "Do it. Anyone else?"

There was silence. "Fine," Jacqueline said. "So we'll start with that. And in the meantime, please hold off on replacing him. I don't want any of the residents having access to the ventilation system until we get a handle on how they're all feeling."

She paused for a few moments and then, watching Olympia's face on her screen, she said, "And I think we can relax the round-the-clock surveillance on July. Please continue to keep an eye on her, but don't do it at the expense of everyone else. Let's focus on the total well-being for now. I'll watch her myself."

The women on the screen nodded and took notes. "And let's just re-member," she said before signing off, "that being here for over twenty years with just one death is nothing short of miraculous. We have nothing to be ashamed about. I'm still very proud of all of you."

She hung up and poured a glass of wine. She spun it around a few times, watching the red legs stick to the sides of the glass, before taking a much-needed sip. She hated compromise.

28

"HE'S DEAD," JULY SAID TO BROOK. "THEY TOLD ME NOT TO tell anyone, but he is."

She'd been trying hard to pretend everything was fine, but she was at her breaking point. They were wandering the quiet tunnels of Inside in the hours after most people had gone to sleep.

"What the fuck?" Brook said, grabbing July's hand. "I can't believe you didn't tell me sooner."

"She made me swear." July started to cry.

"We'll find out what happened to him," Brook said. "I promise."

When she returned to her apartment that night, July's room smelled extra floral, and she accidentally fell asleep before properly getting ready for bed, a deep, dreamless slumber that made her feel heavy and slow when she finally awoke, late and confused. The next day flew by in a haze. She found she couldn't focus on a task without drifting off.

"Are you okay?" Olympia asked her.

"I'm just tired," July murmured, and found herself wandering out of the medical center early to go back to sleep. It was a full twelve hours before she opened her eyes, and she felt no more rested than when her head hit the pillow. Her eyelids felt swollen and heavy. But it wasn't unpleasant. It was like being stuck in the moment between waking and sleep; a delirious sort of out-of-body feeling.

She felt like she was floating as she made her way to the breakfast hall and found Brook staring into her plate of food. Brook barely acknowledged July's presence, and the two girls sat next to each other quietly, not eating, pushing their food around their plates.

"I think you two need to start getting more sleep," Ava said. July hadn't even realized she was there.

Time started to pass strangely. After a few weeks of days that blurred together like dreams, something odd happened: July couldn't remember what it was like to feel sad about Ellery.

He was simply someone from her past, and now he wasn't here. Death didn't have to be sad, she thought, as the brain fog swirled. It was part of life. Everybody dies. There was no escaping it, and that wasn't a bad thing. It just simply *was*.

"Hey," Brook said one day over breakfast, "do you still want to try to find out what happened to Ellery?"

July found it was hard to focus on the words as they came out of Brook's mouth. "Nah," she said. "Let's just let it go."

And then one day she woke up and couldn't remember his name, that boy who had been here and now was gone. She wasn't sure why it mattered, anyway. There was so much else to think about. When she tried to picture what he looked like, she found she couldn't even recall the details of his face.

The next time her tablet asked her how she was feeling, she selected "Good," but it wasn't a lie. She went to bed early and woke up early, too, feeling more refreshed than she had in a long time. The fuzziness was fading. She was okay. Everything would be fine.

29

THIS SITUATION WAS CERTAINLY A SETBACK, JACQUELINE thought, while she adjusted the levels of Xanax that were being pumped into July's room.

It was taking more drugs than she anticipated to get July to let go of this whole Ellery thing. Almost as many as were being distributed to his parent, who for now remained in their room, sleeping through it.

She wasn't sure what the long-term effects of such large dosages would be. But there was nothing she could do about it, because to raise the alarm would be to admit that she had doubts about the way they were drugging people, and she had committed so thoroughly to arguing against that point.

Addiction ran in the family. Jacqueline was well-aware of this even as she emptied another wine bottle and tossed it into the hallway, trusting that Shelby would see the empty bottle and know to ring for more. *But, she wondered, is it really so bad to rely on substances if you function so highly?* Jacqueline had created an entire world with a glass of cabernet swirling in her hand. Sometimes you just needed something to take the edge off.

Brook was easy, though. It only took a little extra push to get her to stop bringing Ellery up to July. Whether that was because she was following July's lead or because she didn't really care was beyond Jacqueline. She only knew what the girls said, not what they thought.

In time, she landed on the right ratio of medications to take the edge off for July. It took a few days, but she could see the weight being lifted from her shoulders. Eventually, it was like the boy had never been there at all. She dialed back the levels, and July woke up looking refreshed and new. *You're welcome*, she mouthed at the screen.

It would take longer to get the boy's parent to forget about him, but that was okay. She could be patient.

Otherwise, as far as Jacqueline could tell, life went on as it always had.

PART EIGHT

DEFIANCE

2078

30

OLYMPIA WAS OVERWHELMED WITH ANXIETY ABOUT WHAT
Jacqueline's vision for the future meant, which magnified how lonely she
felt.

It wasn't a normal sort of lonely; not that alone-in-a-crowd feeling she
used to have in New York City, that total anonymity, the knowledge that if
she disappeared it would take weeks for anyone to realize. No, this wasn't
that. If that feeling was a river, this one was an ocean. Endless depths. She
couldn't see the bottom of it.

For the years that Olympia believed in Jacqueline's vision, Jacqueline
had been her everything. But now, Olympia was alone in the knowledge of
what Jacqueline was planning, and it made her realize how alone she was in
the physical reality of her days. There was no one to anchor her.

She still loved her work—and her patients. But she was also jealous of
them. Their lives were so full, and hers was so one-dimensional. She looked
on with sadness while they formed friendships and love affairs and families.
When she was younger, planning for Inside's future, it hadn't occurred to her
that she might want those things, too. She'd been so captivated by the work
that she hadn't been able to imagine growing disillusioned with it. Now she
was trapped by the choices that a younger, simpler version of herself had made.

Or was she totally trapped? she wondered. She watched her colleagues
suspiciously, wondering how they were coping with their own solitude.
Maybe they had relationships with one another. Or with the residents.

She thought of Ava often. Though she'd been careful to maintain the
boundaries of their doctor-patient relationship, she couldn't help it: she
longed for her.

Olympia had never intended to get brainwashed by Jacqueline. She'd accepted this job with the intention to change things; to take Jacqueline's idea and mold it so that it was more ethical. But somewhere along the way she'd gotten so caught up in the work that she forgot her own motives. She'd come here to make changes, but the truth was she hadn't actually changed anything at all. She'd lost sight of her goals. She'd lost herself, too. And now that she had a full picture of what Jacqueline was capable of—and how deep her delusions ran—she felt unmoored.

So, one evening when the moon was full, Olympia decided to see what would happen if she made an appearance at one of the places where the residents gathered in the night. She was nervous about it but was craving socializing so badly that the consequences seemed unimportant.

She walked toward the so-called secret bar at the top level of Inside, the one with solar string lights around the windows and a small, single bathroom that indicated this space was originally meant for a resident. At some point, when the population grew, it would need to return to its original purpose and become someone's home. And at some point after that, they might not be able to have one resident per room, though she'd probably be dead by then.

Olympia had seen this space on the screens thousands of times, and she always marveled at how it would be overflowing with women who sized each other up in the doorway, their hot breath in one another's faces as they removed their mauve tunics. Their rituals were so predictable, so lovely. So animalistic. It was an odd thing to be on the outside of this community that she knew so much about.

But it wasn't an unfamiliar feeling, this ostracization, this misanthropy. Outside, when she was younger, Olympia had never been part of the queer community. She never understood how they all had so much time to spend with one another while also in school, while also working. Sometimes one of them would be brave enough to pursue her, but Olympia had never figured out how to balance dating with her coursework, and she knew there were several disappointed hearts in her wake. It was never her intention to hurt anyone. She just had different priorities and hadn't been able to find someone who was of the same mind. Perhaps she never would.

The lesbians Inside had the outlines of people Olympia used to know—the same asymmetrical haircuts, toned arms, wide hips, confident saunters—but their faces were different. Other than her patients, she didn't really know any of them at all. She wondered where Ava was. If she would come here.

It was still early, and no one was guarding the door yet, so she was able to slip into the room unnoticed and perch herself on a stool. She wondered what would happen if the residents found out that what they drank had no alcohol in it.

She rested her elbows on the sticky table that was serving as a bar and tried not to look at the woman who was playing bartender, cleaning mugs and wiping down surfaces in a way that struck Olympia as jarringly sexual, perhaps intentionally so. But there was, of course, the possibility that everything an attractive person does appears sexual to the thirsty onlooker, and Olympia averted her gaze. She tried to imagine this woman doing something offensive. Spitting, or maybe picking her nose. It did nothing to help the prickle running up her spine.

Starting to feel flushed, Olympia loosened the top of her tunic.

"You look like you don't belong here," the woman said, but she was smiling, and it clearly wasn't a threat.

"I won't tell if you won't," Olympia replied, and the woman nodded conspiratorially.

The room was filling up with people. Many of them had fashioned their uniforms into things that were smaller, tighter, more corset-like in appearance, and Olympia couldn't help but admire the creativity. It was a compelling aesthetic. Her skin felt hungry. The tips of her fingers ached for the warmth of someone else.

She wondered who, if anyone, she'd be confident enough to speak to. Probably no one, she decided. Better to just observe, at least for now.

31

"I MISS YOU DURING THE DAY," BROOK SAID, AS SHE AND July meandered Inside's passageways together. It had been a few weeks since they'd done this, but Brook couldn't remember why they'd stopped. Maybe they'd just been too busy. When she tried to remember what they'd been busy with, though, it was like trying to recall a dream that was already fading from view.

At any rate, things were back to normal now. She felt great. Better than she ever had, really. "I don't know why they couldn't have given us work assignments together," she said.

"Me either, but I really would not want to work with you in Refillables," July said, and Brook poked her in the stomach, making July squeal.

"What's it like working under Olympia?" Brook asked. "She always seemed kind of intense."

"She's nice, I guess," July said. "But she gives me more work than anyone else. She wants everything I do to be perfect. I don't know why she's not as hard on the others."

"You're her favorite," Brook said. "I don't know why you're surprised. You're always everyone's favorite."

July ignored her. "It's fun sometimes. I learned how to look at blood under a microscope. But other times, she gives me piles of books to study, and then she quizzes me on them without any warning."

"Okay, that sucks."

"And I think everyone else is starting to hate me for it. I would be so much happier just blending into the background."

As if you could ever blend into the background, Brook thought.

Suddenly, both girls stopped in their tracks. They heard laughter, music, and shouting, though it was muffled. It was coming from somewhere very close, and they pulled up the map to figure out which door in the hallway was not claimed by a resident.

"Oh my god," Brook said, and pointed to an unoccupied address at the end of the passageway. "There."

They slowly walked toward the door, which they could see had a sliver of light pulsing underneath it. Now that they knew where they were going, neither was in a hurry. Brook wanted to savor the feelings of excitement, that intangible space between imagining something and seeing it for real. Once she saw it, she wouldn't have to wonder. And imagining was half the fun.

It was fifteen steps to the door. "Are you counting?" July said. "Your mouth is moving."

"Shut up," Brook said, but they were both grinning.

They reached the door, and Brook knocked. Nothing happened. The roar inside the room grew louder. She knocked again, harder. This time it opened, a crack, and a woman stuck her face out. She was older, clearly one of the original women.

"Can I help you?" she said. Someone called out, "Who is it?" and the woman turned and said, "We've got new ones."

The door opened a little wider and a second woman appeared. She said, "Why should we let you in?" They looked like they were trying not to laugh.

Brook and July looked at each other. "Why . . . shouldn't you?" July said, with her signature charm. Brook had to withhold an eye roll.

It worked. "Well, aren't you adorable," the first woman said.

"Oh, fuck it," the second woman said. "Come in, quickly." They ushered Brook and July in, closing and locking the door behind them.

Their ears filled with the tinny sound of music played through multiple tablets, something aggressive and guttural sounding, a far cry from the gentle symphonic sounds that played in the background of the public recreation rooms. The air was hot and stuffy, filled with smoke, smelling earthy and sweaty. And the room was full of people, all behaving in a manner that Brook and July had never seen before. Some of them were dancing, their arms wrapped around each other. Many had taken their tunics off. People were taking great swigs out of their regulation water bottles, and jugs of wine were stationed throughout the room in corners. Some leaned against the wall, taking it all in, while others gazed up at the stars.

Brook recognized a few of the adults, and it occurred to her that this was the first time she'd seen residents from different work units interacting with one another. It clicked for her in that moment how separate everyone was, at least during the day. Inside was supposed to be a collective but instead had been arranged into factions. Why did they need the secrecy of this space to intermingle? But as quickly as that question arrived in her head, it left, because July was pulling her by the arm toward the largest windows Brook had ever seen.

The girls ran over to press their faces to the glass. From there, they could see not just the sky, but the rest of Inside below them. The view was so startling it made Brook dizzy. The peaks and valleys and small bright glows of her home were so dense and endless that it was hard to tell where Inside ended and the starry sky began. And beyond it, they could see the ocean, reflecting the moonlight on waves of angry black ink.

"It looks like it goes on forever," July said.

No one seemed to be paying much attention to the two young women at the window, and it was the first time in a long time that Brook had felt truly uninhibited. She wondered if this was what adulthood would be like: a life lived on her own terms.

Next to her, so close she could feel the warmth of her skin, July's hips were pressed into the glass.

Suddenly, someone yanked July's arm, spinning her around. Standing before them was Olympia.

Olympia began to yell. Not at Brook—it was as though Brook wasn't even there. Something about the sight of July had set the doctor off.

She said, "You absolutely cannot be here, and you cannot tell anyone you were here, either."

July shot back, "But how come *you* get to be here?" Brook knew she was right to ask—they'd both thought the administrators of Inside didn't even know about these rooms.

"Please don't challenge me on this," Olympia said, suddenly sounding very tired instead of mad.

Olympia guided July out of the room, and then Brook found herself alone, until Olympia circled back to her. "You can stay. But you can't bring her back in here."

"Why?" Brook said. "I don't get it."

"She's not like you," the doctor replied, and Brook felt her heart sink into her stomach.

She felt very small, standing in a room of adults who were drinking and laughing, the candlelight illuminating their bare chests. So she left, running fifty steps down the passageway until she caught up with July, who jumped at the sound of Brook's footsteps.

"Why'd you leave?" July said.

"Why would I want to be in there without you?" Brook grabbed July's hand.

They walked back to July's apartment. "Do you want to sleep over?" July asked when they reached the huge locked door.

"You know I always want to."

32

JULY FLOPPED FACE-FIRST ONTO HER BED AS BROOK FOL-
lowed her into the apartment and closed the door. The silence of her enormous
home was still surprising to them both; unsettling in its expansiveness, even
though it was so beautiful.

"They always do this to me," July said into the pillow. A feather went up
her nose and she sneezed into the silk pillowcase.

"I literally can't hear you," Brook said, sitting down next to her.

July lifted her head up. Her face was streaked with tears and snot. "Did
you see the way she only cared about me being there, not you?"

"Ouch," Brook said.

"I don't mean it that way." July groaned. "It's like there are all these rules
that only apply to me." She wiped her face on the pillow and flipped over
onto her back. Brook was staring at the wall.

"Brook," July said, poking her side. "Come back."

"No, you're right," Brook said, after a few moments. "They care more
about you."

"I feel like you are willfully misunderstanding me," July said, growing
frustrated. "I'm not saying I like being treated like this."

"I know you don't," Brook said, and by her tone July knew she was coming back around. "Fuck them, right?" she said.

"Exactly. We're adults now. They can't keep doing this to me. To us."

Brook lay down next to July, and they faced each other. Brook's breath
smelled like the lentils they'd had for dinner, but July didn't mind. It was
familiar.

July couldn't remember the first day she'd wandered over to Brook and

Ava, but Ava had told her the story so often that July could picture it, as though she was a bystander, watching it unfold from above. The woman and child had been sitting on a blanket in one of the VR rooms, the one made to look like a park, and July had been there, too, but with a huge group of babies, the other kids that were being raised communally. Ava had been singing, and July had tottered over to them, still a little unsteady on her small feet, but so transfixed by the sound of the singing, and Ava had simply pulled her into her lap and cradled her. It became a ritual; anytime Ava saw July, she'd absorb her into their duo.

But even if July couldn't actually remember the first time this had happened, she did remember the feeling of wanting so badly to belong to someone. Her envy at seeing how devoted Ava was to Brook. Wondering if she'd be worthy of that kind of love, too, and how seamlessly Ava had adopted her into their little world. Brook was July's second half, and Ava was the ground they stood on. But was that all there was for her? This little family unit that wasn't even hers?

"What do you think it would be like, if we didn't live here?" July asked.

"Where should we live instead?"

"I don't know," July said. "Somewhere outside? Don't you think it's weird that in here, they made it so *different* from how the outside was?"

"Of course I think it's weird." They'd had this conversation hundreds of times.

"What do you think it would be like out there?" July asked again.

"I bet it would be better," Brook said. "At least outside we could go wherever we want."

"I'm so sick of all these walls," July moaned. "Walls, rules, locked doors, secrets. It's getting really old." What she didn't say: *I'm sick of being treated differently. I'm sick of pretending to belong here in the same way that you do.*

Brook rolled over so that she was lying on top of July. July reached her arms around Brook and held her close. She could feel Brook's wet mouth on her neck. "You're drooling on me," she giggled.

"Am not," came Brook's muffled, damp reply.

"You know what?" July said, staring at her skylight. "I think we should leave."

Brook rolled off her and sat up. "Leave where?"

"Inside. I mean, fuck it, right?"

She'd never allowed herself to honor these thoughts before this moment, but as the words left her mouth she knew they'd been lurking there all along. "There's got to be more than this. There's got to be more to life than just getting through the day."

"I think you might be right," Brook said.

They fell asleep holding each other.

33

OLYMPIA LEFT THE PARTY WITH HER HEART POUNDING, THE
tips of her ears turning hot. It was July's transgression, but Olympia knew
who Jacqueline would blame.

When she got home, she immediately called Jacqueline. Putting it off
would only make things worse.

She patched Jacqueline into the video call. Jacqueline had clearly been
asleep—her wig was off, and her eyes were puffy. As Olympia told her what
had happened, she grew very alert.

"I fucking told you so," Jacqueline hissed. "I knew this would happen. I
never should have allowed you to convince me to loosen the watch on her."

"But she's okay," Olympia protested. "She's twenty-two. We can't control
her like we used to."

"No one said anything about controlling her," Jacqueline said. "It's about
keeping her safe."

"Well, regardless of what we call it, at this point I don't see a way to do
that without her figuring out that she's different from everyone else here,"
Olympia said. "She's smart. She already suspects that she's different." Olympia pictured the hurt but unsurprised look on July's face when Olympia had
forced her to leave the party. "We'd need to implement the same rules for
everyone. If July can't sneak out, then no one can."

"So let's do that," Jacqueline said, as though it was the most obvious thing
in the world. "I'll write up some new rules as soon as we get off this call."

"That worries me," Olympia said. "We already increased the amount of
structure just a couple of weeks ago after the boy's death. I'm not sure the

residents are ready for more enforced guidelines. They've hardly adjusted to the most recent ones."

Jacqueline ignored this point, and instead said in a gentler voice, "Olympia, are you happy there?"

Jacqueline's face was slightly pixelated, the connection a little bit choppy thanks to an incoming storm. Olympia said, "Being happy isn't the point."

"Sure it is," Jacqueline said, in that same sweet tone. "If you aren't happy, how will you be motivated to pave the way for a brighter future?"

Olympia swallowed. Sometimes it seemed that Jacqueline spoke in quotes from her own book. She said, "I do get lonely, I guess."

"And that's why you began to spend recreational time with the people you're supposed to be looking after?"

"I guess so," Olympia said. "I just wanted to do something that wasn't work. I'm really sorry."

Jacqueline nodded. She said, "For women like us, the work is all there is. But it's good you were there, to discover July. So, thank you."

"Um," Olympia said. "You're welcome."

"I'm hanging up now," Jacqueline said. "I'm going to patch into July's video feed and make sure she's all right."

They said their goodbyes, and Olympia placed her tablet down on her bed. She checked the time. It was almost dawn. She thought about going to sleep for a couple of hours but didn't see the point. Instead, she got dressed for work, and made it into the labs just as the energy-efficient light bulbs flickered on to signify the sunrise.

As she filled her coffee, Olympia's tablet flashed pink with the new rules. Jacqueline worked so quickly. There was no explanation given. Olympia felt she'd need to brace herself for the backlash.

The energy was tense as everyone began their days, and it remained tense over the days that followed.

As per Jacqueline's instructions, security grew tighter and tighter. Inside's employees were stationed along the residential routes at night, tracking the residents' whereabouts.

Monthly bloodwork became a weekly requirement. Diets were monitored, too, and exercise became required, forty-five minutes each day of cardio and stretching. It was simply easier to keep everyone safe and healthy this way, Jacqueline said. Olympia wasn't so sure.

The point of Inside was not to be a safe home for July and July alone. There were, by then, over a hundred thousand people to look out for, ranging in age from weeks old to people in their mid-forties. All of those people deserved attention and care, too. Especially the older residents. They'd been through so much already in the outside world. The last thing they needed was to feel as though they lived under martial law. She'd always thought they were trying to eradicate oppression, not replicate it.

But that was always the flaw in Jacqueline's thinking. She couldn't understand that the problem in the society they'd left behind was power, which didn't need to be attached to a specific gender to wreak havoc. But it was no surprise that Jacqueline didn't understand how power functioned. She'd never known life without it.

Out of pure defiance, Olympia decided not to stop visiting the bar at night. Jacqueline wouldn't hold her back, not on this.

34

Dear Jacqueline, **THE EMAIL READ.** It is unacceptable that you have missed five directors' meetings in a row. As a leader on the global Inside team, you are expected to, at the very least, make an appearance at our weekly check-ins. We look forward to seeing you at tomorrow's meeting and hearing your updates.

"Well, fuck you, too," Jacqueline said to the screen.

She hadn't realized she'd let multiple weeks go by without dialing in to the meetings with the men who ran the other Insides. She hadn't meant to be absent. There was just so much else going on. So the next morning she fluffed her wig and reluctantly signed into the video chat, where Inside directors from around the world sat waiting for her, oblivious as usual to the alternative world she'd created right under their noses.

As always, the directors took turns sharing updates. Jacqueline was not that surprised to hear they were all having difficulties. How could they not? The other Insides had preserved the culture that had led to the climate crisis. They weren't solving anything; they had created large Band-Aids.

And then one man said, "We can't figure out how to regulate the frequency of sexual assault."

Jacqueline had to dig her fingernails into her leg to stop from screaming at him.

A few others chimed in. They were all having the same issue. Rape had become endemic.

Jacqueline knew they were waiting for her—the token woman—to offer some sort of solution. They were always looking to her to fix the problems that the women in the international Insides faced. But all Jacqueline could think was how simple and effective it would be to just eliminate everyone.

Jacqueline rubbed her forehead. She was more stressed than usual, her brows so furrowed they were a straight line across her forehead. She was too preoccupied even for her dermatologist appointments.

She had a very real reason to be so worried. When Jacqueline had patched into July's video feed the night Olympia had found the girls partying, she heard a conversation that shook her to her core: July and Brook wanted to leave Inside.

July, against all the odds, had somehow decided that the world she was living in—the world that had been painstakingly created to be literally ideal for July, specifically—wasn't good enough. Jacqueline took it as a personal rejection.

Jacqueline began watching the video of the girls on repeat, her pale hands curled into gnarled fists. Every time she heard July whisper to Brook, "There's got to be more to life than just getting through the day," she felt defeated. And that defeat turned to panic, as a few days later she listened to the girls making plans to escape. Jacqueline didn't think they'd actually be able to, but she still let herself indulge in nightmarish visions of it anyway. She imagined them finding a door somewhere and slipping out before anyone could stop them.

She pictured her beautiful young daughter stepping into the sunlight for the first time. More likely, she'd be stepping into a hurricane. Why didn't they understand how dangerous it was to leave? What did they think the entire point of Inside was, if not to keep them safe? *Alive?* The more they searched for a way out, the more Jacqueline could feel her heart breaking. Her daughter—her flesh and blood—did not want to live in this perfect world she'd created for her. What could be more shattering than that?

She'd get it right in the next round. Her future daughters born Inside would love it. They'd love her, too.

35

OLYMPIA DECIDED IT WAS TIME TO FORMALLY BRING UP how poorly Generation A was doing. If Jacqueline wasn't going to care—or worse, if perhaps she'd designed it this way—Olympia would have to just go around her.

It was something her colleagues seemed to have wordlessly agreed to leave unaddressed, because—Olympia assumed—they weren't sure how to handle it. This world was supposed to be great for everyone. Instead, most kids were failing every metric; they were blowing off work, neglecting to take care of themselves properly. They were suffering from anxiety and depression. And now, a young person, dead.

In her memory of her first meetings with Jacqueline, she recalled that she had pushed back on Jacqueline's limited understanding of gender—but she also admitted to herself that she had backed down quickly. Jacqueline had really managed to manipulate her, and very easily at that. Olympia vowed to never let it happen again.

Olympia came to the meeting prepared with research she'd been doing on her own. She spoke at length about Ellery, and how his untimely death could have perhaps been avoided if they were studying everyone more closely; if maybe that in trying to eliminate the effects of patriarchy, they'd still created a hierarchy of sorts.

"The problem of men was a nurture problem, not a nature problem," she said, to a room full of uncomfortable stares. "But we haven't been nurturing *anyone* properly. We've just been replicating power structures and calling them something else."

Someone in the room cleared their throat, but other than that it was silent. Olympia started speaking faster, delving into detail about the rampant OCD and the reliance on drugs and the way they'd failed to instill a sense of purpose in any of the children. But her presentation was met with more silence.

"I'm concerned that instead of equality, we've created a new hegemony, with cisgender women at the top. I don't see how, long-term, this is really a superior place. In a few generations, if not sooner, it'll just be a mirror image of how things were outside."

She knew this was a nearly heretical suggestion. One by one, her colleagues stood up and left.

The last woman to leave paused in the doorway, looking around nervously. "They're afraid," she whispered to Olympia. "It doesn't mean they don't agree."

But whether or not that message was true, after the meeting, things changed for Olympia. Refusing to simply go along with the status quo meant she found herself shut out of the conversation altogether. Her colleagues began to give her suspicious glances in passing. Some staff meetings were held without her.

She began eating dinner by herself. Sometimes she'd even eat in the café with the residents, which was forbidden. Challenging the rules in small doses gave her a thrill.

After another meal alone, she brought her tray back up to the counter, and then entered the tunnel that led to Inside's employee quarters. She knew her movements were being tracked by the tablet in her hands, but that hardly anyone was paying much attention. Though there were cameras everywhere, after July was born, they were mostly trained on *her*. That was how the team that was supposed to miss nothing had missed all the deaths; the drug use, too.

She reached a staircase lit gently with amber-hued bulbs. The walls were lined with paintings the children had done, adorably clumsy stick-figure portraits mostly of their mothers.

To Olympia, the surveillance program was starting to seem symbolic, to maintain the divide between residents and employees. So the administrators could feel superior to the residents in some way. Which of course wasn't true.

Though we're certainly treated as though we are, she thought, as she reached the top of the staircase, pushing the door to the employee wing open. Through the doorway the hall widened into a large lobby set elegantly aglow by a large chandelier. It was much nicer than anything the residents had access to.

She walked through the lobby slowly, her feet sinking into the cream carpeting. It was quiet and empty; most of her coworkers were already asleep.

Olympia remembered the first time she'd read Jacqueline's name on that book so many years ago. Jacqueline's brand was nothing if not consistent. She'd called those spaces Yours!, but perhaps a more accurate name would have been *Mine!* At least, that's what Inside was. It was Jacqueline's. And someday it would be July's.

36

THERE WAS A VICIOUS STORM ON EARTH, SO LARGE IT
could be seen from the windows of the space shuttle. Jacqueline watched
the clouds swirl below her and tried to remember the enormous crashing
sounds of thunder booming.

She was reminded of the strength of a hurricane that had ripped through
New York so many years ago. Jacqueline hadn't been on the East Coast for
it; she'd been on vacation in Greece—a solo trip, like always. She'd returned,
though, to find her house destroyed, a large tree splayed out in her living room,
cleaving her couch in two. That was when she bought the penthouse where
July now lived; the building itself had been converted with Inside's weather-safe
tech, and though the other floors were expanded and changed in almost every
way, Jacqueline had insisted her former home be kept mostly intact.

But the world she'd created for her daughter wasn't serving her anymore.
It hadn't prevented her from feeling pain and suffering. It was driving her
out. Making her crave independence. Which of course would negate the
entire point of having her grow up there.

Plus—Jacqueline was getting close to finalizing her plans to deal with
the other Insides. If she was to move forward with it, and she felt in her
heart that she would, July needed to be in the safest place possible: by Jacqueline's side.

She'd known that this might be a possibility. She'd said so from the beginning. There was always a way for her to remove July from Inside if need be.
What kind of mother would she be otherwise? And so the decision seemed
to be making itself.

July would need to be retrieved. Sooner rather than later.

37

AVA SOMETIMES THOUGHT OF HER LIFE OUTSIDE—THE LONE-
liness she'd felt going to work every morning, the way she'd grow anxious if
she got home before Orchid, unable to deal with being alone in the empty
apartment. She was still haunted by memories of air that smelled like sewage and how the odor seemed to cling to her skin and hair; loud storms, trees
that knocked down houses, water that rushed up from the ground, tornado
warnings on her phone; feeling so exhausted from being anxious, but feeling
too anxious to sleep. She remembered constant fear.

Inside, she had everything she needed. She had friends; smart, interesting, funny friends. And she had her children, who she could love the way
she had wanted to be loved. She also had the ongoing reassurance that no
matter what happened outside, they were all completely protected from it.

She felt as though she'd reached her final form, and she liked that form.
She trusted herself. Inside worked for her.

She was in this place of assurance and calm when one day, her attraction
toward Olympia—which had lurked just below the surface for longer than
she could remember—turned into something more.

Olympia had long been the object of her fantasies, part of her most private inner landscape. But now, when she thought of Olympia, she began to
blush so fiercely that she had to stop herself from doing so in public.

She remembered every single time Olympia had ever touched her. She
remembered the way Olympia had teased her for not wanting to shave her
head. The way she'd smirked and said that the beautiful people would still
be beautiful, with all their heads shaved. She'd been right about that. Did

that mean she thought Ava was beautiful? After all these years, could she possibly still think that? Did she think about Ava at all?

Of course, Olympia was partially responsible for what had been the darkest period of Ava's life—her pregnancy—but had it not ultimately brought the greatest gift? And she had looked out for Ava that whole time, in a way Ava suspected was different from how she treated the other patients. Olympia had visited her daily, regardless of her official appointment schedule. She'd brought her food and books and listened to her. And when she listened to her, Ava could tell that she really heard her, saw her. She made her feel like she wasn't insane. It was because of Olympia that Ava had made it out of the darkness.

Ava had slept with dozens of people over the years Inside, some once and some a few times, but had never felt this strongly about any of them. Or anyone, ever, really—she had never known anyone for as long as she'd known Olympia and that kind of duration felt like it had unlocked something profound within her. Olympia's presence was a constant. It was deeply appealing.

It wasn't explicitly forbidden for the Inside employees to have relationships with the residents, but Ava didn't know of any who did. They didn't even spend their free time together platonically. The employees seemed to always have work to do, anyway, to the point where it was clear that what they were doing wasn't work, not for them. It was their purpose. Ava often wondered how they felt about it, if it had been worth the trade-off. A lifetime of work in exchange for doing something you truly believed was saving humanity. She imagined it would be hard to be motivated to save humanity if you aren't given time to enjoy being alive.

If Olympia felt the same way about her, Ava was certain her professionalism would prevent her from showing it. And in a way, Ava was content to live in the fantasy of it all. Loving someone had only ever led to disappointment.

One afternoon, a friend stopped by Ava's desk and casually mentioned that they and some of the others would be going out later to one of the rooms on the upper level. The mention of the secret bars made Ava laugh with nostalgia. She couldn't remember the last time she'd been out. It had definitely been before the girls were born. She hadn't even been sure people were still doing that.

"I haven't heard someone say that in years," she said. "But I'm in."

"Just a heads-up," the friend added, "some of the others have seen one of the administrators there recently. Not sure what it means, but she doesn't seem to want to stop us."

Ava's heart lurched. "Which one?"

"Who knows," she said. "An administrator is an administrator."

Ava laughed, but she was finding it hard to breathe. Could it be?

She took a long bath that night, taking time to wash her hair and moisturize her limbs. She wore a clean tunic, shaking the wrinkles out; she braided her wet hair so that it dried in loose waves around her face, though she knew that within a few hours it would return to its preferred wild state. She knew she shouldn't get her hopes up that Olympia would be in the room with the skylights, but she couldn't help it. She thought back to the early days of Inside, when the stakes felt low and all she wanted to do was feel connected to other people. Now, she had plenty of connections—but there was only one that she wanted to make deeper.

At the bar, Ava planted herself in a corner, where she could see the whole room. The aesthetic hadn't changed much. The walls were still black. The residents' faces were still illuminated by the moon in that same haunting, alluring way. The fake wine was still plentiful and too sweet; the music was still being played out of those small tablet speakers. But Ava was different, and that made everything else feel different, too. *These are my people*, she thought, smiling down into her mug, *and they always will be.*

When Ava looked up, she saw Olympia, as if she'd manifested her. Olympia was standing near the door; she looked nervous, but eager—she was scanning the room. Olympia looked nothing short of gorgeous, with smile lines around her mouth that had deepened over the years; her neck was long and elegant. Ava imagined resting her hands on it.

Olympia watched Ava approach, her face calm, as though maybe she'd been expecting this. *Maybe she planned this*, Ava thought.

"Fancy meeting you here," Ava said, immediately regretting every single word that left her mouth.

"Is it fancy?" Olympia said, and to Ava's delight, she grinned.

"Do you want some grape juice?" Ava said, with a wink. "I can get us some."

Olympia laughed. "That sounds great," she said. "I'll go with you."

Walking toward the makeshift bar, their shoulders bumped. Ava tried not to assume anything. It was crowded in the room.

She poured two cups full of the watery red liquid, handing one to Olympia, and then they clinked their glasses. "What should we toast to?" Ava said.

"To seeing each other outside of my office," Olympia said.

Ava's breath caught in her throat. Seeing each other, or . . . *seeing* each other? Olympia's expression was impossible to read.

"Should we dance?" Olympia said, but she was already pulling Ava by the hand to the middle of the dance floor, and then, to Ava's delight, she put her hands on Ava's hips. Ava had the urge to pinch herself to make sure she was awake, that this wasn't another dream. But it was very real. All of Olympia's focus was on her. It was as though they were alone.

The rest of the night was an ecstatic blur: Olympia's face close to Ava's, the sweet smell of her skin, and then the warmth of her hands, the clear sound of her laugh, the understanding between them that something was happening, and neither of them was going to stop it.

Ava was leaning against the dark expanse of the window, trying to catch her breath, when Olympia kissed her; a hot, wet kiss that left a trail of saliva on Ava's mouth.

"Oh god," Olympia said, pulling away. "I'm so sorry. I should go."

Ava shook her head. "Do you know how often I've thought about you doing that?"

"How often?" Olympia seemed suddenly shy.

Ava put her arms around Olympia's waist and put her mouth to her ear. "You've been putting your hands on me for nearly twenty years," she whispered. "I can't really quantify the amount of times I wished for a different context." Ava felt Olympia's hips melt into hers.

And then they left, hand in hand.

Ava took Olympia to her apartment. She kept the lights off and guided Olympia over to the bed in the darkness. She pulled Olympia on top of her by the collar of her regulation tunic, which was a different cut from Ava's own, but only just slightly.

Ava couldn't quite believe it was actually happening, and she clutched Olympia tightly, as though at any moment she might vaporize and vanish.

The eagerness seemed mutual: Olympia bit Ava's shoulder, she pulled her armpit hair. She rolled onto her back, pulling Ava with her. She encircled Ava with her long legs and held her so tightly that it made her gasp. But when it came to talking to Ava, Olympia was struggling. She hadn't said anything since they left the party.

Finally, Ava broke the silence. "How do you want me to touch you?"

Olympia looked embarrassed. "I don't know," she said. "Every which way. Whatever you want."

Ava felt her insides soften. There was something endearing about how nervous Olympia was, especially juxtaposed with the masculine confidence with which she usually carried herself. "How do you do it when it's just you?" Ava asked, as gently as she could, afraid that Olympia might change her mind and flee.

Olympia shook her head. "I've never been good at talking about this."

"I get it. How about this: show me. Do it to me the way you want me to do it to you."

"Okay," Olympia said, reaching for her.

Time turned to liquid as they touched each other. Ava stayed on top of Olympia, which wasn't a place she usually was, but she found that she fit there, and Olympia seemed to prefer it.

Olympia came first, silently, lurching forward so suddenly that Ava was almost thrown off her. She could feel Olympia's heart pounding in her throat. As she listened to the hoarse sounds of Olympia trying to catch her breath, she felt the hot glow of her own orgasm take hold—though she was hardly as quiet as Olympia had been. She screamed into the pillow next to Olympia's head, and then, unable to hold herself up anymore, rolled to the side.

"I'm sorry," Olympia said, with a small groan.

"Why?" Ava propped herself up on an elbow. She was drenched in sweat.

Olympia put her hands over her face. "It's just been a really long time since I've done this."

"How long?" Ava asked.

"Well," Olympia said. "There was a girl in college. I think I really loved her, but we were so young. And then there was med school, and then there was Inside . . ." She trailed off.

"And now there's me," Ava said, hopefully.

Olympia turned toward her. "And now there's you."

It took a few days for Ava to ask Olympia the question that had been on her mind; she held off until one night while they lay in Ava's bed together, limbs entangled, waiting for sleep to come. "Did you leave anyone behind?"

"You mean outside?" Olympia replied.

Ava nodded.

"Of course I did," Olympia said, sounding surprised.

"Well, I don't know," Ava said. "I didn't have any family left. My parents died when I was eighteen."

"Oh," Olympia said, her voice catching a little. "Actually, I remember that about you."

Ava knew she should have realized Olympia already knew everything about her—she'd helped select Ava for this world, this life.

Olympia said, into the stillness, "Leaving my family for Inside was the hardest thing I've ever done. I think about them all the time."

Ava didn't know what to say, so she put a hand on Olympia's face and kissed her on the mouth, but Olympia pulled away. "Do you *actually* want to listen to me?"

"What?" Ava said. "I don't understand what is happening."

Olympia sat up. "You asked me a question, used it to talk about yourself, and now you're trying to be physical when I'm telling you how I feel. Why did you even ask?"

Ava rolled away, at a loss for words. She had the sense that there was something larger Olympia was upset about—her strong reaction felt out of proportion to Ava's faux pas. But Ava didn't want to push it, so instead they slept at opposite ends of the mattress, curling in on themselves instead of each other.

In the morning, when they both were stirring awake, Olympia turned over onto her back, staring at the ceiling. "I'd like to tell you about them," she said. "I want you to know me. It's not fair that I know everything about you and you only know who I've been here."

"Please," Ava nearly begged. "I'm listening."

"I grew up in Texas, in a small town where everyone knew each other," Olympia began, staring at the ceiling as though her past was mapped out on it. "Both of my parents were teachers. My mom taught history and my dad taught math. I had a brother who was a couple of years older than me. He was a total pain but also so charming it was impossible to ever really be mad at him. I was his baby."

"Were you close with your parents?" Ava asked.

"Very. They were the best." She was quiet for a few moments. Ava's heart was pounding. She wasn't sure if she should keep asking questions or allow Olympia to tell the story in her own time.

"They adopted me," Olympia said. "But it didn't matter. They were my real parents through and through." Ava thought of July. Would July say the same thing about her?

"My mom and I were especially close," Olympia continued. "We did every-thing together, even when I was a teenager and probably should have been embarrassed by her. I never was. She was my best friend."

Ava thought of Brook and July rolling their eyes at her. A non-embarrassed teenager was hard to imagine.

"She was so pretty," Olympia said. "I used to love watching her get ready in the mornings, even if it made me feel, I don't know. Different. She always said we were the girls of the family but even as a little kid I felt like that wasn't the full story. It's not that I didn't feel like a girl, it's just that I would look at my glamorous mother and think, *How are we the same thing?* I can still remember how she smelled when she was all dressed up, with her makeup and perfume and lotion. Of course, she downplayed her beauty, too. She wanted people to see her for her ability, not her appearance. But some things you can't hide."

That's not so different from you, Ava thought. Even in her drab Inside uniform, Olympia was exquisite.

"Both my parents were really involved in the community," Olympia continued. "And they always wanted us to be, too. I was the top of my class. There were only a handful of other Black kids at school. It was a super-white area."

Ava swallowed, uncomfortable in what she was sure was her deafening silence.

"What was that like?"

"Lonely," Olympia said. "Hard. It was so hard to be different. And then, of course, I also turned out to be gay. I was always kind of a queer kid, before I really knew it. That might have been fine if I grew up on the East Coast, but Texas was still Texas. The other kids seemed to know before I did. There were so many things that made me *other*."

"Kids always know," Ava said.

"I had this best friend . . . We'd practice kissing in my bedroom. My parents walked in on us once and sent her home. My parents were totally fine with me liking girls, they just didn't like the idea of me sneaking around under their noses. They didn't think it was appropriate for me to be alone with someone I wanted to make out with. Her gender was beside the point."

"That's nice," Ava said.

"It was. It was definitely nice at home. But at school, the girl I'd been with told all the kids at school that I was gay, that I'd come on to her in some way, and it was kind of downhill from there for me, socially. My brother didn't let the older kids pick on me, but he had no jurisdiction over my own class. They were pretty brutal. But it didn't matter. All that mattered were my grades."

"Awful," Ava said.

"I remember everything that happened with her in such vivid detail," Olympia said, sounding far away. "Stupid, gross things. The texture of her mouth. I was thirteen."

Ava tried to shake off her jealousy by changing the subject. "Where did your brother end up?"

"The army," she said. "He went to live on the UWG base when I came here."

"What made you decide to become a doctor?"

"It seemed like the job where I could have the most impact. I was good at science. It came naturally."

"Your parents must have been so proud," Ava said.

"They were."

"Do you know where they are now?"

"No," Olympia said. "They were going to stay in Texas. But who knows what really happened. I haven't been able to reach them for some time. All the cell towers out there were destroyed."

"I'm so sorry about last night," Ava said.

Olympia smiled with a sigh and put her hand on Ava's hip.

"It's okay," she said. "Let me forgive you."

"Okay," Ava said. "I'll let you."

Olympia pulled Ava close to her then, and Ava pressed her face into her collarbone. No one had ever told her when she was messing up, and therefore she'd never had the chance to fix it. This felt very new and very different indeed.

"But," Ava said, "is there something else going on? I mean, are you okay?"

"There's a lot going on," Olympia admitted. "I'm really struggling with how much to tell you. I'm sorry if it's coming out in other ways. There's so much you don't know."

"Tell me when you're ready," Ava said. "There's no rush. I'm not going anywhere."

38

BROOK COULDN'T FIND JULY AT DINNER. SHE ASKED
around, but no one else had seen her, either.

Brook left her dinner behind and headed straight for July's apartment.
Trying not to worry, she ran through a mental list of places July could be,
of things she could be doing. Maybe she wasn't feeling well. Maybe she was
still at work. They'd seen each other in the morning, though, and had made
plans to eat together. It was very unlike July to flake on plans, especially with
Brook. She broke out into a run.

Brook reached the door to July's apartment. She typed in the nine-digit
key code, and it swung open.

As she made her way up the long flight of stairs, she heard a loud booming, and a sound like falling water. The sound got louder as she approached.
When she finally entered July's room, she froze.

Above July's bed, one of the skylights was wide open.

Rain was pouring through it in a square-shaped column. The bed was
bloated with water, a huge puddle rapidly extending outward on the floor.
The column of rain as it fell was illuminated by the pink lights of the room,
and small arcs of luminescent color bounced off it.

But otherwise, July's room was empty.

PART NINE

THE OVERVIEW EFFECT

2078

39

AVA WAS CAREFUL ABOUT MAKING SURE SHE STILL SAW BROOK
and July regularly, without Olympia. She knew the girls were technically
adults now, and needed her less, but she wanted to preserve the dynamics
of their little family unit for as long as possible. So they kept some rituals,
like eating meals together, and if not meals, then they'd gather for tea in
the evenings after dinner. On the nights that Ava did this, Olympia would
stay late in her office, catching up on work.

Tonight, Brook and July were late, so Ava left the tearoom and meandered over to the library to wait. She was lying on one of the library's enormous velvet pink couches, hypnotized by a novel she'd found, when finally
Brook burst in, tears streaming down her face.

"What is it?" she said, remembering how Brook had looked after she'd
found the boy in his room. Could it have happened again?

Brook whispered, "July's gone."

A few others looked up from their books. Ava walked Brook into a qui-
eter corner, where she began to sob.

"What do you mean *gone*?" Ava felt all the blood rush out of her face.

Brook said, "We were supposed to eat dinner together, but she never
showed up. So I checked her apartment, and the skylight was open."

Ava asked, "July has a skylight?" And then, understanding that that wasn't
the point, she said, "Do you have any idea where she could have gone?"
Maybe she was only hiding somewhere. Maybe she fell asleep somewhere,
by accident. It simply made no sense for July to no longer be Inside, and Ava
refused to accept it.

But then Brook rubbed her eyes and looked down for a few moments.

"We were planning on leaving," she said, and Ava found she couldn't look away from the truth.

"You were trying to leave me?"

"No," Brook said, backtracking. "No, that's not what I meant."

But, of course, it was what she meant. Ava remembered the day Orchid broke up with her, and how she'd been so unable to say what she really wanted, how they'd both been unable to say it. She knew logically that this wasn't a breakup. But it wasn't not a breakup, either. Brook *had* been trying to leave her. Had she pushed her own daughter away, too?

Ava asked, "Do you have any idea what could have happened to July?" But Brook shook her head. "Okay," she said. "Go to my apartment and wait there. I'm going to get help."

40

SHELBY HEARD A COMMOTION OUTSIDE HER ROOM, BUT
when she peered out of her door, the hallway was empty. Still, she could
hear the sound of a girl screaming somewhere nearby.

Then came a voice that was unmistakable. "Please calm down," Jacqueline said. "Please stop crying."

But the wailing only grew louder. Shelby stuck her head out farther into
the hallway.

After a few moments she could make out some words: "Who are you?
Where am I? What the fuck is going on?"

"July, you need to be quiet," Jacqueline said, in a tone familiar to Shelby.
She was clearly about to run out of patience. "I'll come back and check on
you later."

At that, Shelby ducked back into her room and closed the door as quickly
and quietly as possible. *What did I just hear? Who is July?*

She rushed to her computer. She had an idea.

On Earth, Jacqueline used to ask Shelby to reply to emails as though
she were Jacqueline herself, and it had been something Shelby thoroughly
enjoyed—writing in Jacqueline's voice was entertaining, and she'd loved
knowing about the inner workings of her boss's business and personal life.
But at a certain point, Jacqueline had told Shelby to stop checking her email
for her, under the guise of giving her more important work to do. Shelby had
been tempted to check it many times since then but had always refrained.
Now, though, she needed to know what Jacqueline was hiding. *Who* Jacqueline was hiding.

Sitting at her computer, Shelby pulled up the program that the space shuttle used for email. She had her own account, but she never really used it. There was no one she needed to reach.

But she knew that Jacqueline practically lived in her own inbox, and if there were answers, they'd be there. She typed Jacqueline's email address into the login portal and paused at the field requiring her to input a password. Thinking of the screams from the hallway, she typed in: JULY. The computer made a hideous buzzing sound and told her she had two more attempts before the account would be locked.

She considered other things it could be, coming up short. Holding her breath, she decided to try Jacqueline's birthday.

The buzzing sound returned. "Fuck," she whispered.

One attempt left, the computer told her. Do you need tech support? Hit yes or no.

Shelby reached to click No, but her hands were so sweaty that her finger slipped, grazing the Yes button. She froze.

After a few moments, the phone attached to the wall rang. She jumped, and then, heart pounding, lifted the receiver to her ear. "Tech support," a voice on the other end of the line said.

"Oh, hi," Shelby said, trying to sound normal.

"Hi!" the tech support person chirped at her. "I heard you might be having computer trouble."

"No," she said, as pleasantly as she could. "Thank you, though. I'm so stupid, I forgot my own password. I remembered it now, though. Thanks. So nice that you called to help."

"Can you please confirm your identity, Ms. Millender?" the person on the other line said, assuming she was Jacqueline.

Shelby quickly rattled off Jacqueline's social security number, which she knew by heart.

"Thank you!" tech support said.

Shelby hung up the phone. That was a little too close, and she only had one more try.

Shelby ran through potential passwords in her head, and then it occurred to her that it was entirely possible that Jacqueline hadn't changed it from when Shelby used to check her emails for her. Shelby held her breath while she typed in Yours!1234567. The inbox opened. *Of course she never changed it*, Shelby thought. *Typical millennial.*

And so, she logged in to Jacqueline's email, and began reading.

Most of what Shelby found did not surprise her, but rather confirmed her suspicions. She'd put some pieces together. Now she read for hours, going back years and years. She read the lengthy correspondences between Jacqueline and Olympia, and then she read the emails Jacqueline sent before Olympia was hired. The more she read, the more clearly Shelby could see the full picture of what had transpired. She held her hands over her mouth.

It was obvious to Shelby why Jacqueline thought this was a good idea. It was the logical extension of her legacy. But the holes in the plan stood out even more. Jacqueline had created a world based on fantasies: the fantasy of female moral purity, the fantasy that gender is a coin, with a bad side and a good side.

And—there was no avoiding this line of thinking—was this why Shelby herself hadn't been accepted? Shelby had long suspected herself to be some sort of prop for Jacqueline to prove to the world that she supported trans women. If Jacqueline *really* supported her, though, she'd have allowed her the agency to choose for herself whether she wanted to go Inside or not. Instead, she'd stripped her of choices. She wondered about the trans women who were accepted, and what their lives were like.

She read about the dead kid and the genetic experiments and the drugs they used for mind control. She learned about the girl named July. It must have been July's screams from down the hall, Shelby realized.

Jacqueline's most recent email was to Olympia. Don't look for her, it read. She's with me.

But what Shelby couldn't figure out was *why* Jacqueline had decided to bring July to space. Which also meant that the administrators—Olympia, in particular—might not know, either.

And then, remembering a conversation from so long ago it felt that it might have happened to someone else, Shelby opened Jacqueline's draft folder.

There, she found something that didn't seem to fit with Inside's vision of tranquility. Jacqueline had saved list after list with details about the other

Inside locations, including notes about different kinds of biological weapons and international drone usage.

Shelby made some notes on her pad and chewed her lip. This was worse than she ever could have imagined, but it didn't feel totally separate from the damage Jacqueline had already done. Forcing an entire Inside population to live by her rules was not all that different from eliminating those who might not agree with her; the latter was the conclusion of the impetus for the former. If Jacqueline couldn't force her gender essentialism on the populations she didn't control, she'd simply want to get rid of them.

Jacqueline wanted to remake the world in her image. And Shelby knew she'd stop at nothing to get what she wanted.

41

IT CAME AS A SHOCK TO JACQUELINE THAT JULY, WHOSE
heavy-lidded blue eyes were even larger in person, was absolutely terrified
of her.

They had so much in common. Jacqueline had grown up protected from
the outside world, too. For every layer of weatherproof metal and glass that
now surrounded the chosen women on Earth, Jacqueline had had body-
guards, nannies, maids, and high-tech locks on her doors.

She'd been a precocious teenager, always pushing the boundaries of her
contained universe. So she understood July's urge to see more. Now, approaching the end of her time on this mortal plane, Jacqueline could hardly
believe how quickly her universe had shrunken from limitless possibility to
the confines of the space shuttle. It was nearly impossible to wrap her mind
around the fact that she'd never be on Earth again, that this was the safest
place for her to stay until she died.

She figured she had maybe twenty years left. She wondered how many of
those would be good years, and how many would be spent in pain or confusion. She was concerned about the aesthetics of her own decline.

The reality, though, was that she was far too curious about what would
happen in the immediate future to fully fear it. Because Jacqueline had laid
the groundwork for something quite remarkable indeed: almost everything
Inside relied on her intellectual property, from the Refillables contract to
the curriculum that taught her book. There would be nothing stopping her
from continuing to exert her influence, until it was time to transfer power
over to her daughter, continuing the JM Inc. tradition. And when Earth had
healed and it was safe to go outside and resume life out in the open air, the

people would have generations of trust and affection for JM Inc., and the company's legacy would continue.

But sweet, beautiful July knew none of this, nor nothing of the world she'd come from and the remarkable science that had ushered her into existence. And she knew even less about her mother, from whose egg she was created, and who watched her almost daily, dreaming of a world where they could be best friends. *That dream*, Jacqueline had thought with a smile the night July was airlifted out of bed and brought to space, *is about to come true.*

Jacqueline was sure she knew everything there was to know about her daughter. She'd watched July grow up, after all. She saw her birth, and she stayed up all night for the first few weeks of July's life, watching her sleep. She'd been there for every first milestone. She heard her say her first word and saw her take her first steps. She watched her learn how to read. She'd cried with her, laughed with her, and often she'd even eat meals while July ate hers. She knew that July slept on her left side and that she took long showers and that she liked to doodle pictures of birds from her textbooks. She knew that she had a stubborn streak, that she liked to see how far rules could bend. She knew July was independent, like Jacqueline, and creative, like Jacqueline, too. They could have been best friends in another life. *No, not in another life*, Jacqueline thought. *In this life. We will be best friends in this life.*

But the one thing Jacqueline hadn't counted on, the one thing she didn't know about her daughter, was that July didn't care who Jacqueline was. July hadn't wanted to be rescued. July wanted to go back home. No matter how much Jacqueline tried to explain to her daughter the reason for everything that had happened, July wouldn't stop sobbing, refusing to be touched. The only thing July wanted was to be left alone.

After another fruitless attempt at getting closer to July, Jacqueline left her room, backed out slowly, and closed the door. She could hear July wailing through the walls. She rested her forehead against the cool metal of the door. She felt out of her depth. She needed help.

Jacqueline had July's favorite food prepared and left it outside July's bedroom door herself. She knocked to let July know it was there, and then left.

At least the girl was eating, she thought. She wondered when her daughter would emerge. She tried to will her to. But the door remained closed.

Finally, one morning when Jacqueline was leaving a plate of breakfast on the floor, the door did open. July looked awful. Her face was swollen and puffy. She had clearly not been getting much sleep. She glared at Jacqueline so intensely it made Jacqueline clutch her heart. "What?" she said. "What's wrong?"

July said, "Where did you get this food from?"

Jacqueline said, "I wanted to bring you your favorites. It was made by my personal chef."

"No," July shouted. "I mean where does it *come from*?"

Jacqueline looked down at the plate of food in her hands. It was brightly hued piles of vegetables and quinoa, with a small bowl of sliced strawberries.

Jacqueline began to say, "July, I . . ." But July cut her off.

"You've been making us grow your food," she said.

Jacqueline was speechless. July said, "That's what I thought," and slammed the door.

Jacqueline sat on the ground, her back to July's door. She was at a loss. Of course Inside was supplying food to the space shuttle. How else was she supposed to eat? A special emissary was sent monthly to Earth who would enter Inside through the subway tunnel that was left open. The tunnel led to a locked door that only the emissary knew about, which opened to a room where an Inside employee would leave fresh produce. It really wasn't that sinister. Inside was designed to support three million people, and so far they only had around a hundred thousand mouths to feed. There was plenty of extra food that would otherwise go to waste. It was hardly even a secret.

But, even though it wasn't intentionally a secret, July likely had no idea about the ways things outside of her small universe functioned. Jacqueline could see how it might feel like some sort of evil plot, if you didn't understand how it worked and why. In the absence of transparency, July probably imagined that the people of Inside were like indentured servants, working to create sustenance for the overlords. It hadn't occurred to Jacqueline that her intentions could be so misunderstood, and she didn't know what to say to fix it. It felt irreparable.

All the more reason to begin exploring who would carry her children next, she thought. Perhaps this time, they should know who their mother was. That might instill a better sense of belonging. Of gratitude, even.

When Jacqueline returned to her room, she pulled up the medical files of every childbearing woman Inside and began to search for the ones who were most similar to her. When she had fifteen profiles that fit the bill, she sent them to the woman who ran the IUI center. Let's talk tomorrow, she wrote. I have thoughts.

42

JULY SAT ON THE FLOOR IN THE CORNER OF A ROOM FILLED
with pink couches and white fur, trying to make herself as small as possible. She had spent the past hour dry-heaving over the toilet as her body
tried to adjust to the feeling of the space shuttle, and her mind tried to
adjust to the information she was given: that she hadn't actually been kid-
napped, she was being saved; that the hands that lifted her out of her bed
and carried her up into the darkness weren't trying to hurt her, they were
trying to help.

Out of every lie July had ever been told, this one felt the most glaring.

It occurred to her that she surely must be dreaming. There was no way
something so strange was actually happening. She closed her eyes tightly,
trying to force herself to wake up. But she couldn't. Nor could she stop
thinking about the feeling of strange hands on her body, the shock of having
absolutely no control as they removed her from her bed.

Her pale-pink sheet had clung to her foot until finally it fell, floating
downward and then landing silently on the bed that was getting farther and
farther away.

And now, the horror of meeting Jacqueline, and realizing how extensive
her control and influence ran. The food of Inside was so specific. She remembered a lifetime of meals from a beeping vending machine, meals that
were always fresh, with vegetables picked by people she knew. She knew
many of the adults based on which vegetable or fruit they were responsible for. In fact, looking at the plate Jacqueline was holding, she had clearly
imagined their faces, their hands. Their smells. And now their food, so many
miles from home.

This woman on the other side of the door was not her mother, no matter how many times she insisted. She barely even looked like the Jacqueline Millender in the book jacket photo. Only her platinum-white bob was the same, though July now realized it was clearly a wig.

July eventually got up from the floor and made her way to the bed. Pulling the covers up over her face, July thought about Brook and wondered how long it had taken her friend to notice she was gone. She wished she had a way to reach her, to tell her that she was okay. But, was she actually okay? She didn't know. She didn't feel okay. The only thing she knew for sure was that she was alive. She didn't know where the lies ended, and reality began.

Unless her entire life had really been a lie, which, as she stared out into the sparkling black abyss, was feeling more and more likely. She thought of the feeling that she was always being watched and how she'd written it off as her own narcissism. She thought of the women with clipboards who would swoop down out of nowhere when she was a kid and got hurt playing. She thought of all the digital check-ins, the doctors' appointments; even her food was measured by the vending machine that it came out of. Had her whole existence been simply a test of a theory? And what did that say about her own free will? What was the point of her hopes, dreams, fears?

She was the daughter of the person in charge, but she hadn't benefited from it at all. Instead, she was a hostage.

July slept, hard. She woke up. She ate a little. She did push-ups. She slept some more. She pressed her face to the window. She bit her nails down to the pink, sensitive quick.

She began to feel as though the walls were closing in on her. The next time Jacqueline came to check on her, July was so desperate to leave the room that she decided to try to be nice.

"Hi," she said, opening the door. She tried to smile, but the corners of her mouth remained firmly planted downward.

"Hi," Jacqueline said back.

"Can I see the rest of the ship?" July asked.

Jacqueline looked surprised. "You want me to show you?"

"Sure," July said. "You can. Or whoever. I'm just going a little stir-crazy in here."

"I certainly understand that," Jacqueline said. "Let me give you a tour."

"Now?"

"Why not?"

July took a step out of her room. She and Jacqueline were the same height, which made Jacqueline's intense eye contact all the more disarming. Still, July could sense a shift in their dynamic. Jacqueline seemed to just want to please her. This wasn't all that different from how the administrators of Inside treated her.

"Come," Jacqueline said, and July walked next to her down the hall. Jacqueline took her to a large open area where people milled about, gathering at tables or doing yoga. July had never seen people dressed in anything other than Inside's mauve tunics.

"What are they wearing?"

Jacqueline laughed. "Their clothes, I suppose," she said. "We all brought our own things."

"You own things?" July asked, confused. She didn't own anything besides her tablet, which was long gone. She missed its constant warm weight in her hands.

Jacqueline put a cold, bony hand on July's arm. "You'll get used to it," she said.

A tall woman in a loose-fitting black dress walked by. She glanced at July, and then at Jacqueline. She looked to be the same age as Ava. July recognized some maternal warmth in her, too; the look she gave July was full of concern.

"Shelby," Jacqueline said. "Stop walking away. Come say hello."

The woman paused. "Hello," she said to July, and July noticed Jacqueline didn't tell Shelby her name. She wondered if it was strange for Shelby to see someone new aboard the ship. It must be, but the woman's face didn't give away confusion, if she felt it.

"It's nice to see you," Jacqueline said, though July wondered from the ice in her voice if that was true. "You should come around soon."

Shelby nodded, her eyes darting back and forth between Jacqueline and July. Then she was gone.

"She seemed nice," July said, as Jacqueline guided her out of the open area and back to the hallway.

"That's a good way of putting it," Jacqueline said. "Soon you will learn that lots of people seem nice. But that doesn't mean they are good for you."

Jacqueline took July back to her room. "I hope that was satisfying," she said, lingering in the doorway. "Maybe tomorrow I can take you to the spa."

"I'd like that," July said, though of course she didn't mean it. The only thing she would like was to go home and never see Jacqueline again.

Jacqueline suddenly lunged at July and pulled her into a tight hug. July's soft chest mashed against Jacqueline's bony one. "Ow," July said.

"I'm sorry I don't have an ample bosom to cuddle you in," Jacqueline said, her words dripping in sarcasm, though she continued to clutch July to her. "I had a double mastectomy. Breast cancer. Want to see?"

"No," July said. "Please." It was hard to breathe with Jacqueline's wiry arms wrapped so tightly around her.

"I didn't have reconstructive surgery because I like how much thinner I look without breasts," Jacqueline said. "Is that awful? You must think I'm awful."

July wrenched herself out of Jacqueline's grip. "I don't think you're awful," she lied.

A few hours later, there was a quiet knock on her door, so soft she knew it couldn't have been Jacqueline, who tended to bang on it so loudly it made July jump.

July crept to the door. "Hello?"

"July," a voice whispered. "It's Shelby. Please let me in."

July did as she was told, and Shelby stepped into her quarters. She immediately began to look around, checking the corners of the room.

"How did you know my name? What are you looking for?" July asked.

"Cameras," Shelby said. "But I don't see any. Have you noticed anything?"

"No," July said. "But I wasn't looking."

"Before we speak, let's just check together."

July got on her hands and knees to look under the bed while Shelby searched the bathroom. "I think it's clear," Shelby said, and then her face relaxed. "July, I'm so sorry for what has happened to you."

It was the first time July had heard anyone say something that sounded earnest since she'd been pulled from bed, and she immediately softened. Shelby was clearly someone she could trust. She held back tears. "I don't know what I'm supposed to do," she said. "Everything was a lie."

"I know," Shelby said.

They sat on July's bed, and Shelby took one of July's hands into both of hers, pressing into it warmly. "You were always part of their plan," Shelby said.

"She told me," July said. "She told me everything."

"I . . ." Shelby paused. "I highly doubt she told you everything."

"What else could there possibly be?" July's huge eyes were wide and unblinking.

"Round-the-clock surveillance." Shelby began ticking things off on her fingers. "They were drugging you. It broke more laws than I can think of that she didn't accept any men in the first place. And I think if it was up to Jacqueline, that would only be the beginning. She made it so that the population relies solely on her and her ideas. And . . . she's having the administrators look into new surrogates. I think she's planning on having more daughters. I mean, on forcing more people to have them for her. Like she did with you."

July blinked. She could only hold on to so much of this information. She had so many questions, and no idea where to start. "They were drugging us?" she asked.

Shelby nodded.

"Why?"

"Mind control. They needed you to forget certain things."

"Like what?"

Shelby looked at the wall for a long time before speaking. "Ellery," she said.

"Who?" July asked.

Shelby paused. "The boy who died."

A sob rose in July's throat. "Oh my god," she said. "I did forget."

She began to cry into her hands. The grief she'd felt upon finding out that he was dead came rushing back. She barely even had real memories of him, just things she'd wished she had the courage to say, moments she hadn't taken advantage of. She didn't even really know him, and now she never would.

July felt angry then. There were so many things she'd loved about her home, but there was no denying it now: Inside was evil. No—she stopped herself. Jacqueline was evil. Inside had good things about it. July held very still while this flood of feelings and ideas washed over her. Shelby was waiting for her to speak. Finally, July said, "We need to tell people. They need to know what she's done."

"I know," Shelby said.

"But . . ." July paused. "There are also good people there. I don't want them to get in trouble. Can we report her and leave everyone else alone?"

Shelby drummed her fingers on her knee. "I don't know," she said. "I think everyone who works for Jacqueline might be implicated. But maybe they deserve to be. They carried this out for her, after all."

"I don't know if that's true," July said. "Maybe Jacqueline is the whole problem. Maybe if she's gone, it would give everyone a chance to do the right thing." July closed her eyes and revisited a montage of happy memories; tender moments with Brook, with Ava. Pink walls and soft beds. Ellery's sheepish smile as their eyes briefly met. A ceiling covered in bright blue HD. People holding hands in a circle, singing a song she often heard in her dreams. She wanted to protect it.

"Who do you want to tell?" Shelby said, giving in quickly to July, as July knew she would. "You can use my email to reach the administrators. Jacqueline won't know."

"I want to tell everyone," July said. "But I need to talk to Olympia first."

43

THEIR RELATIONSHIP WAS A SECRET. IT HAD TO BE. OLYMPIA
didn't know what the repercussions would be for being intimate with one
of the residents—one of her patients, no less. But Olympia also knew that
it was foolish that none of them had thought to factor this possibility into
their plans. They were all human, she thought. Their jobs didn't mean they
needed less. She suspected she wasn't the first to transgress this boundary.

Inside's new rules and regulations made seeing each other tricky. It was
hard to have to always account for their whereabouts when most of their
free time was spent with each other. But they got good at lying. And Olympia showed Ava how to turn the camera on her tablet off when they were
together. That meant, of course, that Olympia also had to tell Ava about the
level of surveillance they were under, but Ava didn't seem all that surprised.

"I think I've probably always known that," Ava said. "And right now I'm
too happy to care."

Olympia beamed. She could, perhaps someday, tell Ava the full truth
about what went on Inside. It seemed that Ava might not mind. And then,
once Ava knew everything, Olympia could let the last of her guard down
and be herself.

That their love was born of opposing feelings—Olympia's crushing loneliness and the self-confidence Ava had finally found thanks to long-term
happiness—wasn't lost on Olympia, and sometimes she worried about it.
There would come a time, she was certain, when Ava would grow tired of
her; tired of filling this void. She'd likely start to desire someone whose joy
matched her own. But until that happened, Olympia vowed to let herself
enjoy it.

A few weeks later, Olympia was at her computer looking at some blood-work results when Ava knocked on the door and then let herself in. "Hey." Olympia grinned, but then noticed that Ava looked distraught, and changed her tone.

"What?" she said, turning her computer off. "What's wrong?"

Ava said, "July is . . . She's gone."

Olympia tried to make her face as neutral as possible. "What?"

"Brook couldn't find her, and said the skylight in her room was open? Do you know why she has a skylight?"

Olympia knew that this wasn't a simple matter of July wandering off. The skylight could only be opened from the outside. Beyond that, it could really only be reached if someone were to descend in a helicopter or another air-borne machine—there was no way someone had scaled Inside and actually opened July's window. She immediately understood her disappearance: Jac-queline was the only one who could have orchestrated it. But what Olympia didn't understand was why it had happened now.

"Shit," Olympia whispered. "Hold on."

She opened her laptop. There was already a message from Jacqueline waiting for her: Don't look for her, it read, as ominously brief as the first message Olympia had ever gotten from Jacqueline. She's with me.

"What's going on?" Ava asked, from the other side of the screen. Olympia knew she shouldn't tell Ava anything, but she had long ago abandoned the various shoulds and should nots of their world.

She remembered the first time she'd met Ava in her office the day the residents arrived; how her insides had melted at how nervous and alone Ava seemed. How she'd cared for her and also wronged her, manipulating her into pregnancy at Jacqueline's behest, and then how Ava had overcome it all, as Olympia always knew she could.

Olympia was proud of Ava, but more than that, she respected her. She didn't pity her anymore. And because of that, she decided to tell her the truth.

"There are some things you need to know," she said, closing the computer, and Ava sat down, waiting.

Olympia looked at the ceiling as though the way to tell the story might be written there. But it wasn't. There was only her memory and she was the only one who could pull a narrative from the strange events of the past twenty-some years. "July is fine," she said.

"How do you know?"

"She's not who you think she is."

Ava was silent, waiting. But when Olympia continued to hesitate, she said, "Okay, what does that mean?"

"She's . . ." Saying the words out loud would make them true; would make the betrayal real. "She's Jacqueline Millender's daughter."

Ava laughed, as though Olympia was kidding. "How is that even possible?"

"She was born from a surrogate here," Olympia said. She had lifted a screaming, just-born July from Ava with her own two hands, though this she would never say.

"I'm sorry, what? That's . . . insane," Ava said.

"I know how it sounds." Olympia nodded.

"Who was the surrogate?" This was the question Olympia had been waiting for Ava to ask, and for a moment she thought she might throw up.

Olympia picked at her nails and looked back at the ceiling as she tried to figure out what to say. But in her silence, Ava heard the truth.

"Oh, fuck. It was *me*?"

"I'm so sorry, Ava," Olympia said, finally meeting her eyes. "She wanted it to be me. But in the end it was you."

"How?"

"You had twins," Olympia said.

"I carried her and Brook together? Why didn't you let me raise her from birth?" There was a small tremble in Ava's voice, but Olympia knew it was anger, not fear. Ava's hands drifted to the place on her hips where her stretch marks were the densest.

Olympia felt her stomach lurch with guilt. "Jacqueline didn't want you to. I think she was jealous. She couldn't stand the thought of someone else being July's mother. But in the end it seems July wanted you anyway. Not even Jacqueline could keep you apart."

"I can't believe you've been lying to me all these years."

"Lying by omission, yes," Olympia said. "I'm so sorry."

"And I can't believe she *made* you lie to me! What the fuck kind of place is this?"

"It's still your home," Olympia said. "You still belong here. Jacqueline and I have a lot we don't agree on."

"It's one thing that you've been spying on us. It's another thing that she forced me to carry her baby." Ava's neck was turning red and splotchy.

"I know," Olympia said. "Believe me, I know. That's not even the worst of it."

Ava's fists were clenched. "Tell me," she said.

"She wanted to make it so that people could only have girls moving forward."

"I don't understand," Ava said.

"She wanted us to interfere with the IVF and only implant people with female embryos. This whole thing was an experiment to her. She thinks that how well July did Inside means that all girls are superior."

"Obviously it's more complicated than that," Ava said.

"I know," she said. "I put my foot down about that one."

"But not about other things?"

"I can only say no to so much," Olympia said, and for the first time in a long time she thought she might cry. She was so tired of pushing back, of being the sole force standing between Jacqueline and total domination.

"Is she going to force more people to have her children?" Ava asked.

Olympia sighed. "Yes. That's exactly what she wants to do. We've been fighting about it for weeks. When I said no to her psychotic plan to only allow girls to be born, that was the new conclusion she arrived at. She thinks it's a compromise. She wants to fill Inside with a bunch of little Jacquelines. And I bet she won't give the parents a choice this time, either."

Ava looked like she might flip the table. Olympia kept talking. "It would be problematic on a number of levels. Like a lot of things here. But the problems weren't obvious to me in the beginning. Or at least they didn't seem like that big of a deal at the time. I guess I thought I could change her mind."

"You might as well tell me everything," Ava said.

"You're probably right," Olympia said.

Ava nodded, her fists still clenched in her lap. "Please."

Once the words started pouring out of her mouth, she couldn't hold anything back. "I wanted to help create a feminist world. *Not* a women-only space, but really a place founded on the principles of feminism. A place that would be truly equal, where people would honor each other and the earth, and we could reverse climate change and prevent war and hunger once and for all. We had to start without men because they've proven they'll never fully understand equality. It's their fault the UWG even had to develop the Inside program in the first place. And I think that it could have worked. But Jacqueline's fucked-up politics got in the way. I don't think she necessarily understands what equality means, either. There are too many secrets here. The administrators have so much power and the residents just do what they're told. We decide everything for people. Who are we to tell you what job you're best suited for, or where to live, or who to eat with? Who are we to tell you when to have children and how? It's too policed. When people didn't comply, she had us drug them through the ventilation system. We didn't give anyone freedom. And now Jacqueline is still prioritizing the people who are most similar to her. And in the absence of people on her side, she's going to *make more people who would be.*"

She put her head down on the desk. She was exhausted by the truth. "I don't think we should have done any of it," she said. "Jacqueline never should have been allowed to hand-select a population for survival. I know I enabled her. We could have probably achieved our goals without omitting men if we'd just thought about it harder. But she was so convincing."

She waited for Ava's anger, but it didn't come.

"I think you're being hard on yourself," Ava said, quietly. "Up until you told me all this, I was happy here. It was working for me."

"I appreciate that," Olympia said into the cool metal of her desk. "But your life isn't what you wanted."

"Is it not?"

Olympia lifted her head up. "If you remember, you didn't want kids. I know you love them, but we didn't really give you a choice. And you didn't want to work in the gardens, not after Brook moved out. You wanted to be a science teacher. We didn't let you. And we picked where you live. We picked your friends. We picked where you go at night so we could study it. We took everything you ever wanted away from you. We took your freedom. We altered your perception with drugs you didn't know you were taking. The only thing that wasn't forced on you was . . . well, I guess me."

"Oh," Ava said, the gentleness gone from her voice. "When you put it that way."

"Right." Olympia exhaled.

Ava's face was contorted with grief and confusion, her eyes squinting at Olympia, mouth hanging open. "So where is July?" Ava demanded. "Do you know?"

Olympia answered, "She's with Jacqueline."

"What? Doesn't Jacqueline live on the space shuttle?"

Olympia could hardly look at Ava. "She once said that if things weren't going well Inside, she could find a way to retrieve July. It was always baked into the plan—a fail-safe to make sure Inside's most precious daughter wouldn't be in danger."

"She and Brook imagined they could leave, if they wanted to," Ava said. "Could that be why Jacqueline took her?"

"Maybe," Olympia said, the puzzle pieces starting to come together. Jacqueline would never stand idly by while July tried to escape Inside. Her ego wouldn't allow it.

44

AVA WENT BACK TO HER APARTMENT AND FOUND BROOK
sitting on her old bed, her knees pulled toward her chest. She looked younger
than her twenty-two years. When Ava was that age, she was completely on
her own. Brook had never done anything on her own in her life. It made her
seem like a child, and the urge to protect her was overwhelming. The urge
to protect July was, too. But that was impossible. There was probably nothing she could do for July, her second daughter.

"Did you find her?" Brook said.

"Kind of," Ava replied, and sat down at the edge of the bed, sinking into
the memory foam and, for a moment, losing her balance. "July is with her
mother," she said, once she steadied herself.

"But you're her mother," Brook said.

"That is truer than I can explain right now," Ava said.

"What does that mean?" Brook said.

Ava brushed it off. She wasn't ready for this conversation, not with Brook.
It hurt too much. "Do you remember when you learned about Jacqueline
Millender in school?"

"What does that have to do with anything?" Brook demanded. "Where
is July? Is she okay?"

"Jacqueline Millender is July's mother," she said. "She's brought July to
live with her on the space shuttle."

"What? No. That's awful. She must be so scared," Brook said.

"I'm sure she's fine," Ava said, trying to keep her tone light. "She's in space!"

"This wasn't the plan," Brook said. "Why are you talking to me like I'm
a baby?"

"Sorry," Ava said. "I didn't mean to. This is hard to talk about."

Brook put her hands over her face and began to weep. "Is she coming back?"

Ava bit the sides of her cheeks to keep from crying, too, and put a hand on Brook's knee. "I don't know."

"Why do you seem so okay with this?" Brook said.

"I'm not," Ava said. "Believe me, I'm not."

"This is the worst thing that's ever happened to me," Brook said. "We have to get her back."

"I don't know if we can. Her mother is very powerful. This is way bigger than us now."

They were quiet for a few moments but for the sound of Brook's small sobs.

Finally, Ava said, "Hey. How exactly were you planning on leaving? You know there's no way out."

But Brook wouldn't answer, and after a few moments of silence Ava left her there. Seeing her in so much pain was too much to bear.

Ava got into her own bed, but she didn't go to sleep for a long time. Instead, she pulled up the map on her tablet, studying it closely for what felt like hours. She was looking to see if the door through which she'd first entered Inside was still there. It had to be. But it wasn't noted on the map. She remembered having stepped directly into the medical center, but she'd never seen that door again. Maybe they had boarded it up. Or maybe it only opened one way.

Ava had been hurt that her daughters wanted to leave, but the hurt was quickly fading, replaced by a new thought: Maybe Brook and July were right to want to. Perhaps staying put was the dangerous option.

45

OUTSIDE OF THE CIRCULAR WINDOW BY HER BED, SHELBY could see the huge blue curve of the earth, the weather patterns that swirled white over its surface. Somewhere down there, people clothed in mauve linen were enjoying the benefits of separatism, unaware of what had been sacrificed for them.

Not knowing what else to do, she took out her old off-grid radio and turned it on. One twist of the dial and her room immediately filled with the screams of static from Earth. She turned the dial gently until the noise leveled out, and then she pressed the button that would call the device that this one connected to.

It beeped, loudly. There was no answer for a few minutes. She tried again.

Finally: "Shelby?" A voice that sounded like it was from a dream.

"Dad."

"Shelby, I can't really hear you."

It had only been a few months since they'd spoken, but he sounded years older, like there were cracks in his voice. She'd give anything to see his face; to see how the years in the sun had aged him. A sob escaped her mouth, and she tried her best to muffle it.

"Sorry, I was just catching my breath. It's so good to hear your voice."

"Shelby. Are you okay?"

"I'm not okay," she said. "I think something really bad is happening."

"Bad things are always happening."

"Jacqueline lied to everyone," she said. "I think she wants to start a war with the other Insides. I'm really scared for the people there. And for me, up here. Now that I know what she's done I have to turn her in. But I'm not sure what happens after that."

She'd left everyone who'd ever loved her behind, and she was all alone to face this. She heard the birds chirping in the background and she started crying again.

"Shelby," her father said. "Do you know about the Overview Effect?"

"Tell me."

"When people first started going to space, they realized that seeing Earth from such a distance shifted their perspectives. They could see for the first time that the planet in the context of the universe is fragile and vulnerable, but also that everything on it is interconnected. They called it the Overview Effect. It made some of them religious. Others became climate activists. No one went to space without profound changes in how they saw things."

"I think I've felt some of that," she said, looking out the window at the small blue planet and the smattering of stars and galaxies around it.

"It sounds like you have," he said. "It sounds like things are more fragile and more connected than any of us realize."

Shelby's vision once again blurred with tears. "I love you, Dad," she said.

He sneezed several times in a row, a horrible, phlegmy sound.

"That doesn't sound good."

"Give an old man a break."

"Take care of yourself, please," she said. "Or at least make Camilla take care of you."

"Oh, she does," he said. "She takes care of everyone around here."

PART TEN

YOU KNOW WHERE IT IS
2078

46

OLYMPIA COULDN'T QUITE REMEMBER WHEN EXACTLY, OVER
the years, she had transformed from a loyal employee to a suspicious one.

She wondered how the rest of Jacqueline's team felt. Most of them were younger than Olympia—they'd all been in college when Jacqueline found them, while Olympia had been in her final year of medical school. Olympia was starting to realize it was no coincidence that so many of Inside's employees had been hired as university students to serve the cause. Jacqueline struck when minds were malleable, when idealism ran high and people could be convinced that they were part of something bigger than themselves.

They hadn't really been *hired*. They'd been recruited.

Olympia was at her computer when an email from Jacqueline's assistant came through. *Shelby*, she thought. She hadn't heard that name in years.

But when she opened it, what she found was not from Shelby at all.

Dear Olympia,
Hi. It's July. I'm okay. I wanted to tell you that I'm going to tell people what's going on Inside. Shelby and I are. We're going to tell them everything, starting with the way it was designed, to how Jacqueline has kept us complacent against our will. I don't know what it will mean for you and for everyone, but I thought you should know. We're reporting her to the UWG. I'm sure there will be repercussions. You deserve a heads-up.

Olympia realized she was holding her breath, and she forced herself to inhale before she kept reading.

I obviously can't reach Brook or Ava directly, since you guys never let us have access to email. But please tell them I love them, and I'm sorry it had to come to this. It's for their own good. They're the most important people in the world to me. Please tell them that.

Also—Shelby wants me to tell you this—Jacqueline is the one who doxed you. She put your phone number on a men's rights forum (what even is that? Sorry) after your article came out. She made it so you'd have to say yes to the job (I have no idea what this means but she's insisting I include it). Also—she said she thinks Jacqueline might be planning to start a war with the other Insides. Or at least try to kill the people who live there. We don't know the details, but Shelby saw some weird stuff in J's email. Okay, thanks. Please do the right thing.

Olympia wiped sweat from her upper lip on the back of her hand, and then dried her hand on her linen pants. Of course Jacqueline had fucking doxed her. That's why the timing was so perfect. Jacqueline had orchestrated the whole thing. Just like everything Inside.

As though in a dream, Olympia found herself wandering into the surveillance room. If there was anything good left, she wanted to remind herself of it; wanted to see the administrators of Inside keeping the residents safe.

But when she unlocked the door to the surveillance room, she found it was empty. Perhaps with July gone, there was nothing for them to watch. She stared at the high-definition screens, broadcasting live feeds from the tablets. The residents slept peacefully in their beds, oblivious.

Olympia thought about Ava then. It had been a gamble to tell her the truth, but if they were to have a real relationship, it was the only option. Olympia was so scared of losing her.

She left the surveillance room still thinking of Ava, and, so lost in thought, she forgot to lock the door behind her.

She went back to her quarters. It took her hours to fall asleep, and when she finally did, she dreamed her teeth were falling out.

47

EARLY THE NEXT MORNING, BROOK WOKE UP BEFORE AVA, who was fast asleep with all the covers pulled over her head. The sheets were the same pale-rose hue that they'd always been, the walls as shining and white as in Brook's earliest memories. But the familiar no longer felt like comfort, not now that she knew the truth about July. She dressed quietly and left the apartment, the door barely making a click as it closed.

She and July had never solved the mystery of what had happened to Ellery; at a certain point it was as though July just didn't want to think about it anymore, and they'd given up. Brook didn't understand how July had moved on so quickly, though. There were admittedly moments when she, too, felt his memory fading, but she'd always be pulled back into reality by the vision of his slackened face that morning she found him.

Her feet took her toward the place where Ellery had worked before she even made a conscious decision to go there. If there were answers, surely they began there.

Her canvas shoes were silent on the shiny concrete. Most people would wake up within the next hour and eat breakfast before reporting to their workstations, but for now the sidewalks and tunnels were silent. Little pink lights glowed along the floor, illuminating the way. She held her arm out while she walked, trailing her fingers along the walls, counting corners as she turned them. *Fifteen, sixteen, seventeen, eighteen.* It was so pretty here, especially in the morning. But now, it was hard to reconcile familiarity with her home and her suspicions of it.

When Brook got to the computer department, she walked straight back to the room where Ellery had worked. The room that was always locked. On a whim, she tried the handle; it didn't turn.

It was stupid to think that it would be open. But as she turned and walked back down the hallway, she saw that a different door, one she hadn't noticed, was slightly ajar. A blue light was pulsing from within whatever lay beyond. Adrenaline surged through her, and she had the strange sensation that she was floating above herself, watching herself push the door all the way open.

The room was enormous, and every bit of wall was covered in screens. On the screens were videos of rooms, of people sleeping, of the halls that they'd soon be walking through.

Brook did not have the words to describe what she was looking at, but she immediately understood. They were being watched. They had always been watched.

Brook supposed it made sense. She thought of the cameras in the tablets, which were allegedly recycled from a different life, where people were obsessed with creating images of themselves, and had used those images to define their lives, and even to meet one another. The cameras had no place in Inside's culture. At least, not Inside as she had previously understood it.

Now, Brook could see that she had just believed what she wanted to believe. She had listened to what made the most sense at the time, not to the little voice in her head telling her what was true. She vowed to never make that mistake again.

Brook's vision blurred with hot, angry tears that she furiously wiped away. Looking at the screens that loomed around her and thinking of all the Inside employees who must have known that this was happening, and gone along with it, she thought of the lessons they'd learned in school about all the times men had posed as gurus and brainwashed groups of people and led them to their death. *Jacqueline Millender is leading a cult*, she thought.

She fled the room and ran back through the long glass tunnel between buildings. She knew the way so well that she could have run with her eyes closed. Instead, she had the feeling she was seeing it for the first time.

She ran back to Ava's apartment to wake her up, but it was empty.

She turned on her heel and made her way toward the places she thought Ava might be. Her mother needed to know what was going on.

Brook checked her desk near the gardens. Her favorite breakfast spot, and the library. She ran into someone she knew was friends with her mother, and Brook, now breathless, asked if she'd seen her. The woman pointed toward the medical center, and off she raced, bursting into Olympia's office.

Ava and Olympia sat across from each other at Olympia's desk, holding hands. Brook immediately understood. Her mother had, finally, found love. But there was no time to ask her about it, not now.

"What is going on?" Brook cried, still out of breath. "You've been watching us?"

"Don't speak to her like that," Ava said.

"I'm sorry," Brook said, shaking her head, blood rushing to her face. "But come on! This is insane! Is this why July is gone? Were you spying on us?"

Olympia held up her long, thin hands, signaling for the family to stop shouting over each other.

"We have a larger problem," she said.

48

"COME LOOK AT THIS," OLYMPIA SAID. SHE TURNED HER SCREEN to face Brook and Ava.

"What?" Brook and Ava said at the same time.

"It seems July is going to report Jacqueline to the UWG."

Brook folded her arms across her chest. "Good," she said.

As Ava read the email from July, she remembered when she found out she'd been accepted to Inside so many years ago—that fateful tram ride, all the devastated people around her, the people who had dared to dream for a better future for themselves and had been told no. So many people lied to, she thought. So many people promised hope when they never stood a chance. How many people had applied? Hundreds of millions. And of them, how many survived?

She had no idea what was happening in the outside world. Her life Inside had been rich enough that she'd even stopped being curious about anything else. And even though, deep in the darkest shadows of her brain, she had known there was something off about the whole thing, she had come to believe in it anyway. She'd brushed off her doubts because it was working. She'd felt their society was already more just than outside ever could have been, and not even that much time had passed. But now that she knew what had been sacrificed, "just" didn't feel like a word that could apply.

So she nodded, and put her hand on Brook's shoulder. "I do think this is good," she said. "Olympia, do you not agree? After everything you told me yesterday? And after this email? What does it even mean that Jacqueline is going to start a war? How could she do that from space?" She tried to soften the anger in her voice, but she couldn't. Olympia had betrayed her, in so many ways, for such a long time.

"I don't know what it means," Olympia said. "It's certainly scary. But I also don't know what would happen to us if Jacqueline was found out. We might all be dragged down with her."

A cold sweat was beginning to run down Ava's back. "Well, you did commit crimes," she said. "Against all of us. Against me."

Olympia looked like her heart was breaking. "I'm so sorry, Ava."

Ava dismissed the apology. "It seems like the government needs to know what Jacqueline has done, and what she might be planning to do."

"So what happens if they do find out?" Brook asked. "What does it mean for us?"

"It could mean any number of things." Olympia sounded more anxious than Ava had ever heard her. "The UWG will probably send the military. My best guess is they'll arrest everyone who works for Jacqueline, and then break the population up, interspersing it with people from other Insides until our makeup looks more like theirs. They might force some of us to live outside, and bring some outsiders in, to rightsize what Jacqueline has done." She cleared her throat and looked at her hands folded tightly in her lap. "What *we* have done."

Ava felt a rush of sympathy for Olympia. Despite her anger, she didn't want anything bad to happen to her. "So, let's say that doesn't happen," she said. "Let's say we ask July *not* to report Jacqueline. What can *we* do to change things?"

"We can get rid of the surveillance," Brook said. "I will personally volunteer to smash all those screens."

Ava laughed, proud of Brook's tenacity. "That would be a good start."

"No more drugs in the air vents," Olympia said. Ava watched Brook's confusion and made a mental note to explain it to her later.

"That's all well and good," Ava said. "But we still need Jacqueline arrested. There's nothing we can do if she still has any power. After everything you told me about her, I don't trust that she wouldn't still commit some sort of horrific violence against people who don't see things her way. This isn't just about us. This is about the whole world."

Olympia nodded. "I know," she said. "I know."

"Can we write July back?" Brook asked, in a tiny voice.

Ava turned toward Brook, whose face was streaked with tears. "Oh, baby," she said. She pulled Brook toward her and held her as tightly as she could.

"Can we?" Brook asked again, her face pressed into Ava's collarbone.

Ava let her go and looked at Olympia. "Well?"

"I think we should," she said. "Let's do it together."

Dear July, Olympia started to type, with the other two looking over her shoulder. This is Olympia, Ava, and Brook. We're so glad you're okay and so sorry for what has happened to you. She paused, and then slid her keyboard to Brook. "You take a turn," she said.

Brook didn't hesitate before she began typing. We agree that you should report Jacqueline to the UWG. Don't worry about us. We'll be okay. We'll figure it out. We miss you. We can't believe you're gone. She glanced at Ava, who nodded reassuringly. Brook passed the keyboard to her.

Do everything you can to stay safe, Ava wrote. You're so important to us.

She handed the keyboard back to Olympia, who closed out the email: Please tell Shelby thank you for the information. It has certainly helped me see things clearly. I recommend that she tell the captain of the space shuttle about Jacqueline and have that person be the one to alert the UWG. They will take the complaint more seriously if it's coming from another government employee. We trust you'll be successful. We love you.

Olympia passed the keyboard to Brook. "Hit Send, and then I'm going to shut down the lines of communication with them," she said. "We need to make sure the space shuttle—and the whole UWG for that matter—can't reach us."

"Why?" Brook said, her finger hovering over the Send button.

"I don't know what's going to happen when they find out what has transpired here," Olympia said. "They might do nothing. It might not be worth it for them to get involved at this point. But I'd rather not risk it. If they can't reach us, they can't tell us what to do. This might be the best way to turn Jacqueline in without putting anyone here at risk. Unless . . ." She turned to Ava. "Unless you want to turn me in, too."

"No," Ava said, and she meant it.

"Thank you," Olympia said, looking visibly relieved. "So, in that case, it's not just the communication systems. We need to go into full lockdown."

"Okay," Brook said, and she pressed Send on the message to July.

"Are we not already in full lockdown?" Ava asked.

"Not technically, no. The food entrance is left open for the envoy to take the harvest," Olympia said.

The food entrance? Ava thought.

"We can seal it up," Olympia said, almost to herself. And then, as though this would explain everything, she said to Ava, "You know where it is. It's the only way out."

Ava realized that her brain that used to miss nothing was now just showing her what she wanted to see, believing what was most convenient for her. Like the room in the basement where she left the harvest each week. Of course it wasn't being canned or preserved or tested. Of course someone was taking it. Of course there was a purpose to the alarmed door. At some point over the course of her time Inside, she'd become complacent.

"They take it to the space shuttle?" she asked in a whisper, though she already knew the answer, and Olympia simply nodded.

Their labor in the gardens wasn't just for their community. They were feeding the rich.

"How do they get to the food entrance from outside?" she asked.

"There was one subway station left open," Olympia said. "It's all the way in New Jersey. So the shuttle envoy enters there, and they take a car along the tracks to the entrance here."

"Which station?" Ava asked.

"Some fancy suburb. Cliffside something."

"Cliffside Heights," Ava whispered. "That's where I grew up."

"Oh," Olympia said, her voice filled with compassion. She touched Ava's hand lightly, but Ava pulled it away. She was too overwhelmed to receive Olympia's kindness, because it occurred to her in that moment that a door that could let someone in was also a door that could let someone out.

She looked at Brook, who was wiping her tears on the back of her hand and barely holding it together. She looked at Olympia, who was nearly vibrating with stress, but still so beautiful, so achingly lovely in every way no matter how high her shoulders rose to her ears or how deep her frown.

And she thought of July, trapped with a madwoman claiming to be her mother. July, who didn't step into Ava's arms until she could already walk; whose infancy was spent being passed around instead of with Ava, where she belonged.

"So if we cut them off from our harvest, the space shuttle is going to run out of food," Ava said.

"Yes," Olympia said.

"And when they run out of food, they'll need to return to Earth to avoid starving."

"I don't see any other outcome," Olympia said.

"Mom?" Brook said.

Ava's mind was racing. If the shuttle was to land, that meant that July wouldn't be trapped with Jacqueline forever. July might be somewhere that Ava could get to.

Ava took Brook's hands in hers. "Do you still want to leave?" she asked.

Brook nodded, looking at the floor.

Olympia flinched. "It's really not safe out there," she said, the panic clear in her voice.

"It's not safe in here, either," Ava said.

"Mom, what's going on?" Brook asked.

"I need you to wait outside," she said, and she and Olympia held eye contact until Brook was in the hallway and the door closed.

Olympia extended her arms toward Ava, and Ava stepped into them. In that moment, because she had decided what she needed to do next, all her anger at Olympia melted away.

They held each other tightly, and Ava was afraid for a moment that she'd never be able to let go. Their stomachs pressed into each other's.

Ava tried to picture what it might be like to wake up to Olympia's face every morning for the rest of her life, to have Olympia by her side as they grew old together, to learn all there was to know about each other and be partners, be a family. To argue and make up, to become better people because of each other, to watch over Brook together. To fall deeper and deeper in love as the years went by. She couldn't imagine anything better.

But that wasn't a path she could take. Not anymore. Not knowing what she knew about what had been done to her and her children.

She pressed her nose into Olympia's slender neck and tried to memorize its smell. Salty-sweet. She tried to visualize what it was going to be like after this moment was over, when they would pull apart, when she'd have to spend the rest of her life trying to conjure the smell, the warmth, the sounds of her love. She would have nothing tangible to remember Olympia by, just the echoes of these feelings, which she knew in time would feel like a kaleidoscope of moments, blurry and just out of reach. It would feel like waking up from a dream. In a way it already did.

"I have to find her," Ava said.

Olympia clutched her more tightly. "I know."

"You could come with us."

"I want to. I want to so badly. But I can't. I have to fix what's broken here. It's my responsibility."

"I know," Ava said, clenching her jaw to keep from sobbing. "I forgive you."

"I love you more than anything in the world," Olympia said.

49

WHENEVER AND WHEREVER JULY ENDED UP, BROOK WANTED to be ready to find her.

As Brook and Ava made their way down the many flights of stairs that led to the room in the old subway tunnel, Brook thought to herself that there was an inevitability to this decision. She had inherited Inside, but she didn't want it; its victories weren't hers to celebrate. She couldn't envision a future where she felt satisfied with a life Inside, even once it had fully separated from its creators. She wanted choices. More than anything, she wanted her sister with her.

In one hand, Brook held the emergency kit from Olympia, a pink tin box with a black handle that contained flashlights, water, and some first-aid supplies. Her other hand was free, so she looped an arm around her mother's waist. Ava pulled her close and they walked as one unit, downward toward the depths of Inside.

"Do you smell that?" Brook sniffed the air. "It smells like rotting flowers," she said.

Ava laughed, though she was still crying. "I do," she said. "Though I've gotten so used to it, I don't think I've really noticed it since I first got here."

"It's how they controlled us, right? They messed with the air?"

"To some degree," Ava said. "But I don't know if they completely controlled us. I still feel like a lot of us would have chosen the life they gave us, without being forced to. After all, it gave me you."

Brook didn't know what to say back. She felt guilty. Her mother had been through so much and was willing to do it all again just so she could have been born. She should have appreciated that kind of unconditional love more. Instead, she'd been planning to abandon Ava completely. She vowed to never lose sight of her mother's love again.

Brook had never been down to the level of Inside where they were currently headed. She didn't know what to expect, but she was buoyed by Ava, whose arm was still tightly clutching her waist, and the thought of July, who was somewhere out there, waiting for her.

She didn't think about the possibility that she might want to return. The part of her life spent Inside was over, and there'd be no going back.

50

SHELBY KNEW THAT OLYMPIA WAS RIGHT: SHE AND JULY
couldn't go up against Jacqueline alone. But she also knew that in order to
get the UWG to pay attention, she'd need help. She was going to need to
start a whole movement. And she'd need to do it quickly.

She waited for the dinner hour before she made her move. The support
staff all gathered every evening to eat together. She watched them, waiting
until they were all seated, and then she climbed up on a chair. Whatever
happened next was utterly up to her.

She cleared her throat. The room quieted. "Do you have something to
say, Shelby?" someone said.

"There are things you need to know," she said. "Things about Jacqueline."

People were glancing at one another nervously. Someone coughed. She
gritted her teeth. She wouldn't lose her nerve.

She remembered the first time she'd met Jacqueline, in that huge, ornate
office so many years ago. Shelby had been an adult for all of five minutes before she was brought into Jacqueline's world. She still wondered why Jacqueline had picked her and, for a brief, fleeting moment, wondered if she should
feel guilty for what she was about to do. It was because of Jacqueline that she
was safe, after all. If Jacqueline hadn't brought her to space, she might be
dead.

But Shelby also knew this was bigger than her, and it didn't matter that
Jacqueline provided her with creature comforts. This was something she
couldn't have understood when she was young and working as Jacqueline's
assistant; her personal ambition and success had felt like empowerment on

behalf of all women. She knew now that those things were separate, that just because she was living well didn't mean any sort of equality had been reached.

"Jacqueline didn't allow any men into the North American Inside," Shelby began.

Someone in the room laughed in disbelief and was shushed by another.

"That doesn't sound so bad," someone said from the back of the room.

"Sure," Shelby said. "But she didn't just pick anyone. She picked . . ." She paused, struggling to describe what she'd read. "People that fit Jacqueline's idea of how everyone should be. People from a certain class."

The room quieted. She could tell this got their attention. The chair creaked beneath her. *Don't you dare fall*, she thought.

Steadying herself, Shelby continued, "And then she kept them drugged while she experimented with what I understand to be eugenics. She allowed a young person to die under her watch and she covered it up. She surveilled the residents without their knowledge. She wants to force the residents to have her children, and she wants them all to be girls. It's not just transphobic, it's downright fascist. And she's conspiring to take down the other Insides. She only wants people who agree with her to be left standing. There are countless other crimes against humanity that we may never know about. But she must be stopped. Today."

Shelby looked around her. The support staff looked stunned and confused. Some of them were starting to stand up and walk toward one another. She heard their murmurs.

"What are we supposed to do about it?" someone said.

"We're going to organize," she said. She felt as though she'd been preparing for this moment all of her life. In a way, she had.

"We're not going to let her get away with this." She climbed down off the chair. "Follow me."

And they did. The people who had kept the ship running for twenty years, not just the assistants but professional chefs, waitresses, engineers, workout instructors, the cleaning crew, the laundry team, the IT specialists, doctors and nurses and more, all followed Shelby out of the dining hall, up the stairs and through the corridor that took them to the secluded, nicer part of the ship where the wealthy lived. Many of them had never been to that part of the ship at all.

As they reached the hallway that led to Jacqueline's apartment, Shelby turned around, and saw July's face in the crowd.

When they reached Jacqueline's door, Shelby banged on it with a fist until Jacqueline answered, and then the fifty or so people who had served her and made her life so comfortable forced their way into her glittering pink apartment, and they surrounded her.

Shelby walked right up to Jacqueline and looked down into her face.

"Shelby," Jacqueline said, astonished. "What in the world is going on?"

"You know exactly what's going on," Shelby said. Jacqueline lowered her head. The top of her scalp was patchy.

"I know that I have behaved in a toxic manner," Jacqueline said. "But Shelby, you have to know I've always had your best intentions at heart—all of yours."

There was a sound from the back of the crowd, and the people parted until Jacqueline and Shelby could see July.

"Toxic?" July laughed. "That is not the word I'd use."

"July, I . . ."

"We know what you've done. We know everything," Shelby said, and Jacqueline was, at last, speechless.

Shelby took this as an admission of guilt; up until this moment, there was still a small part of her that hoped it wasn't true. But now that hope was extinguished. She could see Jacqueline clearly. There was nothing redeeming about the woman she'd left her family for.

The group encircled Jacqueline and walked her all the way to where the ship's captain and the security teams worked, a control room with enormous windows and a breathtaking view of the stars. They stayed surrounding Jacqueline while Shelby informed the crew of what was happening. There were so many of them crowded into the control room that only a few could hear that Jacqueline was crying. None of them cared.

The ship's captain was a top-ranking member of the UWG. Despite his status, he was at a loss for what to do. This was beyond any sort of training he'd had. Shelby, seeing the panic on his face, said, "You need to tell the other government officials."

She stayed with him while he followed her directions, and then she said, losing patience, "Now you need to call the North American Inside."

Shelby started to get excited, thinking about being back on land again. Maybe she could find her family.

But when he put the call through, he found that the lines were dead. He tried every channel, but it was no use. The Inside built on the bones of New York City had gone dark.

IN THE EARLY 2050s, IF YOU'D ASKED ANYONE WHAT JM Inc. was responsible for, the answers would probably touch on two major themes: environmental activism (everyone knew about Refillables) and a corporatized interpretation of girl power (most people had at least heard about Jacqueline's book). But I don't think many people would have been able to tell you about the roots of the company: how it got its start, or why it had so much money in the first place.

Here's the truth, as far as I've been able to deduce: the corporation JM Inc. was originally built on the backs of undocumented workers who were bused up from the border to drill holes into the earth.

James Millender, Jacqueline's grandfather, was the founding CEO in the early 2000s, and while some people of that era made their fortunes by investing in internet companies, the first JM preferred to keep things physical. He worked in hydraulic fracturing, better known then, and now, as fracking. He made a lot of money doing this, because it was a lucrative industry in general, but even more so because of the cheap, illegal labor he trafficked. Eventually, growing rich but bored of such a singular focus, he expanded into other industries, buying up smaller companies, and JM Inc. went public.

This bit of sordid history was wiped from archives, as it didn't fit the company's modern, politically correct messaging. Jacqueline herself guided the rebrand. The company's origins were forgotten. People see what they want to see.

It might appear ironic that the heiress of James Millender went on to give so much of the family wealth to Inside, a place that only existed because of climate change—a reality that had only happened because of human-led actions like fracking. It was almost as though the Millender family helped cause a problem in order to be able to solve it: Refillables, after all, were branded as environmental activism, too.

The Millenders' involvement with fracking meant they were heavily involved in the domestic oil business in general, which slowed down any sort of interest in renewable energy. And just a mere fifty years later, the Millender name became associated with forever-reusable household goods and, of all things, female empowerment. The link cannot be accidental.

Fracking is also thought to be responsible for creating the so-called "cancer belt" on the East Coast. Many believe that the drilling in the tristate area released carcinogenic chemicals into the water, causing rates of breast cancer to spike. Jacqueline, of course, was not immune, though she never spoke about the connection between her illness and her family's legacy.

I do wonder sometimes what people like James would have thought about how the world ended up. I wonder if he'd take any responsibility. Jacqueline certainly took no responsibility for the darker parts of her own legacy.

She'd spent years on the space shuttle controlling the population of people that she'd hand-selected to be part of her own personal utopia. Right and wrong melted away; there was only Jacqueline, and a feeling that the future was something to be won. Dominated, even.

She came to believe that growing a civilization to worship her was the easiest way to ensure the success for the Inside she'd funded and the corporation she'd inherited. After all, that had always been the goal—JM Inc. above all else.

Except, then there was July. July was the only thing more important to Jacqueline than the company, and that was Jacqueline's downfall. If she hadn't thought to retrieve July, she wouldn't have been thwarted; July wouldn't have turned her in, and her Inside wouldn't have closed down communication with the UWG, becoming fully separate and independent.

After that, word spread quickly. The North American Inside wasn't the only location forcing its residents to grow food for its investors; as it turned out, that's how the entire system was functioning. Once people found out about the true purpose of their labor, the Insides around the world were inspired to become fully independent as well, shutting down resource sharing with their partner shuttles. There was no need to continue growing food for the rich; their investments had already been made.

And so, running out of food, every space shuttle needed to return to Earth, and no one ever went to space again. Not in my lifetime, at least. Too many people on Earth knew what it took to keep those shuttles in the air, and to keep the people on board alive. They didn't want to spend their brief lives on this fiery planet ensuring the comfort of an elite few.

Jacqueline had wanted to secure her own future, and instead her actions led to the dismantling of the space program, the destruction of an entire class system, for better or for worse.

My goal was to remove Jacqueline from power, which we did. But we couldn't have known that ending Jacqueline's reign over Inside would mean we'd need to land.

I had complicated feelings about it. At first I thought that maybe I could find my family. But the relief I felt at the thought of returning did not last long. The place on the US-Canada border we'd launched from was gone, destroyed by tornadoes. The other shuttle landing spaces around the world were similarly wrecked by unforeseen natural disasters, and there was no one left to make the repairs.

The only safe place to land was New Zealand, which had been one of the most climate-resilient places in the world before the collapse, and I suppose after it, too.

So with nowhere else to go, all the shuttles landed in New Zealand. After weeks of negotiating, the Inside built on the bones of Auckland agreed to take all of us in, though only if the wealthy were treated exactly the same as everyone else. To those of us there as support staff, this seemed like the best option. Equality is only scary if you have to give up power to attain it.

I don't know what would have happened if Jacqueline's actions hadn't inspired such an absolutist response and we still had the option of leaving the planet. Maybe we could have come together and found a way that more people could have benefited from going to space, rather than just a select few. But we'll never know. Thanks to Jacqueline, we're stuck here, watching our only home burn. My one comfort is knowing she'll burn with it.

PART ELEVEN

YOU CAN SPEAK
A NEW TRUTH
INTO EXISTENCE

2078–

51

IN HER HUT UNDER A CANOPY OF DENSE, GREEN TREES, OR-
chid tried to pray to something—though she wasn't sure what would bring
her comfort anymore. She thought about praying to the earth itself and lay
her palm flat on the warm, damp dirt. Her fingernails were torn and dirty,
which made her feel childlike; she'd been a kid with always-dirty fingernails. Skinned knees, greasy hair, ripped clothing—she was destined for the
ragamuffin life, she thought, a word her dad had used, and she smiled at the
ground even though the memory of him made her so sad.

There'd been a terrible storm the night before, which was not unusual.
The kind of storms that had ravaged the East Coast had begun showing up
frequently here, and on nights that were the most dangerous, the hundred
or so people she lived among would crowd into the sturdiest houses, nearly
on top of one another.

Now, the sun was rising, and starting to send its long, hazy beams through
the trees, the branches rustling in the morning wind. Camilla was stirring
in her bed. Other people would wake up soon. She'd be reminded that she
wasn't, in fact, as alone as she felt.

She heard people beginning to speak quietly to one another in the hut
next to hers, and so she gathered up some things—her water bottle, and a
knife just in case—and headed west, up a hill, where there was a clearing
that overlooked the expansive forest. She sat down on a rock and thought
about how grateful she was that there was still this small slice of planet to
inhabit. The warm wind loosened a few bits of hair from her braid.

She sat on the rock for a long time, until the sun was high and hot. The
heat was worrisome. Groups of migrants that passed through had started

to express alarm that her community was so settled in an area that now felt like it was too south for long-term survival, and many told Orchid they were going to head all the way to the north, where the ice had melted and the storms were fewer.

Orchid was reluctant to leave this place, but the climate was catching up with her, and every day felt hotter than the one before it. Her community began making their own plans to migrate somewhere safer, and they were due to leave soon. Orchid, after some convincing, had agreed it was the right thing. Maybe it was time for something new, at any rate.

Her legs were starting to fall asleep, so she stood up and headed back toward the settlement. *These old bones*, she thought. Though she wasn't really that old, especially compared to some of the other people in the settlement. She was solidly middle-aged. Half her life, over. That wasn't so bad. She wondered what her second act might bring.

When she reached the row of scrap-metal houses, she found a group of people gathered around Camilla and her father.

Camilla turned toward her as she approached. "Something is happening with the North American Inside."

As Camilla told Orchid what her father had heard from his eldest daughter, Orchid relived the rejection she'd gotten from Inside so many years ago, and the cool, cleansing rush of relief when she'd been denied. The memory felt as real as the hard, cold ground beneath her feet, as real as the gold light on her face, as real as every decision that had led her to this moment.

For the first time in her life, Orchid knew exactly what she needed to do.

52

A SURGE OF ADRENALINE WAS DELAYING WHAT OLYMPIA knew would be a crushing heartbreak. Ava's decision to leave was permanent. When it finally sank in, it would feel like she'd died.

But for now, there was no time to waste. She couldn't pause to reflect on what she'd lost.

Olympia grabbed her tablet and pulled up the page that would allow her to reach the administrators. Please report to the medical center meeting room, she wrote, in a ping that would be distributed to everyone within seconds. It's urgent.

After a few minutes, the very confused administrators began to file in. There weren't enough chairs for everyone at the white marble table and so people stood, three and four deep, around it. Olympia stood quietly at the head of the table, waiting for them to settle. Her heart was pounding, but her mind felt clear.

Finally, someone said, "What is going on?"

Another, from a different corner of the room, chimed in: "I'm missing my rounds for this." The room erupted into annoyed side chatter.

Olympia held her hands up, and eventually the group quieted.

"July turned Jacqueline in," she said, and did her best to summarize the bewildering events that had transpired.

When she finished explaining, there was silence. Olympia held her breath. She had always hoped that the administrators felt similarly to her but had never been able to confirm it.

"So, what?" someone finally asked. "Are you saying you're in charge now?"

"Would you be okay with that?" she replied. "I don't want to simply take control if you don't want me to."

The person who'd asked the question nodded, and slowly, everyone in the room joined in. A slow clap started, growing louder, until the room erupted in cheers. Someone squeezed her shoulder.

"Thank you," she said, finally letting the tears start to come, but trying to smile, hoping that it would look like gratitude and not grief. They didn't need to know Ava had left, not yet.

"You were the only one of us ever brave enough to challenge her," someone else in the group said. "But we were always cheering you on."

There were nods and murmurs of agreement.

"Thank you," she said again. They waited for her to continue. "Okay, let's do this."

She knew exactly what she wanted to do. She'd been thinking about it for years, and the words rolled easily out of her mouth. "We have a lot of trust to repair. Moving forward, our goal should be transparency and consent. Nothing happens to the residents that they don't know about and agree to. Let's give them their freedom back. No more watching them."

She held up a tablet. "No more of these," she said, and placed it on the table. "We don't need them."

The quiet now felt awkward. "You can disagree openly," she said.

"How will we run things?" someone from the back said. "Everything we do is connected to the tablets."

"We'll figure it out," Olympia said. "I think it's time for some new systems, don't you?"

"But what about, like, assigning the residents jobs?" the same person asked. "How will we know who they are and where we should place them?"

"Perhaps we should see what happens when we let them choose," she replied.

There were nods, and no one else spoke up, so she continued on.

"It's not just internal comms. I'll need someone to volunteer to kill the lines of communication to the outside, so that once Jacqueline is found out, the UWG can't try to tell us what to do."

"We'll get it done," someone said.

And then someone else chimed in and said, "Perhaps we could elect leaders of subcommittees, so that not every directive is just coming from one person."

Someone else said, "More of a community-led model would be amazing."

Olympia clasped her hands together and felt a surge of pride. "Yes," she said. "I love it. Thank you for the suggestion."

There was excited chatter as the administrators turned toward one another and began to lay plans for how to adjust their work to fit the new vision.

"Let's get to it," Olympia said. "I just have one more thing to do."

When the conference room was empty, Olympia turned her tablet back on. She needed to use it a final time.

She pressed a few buttons and then, all over Inside, tablets dinged in unison.

The people grabbed the digital pads that provided the infrastructure for their lives, unsure what it meant, but sensing something important. Adults and their children, clad in mauve linen tunics and canvas shoes without laces, stopped what they were doing. Many were eating in Inside's various dining areas; others were working, tending the fields or cleaning the halls; others still were taking care of babies, their own and others. Some were still lying in bed, many alone and many more alongside another.

Olympia's face appeared on their screens.

"People of Inside," she began, "today we are declaring our independence."

Olympia told the residents as much as she thought they needed to know: that Jacqueline Millender—their investor and director—had been running Inside in a way that was no longer serving the population.

"We will no longer take our orders from someone who doesn't live like us," Olympia said.

In reality, for most of the people Inside, whose lives felt very full and satisfying, cutting off communication from Jacqueline and the space shuttle wouldn't change anything. Many of them had forgotten that orders were being given, at all. But, still, there was a sense of liberation in the air, and the residents felt glad even while not fully understanding the weight of what was happening.

When her broadcast was finished, Olympia collapsed into a chair, but not with defeat. She was exhausted by how successful and quick this transfer of power had already been. She knew she'd be good at this. And her coworkers had accepted her so quickly. It seemed they hadn't been as loyal to Jacqueline as she'd always thought. Maybe they *were* just scared of her, as her colleague had once told her.

The work was only just beginning, she knew. There were still casualties of Jacqueline's reign that needed to be addressed, metaphorically and literally. Ellery's parent Ira was still being drugged out of their mind to keep quiet about their son's death. Olympia would see to it herself that Ira would get the support they'd need to grieve. It was high on what was about to be a very long to-do list.

Alone in the conference room, Olympia finally allowed herself to wonder where Ava and Brook were. If they'd reached the outside; if the outside was safe enough to travel through; if they'd found the road that would take them all the way north to the place where they hypothesized the shuttle containing July might land. She wondered how helpful Brook was being, and then with a pang of sorrow, she thought about July. Ava's surrogate daughter might never get to know that Ava had carried her.

It wasn't only Ava who she would miss; she had come to love Brook and July, too. Maybe it was finally time to have her own children, now that she had a void to fill. That at least sounded better than a life alone. She couldn't fathom having a new lover, though. The thought was too painful.

But there was no need to think about her personal life now. She had nothing but time to mourn what had been lost. And in the immediate future, she had an Inside to run. As her former favorite writer had once put it, it was hers for the taking. And take it she did.

53

THE CAPTAIN'S VOICE CRACKLED OVER THE INTERCOM: "We're about to land in New Zealand, folks, where we've gotten confirmation that Inside will welcome us.

"Once we arrive," the captain's voice continued, "you'll be given a new place to live. Please join me in expressing gratitude to the administrators for taking us in. Let's do everything we can to make this a smooth transition."

Huge dusty tanks were waiting for them in a line when they landed. July stepped off the space shuttle and looked up. The sky was not the blue she'd expected. It was orange.

July breathed unfiltered air for the first time in her life and immediately choked, coughing and sputtering, her eyes filling with tears. The sun was blinding her. And there was a smell—the most horrible, rotten smell to ever hit her nose.

"Keep moving," Shelby said, and pulled July's hand until they were in an air-conditioned vehicle.

From the window, July watched as the wealthy filed off the space shuttle and into the tanks. They looked as shocked as she'd felt.

As they drove from the shuttle's landing place to the gates of the New Zealand Inside, they passed piles of bodies, human and animal. July turned away as quickly as she could, hot stomach acid rising in the back of her throat, before forcing herself to look back. She wanted to see the worst things in the world; she didn't want anything to scare her again.

Next to her, Shelby put a warm hand on her knee. "It's going to be okay," she said, firmly. "The worst of it has already happened."

"What's going to happen to Jacqueline?"

"She's under arrest," Shelby said. "I'm sure there will be a trial. There's got to be some sort of justice system here. She probably won't be allowed to leave her room until they decide what to do with her."

"Good," July said. *Let her feel what it's like to be trapped, powerless,* she thought, though at the same time she also felt a sliver of pity.

"What's it going to be like in there?" July asked.

"I'm not sure," Shelby said. "But we'll figure it out together."

As they approached the looming structure, July felt her stomach begin to sink. This was a world without Brook, without Ava, without anyone she knew besides Shelby. She wasn't even sure if Ava and Brook would know where she was, or that she was okay. She longed for them. They were her whole family.

But then, she felt something new taking shape inside her. Perhaps, she could have a fresh start.

Nobody needed to know her as the girl who was always being looked after and yet always alone. She wished she didn't know anything about herself, either.

In a new home, she could be whoever she wanted. She could remove Jacqueline from the story she'd tell others about herself. She could make up an entire life, in fact, and people would believe her. She could speak a new truth into existence.

Her thoughts became crowded with possibility.

54

ORCHID RAN BACK TOWARD HER LITTLE HOUSE. HER LONG
gray braid bounced violently on her back like a whip urging her to move
faster. She threw some things into her backpack, and then pulled her bike
around to the front and began filling her tires with air.

Orchid was one of the few people who knew how to enter Inside, who
knew about the door left open in the subway tunnel. She had screwed it in
place herself while a coworker held a flashlight over her shoulder. She could
still feel its cold, smooth surface on her palms, and she remembered reading the surprising instructions to leave it unlocked, even after they finished
sealing up the rest of Inside forever.

Orchid imagined sneaking into Inside through that door, somehow finding Ava, and, after a tearful reunion, leaving together, hand in hand. She
knew there were some details in the middle of the plot that needed sorting
out, but she trusted she'd figure it out when she got there.

As she pumped her tires, she looked up with a start and found Camilla
standing before her.

"Where are you going?" Camilla said.

"To do what I should have done a long time ago," Orchid said.

Camilla looked alarmed. "But we're all heading north in a few weeks."

"If I'm not back, just go without me," Orchid said. "I'm sorry. I love you."

"Say bye before you go," Camilla said, and walked away with her head
down.

Orchid didn't know what she would say to Ava when she found her—*if*
she found her. But she felt that it was finally time to fix what had gone wrong
all those years ago, when she'd chosen the ease of freedom instead of the

scariness of staying and trying to work through the parts of the relationship that made it so hard. She tried to imagine what Ava's life had turned into as she planned to save her from it. She'd known when she insisted Ava go Inside without her it would set off a chain of events that she couldn't fathom.

She pedaled her bike to where Camilla and her father were.

"I get why you're going to find her." Camilla knew everything about Ava.

"I have to."

Camilla pulled Orchid in for a tight hug. "Come back, though."

"I'll try my best." Orchid tried to wink, but a tear got stuck and momentarily blurred her vision. Camilla's dad clamped a hand on her shoulder and nodded. She nodded back and left before he could say anything.

Cycling back through the desecrated cities and towns, Orchid wondered if she'd changed at all since the last time she saw Ava. She hoped she had. So much time had gone by. For better or for worse, Orchid was finally aware.

She knew her survival on this trip was not a guarantee. There was a reason everyone had fled that part of the world. As though in a trance, she envisioned the horrific fates that might lie ahead. The deadly winds that could toss her body into the air. The hail that could crush her. The heat that might suffocate her. For the first time in her life, she wasn't soothed by thoughts of eternal slumber. She was afraid. She had something to live for.

It took her days to get to the top of the highway. The road stretched out before her, littered with cars and garbage and, she thought, ghosts. It would be a long, lonely journey south, but she was fueled by a lifetime of regret and the hope that she could be redeemed.

But, she wondered, if she reached Ava, would she be able to prevent herself from making the same mistakes? Would she actually be able to say how she was feeling, as she was feeling it, rather than hiding from things that felt hard? There was only one way to be certain, and that was to find Ava, and to try.

55

THE SECURITY GUARDS AGREED TO LET JACQUELINE KEEP her wig. Other than that, all she had were two sets of clothes, some books—including some coloring books, she fumed—and a pack of cards. None of those things were hers, though. They'd been given to her after she had watched all her possessions get tossed in a large bin and taken away. The punishment, she thought, was starting to feel out of proportion to the crime.

After her things were gone, she was taken away, too.

From her transport to the new Inside, Jacqueline thought she could see July getting taken to a tank of her own. She pressed her hand against the window of her armored vehicle but knew that nobody could see in through the tinted glass. It was for the best. She couldn't stand any more confrontations. She squinted outside at the ravaged landscape. What a waste. She'd had so many wonderful vacations here.

The rest of her journey was no better: when the tank pulled up to Inside, she was yanked out and pushed down a dirt path. Smoke filled her lungs.

"Surely there's a safer way to do this," she gasped, but the guards ignored her. The rest of the trip was a blur that, later, she'd wished she had appreciated more; long hallways and offices and rooms that she'd never see again.

When, at last, the guards brought her to a room the size of her old guest bathroom, she realized how serious things were, and she tried a different approach. "This is really no way to treat an old lady," she said to them with a sweetness she couldn't quite believe she was able to muster, but they ignored her. She tried again; if she didn't have her charm, she didn't have anything. "I should have cryogenically frozen my body and uploaded my consciousness to the cloud when I had the chance." They barely blinked.

She sat on the twin bed. It creaked.

"You'll be allowed one visitor per month," the taller of the two men said. "Otherwise, your food will be brought to you, and if you're having an emergency, ring the bell."

"That's it?"

The shorter man, raising his voice in a way that, a week ago, no one would have dared try with Jacqueline, said, "I think this is a pretty good deal for you."

"When is my trial?" Jacqueline said.

The taller man laughed, a rough, terrible sound. "Someday," he said.

No one visited Jacqueline that month. Or for the month after that or the month after that.

Jacqueline's hair grew out, gray and patchy. Her nails became yellow and gnarled. Her skin sagged and grew rough. She slept as much as she could, which sometimes wasn't at all and sometimes was for days on end.

She imagined that maybe she had died and was living in hell, but then laughed at herself. *Silly Jacqueline*, she thought. *You're not imagining that it's hell. It is hell.*

And then, quite suddenly, an angel appeared.

"Oh my god," July said, floating in the doorway, filling its frame with her light. "You look *terrible*."

"Come in," Jacqueline wheezed. "Please." She couldn't take her eyes off July. She was pretty sure that if she blinked, July would disappear.

Jacqueline sniffed the air, inhaling her daughter's cocoa butter and vanilla scent. She was really here. And she was walking toward her. July sat on the bed next to her but didn't say anything. Instead she looked at the ground, almost shyly.

Jacqueline laid her hand over July's. It was the same size as her own. Even their nail beds were the same shape, though Jacqueline's now held crusty talons while her daughter's were more like pristine seashells.

"Are you doing okay in here?" Jacqueline asked.

July nodded. "I'm happy," she said. "It was an adjustment, and I miss my family, but I like it here. They treat me like everyone else."

"And that's what you want?" Jacqueline asked.

"Yes. It's what I've always wanted. I'm nothing like you, you know," July said.

"Aren't you?" said Jacqueline, still looking at their hands. "I'm your mother."

"No, you're not. I had a mother. She was kind and selfless and she taught me everything I know about how to be a person."

Jacqueline nodded. "Maybe that's true," she said, though it pained her to admit it.

They sat quietly, fingers still interlaced, until the guard knocked to say the visit was over.

56

IN THE MOMENTS BEFORE THEY SAID GOODBYE FOREVER, Olympia said, "Wait!" and began digging through a drawer in her desk.

She pulled out the silver bracelet Ava had been wearing when she entered Inside for the very first time.

"You kept it," Ava said, astonished.

Olympia fastened it to Ava's wrist. "For a long time, I didn't know why I was holding on to it, but now I think it's because I never wanted to take anything away from you."

In that moment, if she'd had more time, and perhaps more energy, Ava could have told Olympia that the meaning of this bracelet was not what Olympia thought; that the person who originally put it on her thin wrist had been Orchid, a thousand lifetimes ago, and that wearing it again was bringing back feelings she'd spent a long time trying to forget.

Instead, she simply said, "Thank you," and then she left. Brook was waiting for her outside the office, and she took her hand.

Ava and Brook were the same height, and as they made their way toward the door that led to the outside, they easily fell into step together.

"I want to prepare you for what's going to happen next," Ava said. "The door is going to take us through an old subway tunnel. We're going to be walking for a long time underground. Longer than you'll want to be walking. It's going to be dark, wet, cold."

They reached the room at the outermost corner of Inside. Before them lay the food table that Ava herself had, earlier that week, filled with the recent gifts of the harvest.

"This is what they've been taking for the space shuttle?" Brook asked.

Ava nodded.

"Mom, I'm sorry, but how did you not realize?" She pointed at the door labeled DO NOT OPEN. ALARM WILL SOUND.

Ava cringed, embarrassed. "We see what we want to see, I guess," she said. "Let's grab as much as we can carry."

As mother and daughter scoured the piles of food for the items that would last the longest, Ava tried to remember everything she knew about the outside.

When their regulation tote bags were so full that the handles dug deep into their shoulders, Brook gave her hand a squeeze. "Now what?"

"Now we walk. We'll walk the whole tunnel. When we get to the end we'll be in a suburb," Ava said. "It's—it's where I grew up. It was so beautiful. But it will probably be completely destroyed. Actually, I don't know what it will be like." Ava wanted to explain how to find shelter and what the storms would be like, but she didn't really know. "We'll need to head north as soon as we can."

"How?" Brook said.

"There's only one highway," Ava said. "There used to be signs for it everywhere. They might not exist anymore. I have no idea what is still left."

"We'll find it," Brook said. "We can follow the stars north just like you taught me, Mom."

"Okay. Yes. Once we find it, we'll stay on the highway for as long as possible," Ava continued. "Eventually we'll get to the border, where the launch station is. Was. I don't know. But that's weeks away. When you think you can't walk anymore, we still won't even be close." This felt like a mistake, but damned if she was going to change her mind.

"We're going to be okay," Brook said. "I can feel it."

"I don't know if we'll find July," Ava said. "I do think the space shuttle will have to land, but it might not end up where it left from. I want you to prepare for that."

Brook nodded, though it was clear to Ava that never seeing July again was a reality Brook could not comprehend; it was as wild and unfamiliar as the world they were about to enter. But Brook would adjust to life unprotected by Inside. She'd have to. In time, Ava knew she would, too. Whether or not they'd ever get used to July being gone was another thing entirely. But maybe they wouldn't have to get used to it. Maybe they *would* find her. She clung to the hope. She had no other option.

Ava used a soldering iron around the edges of the door to seal it to the frame. Her face was wet with tears. She hardly noticed the sparks flying dangerously close to her hair. She paused only to wipe her cheek with the linen sleeve of her tunic.

When the door was welded shut, she dropped the tool to the ground, and it landed with a loud, damp thud.

"Let's go," she said.

As they made their way underground from what was once Manhattan to the coast of New Jersey, Ava relived her last moments with Olympia. She'd miss her forever.

She tried to hide her anguish from Brook, but it wasn't possible. Brook walked quietly next to her, bearing witness. In fact, it almost seemed as though Brook actually *wanted* to be there for her. She was still the mother, but Brook was becoming something more than her daughter. Brook was her equal.

Ava realized this meant that Brook loved her regardless of what she had to give back, which, in this moment, was very little, and it was through this consistency that it occurred to Ava for the first time in her life that her value was not measured by what she could do for someone else.

Perhaps, she thought, it was possible that Brook wanted to leave because she'd been loved enough to understand that she deserved more than what Inside had to offer her. Enough to know that the system that worked for her mother did not have to be the system that worked for her. Ava had imbued Brook with a strength of spirit that she herself didn't have until much later in her life.

But that story, the one she'd always told herself, wasn't exactly true. She was always strong; she had always carved out a space for herself when what was laid out for her didn't work. She had left home as a young kid when she didn't get the love she needed. And she had successfully applied to Inside, and gone, even though she went in alone. No, Ava hadn't been the passive, attention-starved child she'd judged herself to be: she'd been someone who was able to identify the things she lacked and had always sought to remedy that lack in whatever way she could. And she'd passed that quality on to her daughter. Both her daughters: July was also strong, wherever she was.

At the end of the tunnel, they reached a flight of stairs. At the top of it, a blinding light.

As she suspected, the suburb where Ava grew up was gone, and in its place, only ruin. Wild green vines clutched at the skeletons of houses that hadn't crumbled into the sea, and even though it was a frightening sight, it was also beautiful, because it meant that here, things could still grow.

The heat was so intense Ava could feel her skin begin to singe. She and Brook huddled together against the wind and the sun, plodding onward. Their canvas shoes were already soaked with mud. But Ava would get them to safety. There was no other option. They reached the entrance to the highway by the end of the first day.

As they walked farther and farther away from the only place Ava had ever felt cared for, she touched the silver bracelet dangling from her wrist and despite herself, she thought of Orchid. She couldn't help it, especially not now that she was back to wearing something that had allegedly been a token of Orchid's love. It seemed fitting, somehow, if ironic, that Olympia had been the one to inadvertently remind her of the person she'd lost to come Inside.

If it wasn't for Orchid, Ava thought, she might not have gone Inside at all. And if she hadn't gone Inside, Brook and July never would have been born. And if they had never been born, they never would have tried to leave Ava just as Orchid had, repeating a pattern that Ava had spent a very long time trying to understand.

But now the pattern was broken. Now Ava was the one leaving. She was breaking her own heart this time, though there really wasn't any other option.

She thought of all the people she'd known in her life outside and wondered who among them might still be alive. Out of everyone she'd ever met, Orchid was the only one who made sense; if anyone was suited for survival, it was her. Ava couldn't help but look at Brook and think about how she was almost the exact same age that Ava was when she met Orchid on the street so many years ago; and Brook had Ava's same heart-shaped face, those untamed curls. She'd felt like a full adult when she and Orchid met, but looking at Brook, Ava realized she'd been hardly more than a kid.

Ava had no way of knowing that Orchid was traveling south toward Inside as she and Brook traveled north, away from it. If they were to recognize each other when they intersected, it wouldn't be for many long, hot days, probably weeks.

But for now, at the beginning of their journeys, all three people moved with the certainty that comes from making a decision that feels undeniably right. Orchid flew down the last remaining highway on her old bike as Ava and Brook walked carefully along its overgrown median, marveling at the night sky. The full moon bounced light off the concrete and turned the air a ghostly silver. The stars were more infinite than Ava ever could have described.

ACKNOWLEDGMENTS

A million thank-yous to my agent, Nicki Richesin, for championing this idea from the very beginning, and to my editor, Hannah O'Grady—Hannah, our shared enthusiasm for lesbians at the end of the world is something I will treasure forever. Thank you for your brilliance, thoughtfulness, and willingness to let me explore all the ways this story could have been told. This novel became what it did because of you.

To everyone at St. Martin's Press who helped bring this book to life: Jonathan Bush, Amelia Beckerman, Layla Yuro, Dori Weintraub, Alyssa Gammello, and Linda Sawicki. Thank you, thank you.

Thank you to everyone who read early drafts and took the time to tell me what you thought, sometimes in great detail and often after reading multiple versions of the story: Miriam Jayaratna, Amy and Robert Korn, Julia Korn, William Korn, Kristin Iversen, Amanda Montell, Amy Buchanan, Adonis Brown, Mapes Thorson, and Christina Orlando.

The ultimate thank-you to my wife, Wallace May, who started reading this book when it was hardly a book at all and insisted I see it through, and who has given me the love, encouragement, and room I needed to do just that.